BOOK ONE

CONVERGENCE

By Kearstin Dunn

Desmos token illustration by Pinkerchu

Map design by Shanelle Krumbhols

Cover design by designsbyseventhstar

Interior book design by Gillian Collins

Editorial by Gillian Collins

Proofreading by Claire Olivia Golden

To my Great-Grandmother Martha: if it weren't for you giving me a typewriter all those years ago, I would have never found my love for writing. I hope this makes you proud.

To my Husband: Thank you for your unending support, love, and encouragement. Without you, I don't know where I'd be.

FOR MY READERS

To every person who's been told,
"You feel too much."
Your emotions are power.

"POWER TENDS TO CORRUPT, AND ABSOLUTE POWER CORRUPTS ABSOLUTELY."

— Lord Acton

WORD OF CAUTION

Convergence is set in an action-packed, dystopian world where humans bond to animals, which includes elements regarding animal abuse, death, violence, and descriptive injuries. Please take note and proceed with caution.

CONTENTS

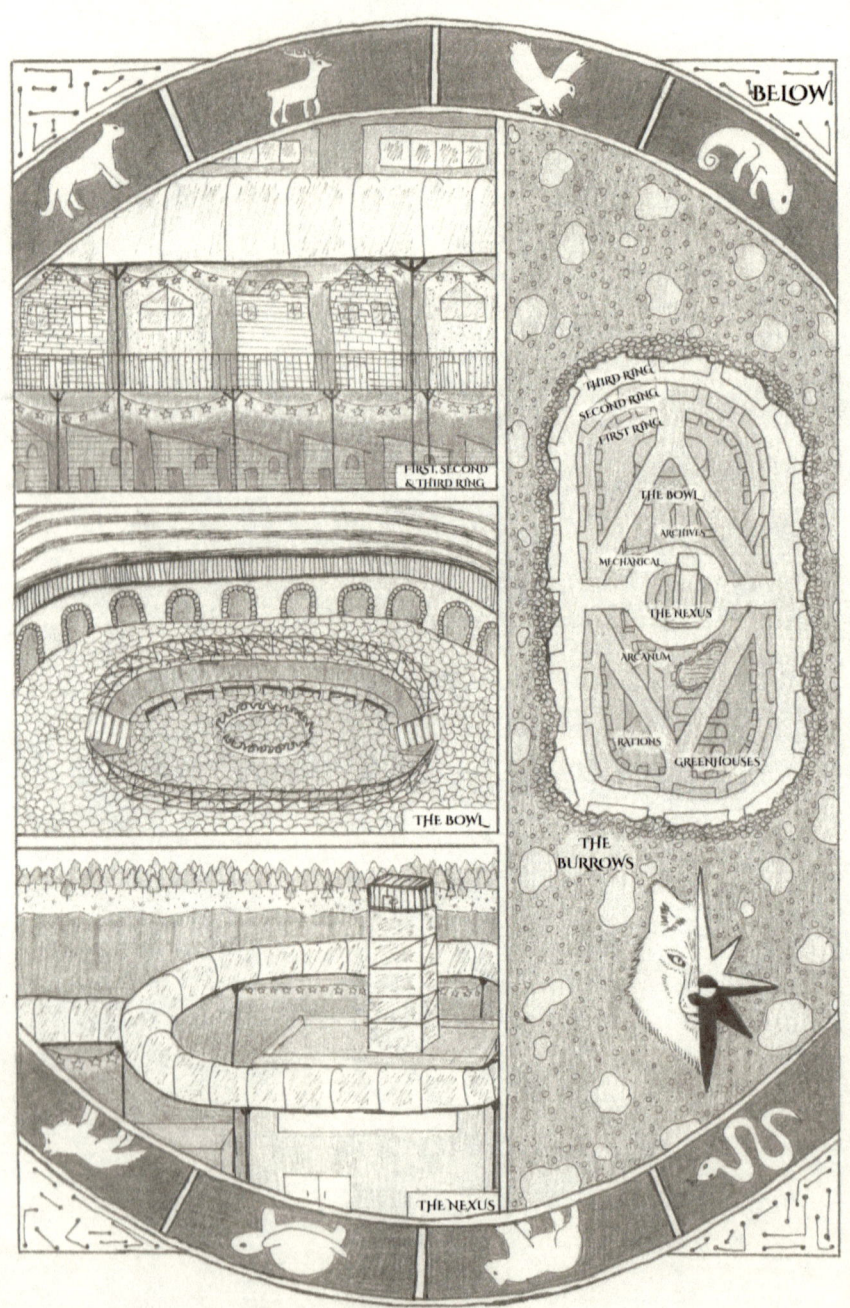

ABOVE

EXION

THE WILDWOODS

THE POND

THE PLATFORM

CAMP SOLIS

THE TRAINING FIELD

Auryth : Ah-ruth

Kaleu : Kay-loo

Eronaeic : Er-ronic

Lief : Leaf

Wilder : Wild-er

Vesper : Ves-pur

Quor : Core

Caius : Kai-us

Cognis : Kagn-ness

Exion : Ex-ee-on

CHAPTER I
LENNON

Today will decide my fate. The Convergence is supposed to be a privilege—or at least that's how we're expected to look at it. From the time we are old enough to wonder why our parents always have an *Auryth* by their side, and why they have abilities we don't, they shove that nonsense down our throats to feed our ever-curious minds. But it's not a privilege; it's a gamble, and only the worthy survive.

I walk through the center of the Burrows toward the city's main greenhouse, doing my best to ignore the signs now plastered on nearly every building and light pole in preparation for the ceremony. One phrase written in bright white catches my eye, standing out against the faded brown of an old building. Despite already knowing what it will say, I can't stop myself from reading it: *"The worthy will rise."* More like the *unworthy* will rise ... on a platform ... to their deaths.

I roll my shoulders, releasing the tension from a poor night's sleep, and use the ladder to climb onto the greenhouse roof. Nausea seeps through my bones as I stare at the three

1

rings of houses coiled around the Burrows like the strangling roots of a tree, each layer feeding off the one below.

The homes on the First Ring are identical copies of one another, with charcoal-grey siding and dust-covered windows; they're poor in comparison to the homes on the Third Ring, with their enclosed walkways dripping in purified air and bright red exteriors. In between the two sits the Second Ring, a buffer between the low and high-born members of society. The houses are a touch nicer than those on the First, with a second story and a pale blue exterior, but they're still nowhere near as luxurious as the Third's.

Walkways of iron and rust—added during the Second Ring expansion thirty years ago—cross overhead underneath Third Ring's enclosed ones, offering easy transportation from one side of the Burrows to the other. I watch them pass, undisturbed by the sheer drop or the low-born beneath them. Ironically, the expansion left us with an abundance of homes, making them the one thing we don't have to ration or struggle for.

So many empty houses, yet we send those who could fill them to their deaths.

I'll never understand how a belief can be held so strongly by so many to the point of craving the death of others, but then again, no one here has ever known any different. We only know what we're taught. The *Auryths* were worshipped long before humanity moved underground, and their decision is law. If they judge you as unfit for a bond, there's nothing anyone can do to sway the Regime's mind.

It's inhumane, disgusting, and utterly mad.

"I thought I'd find you up here," a voice calls from behind me, and I don't need to look to know who it is.

The humidity has Wilder's blond curls sticking to his forehead, framing his pale blue eyes that sparkle against the dull, mechanical light hung high above us. Supposedly, they represent the stars—something we'll never get to see. They're meant to make us feel less trapped, but it's hard not to feel that way when you live in an underground cave with no end in sight besides your own death.

He scoots closer to me, and I lean a weary head on his shoulder. "You're not nervous about today, are you? An *Auryth* would be crazy not to bond with you."

I sigh. "Personally, I don't think there's any rhyme or reason for who they deem worthy or unworthy of bonding. So yes, I'm nervous. About me … about you. If something were to happen to you—"

He cuts me off. "Nothing is going to happen." His lips brush the top of my head tenderly, then he pulls me closer to his chest. "Not to me, and not to you." Tears prick my eyes, but they don't fall. I've cried so much in the last few days that I hardly have anything left. Wilder's scent wraps around me, a mixture of sweat and fresh mint. I began pocketing a few leaves from the greenhouse for him years ago to mix into his soap, and he always uses them, knowing how much I adore the smell.

I've always loved Wilder, not that I'd ever tell him. He's my safe space, my home, and I dread the idea of him not bonding far more than myself. We met when we were ten; he found me sitting alone in the courtyard, sobbing my heart out. I'd lost my mother that week.

He didn't ask why I was crying; he simply sat down next to me and asked if I was going to eat my rations, earning a quivering smile from me as I handed him my untouched pouch.

We've been inseparable ever since.

"At least if we don't bond, we'll get to see the sun," I say softly, watching the little lights flicker in and out of view.

"Yeah, right before we choke to death on the chemicals," he replies bluntly, and I pull away to scowl at him. "What? It's the truth."

"I'm trying to be positive."

"Right, because 'we're going to die' instead of 'we're both going to bond' is way more positive." He raises an eyebrow at me and smiles enough for his dimples to shine through.

I've always loved his dimples, too.

"Fine. We're both going to bond. And after we bond, we'll find someone to marry, and if we dare to ever have children, we'll get to watch them go through this entire process in eighteen years. I. Can't. Wait." My words ring true, but they carry no heat. I don't have the energy for anger today. "Maybe we'll at least get a house with a prettier view out of it all if we bond to an elite."

He forces me back into the crook of his arm, placing a hand on my head to squeeze me in tighter. "That's my girl," he says sweetly, sending a rush of heat through my body.

You'd think now would be a good time to tell him how I feel, in case one of us doesn't make it, but I can't find the words. I cling to him, trying desperately to hold onto this moment for just a minute longer.

"We've got to get going soon. We still have to finish our shifts and pick up our ration packs before it starts," he says. I pull away to look at him, to memorize the lines of his jaw, the way his hair slightly curls around the tips of his ears. Just one more minute.

He stands and extends a hand to me. "We'll either go home after this, or I'll meet you in the sun. You know nothing could keep us separated for too long, Len."

His words steal the air from my lungs, and I take his hand and fold myself into his open arms, just in case this is the last time I'll ever get to.

I nearly squeeze the life out of him, and he does the same to me.

Just in case.

Once I reach the ground, I head into the greenhouse, waving goodbye to Wilder as he leaves for his work detail at the mechanical building. My mother was bonded to a red-tailed hawk before she died, and although it'd be a nice sentiment to follow in her footsteps and develop foresight, my heart has always been with the stags. Those bonded to stags have the gift of chloromancy—the ability to create plants and vegetation from nothing. Being surrounded by fresh greenery always relaxes me. With every bond having a unique form of magic, jobs are generally assigned based on which species you bond to. At least if I did bond with a stag, my greenhouse position would be secured.

I open the door and am instantly met with sticky air and the smell of fresh plants of all varieties. Leaning down, I gently lift an orange blossom to my nose and breathe deeply, savoring the scent. This is the one place that truly makes me feel like I'm on the ground, even if everything in it is either genetically or magically made.

As I step away and start toward the front of the facility to begin my rotation, a hand jumps out from a wall of greenery and grabs my arm. I scream, then instantly cover my mouth in embarrassment as Quor doubles over laughing at me. His smile is bright against his green skin, and I watch as he transitions back to his normal, human color.

"What the hell is wrong with you?" I say exasperatedly, placing a hand to my forehead, the other still hovering over my heart.

"Don't be such a killjoy, Benfield. I figured you could use something to get your mind off of today," he says, still grinning. Quor is *technically* my boss, given he's a few years older than I am and is already bonded, but most days, you'd think it was the other way around.

I ignore his comment as I scan the room for his *Auryth*. "Where's Miko?" A head pops out of his pants pocket right on cue, revealing the small chameleon who has turned himself a dark shade of green to match Quor's work uniform. I hold out my hand, and he passes Miko over. My laugh rings out as he climbs up my shoulder and slowly begins changing to a deep black, matching my shirt. If there's one thing I'll never get tired of seeing, it's the magic of *Auryths*.

My mind reels for the next two hours as I carry buckets of water in from the central pond and mix supplements into the soil, the fear in my belly coiling tighter with every passing minute.

"How many do you think will be exiled this year?" Ruby, one of the other workers usually on my rotation, asks Quor.

I keep my eyes trained on the soil, pretending that I'm not listening in on their conversation, but I can't stop my ears from pricking up. Quor straightens, wiping his damp hands on his pants, and the earlier playfulness in his expression vanishes. "It's hard to say. Seems like there are more every year."

Ruby shrugs and digs her hands into the soil, her lips curling into a smile. "I guess worthy people are more difficult to come by these days. I say good riddance." Her *Auryth*, a small raccoon named Poe, lets out a low growl as if in agreement.

The silence is deafening, and I can't bear to look toward Quor to see his reaction; the idea of him agreeing with her makes my insides twist. It's difficult to swallow the realization that most people in the Burrows see things the way Ruby does: that if I don't bond, my life isn't worth saving.

"I'm only saying what everyone else is thinking," she presses, attempting to fill the void with her misguided justification. "The *Auryths* are our moral compass; they decide who is good and who is ... well ... *evil*. If someone isn't chosen for a bond, there's a reason."

The soil pot slips from my hands before I realize what's happening and clatters to the ground. Both of their heads snap toward me, as if they've somehow forgotten I'm here.

It isn't uncommon for people to say things like that; hell, most of our everyday citizens were the ones who put up the signs around the Burrows. Still, it's not an easy thing to hear. "You shouldn't say things like that," Quor scolds her, then gives me a sympathetic look. "And our beliefs don't make today any less difficult for those going through the Convergence. Death is never something to be celebrated."

My hair falls into my face as I crouch down to scoop the soil back into the pot, and I yank the long strands into a tight bun. Despite my trembling, I force my attention on the ground, desperate to quiet the rising panic.

Quor sits on his knees and slowly takes the pot from me, offering a soft smile. "You need to go get ready; it's getting close to time. You don't want to be late today." I find I can't smile back. I stand, wipe my dirty hands on my pants, and walk out the door without another word.

Marching through the busy streets of the Burrows, I can't help but tune into the buzz of the crowd that grows louder as people and *Auryths* shuffle toward the Bowl to secure their seats. You can't miss the massive structure; it takes up nearly half of the city's center with its round shape and pure white walls that always seem clean despite the film of filth covering everything else down here.

Someone in the crowd takes bets on how many will try to fight the guards after being deemed unfit for a bond; another complains about how long the ceremony has taken in recent years and insists that sitting on the stone benches for hours hurts their back.

It's a funny thing to hear people gamble and grumble about such trivial things when it's your life on the line.

My eyes catch on a few of the larger *Auryths*—bears, panthers, stags—following closely behind their polished humans who march through the square with their heads held high. Their fresh suits and gowns are neatly pressed, and many of the women wear hues of gold and silver smeared around their eyes and lips like warpaint. We can hardly survive on the rations the Regime provides, but at least the elites look good.

Some of the smaller *Auryths* cower to the side as they pass, clinging to their humans for protection. Even within the *Auryths'* world, there's a hierarchy, and the humans who bond either benefit from it or find themselves stuck on the bottom.

My boots slip against the cobblestone at my feet, its worn surface marred with faint cracks and grooves from generations of use. The Second and Third Rings of homes loom over us, and I admire the finely painted houses. If Wilder or I bond one of the elite *Auryths*, we'll be moved to one of those rings, torn from our families, and hoisted out of poverty by the "generous" hand of the Regime.

I let the fantasy play out in my mind, imagining the soft silk fabrics and plush beds. No more early morning work duties. No more growling stomachs at the end of the day. But if I don't bond to a stag, that would also mean leaving the greenhouse, my *sanctuary*, behind, because most elites don't dirty their hands in the mud; they're *far* too sophisticated for that. Not to mention having to leave my family down below. At least the Regime is 'kind' enough to let them visit and admire my newfound luxury every once in a while.

The ration building comes into view, a square, blocky structure built from rusted steel with a line already spilling out into the streets. People are arguing and attempting to push their way to the front. Guards interject where they see fit, mostly giving stern looks and flashing the guns secured at their hips. Not much more is needed to make people quiet down than that. With the threat of having your chip activated —a bonded's instant kill switch—no one dares to fight. Not about food, not about orders, not about anything, really. That's one thing I'm certainly not excited to receive if I bond.

Strings of lights loop lazily overhead, swaying slightly in the artificial currents from the ventilation fans. Their warm glow bathes the line of people in soft rays of light, reflecting off the steel. When my turn finally comes, I step up to the counter and slide my identification card into the slot. The attendant barely looks at me as he hands over three silver ration packs: one for each person in my household. As the Regime likes to say, *"It's everything your body needs in one easy meal."* They don't like to talk about the fact that everyone on First is comparable to a sack of bones these days, though.

We produce the synthetic protein paste in the greenhouses, derived from a variety of mutated plants that smell about as good as they taste. There's no sweet scent of fruit trees or blooming flowers; they're just *bland* in every sense of the word. But somehow that blandness led to these tiny little packs that are supposed to be so incredibly rich in nutrients, we only need one a day. What a joke. I slip them into my pocket without looking.

The crowd thins as I turn down a quieter path toward home, and the noise settles into a gentle hum as I retreat from the center. The ground beneath my boots is damp and slick from the humidity, and the faint smell of moss poking through the cracks where the stone meets the edges of the buildings fills my nostrils. It's calmer here; almost peaceful.

I round the final corner and spot my house, its crooked, crumbling roof barely visible in the poor lighting. My fingers brush over the ration packets in my pocket before I shift the creaky door open.

My little brother, Shiloh, looks up from his book to greet me. He doesn't say it, but I can tell he's nervous for what's to come today. His broad smile is clearly forced as I pull out the packets and set them on the counter.

Peeking around the corner to the living room, I note my father sprawled across his disgusting recliner, either asleep or pretending to be. An empty glass sits on the table beside him, no doubt reeking of illegal moonshine—the only thing he tends to leave his chair for these days. I have half a mind to pick it up and throw it against the wall just to get his attention, but there's a brokenness in him that always makes me hesitate. He hasn't been the same since Mom died.

To be fair, none of us has.

"I'm gonna change, and then we'll head out, okay? We'll swing by Wilder's house on the way. You'll sit with his family, and I'll find you once it's all over," I tell Shiloh, forcing myself to keep it together with what little energy I have left.

He stares at his hands, meticulously cracking each finger. "I don't need a babysitter."

"I know you don't," I answer softly. "I just thought it'd be nice for you to have someone to sit with."

His glare wavers for a heartbeat before he turns away. "Stop treating me like I'm still twelve." He disappears down the hall, his door shutting with a thud.

I press a hand into the counter, its rough surface digging into my skin. I'm not sure what bothers me more: the idea of dying, or the idea of him no longer needing me if I survive.

CHAPTER 2
LENNON

I slip on the ceremonial white pants and matching shirt that were delivered to our door a few days ago and glance at myself in the mirror. Pure. Clean. Worthy. That's how we must present ourselves to the *Auryths*—as if wearing the wrong thing will somehow sway their decision to bond with us.

My mother hated this day. She dreaded the idea of my brother or me having to go through it and despised the thought of us not bonding even more. She thought the entire concept of exiling people in general was ludicrous, and though she was always careful with her choice of words when it came to such delicate matters, she and I always understood each other in a way no one else ever could.

Those deemed unworthy by *Auryths* are considered a threat to society. After all, if you ask the Regime, the unbonded were responsible for our ruin. Their jealousy sparked a war that destroyed the Earth's surface, allowing only a small fragment of bonded to flee underground before the air turned murderous. But if you ask me, it's been 152 years since the world as we knew it ended; maybe it's time to finally leave the past where it belongs.

No one ever asks me.

Of course, that idea would not only be considered absurd but also treasonous within the rock-carved walls of the Burrows.

I neatly twist half of my hair up and out of my face, my chest aching as I stare at my reflection. All I see is my mother's brown waves, her hazel eyes, her slightly rounded chin. So many reminders of her that haunt me endlessly. I wish she were here, especially today, but I swallow my pain and force my shoulders back. Whatever fate awaits me, I'll face it head-on. It's not like there's another option, anyway.

I head back into the living room and find Shiloh dressed in his best clothes: a black button-up and matching pants. The set is big on him, passed down from Wilder as a gift. Even though he's only sixteen, he seems to grow every day, already standing at least six inches taller than me. Granted, I hardly surpass five feet, so that's not saying much. At least we still have two years before he'll find himself in this very same situation. For one selfish, fleeting moment, I hope I won't be around to watch it.

Shiloh doesn't say a word but follows me over to Wilder's despite his earlier comments.

Wilder's mother, Willa, stands in the doorway, fretting as usual. She's a busy woman, always rushing despite the seemingly still time we have down here. She ushers Shiloh inside with a warm smile and a quick pat on his shoulder before offering me a hesitant look. "You two better hurry," she says, her voice unsteady. "Don't keep them waiting. Especially not today." She stares at Wilder with such adoration that my stomach turns sour, then pulls him in for a hug. "I love you."

I can't help but consider what it'd be like to have my mom here today, to embrace her. Would it ease some of the worry etching itself into my core? As if she can read my mind, Willa pulls me in to join the hug.

"I love you too, Mom," Wilder tells her.

He extends a hand to me as we step back onto the street, and I take it without hesitation. His fingers are rough and warm against mine, and before I have time to adjust, he yanks me forward, leading us into a fast walk that has me nearly jogging to keep up. "Let's go, slowpoke."

I stumble after him, unable to process the reality of where we're headed. The narrow roads wind like veins through the Burrows, twisting and branching every which way, pulling us into its heart.

"Wilder, slow down!" I gasp, trying to keep up without tripping over my own feet.

He slows, but only a fraction, shooting me a grin that doesn't quite meet his eyes. He's putting on a brave face for me, trying to ease my worries, but I know him well enough to see through the facade. "What's wrong? You worried they'll deem you unworthy if you show up sweaty?"

"That's not funny." My voice cracks, betraying me. Normally, I'd fire back, maybe roll my eyes, shove his shoulder a bit. But my hands won't stop trembling, and no matter how much air I suck down, my chest feels tight, starved. The reality keeps hammering through me relent-lessly: *if we don't bond, we die. If we don't bond, we die. If we don't bond, we die.*

He stops suddenly, pulling me behind a building. For once, there's no sign of humor in his expression, no mischievous glint in his eyes. He grabs my shoulders sternly, his tone more serious than I've ever heard it. "Listen to me. You, of all people, have nothing to worry about. You know what's inside here." He taps my chest, right over my heart, and I swear it skips a beat. "The *Auryths* will know that too." I open my mouth to answer, but he leans in closer, his arm above my head, his eyes burning a hole into my soul, and I find myself entirely speechless. "You are everything bright in this dark place, Len."

His body is pressed so close to mine that I can feel his every breath, smell the mint stuck to his skin. This moment is everything I've ever waited for, and when he leans in, his breath hot against my lips, my legs nearly buckle. My body is begging. Begging me, begging *him* to do it, but when I close my eyes—

"Keep moving!" My eyes instantly snap open to find a guard glaring at us, and Wilder moves away so quickly that I start to wonder if I somehow dreamed the entire encounter. My heart sinks in disappointment, my chest aching with the curiosity of what it might have been like to finally taste his lips.

We walk the rest of the way together in silence, his hand still in mine, steadying me when the road grows uneven. The air thickens as we approach the Bowl, a heavy concoction of sweat and fear that clings to all of us. We stop with the rest of the group in front of the building, and I turn to face him with one last request. "If I don't bond, will you look after Shiloh?" Even if he claims he doesn't need me, I can't bear the thought of leaving him entirely alone.

"Don't ask me that. It's not going to happen. It's not even a possibility."

"But if it does?" I ask, more to myself than to him. "I'm all he's got left."

"There is no situation in which you do not walk out of this

16

bonded. You're Lennon Benfield." Something in the way he says my full name brings me back to reality, grounding me. I nod, and he pulls me in for one final hug as they begin to call us up alphabetically. I make my way to the front of the line, and he heads to the back.

They guide us through a door on the side of the building opposite the crowd entrance. Once inside, I twist around to check for Wilder one last time and let out a breath when his blue eyes meet mine. He winks, and I fight the urge to run to him. My stomach churns with the reminder that I may never get to again.

The middle of the auditorium floor is set ablaze in a flaming white circle, and in its center sits a painted replica of the Desmos Token—an ancient coin that's plastered on nearly every government building inside the city. Its normal, rusted gold color shimmers in the light, highlighting the eight elite *Auryths*—a wolf, bear, chameleon, bird, panther, serpent, turtle, and stag—with a sun in the center. The words, *Auryth coniungere summum hominis propositum est,* form a ring around the outside. It's meant to represent the importance of the Convergence and supposedly means, 'to bond to an *Auryth* is man's greatest purpose.'

No one's ever actually seen the physical token; allegedly, it's kept locked up and safe from thieving hands—as if any of us would risk our lives to steal an old hunk of metal.

Stone benches are arranged in tiered circles from the floor to the ceiling, giving spectators a near-perfect view of the stage. We file in, one after the other, stopping right in front of the ring of flame. I don't miss the box seats positioned in the highest part of the stands, closed off from the rest of the crowd and filled with Third-Ring elites dressed in their finest wear.

"Welcome to the annual Convergence." President Blane's voice echoes through the microphone he's holding, silencing the crowd. He stands on a wooden, raised stage adjacent to the center circle; his *Auryth*, a terrifyingly large Kodiak bear named Maerock, sits calmly at his side. "As you all know, this is the tradition that we hold most sacred in the Burrows. To bond an *Auryth* is man's greatest purpose. Without them, we wouldn't have magic, and without magic, the creation and sustainability of the Burrows would never have been possible." Cheering and applause ripple through the space, bouncing off the walls.

There's a clear differential in the crowd: those who devour every word he says as if it's prophetic, and those who are simply terrified of what will happen if they don't at least pretend. Eager spectators sit at the front, likely getting here hours before the Convergence was even scheduled to start. Unsurprisingly, that section is full of mostly mid to high-ranking *Auryths* and humans, likely Second-Ring citizens. They're granted more privileges than those of us on First, such as getting released from their work details early enough to get seats. Not that most of us First-Ringers care about getting good seats anyway.

"Long before the war that forced us underground, humans and *Auryths* bound themselves for life. Our ancestors believed they were sent to separate the wicked from the virtuous, and we still hold that belief today. Since the day the Burrows was established, the Convergence has been implemented as a means to preserve the integrity of what remains of humanity. If we are fortunate enough to ever return to the surface, it will be as a people who surpass our predecessors—only the *best* humanity has to offer. Let the *Auryths* decide which of us is worthy. Only *then* can we rise."

He turns away from the crowd to where our class stands, his expression blank. "Some of you will not be chosen today, for reasons unbeknownst to us. Know that your life will not be taken in vain, but for the good of humanity. There is no greater sacrifice." Blane steps off his podium and disappears from my line of sight, leaving us to our fate once more.

"There is no greater sacrifice," the crowd echoes after him.

"Maggie Abbot." The female attendant leading us gets right to it, and I watch as the girl two spots ahead of me in line approaches the circle. Her bright red hair trails down her back, nearly reaching her hips, and her green eyes are wide with fear. She steals a look at the rest of us, and I force what I hope is a comforting smile. The attendant places a stern hand on Maggie's back, then forcefully pushes her through the flames and into the circle. A gasp leaves my lips before I can stop it, but I'm not the only one.

Once inside, she does a slow spin, likely overwhelmed by the massive crowd watching her intently, and, without warning, the flames erupt, creating a ring around her that reaches from floor to ceiling, concealing her from view. We all watch, mesmerized, and I realize that I'm no different than everyone else inside the Bowl; I'm anxiously waiting to see what *Auryth* she'll emerge from the flames with, and find myself curious about what will happen if she comes back alone. Will she fight? Cower? Run?

Five minutes later, she returns, a small, fluffy white rabbit in her arms. Her smile is big and shining as the crowd cheers, and she even does another spin to showcase her new bonded. They direct her to a row of benches on the other side of the circle, set up specifically for the newly bonded, then call the next name. "Banks Abshire." A boy with curly black hair steps through the ring next without hesitation, and the flame goes up once more. My feet continue shuffling forward until I realize there's no one left in front of me.

I'm next.

Again, the flames retreat, only this time there is no *Auryth* by his side. Cold-blooded fear floods through me as his eyes meet mine, suffocating and relentless. He's terrified—his brown eyes frantic as he fidgets with trembling hands. I want to help him, but I can't. There's nothing anyone can do for him now.

Guards swarm the inside of the circle immediately, and I can't help but watch as he panics, searching the room for any way out. Nothing in his movements is cruel or rebellious; he simply doesn't want to die. "Please!" he shouts, holding his hands up in surrender while moving away from the approaching guards. "Please, I don't want to die. Please! *Please!*"

The guards do not waver. In fact, another set approaches from behind him, blocking off any potential escape plan he could concoct. I breathe a sigh of relief when he doesn't fight as they handcuff him; I don't think I could bear seeing him beaten. He's still pleading as they haul him out of the building toward wherever they hold the next group of exiles.

"Lennon Benfield." A knot of nerves takes root in my throat. I swallow hard, trying to force it down, and my mind decides to focus on the potential burn of the flames, rather than my impending life-or-death situation.

I hesitate.

"Step into the ring," the attendant commands, and I give her a sidelong glance. She shoves me through in response, and I hardly manage to stay on my feet. Thankfully, the flames don't hurt at all, but my body instantly freezes as I take in the sheer number of eyes trained on me. It would be impossible to locate any one person out there, but I do my best to find Shiloh and Wilder's family anyway.

When I can't find them, I attempt to rotate back toward the Convergence group and find Wilder instead, but the flames explode before I have the chance. There's a piercing sound in my mind, and every piece of me fractures. The flames are suddenly hot against my skin, and beads of sweat drip from my brow onto my lashes. I drop to my knees, covering my ears like the action can somehow block the noise out of my mind.

It's excruciating.

As the sound finally dissipates, I realize I'm in a white, blank space. There are no floors, no furniture, no markings, no guidance. The Convergence is considered sacred, and though we are taught an overview of how it works, no one speaks of what happens once you're actually *inside*. In fact, they forbid it.

All I know is that this is the "in-between"—a place where *Auryths* and humans find themselves on the same plane while they decide to return with you or discard you altogether. The latter makes me tremble.

"Hello?" I whisper as I stand, my voice barely audible in the emptiness.

"What is one thing you would never sacrifice?" The voice speaks directly into my mind as if it has always been there.

My heart beats erratically, and I do my best to slow my breathing. I don't need to think before I blurt out my answer. "Any living thing."

"Why?" It replies. My body tenses. Is it a trick question? A test of my character? What happens if I get it wrong?

I consider each word carefully before speaking it. "Because I believe every life is worthy. No one life should outweigh that of another," I answer—and mean every word of it.

"What if you had to sacrifice one life for the good of the many? Would you still refuse?" It presses.

A tremble shudders through me, and I squeeze my eyes shut as if the motion will somehow force an answer past my lips. "I ..." I start. Would I sacrifice one for the many? I'd sacrifice myself without question, but someone else? How could I ask someone to do that? Would I be willing to sacrifice Wilder? Shiloh? Where is the line drawn in this equation?

The piercing starts again, and memories begin to flash through my mind in rapid succession. They're from every aspect of my life. One second, I'm five and helping my little brother with his alphabet, and the next, I'm ten and helping him through the grief of losing our mother while simultaneously trying to keep myself together.

There are countless nights of a grumbling stomach after giving up my ration packets for him. Countless examples of me watching over him, then trying to look out for Wilder and his family after I got to know them. Even the times I'd forced water down my father's throat or covered him with a blanket after he passed out make an appearance. I don't understand why it's showing me these; why do they matter?

The memories stop flashing when they reach a mere hour ago, when Wilder and I said goodbye outside the Bowl. The piercing dissipates once more, and I spin through the nothingness in a slow circle, searching for the voice, but it's gone; I'm alone again.

It didn't let me respond. I didn't give it what it's looking for, and now I'm going to die. How could I be so stupid? So tongue-tied during the most important moment of my life? "No! Please! Let me answer! I can answer!" My voice cracks as panic grips me, but the room remains silent. The air thins, and every passing second squeezes more from my lungs.

And then I see it.

A white wolf with golden eyes that bore into mine, hauntingly familiar, emerges from the light like a figment of my imagination. It's barely visible against the starch whiteness that still envelopes us.

I blink, a heavy weight dropping into the pit of my stomach. I've spent countless hours in the Burrow's archives, studying not only the eight elite *Auryths* but all of the variations of species that have ever been recorded.

No one has bonded with a wolf in the history of the Burrows. 152 years.

"My name is Kaleu, and you are mine.*"* His voice reverberates through my mind like the distant rumble of shifting earth. *"From now until our dying day, Lennon Benfield."*

What can only be the bond snaps into place, and a searing energy courses through my body. I collapse to my knees, trembling as fire blazes through my veins, branding itself into every piece of me. It's painful yet exhilarating, as if I'm being melted down and forged into something entirely new.

For the first time in my life, I'm whole, and I hadn't even realized I was broken until now. *"Stand,"* he commands, and I do. *"Now, prepare for the flames to fall and steady yourself. I will be at your side and in your mind. We are bonded now—you no longer need to worry about exile."* My arms are riddled with goosebumps as I process that his speaking into my mind is going to be an ongoing addition to this new bond.

I do exactly as he asks and stand on shaky legs. The moment the flames recede, the entire front row audience is on their feet, screaming and applauding in amazement at the sight of us. A few stare with predatory intent, as if envious of what I now hold. I briefly scan the rest of the room, staring at the rows and rows of people behind them who either clap with blank faces or do nothing at all.

An attendant I recognize, Amelia, grabs my arm and pulls me from my trance. She had been a friend of my mother's growing up, and always went out of her way to be kind to me when she passed. "Step over there with Maggie," she whispers, lightly tugging me out of the ring. "A *wolf*, Lennon. You bonded a wolf. Your mother would be so proud of you." The sentiment draws my attention, and she lightly brushes my cheek before rushing back to help with the others.

I sit down next to Maggie, unable to pull myself out of the shock to speak, and Kaleu sits down near my feet. I can't even bring myself to focus on my new bond. All I can think of is Wilder as they call name after name, each coming out either bonded or dragged off to their deaths. What questions will they ask him? How will they measure his worth? Is it the same for everyone?

"No," Kaleu says, startling me. *"Every Auryth has different questions and reasoning behind who they choose."* This mind thing is going to take some getting used to.

A symphony of screams draws my attention back to the ring. In the center is a girl with bright blond hair, panicking as she returns unbonded. *Delilah.* We've had several classes together, and she has always been soft-spoken and kind. Every scream that leaves her lips is so chilling, I'm convinced they'll haunt my nightmares for the rest of my life. I can hear a few sobs from the crowd as she fights for her life, which assures me that I'm not alone in my sentiment.

She gives them a hell of a struggle—kicking, punching, thrashing. Anything she can possibly throw at them, she does, but in the end, it isn't enough. One of the guards cracks her over the head with a baton, which I suppose is kinder than shooting her, but I cringe nonetheless as she hits the floor. The careless way they drag her dead-weight body across the ground makes me sick.

Across the stadium, a few people in the first three rows shoot to their feet, cheering for the guards and relishing the violence. My rage is a pot waiting to boil over. How can anyone sit and watch someone so desperate to live have their life stripped away, then cheer as it happens?

No one says anything to them, though, myself included. All that would do is put a target on my back, and my life is no longer only mine to protect.

The next name is called, and I turn to see Isla Dade eagerly walking toward the ring. Her jet-black hair is tied into a neat braid down her back, and I can't help but admire the sheer confidence in each step she takes. Minutes later, she emerges with a massive panther, as black as her hair, by her side. I'm not surprised she bonded. Growing up, she's always been the kind of girl who does whatever it takes to get her way, and I doubt even an *Auryth* could stand in her path. She devours the attention from the elites, prancing in a slow circle around the ring, encouraging everyone to stand for her with waves of her arms.

Name after name. Bonded after bonded. Exile after exile. My heart bleeds for every person who returns alone. There are over a hundred in our class this year, and I don't even want to consider how many of those will be sent to their deaths today. I stopped counting after twenty-two.

"Wilder Ray," The attendant calls, signaling him over, and my breath catches. I watch as he walks to the ring, his sandy blond hair gleaming in the beaming light. His blue eyes meet mine, and he gives me a subtle wink. I don't miss how his body trembles, though.

My best friend. The one person who knows me wholly inside and out. The *only* friend I've had my entire life. My family.

The thought of losing him makes my heart clench.

The flames shoot upward, and I've never felt so helpless, so useless. And, because I don't know how else to calm my nerves, I start counting. When I reach 272 seconds, the flames begin to descend. I stand and move toward the ring, each step more difficult than the last.

There's no way he'll come back without a bond—he's the best of us. He always has been.

I try to trick my mind into thinking everything will be okay, but the flames recede.

And he's alone.

CHAPTER 3
LENNON

M y body rushes into the ring before my brain can register what's happening. Panic surges through me, pushing my pulse into my ears. Kaleu moves quickly, staying underfoot as I race towards Wilder. We're faster than the guards, and I step in front of him as if my body can somehow shield him from this fate, from the punishment he does not deserve. Wilder stares at me, his expression silently begging me to stand down. Kaleu positions himself between me and the approaching guards. Every hair on his back stands at attention as saliva drips from his barred teeth.

"I don't have a plan," I admit as the guards strategically attempt to surround us, their weapons raised ever so slightly.

"I gathered that much," Kaleu scoffs, holding his ground. Right. He's in my head now. I'm not just talking to myself anymore. My breathing is rapid and uncontrolled as I process his words and our surroundings, trying to piece together a way out of this.

I'm small in stature compared to them, and considering the lack of rations, I hardly have any meat on my bones. Not to mention the fact that I have no weapons, and they have *guns*—rifles with polished barrels—and a steady aim; this is far from a fair fight.

"Stand down, girl," one of the guards seethes, stepping closer. Kaleu snaps his teeth, and the guard jumps backward, his grip tightening on the gun.

I push Wilder backward slightly, aiming to get our backs against the wall. I watched how they cornered Banks and Delilah; if we aren't careful, they'll send another batch to come up from behind, giving us no way out. *Is* there a way out of this? We're underground. It's not as if we can run or hide.

To my surprise, President Blane emerges from behind the guards, his face a mask of cool indifference. His Kodiak bear, Maerock, walks steadily behind, towering several feet over him. Her paws are massive, and all I can think about is what will happen if she gets too close. "Now then, that's enough of that. I can see you care a great deal about him, but you know the rules. No exceptions. Not for him. Not for anyone. The Regime's mercy for the unbonded has limits, and you're testing them."

I clench my fists, feeling the sharp sting of my nails digging into my palms. "Mercy?" I shout, my voice trembling with anger. I want them all to hear this—to understand. "You call this mercy? This is *wrong*. He hasn't done anything to deserve this."

"Kill him!" Someone in the crowd shouts.

"He's unworthy!" says another.

Cowards, all of them.

Blane tilts his head, his lips twisting into a mockery of a smile. His voice is low and calm, only loud enough for me to hear in the chaos. "Oh, but it *is* merciful. The unbonded are the reason we're down here in the first place. *Mercy* is not forcing their families to watch them die down here. Give the boy the privilege of a good, honest death like all of the other exiles. Don't be the one to take that away from him." He nods to the guards. "Take him."

I back up even closer to Wilder, my body trembling but resolute. "No!" The word tears from my throat, raw and desperate. "I won't let you."

"Lennon, please. You're going to get yourself hurt. I can't —" Wilder falters, the words stuck in his throat. "I can't watch them hurt you." He grabs my arm, trying to reel me in and hold me down, but I wrench free from his grip.

The guards hesitate, their weapons twitching slightly as if they're uncertain about how much force they can use. It's always the unbonded who fight, and their lives are seen as useless. Mine isn't, and I'm still unchipped. They can't threaten me with the kill switch, not yet.

"I don't want to hurt you," a guard says, stepping closer and leveling a baton crackling with electricity. Such lovely words for such a threatening gesture. Kaleu's growl deepens, and my stomach twists in fear and fury. I will not move. I will not let them take Wilder from me. I don't care if they hurt me, exile me—I'm not going anywhere, not without him.

"I don't want to hurt you either," I tell the guard, doing my very best to sound threatening despite my shaky voice. It's an empty threat, but he doesn't know if I'm capable of following through with it. Or if I'm capable of *anything*, for that matter.

My heart pounds against my ribs, every beat screaming at me to fight, to do something, *anything*. Blane's expression darkens. "Enough of this." He gestures to one of the guards, who grabs my arm harshly, and my body fills with an odd, burning sensation.

The guard jumps backward, his palm new shades of purple and blue. "What the hell?"

I look down at my skin, toward Kaleu, and back to the guard, trying to understand what happened. *"What was that?"*

"Magic," he says plainly, and I turn my attention back to Wilder as Kaleu lunges at the guards, pressing them further back. The audience is locked in. Tears trickle down some of their cheeks as if they hurt for our situation, while others look far too excited for the guards to win.

I don't know what gifts our bond has given me, but if it will help us at all right now, I'm willing and ready to use them. I allow that rage, that panic, to fill me like it's tangible, burning me from the inside out in a combination of fire and ice that I can't explain or begin to understand.

A guard rolls something toward us, and I'm too focused on my emerging power, on Wilder, on everything else to consider what it could be. Seconds later, a green gas pours from the small black tube, and reality itself shifts. My eyes droop, my body unsteady, and as I pivot to check on Wilder, I collapse from exhaustion.

I crawl to him, desperate to save him. My hands find his, and I cling to them for dear life as the darkness overtakes me, whispering "I'm so sorry" like a mantra.

I wake in a cell with thick metal bars, no windows, and no way out. I didn't even realize we had a prison inside the Burrows. We have no need for one when the chips loom over our very existence.

In my lifetime, I can only recall one instance where someone's chip was activated. The memory itself is hazy; I couldn't

32

have been older than eight when it happened. It was a father who had lost his only child to exile after the Convergence. He didn't cause a scene during the ceremony like I did. He waited, plotted, then used his magic to set fire to one of the greenhouses right outside the main square.

Then he watched it burn.

He didn't bother putting up a fight when they came for him; I think he wanted to die. He was bonded to a red fox. In my mind, I always thought it would be quick, but it wasn't. It was torture to watch them both go down, screaming as their bond faded into absolute nothingness and their hearts ceased to beat.

Needless to say, people tend to back down when faced with the threat of the chips. The fear of dying outweighs the idea of rebellion every time.

The sound of clanking keys echoes through the hall, and I stand up to peer through the bars. President Blane strides forward with measured grace, his polished boots clicking against the floor in a steady rhythm. He doesn't look to the guards flanking him; they orbit him like silent watchdogs. His gaze is fixed, unwavering, and each step is calculated. His bear is nowhere to be seen, and I suddenly realize I have no idea where Kaleu is either. I quickly wipe my tears and steel myself, crossing my arms tightly against my chest.

"I'm sorry it had to be this way, Miss Benfield. You caused quite the scene; everyone will be buzzing about this for weeks." His tone is almost sympathetic, like he hates what I've done but understands why I did it. He approaches the bars, his face so close I could touch him—if I were brave enough. "I need you to understand that I don't enjoy exiling anyone. In fact, it killed me to see how much you care for that boy and having to be the one who ripped you apart. But rules are rules. Without order, there is only chaos. With chaos comes death and possibly the end of the human race. You don't want that, do you?"

Liar. Manipulator. Murderer.

I fight the urge to bark insults in his direction, but I still don't know where Wilder is. Have they already exiled him? Is my brother safe somewhere, or will his life be threatened next if I don't fall into line?

"Of course I don't want that," I snarl, attempting to dull some of the bite on my tongue. "But that doesn't make any of this right. We're just *kids*. It's not any of their faults that they weren't chosen; why should they have to die for it?"

He cocks his head slightly, his eyes burning a hole into me. "You know the history between bonded and unbonded. The unbonded will always covet what the bonded have. Before we were forced underground, they were so envious of our way of life that they created nuclear missiles to destroy us. Do not think for one moment that the same thing would not happen again if we allowed that jealousy to fester down here. The Convergence *protects* our people."

"They're our people, too," I seethe, lifting my chin to him. "Them being unbonded doesn't change that. How can you only care about a fraction of our society? How can you pretend the rest of their lives have no meaning? They grew up here; they work the same jobs, eat the same food. They have families and people who love them!"

He stares blankly at me, seemingly unfazed by my words. Something about the way he refuses to acknowledge their lives infuriates me further. "You're not a leader, you're a coward." His eyes widen as he takes a step back. I've hit a nerve with that one, perhaps even pushed him too far.

He stays tortuously silent, simply nodding to one of his

guards before disappearing into the shadows once more. The guard unlocks my cell, and I begin frantically searching for anything that could be used as a weapon against him, but there's nothing. Not even a pot to relieve myself in.

Rough hands grab my arms, dragging me down the dimly lit corridor. My feet scrape against the stone as I thrash against their grip. "Where are you taking me?" I demand, winded.

"You'll find out soon enough."

We stop in front of a thick metal door. The other guard unlocks it, and my eyes have to adjust as I'm dragged inside. The room is small and barren, save for a single chair bolted to the floor and two thick, black straps hanging from its armrests.

I dig my heels in further as I realize the chair is meant for me. "No. No, you can't—"

They shove me toward it and twist me around. My back hits the chair, and before I can attempt to fight back, they strap me down. "The Regime does not tolerate rebellion. It's a poison, and poison must be eradicated," one of the guards says as bile rises in my throat.

"What are you going to do?" I snap, though the tremble in my voice betrays my facade.

The guard reaches into his pocket, pulling out a sleek device no larger than a pen. He presses a button, and a faint hum fills the air.

Before I can brace myself, the hum intensifies, and a sharp, searing pain shoots through my body. It's as if my very nerves are unraveling, each thread of my being exposed and torn apart. I scream, unable to hold it back, the sound ripping from my throat in a way that's foreign and animalistic.

After what must be hours, the guards unstrap me and take

me back to my cell on shaky legs, and I collapse onto the cold floor. The cell door slams shut, leaving me in darkness. I can still feel the lingering pull on every cell in my body; the pain radiates throughout, like thousands of needles piercing my skin.

When Kaleu's voice finally finds me, it's soft and tentative. *"Lennon?"*

"I'm here. I'm okay," I lie.

"Oh, little wolf, what did they do to you?"

I don't answer. Instead, I curl up, wrapping my arms around myself as if I can somehow hold my shattered pieces together. I tried to protect Wilder. I tried to fight. And now, I don't even know if he's alive. And if he is, he'll be dead soon anyway. Was it all for nothing?

Blane returns to my cell once more, his exterior calm and bored. "I see you've met our Dissonex. It temporarily severs the bond between human and *Auryth,* creating excruciating pain in the process. Our ancestors stole it from the unbonded before we built the Burrows. It seems their only purpose as a society was creating tools to use against us." He smiles, and the gesture sends chills through my body. "And now we can use them to help keep our people safe."

He lets out a long breath. "I'm going to give you a choice: comply with the Regime, receive your chip, accept your place in society, and in return, I'll allow the boy you tried to save to be exiled with the rest of them. You will be placed on military duty, allowing us to keep a closer eye on you, effective immediately. Refuse, and I will allow my guards to continue practicing with the Dissonex until you break, and I'll kill the boy here, in front of you. The choice is yours."

Choice? I'd laugh if I weren't so scared of him. This isn't a choice—it's a promise. If I can't save Wilder, the least I can do is give him the honor of seeing the sun before he goes. If I refuse, they'll kill him and force the chip into me anyway. Not to mention the pain of that device ... I'm not sure I can go through that again. And then there is the reassignment. Military duty has never been a dream of mine, and my heart clenches at the idea of losing my greenhouse shift, though I suppose that was inevitable given that Kaleu and I bonded.

There is no scenario in which I win.

"I will comply," I whimper, defeated.

He claps his hands together and smiles. "Good. And to be clear, you will not speak a word of what's transpired today with *anyone*. If you do, you'll either find yourself or someone you love, perhaps that little brother of yours, back in that chair. The Dissonex is just one of many tools we have to inflict pain. We'll be watching you, Miss Benfield. Be careful of the choices you make going forward. I wouldn't want us to have to have another conversation."

"Of course. I'd hate to ruin your reputation as a kind and caring government." I'm unable to stop the words from tumbling out at the mention of Shiloh, but Blane refuses to acknowledge my comment, leaving me alone with his guards once more.

"Let's go," one of them says as he opens my cell door, and my panic kicks in. The thought of their hands on my body again makes me tremble, and I can't force my legs to move despite my desire to leave. He grabs my arm harshly and tugs, tearing another scream from my throat.

I'm taken through a maze of halls to another room, only this one has a medical bed rather than a chair with restraints. A nurse waits for me there, an array of tools laid out meticulously beside her: a pair of small, silver scissors; a tiny blade; thread; a needle; and a small black chip no larger than my pinkie nail. The room is surprisingly pristine, given the dullness of the rest of the halls, and reeks of antiseptic. At least I don't have to worry about an infection.

A plate full of savory pastries sits on a little table beside the bed. A guard catches my line of sight and says, "A gift from Blane from the celebration."

The smell of the baked goods mixed with antiseptic is a nauseating concoction. That, coupled with the fact that it's from the celebration for the newly bonded, makes my stomach drop. Celebrating while nearly fifty kids were just sent to die. While Wilder ...

I slide onto the table and bite my tongue as she creates a small incision in my right arm, shoves the chip inside, and stitches me back up. I hardly feel it; I'm not sure any pain will ever compare to the kind that device inflicted.

The door swings open, and I snap my head around, preparing to see Blane. Instead, it's a guard, and Kaleu stalks in right behind him. He doesn't appear to be harmed, and relief floods my lungs, letting me breathe for the first time since the Convergence.

They release us back into the streets of the Burrows, my feet like lead against the stone path as my mind struggles to reconnect with my body. I'm both here and not, torn between the desire to fight and the knowledge that if I do, Shiloh will be their next target. Wilder is gone, there's nothing I can do to change that, but my brother ...

I take a seat on a nearby bench to collect my thoughts, my chest heaving as I gulp down the heavy, earthy air. There are so many things I should have said to Wilder, but I was too afraid. Afraid that he would reject me and that I'd ruin what we had. Afraid that he might actually feel the same way, and that something I've always dreamed of would become real. I should have leaned into that kiss this morning; now that's one more "what-if" I'll have to learn to live with.

Kaleu presses against my legs, and I place a tentative hand on his head. There's an unspoken comfort between us, a familiarity that I'm still getting used to. *"Do you think it will hurt? When they reach the surface?"* I ask.

"I think it will be beautiful."

CHAPTER 4
LENNON

S hiloh races for me, his voice echoing through the street. "Lennon?" I stand slowly, still slightly unsteady from the effects of the Dissonex, and throw on a mask of pure indifference.

He throws his arms around me, squeezing as though I might slip away if he lets go, never to be found again. My throat tightens at the contact, but I hold the broken pieces of myself together despite the exhaustion and allow myself to fold into him, burying my face in the crook of his neck. I can't remember the last time we've been this close. "I thought … I thought they were going to exile you, too. Where is Wilder? Did they take him? Where have you been? Did they do something to you?" He pulls away to look me over as if checking for injury. I wish I could tell him that the kind of pain they inflicted isn't visible on my skin.

I pause, considering my words carefully. The last thing I want is to put him in danger by telling him the truth—Blane made that threat crystal clear—but the thought of lying to him nauseates me.

"They gave me a stern talking-to for my behavior today and put me on military duty." Saying it makes it all too real, and my heart sinks.

"It's been hours." He looks at me through a set of thick black lashes, skepticism lining his brows. "Why did it take so long?"

"They had questions about Kaleu." I gesture toward him, and his ears fold back against his head. "It's nothing to worry about, I promise. I'm here now, and that's all that matters."

"They still took Wilder, didn't they?"

"Yeah, they still took him." If there were a way to save him from that truth, from the pain, I'd take it. But tomorrow will still come, and Wilder will still be placed on that platform.

His body tenses, and I pull away to find his hands clenched into fists. I'm not the only one losing someone I love today. Wilder's practically a brother to Shiloh.

A hand slips into his pocket and pulls out a folded piece of paper. "He left this for you. In case …" he trails off. "He made me promise I'd give it to you if he didn't bond." He extends it toward me, and I take it blankly. "I'll give you some time and meet you back at the house—unless you want me to stay. I can stay—"

"I'll meet you back at the house," I tell him with a sad smile. He nods and walks off, leaving Kaleu and me to our silence once more. I sit back down on the bench, my hands shaking as I trace a finger over my name on the front, written in Wilder's handwriting. Kaleu rests his head against my legs as I begin to unfold the paper.

Lennon,

If you're reading this, I didn't bond, and I'm probably on my way to a pretty crappy death. I know you're somehow surprised by the fact that I wasn't deemed "worthy," but I'm not. I knew I wouldn't be chosen for this. Call it a gut feeling. When it came to you, though, I didn't doubt it for a second. I bet you're buddied up with your Auryth right now. Is it bad that I hope it's a snake? I know how much you love them.

Tears fall silently onto the page, and I quickly wipe them away to avoid smearing the ink.

I'm only joking. We both know the snakes only bond with the slightly questionable humans around here, and you're as pure as they come. Hell, you probably got a wolf to climb out of the shadows this year. That would surely make Blane lose his mind, and I know your mom would have loved it too. Anyways, I wanted to write you this letter because I have no doubt you're distraught and worried about me and probably trying to come up with some solution to keep me safe. Although I love you for that, I needed to remind you that there is nothing that can save me from the fate I've been dealt today, and I'm okay with that. I'll get to see the sun, just like we both always dreamed about.

Meet me there one day, would you?
Love,
Wilder

The sob that escapes me is nearly inhuman, but I let it out all the same. It's like I'm boiling from the inside out, fueled by a pool of rage and sorrow so deep it seems endless. I tried to save him, did everything I could possibly think of doing, and it still wasn't enough.

Kaleu stays with me until there is nothing left but numbness, and we begin the walk back home—or at least our home for now. We'll get our new housing assignment as soon as I muster up enough energy to go to the Nexus and receive it. For now, I want to crawl into my bed and do my best to pretend this day never happened.

My stomach sinks as I walk past Wilder's family's house. Had I not spent nearly every day there for the last ten years, I wouldn't be able to tell it apart from ours. A huge part of me wants to go inside and check on his parents, who have practically become my own, but the idea of seeing them right now … it's too much. How can I look them in the eye and tell them I failed? That he's gone and yet, for whatever reason, I'm still here? I know they wouldn't blame me, but I feel the guilt all the same, and I just can't *feel* any more today.

I turn the knob to my house and force it open, taking in the small living room and my father sitting in his faded recliner. His *Auryth*, an all-white ferret named Pip, is perched near his head. Shiloh's at the dining table reading what's probably his tenth book this week, trying to appear interested in whatever is written on the page. "I'm home," I call out and head to where my father can see me.

He didn't bother showing up to the ceremony, as I anticipated, and I'm honestly not sure why I bothered looking for him anyway. I turn toward my room, resolved to just let him be and lacking the energy to try to force him to care. It's been a long time since he cared for anyone.

"A wolf?" He says casually as I pass. "It's big." They're the first words he's spoken to me in months, and my temper flares.

I don't care that he fell into depression after Mom died. We all did, but the rest of us had to keep moving. I had to keep moving because he refused to get up and take care of his children.

"I'll be sure to head to the Nexus tomorrow for my new housing arrangements. I'd hate to *inconvenience* you," I snap, Kaleu's rage swimming down the bond in agreement.

"Lennon—" my brother starts, but I give him a look that stops him from saying anything else.

Our small home only has two bedrooms, but since my mother died and my father practically moved into the living room, my brother and I each have our own space. Being the oldest, I drew the unlucky straw of getting our parents' old room. I didn't want Shiloh to have to live in a constant reminder of her, so I chose to instead.

I storm toward my room and slam the door shut, hard enough to rattle the wall.

I swear I can still smell her when I come in here sometimes. Even the curtains seem to hold her scent, like they're just as determined to hold onto her as we are. Maybe getting my own home will be a good thing—a fresh start. There are too many things that remind me of her. Too many that will remind me of Wilder now, too.

"*You've been awfully quiet,*" I tell Kaleu as he climbs onto my bed.

"*You are not alone.*"

"*That's comforting.*" He nuzzles into my side, and I reach to cut off the light as my eyes grow heavy. Crying always does that to me. "*Thank you for having my back today. You didn't hesitate. You just acted.*"

"*You are mine. From the moment I chose you, I chose to have your back always—even when the choices you're making will likely get us killed, tortured, or both.*"

"*Do you think people's minds can ever be changed … about the Convergence? Can they ever be convinced that every life—even those of the unbonded—matter? Or do you think people will always follow the herd?*"

"*I think it is difficult, but not impossible. Sometimes, it only takes one choice to ignite the flame of change, and others will follow. Perhaps that is what you did today.*"

His heavy breathing as he drifts to sleep soothes something deep inside me, and despite everything that has happened and is still to come, I know I'm safe with him. The bond is strange, filling me with a sense of all-knowing certainty that I can trust him fully, and he can trust me. We will protect one another … always.

From now until our dying day.

CHAPTER 5
SLADE

J une 24th. Same day, same time, same type of kids—
either trembling behind one another or embracing their
supposed impending death. They might not be the
exiles from last year, but their behaviors, their look, are
always so similar that it really doesn't matter. I sheath my
machete and follow the rest of the group to the platform,
hoping there won't be any fighters today. I'm not in the mood
to get blood on my clothes.

*"It's a large group this year—maybe fifty or more. I can smell them
approaching,"* Vesper says, already showing her teeth. Her
black coat gleams in the overhead sun, and I can't help but
wonder how hot it has to be under all that fur. Hell, I'm
sweating in my worn T-shirt and pants.

"I am not weak like you. I don't sweat," she purrs.

I snort, knowing if I were to touch her right now—if I
didn't think she'd bite my hand off—I'd find her fur damp.

*"Whatever you say. Just try not to kill any this time, okay? We
need the extra hands around camp."* She ignores me entirely, then
proceeds to block me out. Fine.

The mechanisms groan to life as we approach, the rusted crate grinding open to reveal a small army of new recruits, all packed tightly together.

Some cover their faces with their sleeves, their movements panicked, as if the air outside might still carry poison, which is a reasonable assumption, given what they're taught about the ground in the Burrows. The rest stand rooted in place, their wide eyes darting between us and the platform's edge. One girl steps back against the cage, pushing herself behind the others. Human shields. Smart.

It takes them a moment to process that we're alive and breathing, and that the air is no longer toxic, before the questions start loading in.

"We aren't going to die?"

"How?"

"I-is that an *Auryth*? How is that possible?"

"Stand up and form a line so we can search you," I shout over the murmuring. "Once we know you're clear, we'll direct you back to our camp. I understand many of you are likely wondering what the hell is going on, and rest assured, we have answers for you, but we need to do this first."

"Search us for what?" a blond-haired boy asks, his chest slightly puffed as he glares at me with narrowed eyes.

"Is he really about to try to act tough right now? He was just crying," I say to Vesper, only to be met with silence. I look in her direction, but she's too busy sizing up the group to notice.

"Anything they may have placed on you down there to see if the ground might be viable. Wires, radios, vital sign recorders, whatever. And let me go ahead and re-emphasize that we don't want any trouble. I'd hate to give her what she wants right now," I reply, nodding my head toward the drool dripping from Vesper's maw. She can be quite the terrifying beast, which is exactly why I love being bonded to her.

He takes the hint and falls in line with the others, extending his arms as they pat him down. "I'm sure this is a lot to process," I continue, "and I promise we'll answer all of your questions once we know you're not being tracked."

Within a few moments, they're all cleared, and though I doubt the underground civilization cares enough to see if they live or die, it's better to be safe. The last thing we want is the Burrows coming after us.

"Keep close and stay away from the woods. There's nothing out there you want to see, trust me." They begin to form a crowd around me, staring in all directions as they try to adjust to their new world. "It's around a four-hour walk to camp, which means it's four hours until you get food and water. Better keep up." A few of them look uneasy, as if they aren't sure they can trust me, but I simply grin and lead the way.

We begin the trek back to camp, the newcomers following silently behind us, though I don't miss how some of them tremble when Vesper gets too close. Clearly, no one has bonded a wolf since I was forced out, which is good.

I like it that way.

Many of the new recruits stare in awe at the forest, taking in the new sights and smells that are no doubt overwhelming their senses. After about three minutes, a muscular guy with long black hair takes off, running toward the woodline.

There's almost always one who thinks they can survive better on their own, and it's almost always the strongest looking one. They stupidly assume they're safer on their own, playing into the foolish notion that they're in control of their own fate. Little do they realize that none of us are in control up here.

As soon as he crosses the boundary, a massive white bear steps into his path. The ground shifts from its weight as coiled muscles contract beneath thick fur. A menacing growl reverberates through the forest, and the boy's knees wobble. His scream shatters the silence, and he takes off running through the woods, the bear hot on his trail.

"We have to help him!" the blond-haired boy, who was full of bravado earlier, shouts, looking between me and the rest of our group for help. Everyone stops walking, waiting for a command or instructions.

"No. He made his choice, and now he'll die for it. I couldn't have been clearer about the importance of complying with my rules. I specifically said *do not* go near the woods, and he went in anyway. We don't have the space or time for liabilities in our camp." I ignore the desperate pleas from the boy behind me until my machete slides out of its sheath, and I whip around to see him running towards the woods with it.

Anger ripples through me, and I consider using my power to knock him flat on his back. It would be so simple—just a wave of my hand. But then again, if he goes after that bear, it will probably kill him, too, and that will be one less problem for me to deal with. Even if that means I'll have to find a new weapon, which is a surprisingly difficult thing to scavenge for these days.

"Let him go," I tell the group, continuing on. "That bear will kill them both before they can make it back over the line. As for the rest of you, *listen* when we tell you to do something. The woods are wild *Auryth* territory, where they live and hunt as they please. If you want to stay alive, try following orders."

We make it all of five minutes before a scream rings out. A few shudder at the sound, but I ignore it. A few minutes later, Vesper's ears perk up and her nose twitches as she smells something in the breeze.

I follow her line of sight to find Blondie jogging toward us, his clothes stained red, tears sliding down his cheeks in a steady stream. He appears unharmed, but the first boy who'd taken off isn't with him.

"It—it ripped his head clean off. Th—there was so much blood. So much. I couldn't stop it. I couldn't—"

I walk toward him and snatch my machete out of his hand, sheathing it back in place. "So you ran and left him to die instead?"

"I—I couldn't save him. I tried to stab it, but it already had him cornered and wasn't remotely phased by the wound. When I ran, it was … it was eating him alive. Tearing him limb from limb."

I raise an eyebrow, crossing my arms. "Had you listened to me the first time, you would've saved yourself the trouble of seeing that. The wild *Auryths* are ruthless. We believe it's something about the chemicals left over from the war that's affected their brains. Stay far away from them." I allow a moment for that to sink in, savoring the visual of several eyebrows attempting to fly off faces. "For whatever reason, they won't leave the woods, so you're safe as long as you don't go near their territory. "Oh," I spin to glare at Blondie, "and if you *ever* touch my machete again, you'll find it in your neck. Now, let's go."

The field stretches on forever, its tall grass rippling in waves as the wind passes through. Here and there, broken pieces of concrete jut out at odd angles, remnants of an old road or a foundation long since swallowed by the earth. As we walk, someone stumbles over a rusted pipe half-buried in the dirt and curses under their breath. I don't bother turning around to check on them. Until we make it to camp, they're just bodies. Potential recruits.

Beyond the field, the hills roll out in uneven swells, dotted with crumbling buildings and the skeletal remains of what look like crawlers, rust-eaten and hollow. One leans against the slope, its body cracked open like a rib cage picked clean, the weeds slowly pulling it into the dirt. I remember the sketches from our history lessons—hulking metal shells on wheels, packed with seats, meant to carry people and *Auryths* across the surface before we went underground. Now, it doesn't look like it ever moved at all.

The group is quiet, and it isn't the kind of silence that comes with comfort—it's heavy, tense, like everyone is waiting for the other shoe to drop. The blond boy is a few steps behind me, his shoulders square, his hands clenching and unclenching at his sides. His anger and fear linger in the air like a tangible thing.

"Is it always like this?" one of the girls asks, her voice barely above a whisper. She's smaller than the others, her near-white hair sticking to her forehead from sweat. She keeps glancing at the horizon, like she's expecting something to appear out of nowhere.

"Like what?" I ask.

"Empty," she says. "Broken."

I glance at the ruins covering the landscape. "It's better than that underground prison you used to call home."

~

Our camp always makes my heart swell with pride when I see it. What we've built, despite being thrown to our deaths with nothing but the clothes on our backs, will always be impressive to me.

The inner area is a patchwork of tents and makeshift shelters, some reinforced with scavenged metal sheets from abandoned crawlers and buildings, others covered in tattered tarps weighed down with bricks. Woven branches and old ropes serve as walls for a few structures, while others are reinforced with bent rebar and scrap wood. Fires burn in stone pits spread out around camp, their smoke curling into the sky in thick, lazy plumes that carry the sharp scent of charred wood and leaves through the air.

"Welcome to Camp Solis," I tell the new group, giving them a smile I rarely wear. "This can be your home, or you can try to face the world outside of our walls on your own. We're all about choice here. Though I do suggest you make yours wisely."

Around camp, clotheslines sag under the weight of patchy garments and threadbare blankets, fluttering halfheartedly in the breeze. Tools lay scattered across workbenches pieced together from broken doors and rusted metal.

"Tomorrow, you'll be given your work details based on your previous job in the Burrows and what interests you might have. We have five divisions: guardwatchers who help protect our village; scavengers who hunt for materials and supplies; medical; farming and food preservation; and patchers who help repair structures, tents, and anything else we might need them to. Think about what you might want to do and be prepared to provide us with some sort of reasoning tomorrow."

I pause, giving them time to process before continuing.

"Some of you might think that this is just like the Burrows, that we're using you for free labor and providing scraps in return, but we're not. We won't force you into a role that you don't agree to, but everyone here plays a part to keep this place running. We don't tolerate freeloaders. Once you agree to your assignment, you'll be expected to show up to work and *do* the work expected of you. If you refuse ... well ... you might just find yourself sleeping with the wild *Auryths*."

Despite the constant grind of survival, the place sings with a quiet resilience—an energy born not from hope, but from sheer determination to stay alive. It's ugly, yeah, but it's ours.

The newcomers stand frozen, their eyes darting around the camp, taking in the layers of ingenuity that surround them. Much of the initial shock from the bear massacre—and being sent to their deaths mere hours ago—falters as they realize what this means for them. For all of us.

"Go on. You're free now."

Cheers erupt from both sides as they flood the open gate, joy visible on almost every face. I remember how I felt when I was in their shoes: the fear, the happiness, the desperation for release from the rules below. It's only been two years since my exile, but it feels like an eternity now.

As night approaches, I take my place around one of the many fires and listen to Sage, one of our oldest residents, tell stories about when she first arrived. I've heard every single one before, but I never miss when she tells them again.

"I was one of the first to be sent here from below and survive. Fifty-two years I've walked this ground. I still remember the warm sun on my face and being terrified that I was going to die. Only I didn't die. Instead, the twenty of us wandered aimlessly, looking for any other survivors. We lost two on the first night and three more over the next few days.

The wilderness can be quite ruthless—as I'm sure you've discovered—and back then, the air wasn't perfect either." Her eyes gleam with tears, but they don't fall.

"We started small, collecting rubbish to build our home and creating a boundary map to keep us safe from the things that lurk in the shadows. Before we knew it, a year had passed, and a new group was being sent up right where we once were. Thank goodness we checked that stupid platform, hoping there'd be more of us one day—or at least that they might send up some food. Since then, we've grown into quite a bunch. We work hard, but we do it together. You will all find happiness here. A family of unwanteds, if you will," she finishes, giving them a sweet smile.

"What about the others down below?" Blondie from earlier asks, immediately jumping to the top of my list of grievances.

"They don't care about us, so we don't care about them. Let them live in their 'utopia'. Let them believe they're sending people to their deaths for the good of the city. We'll be here to take in the unwanted and give them a place where they belong. Trying to bring everyone up here will only open the door for the Regime to gain a new foothold, and I'd rather die than see that happen," I seethe.

"The people we love down there deserve to be free, too!" he presses.

"What's the matter, Blondie? Have a hot girlfriend down there? Maybe your mommy? The fact of the matter is, if we tell them they can come up here, *no one* will be free. If you try to get a message to them, it will be considered an act of treason, and it will result in your death. It's one of the few rules we abide by here. Is that clear?" I tilt my head, daring him to breathe another question in my direction. I do not have the patience for this, least of all on the day of the Convergence. Taking in an entire new group is enough work as it is. I don't need to deal with him on top of it.

His blue eyes shine with malice as they narrow on me in the firelight. "Clear, *sir*. And my name is Wilder."

"Can I kill that one?" Vesper asks.

"Nice of you to join me again, Ves. As for the boy, I'm not sure yet. Quit blocking me out, and I'll be sure to let you know when I decide." Her growl rumbles through my mind, sending vibrations all the way to my toes.

"How did you bond up here?" a girl asks, her eyes fixed on Vesper, mesmerized. "I thought we were all unworthy."

The rest of them lean in, either genuinely curious or trying to plot how they, too, can gain a bond. "I'd be lying if I said I understood it. She found me, and I became hers. I would highly suggest that you don't go looking for a bond, though. Most of the *Auryths* up here are more likely to eat you than bond with you."

It *is* unusual for an *Auryth* to decide to bond up here. I'm not sure if it's because the chemicals messed with their minds, or if there's truly something to us being deemed unworthy, but I can count on my hands the number of bonded that have been inside Camp Solis. Most days, Vesper likes to claim she must've been delirious from dehydration when she stumbled upon me.

I leave them with one final message before heading to my makeshift home. "Here's the thing: the Regime lied to you —*shocking*, I know. They needed you to believe you were nothing without their approval, without a bond. And you believed them, didn't you? We all did. Well, let me be perfectly clear: you're here because you're unbonded, not because you're unworthy. That crap they drilled into our heads was their way of keeping us on our knees. Now, you get to prove them wrong. Or not. The choice is up to you. Either way, I'll see you bright and early for breakfast and assignments."

I say it for them, but sometimes I don't even realize how much I need the reminder, too.

CHAPTER 6
LENNON

The lights flicker more than usual as I walk to the Nexus. A power outage is almost inevitable, given it's been nearly a week since the last one. The Burrows are *technically* kept alive by generators older than any living human, but the magic imbued into them from the technomancers—those bonded to serpents—keeps them from going out entirely. Using so much magic, though, can be costly and exhausting—hence the blackouts.

I focus on it more than I ordinarily would, mainly because it's better than thinking about all the other things currently fighting for space in my mind. Kaleu walks beside me, and I try my best not to panic about getting a new home placement or my new military assignment, or to think about Wilder.

Besides the Bowl, the Nexus is by far the most noticeable structure in the Burrows. Nearly five feet taller than the rest, it isn't just a building: it's the heart of the Burrows. Here, life begins and ends: marriages are officiated, births and deaths are recorded, homes are assigned, rations are organized, and futures are dictated. Everything flows through it.

I face the heavily guarded entrance and pull out my identification card. One of the taller guards takes it silently, and I watch as he looks between me and the picture a few times before finally buzzing us in. The gate shifts open, allowing Kaleu and me to pass before slamming shut behind us. Another guard motions for me to follow, leading us down a long hall and into a room on the right.

Inside is Isla Dade, and her black panther; Rudy Zepp, and his creepy red serpent coiled tightly around his neck; and a middle-aged woman with shoulder-length, curly blonde hair. I swear I've seen her somewhere before, but I can't remember when or where. "Lennon Benfield," she says as everyone's heads pivot toward us. "I see you also came for your next steps today. Please, join us. We were just getting started."

I give her a soft smile and move to stand with the others. Kaleu pushes so hard against my legs that I have to fight to keep my balance. *"What are you doing? You're going to knock me over!"*

"I'm staying close. I don't have a good feeling about any of these people or their Auryths. Stay alert." Well, at least I'm not the only one who doesn't like snakes.

"My name is Lyric Calwyn, and I oversee post-bonding affairs. As you likely already know, you have two days post-ceremony to come here and get everything in order, but I can see you three are ahead of the game!" She adds a soft laugh, to which no one joins in. There's something about her that makes me nauseous.

"Okay, where were we?" she continues. "Oh, yes. Housing arrangements. You'll each be given your own accommodations for up to three years before you're obligated to fulfill your duty to the Regime and marry. If you don't choose a partner before your allotted time is up, we will provide you with a few potential matches based on both genetics and personality. We believe that everyone has a right to choose their spouse, but if you are unable to, it is in the best interest of the Burrows to create partnerships with superior bloodlines, so the children are more likely to bond."

My head is spinning. Arranged marriages? Superior bloodlines? Every day in this place, I learn something new that pushes me closer to the edge of wanting to burn it all down. Was my parents' marriage arranged? Will I be forced to be with someone I despise?

"I won't let that happen," Kaleu growls. *"I'll rip out their throats with my bare teeth before you can lift a pen to sign a marriage contract."* Well, that's comforting.

She scans our faces, and I do my best to keep my expressions neutral. "That will give you ample time to get acquainted with your *Auryths* and begin your lessons, which will begin two days from now. This is a topic we do not speak openly about within the Burrows. It's a conversation we have with every bonded, but it is a conversation for *us* to have with *them*, not for it to be spread around the city. If you are caught telling anyone about what we've discussed inside this room, we may be forced to activate your chips. Any questions?"

A million, actually, but considering I'm already on thin ice with the Regime, I keep my mouth clamped shut. No one else says anything, either. Lyric sits at her desk and gets to work assigning us homes. Within ten minutes, I'm holding a key to mine: number 363—the Third Ring. I do my best to hide my sneer. At one time, being assigned to the Third Ring would have been a privilege, but now it feels like salt in an open wound. Generally speaking, First Ringers who bond to elites move to Second, and Second Ringers jump to Third. It's rare to have someone jump straight from First to Third. Blane is trying to keep an eye on me, and the easiest way to do that is to keep me close.

As we head out of the room, she calls out, "Remember, your lessons will begin in two days. They'll be in The Arcanum, located right past the greenhouses on the south side of the Burrows. If you have any issues finding it, please return here to the Nexus, and we will have someone escort you. Congratulations! Oh, and Lennon, stay behind for a moment, please."

My entire body goes rigid at the request as the memory of yesterday's torture flickers in my mind. Isla and Rudy file out of the room, leaving me to my demise. We should run. There might not be anywhere else to go, but anywhere is better than here.

"You won't need to run. She's bonded to a frog," Kaleu says, his eyes darting toward my own.

"What? What does that have to do with anything?"

"Her Auryth is a frog. It's not an elite. I could eat it like a snack with ease. Look at her front pocket." I do as he asks, focusing my eyes on the front pocket of her grey shirt. Lo and behold, I can barely make out the small, yellow frog sticking out.

"Cute. If only I could carry you in my pocket. Now, why is it so important that I look at it?" I ask him, nudging his body with my leg.

"You must learn to watch more carefully and notice the things others do not. Always know who you are up against, even if you are not actively threatened."

"I didn't know you were such a poet," I tease. He has a point, though I'm not the type to discredit any *Auryth*—even some of the so-called "weaker" species can still be utilized in deadly manners.

"President Blane has informed me of your transition from

the greenhouse to military duty. With you being in classes, you will only spend three hours a day there until graduation. Meet the guards at the front of the Nexus after your lessons, and they will direct you from there. That is all." Her lips twist into a fake smile, her kinky curls bouncing as she motions toward the door.

I was hoping Blane had forgotten to move my work detail. Despite all the things that have transpired over the last few days, there's still something incredibly excruciating about losing the one thing I actually enjoy down here. What is there to even do on military duty? The citizens inside the Burrows hardly revolt against the Regime, and it's not like we're going to war. Shouldn't our priority be optimizing our crop yield? Wouldn't I be more useful there? Of course, I would be, but I'd also be more difficult to keep an eye on. I know it as much as Blane does. It was all worth it, though, if only to know deep down that I did everything I could to keep Wilder from his fate.

Even if it was a failure.

The moment I step out of the Nexus, I'm greeted by Isla and Rudy. "Pity about Wilder. Who will you possibly find to marry you now?" Isla's voice rings out, and I turn to face her and her enormous panther.

She's annoyingly pretty—tall, smart, and eyes a perfect shade of ice blue—but mean as hell, too, just for the sake of it. She always wants to be the best at everything, and I know she likely despises that Kaleu chose me instead of her. "I don't know, Isla. I guess it's a good thing they'll pick for me if it comes to that."

"How unfortunate for that person," she replies curtly. I propel myself in the opposite direction, attempting to both run from the confrontation and hide my trembling fists.

"Why do you run? Why let her intimidate you?" Kaleu asks, easily keeping stride with me. *"I could take that panther easily."*

"Would you quit threatening to 'take down' every Auryth you see? It's not worth the argument, and, despite recent events, I'm not a confrontational person. Not to mention, we aren't supposed to speak about the arranged marriage thing openly, and we both know the Regime is watching me closely. I don't want to give them any more ammo. Just drop it, please."

He lets out an overdramatic huff. *"I am the only wolf, and you are the only human to bond a wolf, within the walls of the Burrows. They should fear us. You should not fear them. I guarantee you that the wolf-bonded who lived above before the war were feared by many."*

I ignore his sentiment.

We stop at my family home first to pack and inform my brother and father of my new house number, not that my father will visit anyway. There isn't much to take with me beyond my clothes, daily essentials, and my mother's journal, which I stuff into a wheeled basket cart.

I grab an old Polaroid of the four of us before everything went to hell and stare at it. I remember the day fondly: all of us dressed in our finest clothes, eager to secure our spot in line and document our family in film for an eternity. Shiloh was so small then, a frown plastered on his tiny face. Dad has his arms wrapped around Mom tightly, smiling like he doesn't have a care in the world. It's strange to see him like that. I can't even remember the last time I've seen him smile.

My parents' marriage couldn't have been arranged. My mother was bonded to an elite, a hawk, and my father to a ferret. For a family to gain access to the Third ring, *both* parents must be bonded to elites, which makes sense as to why they create arranged marriages for those who don't choose their own spouses. It's just another way for them to keep the elite bloodlines "pure" under the illusion of choice. My mom chose to leave that life behind for my father. She loved him. Though now, it's hard to see why.

They both worked incredibly hard to try to get us moved up to Second, but now I know that those spots are reserved for those who agree to do the Regime's bidding. My parents would do nearly anything to give us a better life, but never that.

The platform that rises to the Second and Third Rings is far more exquisite than anything should be down here. Constructed entirely of glass, the walls and floor are so clean that it's as if you're levitating. I roll my squealing cart into it, making Kaleu's ears fold back with each screech of the wheels. Someone else enters next to me, a woman who smells of what I think is vanilla and something more lavish than my senses have ever experienced. She's draped in a glittering, royal blue gown, and gold is painted on her waterlines and around her lips. Her curves spill out in the tight dress, making it evident that she's never known a day of rationing. Or maybe she has. Maybe she was like me once but has spent the last however many years indulging in the lifestyle change.

Her *Auryth* looks just as well-fed: a plump, electric-blue snake that curls around her neck like a piece of jewelry. Its beady eyes slide toward Kaleu and me, its tongue flicking incessantly as she runs a finger against its scales.

I face the opposite direction, desperate to avoid their gazes. The ground below seems so small from up here; lights flicker in and out of view, and the deterioration of the buildings I've come to know fades into oblivion. The ration building is impossible to miss, though, with a line already curling around the side as people wait with their cards in hand.

I won't let myself become like this woman. I won't forget the people starving below.

"First day?" she asks, looking between Kaleu and me. I nod, finding myself at a loss for words for once. "You'll want to take a left when we get to the top. Your attendant will find you, explain the rules, and get you a new wardrobe." I don't miss the way she scrunches her nose as she looks me up and down. "And a bath."

"Thank you," I force out, and my stomach drops as the platform comes sliding to a halt. The woman exits first without another word, the train of her dress dragging behind her. I've never owned a dress, and I can't help but admire it as she goes.

I place a hesitant foot out of the platform and onto the marbled floor, suddenly feeling exceptionally dirty in comparison to the sterility of my new home. Even the air itself seems to be cleaner, making each breath feel more luxurious. Large glass windows line the enclosed walkway, showcasing the view below. It all seems so small from up here.

"Miss Benfield, I presume?" a voice calls from behind me, and I jump, startled. I turn to find a thin, older man wearing a small, oval hat and stark white uniform to match. His face is riddled with wrinkles, and his eyes are soft and soulful.

"Yes?"

"My name is Archelaus, but you can call me Archie. I'll be your personal attendant from now on. At least until I finally croak, that is." He laughs, but all I can do is stare. My own attendant? And an elderly man, no less? I feel sick. "That was supposed to be a joke, Miss Benfield. I didn't mean to offend you."

"You didn't," I say quickly. "I'm sorry. It's been a long few days."

"I understand. Let's get you and your *Auryth* to your new home. I'll push your cart for you."

"I've got it, Archie. Just show me the way." His face sinks in a way that instantly makes me feel horrible, and I can't for the life of me understand how I've managed to offend him. Surely he doesn't enjoy serving a group of pompous, entitled elites, right? There's so much I don't understand about this place, and probably never will.

I roll the cart toward him and watch as he lights back up, grabbing it and leaning his frail body on the handle. This is so wrong. How did someone who should be enjoying the remainder of their life end up becoming a personal servant for people who don't even *see* him?

"Do you sense his Auryth anywhere?" I ask Kaleu after looking Archie over a few times.

"No." Interesting. I haven't known many people who go without their *Auryth*, especially at work detail. Do they not allow "attendants" *Auryths* up here? If so, why not?

He leads me through a maze of corridors, proving the Third Ring is even more complex and vast than I gave it credit for. Doors leading into homes line the sides of the walkways with numbers engraved above them, but he keeps going until we get to 363. Reaching into his pocket, he pulls out a twisted, gold key and hands it to me. "You should do the honors. Welcome to your new home. And when I say new, I mean *new*. You're the first person to ever live in this one."

He's beaming with excitement as I turn the key over in my hand, my mind racing. Why would the Regime give me this place?

I insert the key and twist until I hear it unlock, then push the door open gingerly. My breath hitches as I take in the high ceilings, marbled floors, and full kitchen with new appliances. There's even an oven; all we've ever had is a stovetop. With rations coming in packets, we've never really had a need for anything else. Is the food different up here, too? *Real?*

Everything I've heard regarding how the elites live on Ring Three has been contradictory and, no doubt, various forms of conjecture. Some say they have food delivered three times a day to their very doors. Others say their process is similar to ours on the bottom, but they have more rations and actual full-course meals.

Two plush, white couches are positioned around a coffee table in the living room. Kaleu takes off ahead of me, his nose twitching in investigation as he inspects every corner of the house. It appears to be one story, but from where I'm standing, I count at least four bedroom doors stretched open on either side of the kitchen and living room: two on the left and two on the right. Another friendly reminder that they want the elites to breed and give them better genetic pools for the Convergence.

Archie rolls my cart in and straight for one of them, motioning for me to follow. This must be the master bedroom. A giant bed, decorated with lilac pillows and a white quilt, takes up almost an entire wall, and there's a bathroom *inside* the room, containing a massive tub that I selfishly can't wait to sink into.

"Before I leave you to get acquainted with your new home, there are a few rules we need to discuss. Care to join me in the living room?" Archie asks, giving me a soft smile. I nod and follow him back out, then take a spot on the couch.

It's incredibly soft and warm, and I slip off my shoes and curl my legs up underneath me. "First, congratulations on

70

your bond to an elite. It isn't every day that someone rises so highly in station, and to a wolf, no less. That being said, this new lifestyle will be vastly different than what you're used to. Your family is welcome to visit you as long as you notify me for documentation purposes. No more than two consecutive overnight stays are allowed without special permission, which you can request through me. Only one visit per guest per month."

Well, at least Shiloh can visit. I wish I could just drag him up and out of that house to live here permanently, though. "Second, rations operate a bit differently here. Meals can be either delivered to your door or you're welcome to go to the mess hall and receive them. I'll provide you with a map in case you want to navigate there on your own, but I can always lead you there until you get comfortable. The meals here are a bit more ... extravagant than what you're used to. It's recommended that you don't overindulge in your first few weeks, or you'll likely make yourself sick. You'll receive three per day."

He pauses, coughing into the crook of his elbow. "No giving away rations under any circumstances. If you don't finish it, you're welcome to keep it in your refrigerator or throw it away. If you have a visitor, they may share your rations with you during the length of their stay, but they will not receive their own. There are weekly, random security sweeps of all homes to ensure everything is in order. Failure to comply will, again, result in consequences. Lastly, the use of magic in any capacity within the Third Ring is prohibited. There aren't many rules here, but if you were to break any of them, it would mean your immediate relocation to the First Ring and possibly worse, depending on the transgression. Any questions?"

Throw the food away? We can't supply enough food to

healthily support our people below, yet they tell us to *discard* the extras? How can they have so much food up here when people are starving in the First Ring? When they're eating damn plant goop? How is that even legal? And no magic use up here? What's the point of bonding to an *Auryth* if we can't even use our gifts?

I open my mouth to spout out snide comments, but my mind lingers on that last bit. *Possibly worse.* I know what that means all too well. My eyes scan the room, looking for the cameras I can't see but swear I can feel watching me.

"Any way you can write these down for me? That's a lot to remember," I choke out. He looks slightly surprised by my question, then reaches for a pen. "That was supposed to be a joke, Archie. Sorry. No, I don't have any questions." He lets out a wheezing sound that I think is supposed to be a laugh, then smiles.

His voice lowers. "I like you, Miss Benfield. You're not like other folks up here, though I've known that since the day you fought for that boy. I shouldn't say things like that, but I thought you should know that you weren't alone in your sentiment."

My throat tightens, but I force myself to smile. "Thank you, Archie." He points to an old phone connected to the wall and instructs me to dial 333 if I need him for anything before leaving us to the silence.

I saunter back to my new bedroom and climb into the bed, doing my best not to let myself enjoy the way my body sinks into it. This is a bribe from Blane. I don't know what his endgame is, but I will not allow him to win at his mind games. Kaleu crawls up with me, releasing a low, satisfied growl.

My heart is heavy with the weight of what I've lost. I stare at the perfectly placed curtains, the intricate rug extending from underneath the bed, and the bathroom only steps away. This is what they sacrificed Wilder's life for. So we can live up here in luxury, pretending we don't spend an entire day each year sending kids to die.

I'm filled with rage. My blood heats to the point of boiling, my chest so tight it hurts to breathe. I can't look at it anymore. I can't pretend to be a part of this.

I crawl out of bed and rip at the velvet curtains, letting them pull from their rod and clatter onto the floor below. It's not enough. My eyes catch the bedding, and I move straight toward it, throwing the lilac pillows around like they're daggers. All Kaleu does is stare at me, silent. It's stupid. None of this changes anything; it can't undo the things that have already been done. But it's the only way I can get at the Regime, the only thing of theirs I can destroy without risking them hurting Shiloh.

I want to scream, cry, vomit, fight, *something*, but I am a useless shell of the person I was two days ago. Dropping to the ground, I curl my legs to my chest, letting the firm hand of grief wrap her claws around me. Out the window, I can make out the little lights lining the streets of where I used to call home, flickering in and out of view.

I wonder if he got to see the sun before he died.

The bed sinks under my weight as I curl next to Kaleu. *"Why did you choose me?"* I ask Kaleu, my voice cracking. *"I'm not strong. I'm not confrontational. I'm not outspoken or a leader. I can't fight. Why choose me when there were so many other options? People like Isla? People like Wilder?"*

"The fact that you still worry about the others suffering below is exactly why. Your heart is pure, your intentions always good. I saw that when I looked inside your soul."

"The people below are suffering, Kaleu. Suffering while all of these people sit up here, plump and spoiled. Not to mention the ones who died. Who will die. How can I let myself enjoy any of this? How can I live like this? How can I go on pretending I'm someone I'm not?"

"There is always suffering, little wolf. You simply have to decide what you're going to do about it."

CHAPTER 7
SLADE

After two weeks, we've managed to get everyone assigned to a work detail, establish the ground rules, and provide each of them with their own tent, but keeping them in line has been another story altogether. There's something about the way their minds run wild with freedom that makes them act like a bunch of delinquents. Unfortunately, I've caught several of them doing rather *suggestive* things, and as the Warden, it's my responsibility to scold them and send them back to their own tents.

Sometimes it's like I'm an elder despite being only two years older than them.

When I first came to the surface and realized I wasn't going to die from suffocation, joining leadership certainly wasn't exactly part of my plan; survival was. But then Ves found me, and everything changed. She didn't ask, she decided. She bound herself to me, and suddenly, people started looking my way for answers. Answers I didn't have and didn't want to give.

Commander Keelan calls it fate. I prefer to call *her* a headache.

There's something about bonding with a wolf that makes people look at you differently. Most out of fear, some out of jealousy, and some simply out of curiosity. It's rather backwards: being bonded in a group full of unbonded exiles. Despite all the conversations we've had about equality and how having an *Auryth* doesn't make those in the Burrows superior, they all look to me as a protector, a leader of sorts. But I never wanted any of this.

I splash my face with a bucket of lukewarm water I pulled from our camp's small pond and watch it drip from my chin onto my shirt. There's hardly anything I miss about the Burrows, but running water is a luxury I did not appreciate when I had it.

"Slade?" It's not a voice I recognize, and I bristle.

"It's the boy from the platform. The blond one you're still debating on killing." Vesper says, and I groan, dragging a hand over my face.

"Wilder. What does he want now?"

"To amuse me, if nothing else." She stretches near the entrance, her tail flicking lazily as her amber eyes glint with mischief. *"Let him in. I'm curious how long it'll take before you lose your temper."*

"Great." I pull on my boots. *"Glad someone's entertained."* When I step outside, the air is thick with the scent of lingering smoke and pine. Wilder stands rigid, his arms crossed and chin raised. A poor attempt to appear intimidating.

"Speak," I say flatly.

"I think we should bring them up," he blurts, his voice

cracking on the last word. "The ones in the Burrows, the kids, the families, they deserve a chance."

I arch a brow, leaning closer. "Do I look like someone who cares about people who never cared about us?"

Wilder flinches, his jaw tightening. "Not everyone agrees with what they did to us. There are innocents down there, people who don't know the whole story. If they knew—"

"*If.*" My laugh is anything but amused. "Do you know what would happen if word got back to the Burrows? If they found out they could survive up here?"

Wilder opens his mouth, gaping like a fish, but no sound comes out. "They'll come," I say, stepping closer. "Not with questions or negotiations, but with force. They'll take everything we've worked for and claim it for themselves. And people like us? They'll shove us back into the ground or string us up for living when they meant for us to die. Do you think your noble ideals are worth that price? Would you trade everyone's life up here for the ones down there? They *despise* the unbonded."

I lean in close enough to see the panic flicker in his eyes. "They don't even track the people they send up here. We're dead to them. And that's the only reason we're still breathing. So, unless you're prepared to rain down hell on all of us, *drop it.*"

Wilder's jaw tightens. "It doesn't have to be that way."

I snort. "It does. So here's what's going to happen. You're going to forget whatever brilliant idea you think you have, and you're going to focus on surviving, like the rest of us. And if I hear even a whisper of you going behind my back, I'll make sure you never have the chance to go against me again. Understood?"

Wilder's face pales. He nods stiffly. "Understood."

"Good." I turn on my heel and head back into the tent, brushing past Ves.

"I think I'm rubbing off on you," she muses, ears twitching as she focuses on sounds I can't hear.

I tense. *"What is it?"*

"The bell. Someone's at the gate." The bell. My stomach twists. I'm already moving, my boots pounding against the packed earth as Ves keeps pace beside me. We don't get visitors out here.

By the time I reach Commander Keelan, the figure at the gate is fully visible. A man, barely older than me, staggers forward, leaning heavily on a panther as dark as midnight. The *Auryth* moves with liquid grace, supporting him with every step. Blood seeps from his abdomen, dripping onto the grass below.

"Opie," Keelan breathes, his voice breaking. Before I can stop him, he runs to meet the man, hauling one of his arms under his shoulder. I'm glued in place. I've heard stories of Opie; he left right before I arrived. He's also one of the few others to bond an *Auryth* on the surface.

"Slade, go get Caius! I'll try and get him inside the gate as quickly as I can," Keelan barks, his voice snapping me out of my daze. I hesitate. We have very few rules here, but the one we always put the most emphasis on is *no* outsiders. Opie isn't the only one to have left our camp over the years for one reason or another, though none have ever returned and made us enforce that rule—until now.

"With all due respect, sir, he's an outsider," I say sternly.

Keelan's glare is dark enough to make my stomach twist. "He is not an outsider. He's one of us. Do as I say. Now!" I swallow the protest rising in my throat and sprint back toward the camp. I could have told Caius mentally—one of the few benefits of being bonded to a wolf—but I need the space, if only for a moment, to collect myself.

When Caius and I return with a med kit in hand and his stag, Mage, trailing behind, Opie is barely clinging to consciousness right inside our gate. His breathing is shallow, each gasp ragged and desperate. Caius wastes no time, cutting his shirt open to reveal a jagged gash stretching across his abdomen.

"Hold him steady," he orders as he reaches for a bottle of alcohol to sterilize the wound. "This is going to hurt." The moment he pours the liquid, Opie returns to life, screaming in agony as I pin his arms down, struggling against his inhuman strength. His panther growls low and approaches closer, lying near Opie's head and nuzzling up against him. There's no doubt the beast is hurting, too, thanks to the link they share.

"Keelan, apply pressure here," Caius orders, handing him a strip of cloth. The Commander does as he asks, his hands unsteady.

I watch, mesmerized, as Caius's hands began to glow in that pure white color his healing abilities always seem to produce. One brushes the skin of Opie's forehead gently, then both move and dig into the dirt. The light trails through the soil, breaking through some of the looser patches until it reaches Caius's stag. Soon, all of us are bathed in the warm glow of his power.

A tingling sensation trails up my arm as plants begin to sprout sporadically around me, blooming into purple and white flowers that are absolutely breathtaking.

Caius mutters something under his breath—a prayer or a spell, I can't tell—and plucks a handful of the purple blossoms from the patch that shimmer faintly in the light. Lumia vine. I've heard the name before. It's a rare plant that's said to have exceptional healing qualities, though I always thought it was a myth. He mashes it in his hand, creating a paste-like substance that he smothers over Opie's wounds. Within minutes, Caius carefully lifts the rag off Opie's body, revealing nothing but an angry, thin line of redness and dried blood. "He will be fine. I need to rest, and so does he," he says, resting a shaky hand on his stag as he gets to his feet. Using so much power has taken its toll on his body.

Eventually, the others disperse, leaving Keelan, Opie, and me on the ground. "He left, and you don't know why he came back. We have rules, Keelan, rules that you helped create. Rules that *you* taught *me*."

"It doesn't matter why he came back. He's one of us, Slade. He's always been one of us. We need to find an empty tent where he can rest, and we'll ask him all the questions you want when he wakes," he replies, and I bite my tongue to keep from spewing all of the reasons this is a terrible idea. Keelan lifts Opie into his arms, his muscles straining with the effort, and heads to the tents, the panther right behind them.

"Something doesn't feel right about this," I tell Ves.

"I can't say I disagree with you. I want to know how he got this injury and how he just happened to be close enough to our gate for Caius to repair it before he bled out. I don't particularly like panthers either." Her eyes meet mine, her lip curled upward just enough to bare her teeth.

I follow Keelan to an empty tent and help him clear a path to the bed before dragging one of the two chairs inside the tent to Opie's bedside and leaning back. "I'll wait here until he wakes up," I say, watching the panther climb into the bed with him while Ves lies at my feet, her eyes locked on the pair.

"I think it would be best for him to wake up around someone familiar. Head back to your tent or find something to do with the newcomers. I'll call for you when he's awake," Keelan counters, taking a seat in the other chair.

I clench my fists at the dismissal but do as I'm told. My power presses against my skin like a storm, desperate to break free. *"Keep it in check until we're outside the perimeter,"* Vesper warns, nudging my leg as I jog toward the gate. My chest tightens with the effort to hold it in. I need to go somewhere I can unleash it without anyone seeing.

I sprint through the gate and well beyond it, each stride pounding the earth, my heartbeat thundering in my ears. My lungs burn with every step, and it's as if the ground beneath me is vibrating in sync with my rapid pulse. When I'm sure we're far enough from the others, I drop to my knees, unable to hold it in anymore.

It comes in waves, crackling and snapping through the air. The ground trembles beneath me as I let it take control. The world slows as the anger surges, rising from somewhere deep inside until I can't remember what it's like to hold back anymore, and I don't want to.

When I finally look up, I realize the grass in the field has been reduced to smoldering embers, the ground scorched and blackened in every direction.

It took me a year after bonding Ves to learn that my power is tied to emotion. Keeping them in check, especially when I'm worked up, is the most challenging part.

I've spent the majority of my life learning to be emotionally numb, an asset that I once despised and have now learned to appreciate. But in rare times like this, when my emotions are running rampant, I can burn the entire world to ash.

There's still so much I don't understand about what I'm capable of, and there's no one I can ask, either.

"Breathe," she commands, and I obey. I always obey her in this state, as if something in the bond allows her complete control over every part of me. It's the only time I ever let someone—let anyone—have that kind of hold over me. And I loathe it.

No one knows how explosive this gift, this ... power can truly be, and telling them would label me a threat. Something to be feared, which I'm not. I'm just ... alone.

I will always be a threat for my people, but never to them. Not if I can help it.

"You are not a threat. Now breathe. Force it away," she demands, and I do.

CHAPTER 8
LENNON

As we approach the Arcanum, I prepare myself for the first day of magic boot camp. Despite my nerves, I'm somewhat excited. Determined. I need to learn how the hell to use my powers, especially with Blane on my back. If it comes down to it—if he threatens Shiloh—I need to be ready to fight.

I've had plenty of chances to see the other *Auryth* bonds at work in the Burrows, but never a wolf, and Kaleu's and my efforts to locate any information on the topic in the archives were useless. There's nothing there but a bunch of dusty tomes and over-appreciated artifacts from our time above ground. It's as though all of it has been scrubbed from history. Even Kaleu doesn't know what, exactly, we can do: only that it's dangerous in the wrong hands, and therefore makes us a special kind of powerful.

That's the problem with history; it all depends on who writes it, and who has the power to erase it.

So far, there haven't been any indicators that I even *have* powers, aside from that one instance with the guard, and I'm not so sure I didn't make that up in my head. I don't care how long it takes, though. I'll figure it out. For Shiloh.

"Do you even have an idea of what powers we might have?" I press, eyeing the steel structure before us.

"I have a general understanding of our power, but it's different for each person and animal that bonds. You know that," Kaleu says. *"Besides, it's the strength of the bond that matters. Learn how to do the small things first. Focus on mastering control. You don't want to accidentally kill us in your sleep, do you?"*

I stop walking and place my hands on my hips. *"That's not a thing. I've never heard of that happening to anyone."*

"Just like you didn't know they had a prison and a torture device? How about the arranged marriages part?" He slides his piercing golden eyes toward me. *"Fear surrounding the bonding wouldn't be wise when everyone here is forced to endure it or die."* I glare at him as he turns and walks through the open door ahead, completely ignoring me.

Maybe he can smell the other *Auryths*, or maybe he simply has an uncanny sense of direction. I don't ask, but he leads us straight into the large auditorium where the others who survived the bonding ceremony are already waiting. Isla and Rudy stand off to one side, probably talking about how superior their *Auryths* are to everyone else's. I make a point to stay as far away from them as possible, standing with Kaleu on the opposite side of the room. I'm here to get through this and learn how to harness my abilities, not to make friends. Or more enemies.

"Congratulations," a voice calls out. I look up to see Tallie Black accompanied by her new, majestic reddish-brown stag.

We aren't close, but she's always been kind to me. I also caught her sneaking glances at Wilder more times than I cared to count, though he never returned the sentiment. She grins at me, but I can tell she's uncomfortable with Kaleu's presence, which is a reaction I've been getting a lot since the Convergence Ceremony.

"Ardelle," Kaleu says as the stag approaches.

Tallie's eyes sparkle with pride when she sees me staring and quickly gestures to Kaleu in response. "A wolf. I can't believe it. His fur looks so soft, too," she says, reaching her hand towards Kaleu's head.

Suddenly, her stag takes a few steps back, throwing its head up and pushing Tallie behind her. Tallie's face quickly falls from joy to anger, and she narrows her eyes at me. *"What was that about?"* I ask Kaleu.

"I informed her stag that if her human touched me, she'd lose a hand."

"Could you make it any harder for me to make friends? She was just trying to be nice."

"If you pet her head, how would she like it?" Kaleu grumbles.

I shoot him a pointed look. "You never seem to mind when I do it."

"That's entirely different. You are—" A sharp whistle cuts through our conversation, and I turn to see where the sound is coming from.

A man strides toward the center of the room, his presence immediately demanding attention. He's older than us, maybe in his mid-forties, with a scruffy black beard, slicked-back hair, and tattoos snaking up his arms—and he's carrying a turtle.

Naturally, people are already snickering.

Those who didn't bother to listen in class about the elite eight and their gifts won't understand that his *Auryth* makes him perfect for this teaching role.

"It's good to see you all bright and early," the man calls,

his voice loud enough to quiet the murmurs in the room. "I'm Magnus Cray, and I'll be your magic instructor for the next four months. You should all have a general understanding from your schooling of the eight elite *Auryths* and the powers they grant, but every bond is different, and there are plenty of you not bonded to elites. However, all of us can also wield basic magic that helps us flourish in the Burrows and keep things running smoothly. We'll start with the basics, then eventually break into individual training, but we've gotta get through this part first. Any questions?"

One of the boys, Galen, raises his hand. His red-tailed hawk is perched on his broad shoulder, a cocky smile on his face. "What are we supposed to learn from someone bonded to a *turtle*?"

A few of the others laugh at his jibe, and I wince. They're all such idiots.

Magnus doesn't seem bothered by the comment. Instead, he looks around the room, raising an eyebrow. "Anyone care to answer his question?"

Kaleu nudges me gently, but I ignore him. I'm not interested in being the teacher's pet today, especially not with Isla and Rudy already eyeing me like I'm prey.

Magnus lets the silence hang for a moment before speaking again. "No takers? Fine. Let's do a demonstration, then. Galen, since you were so eager to cause disruption this early on and attempt to assert your position as the class clown, I'd like you and your *Auryth* to join me in the center." He sets his turtle aside before walking to the middle of the room.

Galen strides toward him, that smug smirk still plastered on his face. Magnus extends a dagger to him, which he accepts, then walks about ten feet away. "Throw that dagger at me as hard as you can," he tells him.

Galen's smile drops, replaced by fear and confusion. "What, and risk exile? No thanks."

"Only minutes ago you insulted my capabilities, yet now I give you the chance to prove your theory and you refuse? Don't be weak, Galen. Prove your point so we can move on with the rest of class. You've been on military duty since your first assignment, if I'm not mistaken, so your aim better be good."

Everyone stands as still as stone as we watch the two of them, myself included. I'm not afraid for Magnus; I know there's no way the blade could hurt him, let alone kill him. Honestly, I'm more amazed that no one else understands that. Did no one bother to listen during class but me? Or did they zone out when our teachers said the word "turtle?"

Galen grips the hilt firmly and moves it back and forth several times in an attempt to perfect his aim. On the fifth time, he draws his arm far back over his head and releases it, centering it on Magnus's heart. There are a few dramatic gasps from the crowd as it flies through the air, but I only smile.

The blade hits its mark but warps on impact, as if hitting a piece of solid steel at maximum speed. Now it's Magnus who's smirking as he leans down to pick up the bent blade, then picks up his turtle. "First lesson," Magnus calls out, "never underestimate or overestimate someone's abilities based on their *Auryth*. In the unlikely event you'll ever have to fight, that mindset could cost you your life. Oh, and perhaps pay attention. I'm certain your teachers discussed what sort of abilities turtles provide to their bonded—armored flesh."

I note the advice about never underestimating or overestimating *Auryths* and emphasize it through the bond, thinking back to Kaleu's comments about Lyric's frog.

"Well, that was fun," Magnus says, amused. "Now let's get to something actually useful—basic magic. We'll start with your flare: the ability to create light in the darkness. Trust me, you'll need this sooner than you think, unless you want to keep tripping over your own feet during a blackout."

The room dims, though no one has touched the lights. Magnus raises his right hand, and a soft green glow spreads from his palm, illuminating the space around him. It isn't blinding, but steady. "By the end of the week, you should all be able to do this in some capacity," he says. "It might not look the same for everyone, but the important thing is that you figure it out. Some people produce orbs, and some produce it straight from themselves. Some have the ability to do both. Practice makes perfect, of course."

He scans the room before his gaze falls on me. "Lennon, let's see what you've got."

I freeze. "What? Me?"

"You're not allergic to magic, are you?" Magnus raises an eyebrow, and a few people snicker.

"No," I mutter, stepping forward. Kaleu nudges me again as if I'm not already under enough pressure.

"Good. Close your eyes. Focus on your bond; let it out. It doesn't have to be perfect. Tap into that link. Ask your *Auryth* for help if you need it."

I close my eyes, blocking out the sounds around me. I stretch my senses, searching for that spark of energy, the golden thread of connection between Kaleu and me. I focus on it, willing the magic to appear.

Nothing.

"A little help here?" I beg, panic creeping into my voice.

"Close your eyes and focus on me," he says softly. Unhelpful. I'm already doing that. I do my best to refocus, squeezing my eyes shut tighter and reaching again for that invisible connection.

When I open my eyes again, I stare down at my hands. There's still no glow. *"Nothing is happening,"* I tell him, disappointment creeping into my voice. But then I turn to look where Kaleu stands beside me. His eyes are gold, like two burning embers, and his coat gleams as if it's catching every flicker of light in the room. *"Is that coming from you?"* I ask, confused.

"Use your brain, Lennon," he says excitedly. I follow his gaze toward where Magnus stands, and my breath catches. I can still see him, but not in the way I expected. He isn't sharp and defined, like someone standing under full light. No, he looks more like a dark shape in the shadows, his eyes glowing like two bright orbs in the darkness.

"Night vision?" I ask Kaleu, not wanting to say the words aloud until he confirms I'm right.

"I think your eyes may be becoming more wolf-like," he jokes. My heart pounds with adrenaline as I scan the rest of the group. The world around me has shifted; everything is more vivid now, more defined through these new ... lenses. The edges of shadows are more precise, the outlines of people sharper, and the details I haven't noticed before are almost blinding in their clarity.

"I think ..." I swallow, my voice barely a whisper. "I think my flare manifested as night vision. Like I'm seeing through a wolf's eyes. Is that normal? Shouldn't I produce some sort of light?"

Magnus lets out a soft, impressed breath. "Fascinating. When it comes to bonds, nothing is ever really considered normal, my dear." Then the lights flicker back to their usual brightness, and the sharpness of my vision begins to fade, returning to normal as my surroundings adjust. "Now, who's next?"

After military duty, I race back to my family home to retrieve Shiloh. Archie was able to get a one-night stay approved for him, and there are so many things I can't wait for him to see. My first two days were full of more food than I ever thought possible, warm baths, and sleep like I've never known. Every bite I take makes me nauseous—not so much from the richness of every plate they put in front of me, but because one day's rations up here is equivalent to nearly a week's worth for someone on the First Ring.

I spent my entire life on the First Ring, never knowing that the people right above us lived a vastly different life. Do they keep it a secret to avoid uprisings from those starving below? In retrospect, it would almost make sense for them to show it, if only to incentivize people even more to create advantageous marriages.

I knock on the crumbling front door, feeling like a guest in my old life. Shiloh answers, his grin wide as he yanks me into a tight hug. His small backpack is already prepared, and he shuts the door behind him without a second thought. "I figured you didn't want to go in," he says with a shrug.

"How is he?" I ask, more out of duty as a daughter than genuine care.

"Same as always. I'm not even sure he's realized you're gone." The words sting, but I know he didn't say them to hurt me. It's the truth. We could both disappear tomorrow, and our father wouldn't even notice.

"Well, he's on his own for tonight. You ready?" He nods, practically teeming with excitement as I lead him toward the platform.

He's like an overgrown child in a room full of toys as he moves from spot to spot on the glass, pressing his face and hands up against it, leaving fingerprints everywhere. I have half a mind to tell him to stand still lest the attendants have to do more cleaning, but I don't want to dull his enthusiasm. It's been a long time since I've had the privilege of seeing him act like a kid.

When it comes to a slow stop and opens, Archie is already waiting for us, a small glass of red liquid in one hand and a smile on his face. "You must be Shiloh. Welcome to the Third Ring."

Shiloh looks at me with wide eyes, his face scrunched into what I think is an expression of joy. "This is Archie. He helps take care of our needs," I tell him, motioning for him to move forward.

In typical Shiloh fashion, he offers Archie an awkward handshake and thanks him for the drink. Archie's face is red and overjoyed, like he's never received that kind of greeting from anyone up here. We're led back through the maze of halls to my home, and Archie says his farewells as we go inside.

Kaleu immediately nuzzles up on the couch, already snoring, while Shiloh moves from room to room, offering breathless sounds of excitement as he goes. I curl up next to Kaleu, letting Shiloh take his time exploring.

I watch as he makes his way to the fridge, already finding

the leftover rations I kept for him. "Can I have this?" he asks, holding two plates in his hands.

"Of course. I saved it for you." He sits at the dining table and inhales every bite as I head to the kitchen to grab him a glass of water. Seeing him like that, so starved and thin, kills something inside of me. One visit a month here won't change that, even if I save a week's worth of food for him to devour.

"I still have lunch and dinner rations later this evening," I tell him, unsure what else I can say.

"More?" he asks, chugging the water desperately. "It really is a different world up here, isn't it?"

"You have no idea."

I get him set up in one of the guest bedrooms, and he lies down on the bed, releasing a sigh of relief at the coziness. Suddenly, he sits up and grabs his bag, reaches inside, and pulls out a brown T-shirt.

I'd recognize it anywhere. It was one of Wilder's favorites, worn so many times that some of the stitching has started to fray. "His mom dropped a few bags of clothes off at the house for me. Said she thought he'd want me to have them. But I know this was one of his favorites, and I thought it would mean a lot more to you."

I take it with a shaky hand, holding it close to my chest, my eyes growing watery. It still smells like him. "Thank you." I leave the room before my tears have the chance to fall.

His snoring fills the house, and I smile, knowing that at least for the next night, he'll have a full belly and anything else he needs to be comfortable. It may not be permanent for him, but it's still a small win. Though I still don't agree with anything going on up here, at least I can give him that.

Maybe that's why other people don't oppose the luxury up here: not only because they get to enjoy it themselves, but because they allow the people they love to enjoy it as well. It's a brilliant tactic on the Regime's part. Even with my absolute hatred of them, a part of me considers keeping my mouth shut if it means Shiloh can spend a few days a month like this.

I curl up next to Kaleu on the couch and tug on Wilder's t-shirt, wrapping my arms around myself. My throat becomes tight, and my eyes sting with the memory of him. He should be here, not me. How am I supposed to survive without him?

Shiloh's screams interrupt my hour of sulking. "I've got to get to it! Please, tell me how to get to it! Tell me how to stop it!" I'm up and running before I can think. I swing his door open to find him shaking, sweat soaking his body as he continues to repeat the words over and over again.

I shake him, gripping his shoulders firmly as I try to coax him back to reality. Kaleu sprints in after me, jumping onto the bed and placing his head on his chest in an attempt to anchor him, whining softly. "Shiloh, wake up! It's just a bad dream." His eyes fly open, frantic as they scan the room for something. They finally meet mine, and he takes slow, ragged breaths to calm his trembling. "Hey, it's me. It was just a bad dream."

"Sorry," he whispers, squeezing his eyes shut softly.

"What was it about?"

"I can't remember. Just a nightmare, I'm sure. I haven't slept that deeply in a long time." There's something in the way his throat tightens, every word squeezed out, that makes me feel like he's lying, but I don't press him.

This is *supposed* to be an enjoyable trip for him, and I refuse to let anything, even nightmares, take that away from us.

A knock sounds at my door, and I open it to find a cart and

a dome cover over what I presume to be a plate. I look both ways in the hall for Archie, but no one is there. Rolling it inside, I close the door behind me and begin to lift the dome off to see today's meal. Underneath, there are two plates, stacked on top of one another. Two plates? But Archie specifically said guests wouldn't receive rations up here. I lift the plates to move them to the dining table, then stop.

Underneath one is a note, and I set them down before picking it up to read.

An extra plate for your brother. Our little secret.
— Archie

I'm shocked by his generosity, but even more floored that he broke the rules for me. Is this a test? A way for the Regime to see if I'm still willing to keep secrets and break rules? Or is this simply an act of kindness from the attendant I've come to adore?

I rip it into a million different scraps until it's entirely illegible, then throw it in the trash before rolling the cart back outside. Shiloh seems to have calmed down as he makes his way out of the room, likely following the scent of fresh food. "I could get used to it up here. Is that glazed stonefruit?" he asks, eyes wide as he hurries over to the table.

The plates are almost too beautiful to touch. One holds a thick vegetable medley with roasted potatoes and mushrooms, drizzled with something fragrant and spicy. The other has a small cut of fish, seared and topped with a citrus glaze. I hadn't realized we even had tanks here. A small, warm, baked roll sits on the side of each plate, still steaming, and a tiny bowl of deep purple berries soaked in syrup sits in the center.

Shiloh is already licking his fingers before he finishes his first bite, not bothering with the utensils. "This is a far cry from the ration packets," he mumbles through a mouthful, eyes practically rolling back in delight.

I sit across from him, watching as he scarfs down the food like it might vanish if he blinks. He doesn't know what half of it is or how rare it is to get the spiced oil that coats the vegetables. How difficult it is to grow citrus trees underground. How these berries only bloom in the deepest corners of the greenhouses and are so scarce, we had to place them in an entirely different preservation unit.

So many of my days were spent in those greenhouses, wondering where these exquisite harvests were going. I always assumed it was going to the Regime's council, and I never asked. But somehow, seeing that all of this has been funneled *here*, to the Third Ring ... this is indulgence. We eat one packet of plant goop a day, and they've been eating all of this? Not only eating, but throwing the extras away?

Another knock at the door has me rising to my feet, and I find yet another plate sitting on the cart. This one I expected: Kaleu's dinner. Two massive fillets of fresh fish.

CHAPTER 9
SLADE

Too many things about Opie don't add up. I've been retracing his steps all morning, trying to understand what, exactly, attacked him, and where he came from. There's a trail of blood leading from the very edge of the woods to our gate, but it doesn't go any further into the forest than that.

Sure, hypothetically, it's possible that he was attacked by a wild *Auryth* right before crossing the threshold, but why would it wait that long? He had to have been traveling through the woods prior to that, so it doesn't make sense. A typical wild *Auryth* would attack the moment it set eyes on its prey, not give it time to get away. Not to mention his panther didn't have a scratch on her. Perhaps all *Auryths* aren't quite like Ves, but I can't imagine one not defending their human's life, especially considering their very existence is linked to ours.

So that brings me back to thinking the wound was self-inflicted. But *why*? If there's something he wants, why not go on and say it? Clearly, Keelan has a soft spot for him and would've allowed him in regardless. Was it all for show? To make us let our guards down? What is he hiding?

I walk back toward camp after finding nothing else to help build my case, then head toward Opie's tent. Half the day has already passed, and still I've heard nothing from Keelan. His wound is healed, so why haven't I been notified that he's awake and ready to talk? As I approach, I can hear the sound of laughter from inside, and I look toward Vesper.

"What do you hear?"

"Oh, he's awake, alright. He and Keelan are playing catch-up and giggling their troubles away." I begin pacing quietly, trying to decide if I want to interrupt or wait for Keelan to come find me. I quell the growing unease building inside, itching to release itself in the form of power.

Right as I've finally decided to enter the tent, the flap opens up and Keelan steps outside. "Ah, Slade! I was on my way to find you. He's awake and ready to answer any questions you have." I step past him, but he puts a steady hand on my chest to stop me. "I know that you always have our people's best interests at heart, and you know I do too. I'm also aware that when it comes to a fight, you will always have the upper hand between the two of us, but I do hope you will hear me out. He's been through a lot, and he has a good heart. Please keep an open mind when you listen to what he has to say."

My jaw tightens. From the moment I stepped onto solid ground and off the platform, Keelan has been like a father to me. There's something about seeing him with Opie—the way he coddles him, protects him—that leaves me feeling so … inadequate. Unnerved. Like I'm some sort of replacement for the makeshift son he thought he lost, only to be cast aside now that he's returned.

It's a ridiculous sentiment, and I've always known better than to get attached. There is only one person in this world who has my best interests in mind, and that's me.

I take a steadying breath before entering, and my eyes immediately find Opie propped up against a few pillows stuffed with milkweed. The color has returned to his face, his green eyes shining with a hint of restlessness, his smile clearly insincere as he takes me in. I suppose he sees me the same way I see myself: his replacement.

I've done a hell of a better job than he ever did.

"Why did you come back?" I sit down in one of the chairs, not bothering to waste time with pleasantries.

"It's wonderful to meet you, too, Slade. I've heard so much about you and your ... wolf." He gives me a lopsided grin, steadily petting his panther's massive head as it purrs.

"Then I'm sure you've also heard that I'm not the type for small talk. Now answer the question." He raises an eyebrow as if this is some sort of game, and I cross my arms over my chest and lean back.

"There are other civilizations out there. I've spent the last few years with one called Exion. It's how the unbonded survived the war. I told them about our people, about how we were exiled and our village. But Exion ... they have everything we could ever dream of. Endless food, working showers, rooms with warm beds. It's a safe place where our people can flourish. They're willing to accept us and anyone else who comes up on the platform, no strings attached. I've come to bring my people to their new home." He stares at me with sheer pride, and every alarm bell in my head starts to go off.

I scoff and roll my eyes. "Right. You're telling me there's an entire other civilization out there that survived the war, and, despite Solis being here for over fifty years, they just magically want to take us in now? If you're going to make up stories, at least make them believable." My chair scrapes in the dirt as I stand and walk toward the tent opening.

"I'm not making any of this up," he calls after me. I hesitate, my curiosity momentarily outweighing my logic. "You can think whatever you want, but it's the truth."

I whirl around. "Why now? You've been gone for nearly three years, Opie. Did "negotiations" really take that long, or is there something else you aren't telling me? Because from where I'm standing, Exion has nothing to gain from taking us in but more mouths to feed—if they even exist, that is."

He swallows hard, the first clear indicator that whatever words are about to slip past his lips will be untruthful. "It's taken them this long to trust me, to be willing to extend a helping hand. They are wary of the bonded. After all, our people have been killing theirs for centuries simply because they weren't chosen by an *Auryth*. You can't blame them for being protective of their home."

I scoff. "That argument carries no weight. We were *exiled* by the Burrows for not forging a bond. That makes us no different than them. If you ask me, their refusal to aid us until you "negotiated" makes them no better than the Regime. Why would we subject ourselves to another dictatorship when we're perfectly fine on our own and have been for years?"

He puts his weight on his forearms and swings his legs over the side of the bed, inching closer to me. "I can understand your perspective, and I respect it, I really do. But don't you think it's a little selfish to keep everyone here, struggling, when there is an entire fortress willing to take them in with open arms? No one will ever have to wonder if they'll survive the harsh winters or where their next meal will come from. If there's illness, they have some of the best medical teams out there. Not to mention if the Regime ever comes back up—and neither of us is dumb enough to believe that won't happen at some point—we'll have an entire army willing to fight against them."

I despise the fact that he makes valid points, but I can't ignore my gut telling me that something is off. So many years our people have been out here struggling, and this "Exion" has never interjected. I have a hard time believing two civilizations can be near one another and yet never interact or know about the other's existence. But what is his motivation for making it all up? Fearmongering? Gaining his position back in Solis?

Something doesn't feel right; I don't trust it. I don't trust *him*.

"I need some time to consider this information. Keelan has informed me that you're a guest here, so please let *him* know if you need anything. In the meantime, let's keep this quiet until I have a chance to discuss it with Keelan and consider all potential outcomes. I'm still not convinced this place even exists. Do not stir up discord within *my* camp. You may have been the Warden over these people once, but you aren't anymore. You lost that privilege when you left and spent years living in your perfect little world."

He opens his mouth to speak again, but I'm gone before he can croak out a syllable. Keelan is still waiting for me outside, and I throw a sound barrier around us as we begin to walk the perimeter. Vesper has been uncharacteristically quiet, but I'm sure there are plenty of questionable ideas circulating in that head of hers.

"I take it he told you? About Exion?" he asks, and I nod.

"He did. I'm not sure how to feel about it. On one hand, it

sounds promising. We barely survived last year's winter, and we're having to ration food most days to try and preserve what we can for the colder months when things won't grow. But I can't shake this nagging feeling that something's off. We have no way of knowing this place even exists. And if it does, why haven't they helped already? And why now?" I kick at the dirt as I walk.

"I think it's fair to say that we're all a little traumatized by the Burrows from the way they conned us into a belief system, but who is to say that this place isn't different? What if it's our second chance? A place where we finally belong? What if they are good and fair and just?"

I don't really belong anywhere. Certainly not in the Burrows where I was sentenced to death for being unworthy, but also not in a place built for the unbonded now that I have Ves. Here, in our camp, is the only place I've ever felt like I fit in—where I've been important. This is my home.

"There's no such thing as a *fair* or just *government*; you know that. Corruption always flows beneath the surface, no matter how well it's hidden. Sometimes it's harder to see, but it's human nature to act only when there's something to gain in return. That's why I can't understand what Exion's endgame is here. If they're building an army to take down the Burrows one day, fine, just say that. But they certainly aren't doing this out of the goodness of their hearts, and the fact that even Opie doesn't know—or won't admit—what their true intentions are makes me uneasy about it all."

He sucks in a deep breath and stops walking, propping an arm against the makeshift fence that surrounds our camp. "I understand your points, but I still think it is something to consider. I know that I'm technically in charge here, but I value your opinion and the lengths you go to in order to keep us all safe. I want you to truly consider this as an option, even taking Opie out of the equation. Perhaps we let the people decide if they'd rather stay here or go to Exion. They haven't been given many choices in life, but if we decide for them, we become no better than the leaders we've endured before."

My first instinct is to argue that people *need* leadership because they don't always understand what is best for them, but everything clicks into place in my mind. The Regime assumed that what was best for *their* people was to protect them from the unbonded. Maybe Exion thought they were doing what was best for their people by protecting them from those who grew up thinking being bonded was the ultimate life purpose.

If I decide for them, I'm no better than the Regime.

"You're right. They deserve to choose. But we need to present *all* of the options. If they go to Exion, they'll no doubt have to live by their rules and standards. We need to get a clearer understanding from Opie of what those are. I will stay here with anyone who doesn't want to go and receive any newcomers on the platform. If you want to go with them to Exion, you should. They'll need a stable leader to guide them."

He looks at me with sincere pride, his eyes softening at my words. "I wish you'd reconsider going with us, but regardless, I respect your choice and am so proud of the man you've become."

My throat tightens, and my eyes cloud. In all my years, I've never had anyone tell me that.

LENNON

S hiloh spent most of his visit battling sleep and eating, which means I spent most of my time snuggling with Kaleu on the couch. He had the same nightmare again that night and shouted the same words, but still claimed not to remember anything. My older-sister intuition tells me there's more to it than just a bad dream, but I also know he's not the kind of person I can easily pry information out of. He didn't say much when he left other than "thank you", and it's been nearly three weeks now since I saw him last.

It's also been three weeks since I've seen Archie.

I tried asking someone I passed on the platform if they'd seen him, but no one seems to even recognize his name, which is unsurprising given that they see attendants as servants rather than actual people. I'm hoping that no one knows about the extra plate, and that he isn't being punished or something for his kindness. I even tried dialing 333 to reach him, but the line only rang endlessly.

Military duty, as I expected, absolutely sucks. For the most part, I serve as a personal assistant to egotistical guards who

109

dislike doing grunt work. Thanks to my track record of being a delinquent, the guards are under strict orders not to let me out of their sight.

In the last few weeks of magic lessons, I've learned to see in the dark, regulate my body temperature, light a candle, and put up a sorry excuse for a shield. Magnus hasn't taught us anything about our individual bonds yet, which is starting to drive me a little insane.

I haven't felt any new powers develop either, and Kaleu has practically no information. Even the heat I created during my protest at the Convergence Ceremony refuses to reappear, despite my best attempts.

Kaleu and I enter the Arcanum bright and early today, finding we're the first to arrive. *"Well, aren't we a punctual pair?"* I joke, giving him a sweet smile.

"This only proves that you didn't need to wake me so early," he grumbles, sitting at my feet as I take up a spot against the wall.

Isla Dade and her panther enter the building next, and I don't miss the side-eye she gives us as she heads to the opposite side of the room. Whatever I did to earn her disdain, I'll probably never know, and, thanks to Kaleu and our interaction with Tallie and her stag on the first day, she hates us now too.

"What do you think it is about me that makes it impossible to make friends?" I ask Kaleu, my expression neutral as I watch the others file in.

"Because you intimidate them. You bonded me, and they are jealous. It should be considered an honor to be disliked by so many," Kaleu replies, and I try to hide my smile as Magnus enters the room.

Oh, Kaleu, the ever-humble wolf.

Once we're all in a circle surrounding Magnus on the floor,

he quiets the room with a sharp whistle to begin today's lesson. "Alright, kids. Today is the day we'll finally begin working on your individual gifts. You probably thought you'd get one-on-one time with me, but you thought wrong. We'll do this in a group session as well. It's important for everyone to learn what the other bonds can do in case you ever encounter a situation where you're against another bonded. Who would like to start us off?"

Isla raises her hand and stands, her panther rising with her. "Perfect!" Magnus says, extending a hand toward them. "Show us what your *Auryth* has taught you so far, Isla."

She gives him a playful smile as if she's been waiting for this moment her whole life and looks toward her panther. "Can everyone shift to one side of the room?"

When we've given them half of the floor, I watch the pair disappear entirely, then reappear several feet away. *Teleportation*. "Right now, Nyla and I can only go small distances, but we're working to improve that." Magnus is beaming with pride and amusement now, eager for the next person to go as we readjust back into our circle.

Hands fly up all around, and everyone suddenly becomes eager to showcase their new gifts in an attempt to top what Isla did. Rudy and his serpent utterly terrify me when he shuts off the power to the entire building, then flips it back on. Technomancers are unique in their abilities, possessing a large range of powers. Some can imbue, like the ones that keep our generators running, and others, like Rudy, can control anything technologically powered. In my opinion, it's always been one of the most powerful gifts out there—and perhaps the most intimidating.

The most interesting set of powers to watch is Juniper and Cleo Langston, twins who both bonded chameleons. They go one after another, displaying an incredible ability to blend into their surroundings. One touch of a brown wall has every inch of their bodies shifting color, making it nearly impossible to see them if you don't know they're there. Chameleons are generally on the opposite side of the unique spectrum. Almost all of them can simply blend into their surroundings, though some are better at mastering it than others.

Kaleu's and my turn is next, and all I can do is stare blankly at Magnus, unsure of what to showcase. Outside of the one-time ability to heat my skin and the night vision, I have no idea what I'm supposed to be capable of doing. Compared to the rest of the class today, we seem incredibly underwhelming.

"We are not underwhelming. We just don't care about flaunting what we can do," Kaleu says, sending a course of irritation down the bond to accompany his words.

"We don't have anything to flaunt, and you don't even know what else we can do, or if we can do anything else."

"Maybe you should've bonded to a precious chameleon. Perhaps then you'd be proud of your bond." His words strike a chord deep inside my chest, and I absorb the hurt in them like a physical ache.

"I am proud of my bond. I would never want any other Auryth, you know that. If these are the only gifts I'm ever given, I am perfectly content with that. Now quit pouting, they're staring at us," I reply as gently as possible.

"Miss Benfield, if you and your *Auryth* are finished conversing, we'd love to see what you've learned together," Magnus says, drawing my attention from Kaleu.

"Sorry," I tell him, looking between him and Kaleu.

"Kaleu, what do we do?" I plead as the group stares us down.

"Maybe try burning him?" he suggests.

"Burn him? That's seriously all we've got?"

"I mean, he does have armored flesh. You did it when you tried to save Wilder. Shall I provoke you to anger and try to make it appear?"

"Lennon? Are you okay?" Magnus asks, and I open my eyes to find everyone staring at me.

This is useless. I can't feel even a twinge of power inside, despite my best efforts to tap into my own rage. "I-I'm sorry. I don't have anything to show at the moment. We're still … working on it," I say, my voice trembling with each word.

"That's perfectly fine. Some bonds take a little longer to develop than others. There's always tomorrow," he replies kindly, but I can't bring myself to meet his gaze.

"I'm sorry I failed us," I tell Kaleu. *"I'm useless. You should have chosen someone else."*

"You never disappoint, little wolf," he says, filling the bond with swelling pride. *"I chose the right person, whether you see that now or not. Now lift your chin. A wolf has no need for weakness."* I force myself to pretend that what's transpired isn't bothering me and nod in response to Magnus.

"What a pity. No one's ever bonded a wolf, and she can't even be bothered to learn what she can do? Why the hell would that *thing* choose you? Pathetic." Isla's voice rings out through the room, earning a couple of snorts and laughs from the others.

Kaleu growls low beside me. My hands curl into fists, fingernails biting into my palms. I feel that same pressure I'd felt when trying to save Wilder, like something too big is building beneath my skin. Hot. Unsteady.

"What's the matter, Benfield? Ashamed that you're completely and utterly useless?" she presses.

"Shut up," I seethe.

She laughs. "Or what? You'll cry? Glare me to death?" She

goes to move past me, intentionally slamming her shoulder into mine to offset my balance. I whip around to push her off me, my hand catching her arm.

Isla screams. She drops to the floor, clutching her forearm, skin bluish and blistered where I touched her. Gasps erupt around the room. Someone curses. Magnus kneels instantly beside her, shouting for help.

I back away in horror, staring at my hand like it betrayed me. "I—I didn't mean to—I didn't know—"

"She needs to go to the infirmary," someone shouts.

Isla glares up at me with tear-filled eyes and trembling lips. "What the hell *are* you?" No one dares step closer. Even Kaleu is silent.

My chest tightens so much it hurts. I stumble back another step, the weight of every stare pressing in around me like walls are closing in. "I didn't mean to," I whisper again, more to myself this time than anyone else. "I didn't know that would happen."

Isla's still whimpering on the floor. Magnus has already wrapped her arm in a cloth, but it's shaking—she's shaking—and the image of burned skin won't leave my mind.

My vision blurs. I blink hard, trying to make it all go away.

"You saw that, right?" someone mutters. "She just burned her by touching her."

"She shouldn't be allowed in training," another says, quieter.

The burn on Isla's arm. The way no one's stepping closer. I wrap my arms tightly around myself. I want to apologize, to fall on my knees and beg them to believe I didn't mean it. But all I manage is a whisper. "I'm sorry."

No one answers.

I stand there for a moment too long, rooted in place as I'll disappear if I stay still long enough. Magnus's eyes meet mine, filled with both panic and sincerity. "Lennon, you're due for your work duty. *Go.*" The words land like a punch. I nod once and force my legs to move.

I don't look back as I leave. I can't. Not when I'm terrified of what they'll see on my face. Not when I'm terrified of what I'll see on theirs.

"She deserved it." Kaleu breaks the silence as we walk, my hands still trembling as I keep them close to my body.

"No one deserves that."

"I disagree."

My usual two guards are waiting for us outside, whom I've nicknamed Stick and Stump. It's fitting, given neither has bothered to share their actual name. Kaleu prefers to call them something else, but I'm not a fan of his word choices.

Stick is tall, slender, and painfully quiet, though when he does speak, it's always to give some curt order delivered in a cruel and demeaning tone. Stump, by contrast, is short, round, and perpetually irritating. He thinks himself to be funny, spitting out an incessant cycle of humorless jokes between mouthfuls of food, which is an infuriating sight, given how many people barely scrape by on their rations.

"Where's your uniform?" Stump asks, looking me over. In all the commotion, I hadn't thought to change, and I'm still wearing my white training uniform versus my black military one.

"I didn't have time to change."

He rolls his eyes but thankfully doesn't press the issue further. They open the gate and lead us back to the control room. I'm not sure what I was expecting to do on military duty, but sitting in a room and watching more than fifty screens full of people all afternoon was certainly not it.

Clearly, the Burrows had a list of technology they needed to take from the unbonded before moving underground. A chip to deactivate bonds, a device that won't kill you but will make you wish you were dead, cameras to hide in every nook and cranny of our city, and monitors to help them spy on us.

Blane put me here on purpose. He wants me to understand that when he says they're keeping a close eye on me, they mean it. We've never had any privacy here, except maybe in our homes. But even then, the Regime has been hand-picking who knows how many families, forcing marriages, and creating bloodlines.

Stump is already asleep in his chair, snoring loudly. Stick didn't even bother coming into the room with us or explaining where he was going. Not that I care. Kaleu slumps down at my feet and dozes off. My eyes slide back to the screens, watching everyone go through their daily routine. Everything appears so dreary from here. There's nothing to look forward to, nothing to work toward. You do your job, pick up your rations, and go back home to the household that was more than likely created for you. No wonder people enjoy the Convergence every year. It's a disruption from their normal, tedious lives.

What the—

Our screens begin to flash red as an alarm sounds above, and Stump nearly falls out of his chair, his eyes wide with panic. My eyes scan the screens frantically, trying to locate the cause.

It's a boy, running like his life depends on it, but I can't see what, or whom, he's running from. My first instinct is another townsman, angry with the little instigator for stealing a ration card, until I see the swarm of guards run past the camera.

The door swings open to reveal Stick, looking just as frightened.

I turn slowly back to the screen to see that the boy has now been cornered, and he's hiding something behind his back. I check the other cameras for a better angle, and my heart stops when I get it.

It isn't just a boy.

It's Shiloh.

CHAPTER II
SLADE

I t's been three weeks since Opie first arrived in our camp, and though I agree with Keelan that our people should be able to choose their own paths, I don't trust the panther-loving jackass as far as I can throw him.

I know he's been sneaking around camp, filling everyone's heads with ideas of Exion, despite me explicitly telling him *not* to do that. The chatter around camp is enough of a tell. People keep watching me as I pass like they're waiting for an explanation or an announcement, and though it annoys me to no end, I can't confront him without proof. So here I am, following him around and waiting for him to slip up—which he will.

Tonight he's inside Wilder's tent of all places, which truly has me intrigued. My two biggest problems in camp becoming buddy-buddy can't be good. Honestly, I hope he takes Wilder with him back to dreamy Exion so I never have to listen to his constant, self-righteous complaints ever again.

I release myself from the shadows, prop my back against a

tree outside the tent, and wait. The second Opie's outside, his panther, Selene, senses us, and he pivots in our direction.

"Slade?" he questions, raising an eyebrow. "To what do I owe the pleasure?"

"I was coming to keep the two of you company. I must have missed the invitation."

"You seem a little jealous. Or are you just terrified I'm going to take all of them with me and you'll be left all alone?" His accusatory tone sinks under my skin, making my blood boil.

"Do you really think I'm threatened by you?" I counter, allowing tendrils of black flame to slip from my fingertips as I offer an insincere smile. "Surely you can't be that stupid."

"If you weren't threatened, you wouldn't be following me, now would you? Or attempting to unnerve me with your power, for that matter." One minute, he's several feet away, and the next, he's right in front of my face, his panther snarling at his hip. I stand a little straighter, hiding my unexpected discomfort.

Did they just … teleport?

"Can you not appear like a scared little boy? You have powers too, you know," Vesper growls, and I immediately snap back to reality.

"Nice trick. I'd show you what I'm truly capable of, but I don't think Keelan would appreciate me turning you into ashes." I smile wider.

"You really think you're something, don't you?" he laughs. "Well, you're not. People don't follow you because they *want* to. They do it because they're scared of you. You and that unbridled temper you wear like a medal of honor. Sad, really."

"On second thought, turning you into ashes sounds like a great idea." I wrap the flames around him, leaving just enough space that his skin doesn't blister, and watch as sweat drips from his brow. He maintains a calm exterior, his eyes bored, collected, like he doesn't have a care in the world, and my anger flares.

"Slade? What the hell are you doing?" Keelan's voice breaks the silence before I can completely incinerate him, and I snuff my flames out like an ashamed child. Pure disappointment fills his features. "Go back to your tents, both of you. We'll discuss this tomorrow."

Vesper sends a few curses in my direction for bowing down before I swiftly block her out. If it were up to her, I would've accepted the position of Commander last year when they offered it to me, but I never wanted it. Some people are meant to lead, and others are meant to help keep those people in their positions.

"Voltage storm!" someone screams right as our warning bells start ringing. My head snaps toward Keelan, panic consuming me. Before I can get a word out, the first blue bolt strikes across the night sky, rumbling through the ground as if shaking it to its very core.

A second crash follows, then a third. Rapid-fire bursts of electric light split in jagged cracks. The air shifts, hums, charges. Every hair on my body lifts in warning. "Get everyone inside a tent or shelter, NOW!" Keelan orders, and I take off running through camp to get people ushered inside. I tap into my power, letting my vision shift until the world brightens around me, making it easier to navigate the darkness.

Sage is struggling to get up off a campfire bench, her gray hair wild from the spiraling wind. I scoop her up in my arms and practically toss her into a packed tent, commanding her to stay put until I say otherwise. People are running frantically in every direction, helping one another into shelters or trying to save their own skin. A few are trying to secure food safely inside a building, and I scream at them to leave it and get inside. Food can be replaced, but lives cannot. Across camp, Opie is teleporting people from the camp center into various shelters, moving at a pace that I never imagined possible.

The air cracks again, louder this time, sharper. My ears ring as the voltage burns across the sky like it's trying to tear the world open. I duck under a low-hanging line strung between two poles and see Vesper's eyes lock onto something —someone—out in the open. I follow her line of sight, seeing long hair whipping in the wind.

Florence—one of last year's recruits. She's sprinting toward the west edge, where the supply tarp has collapsed into a tangled heap. "Are you *kidding* me?" I mutter before launching after her. "Florence, leave them!"

I know what she's doing; she's trying to save the seedlings, but volts continue to tear through the atmosphere without warning, drawn to anything metal, anything living, anything warm. She's going to get herself killed.

My boots skid in the mud as the storm surges. Light breaks the sky like shattered glass, and thunder crashes down so violently I feel it in my bones. I shove forward, dodging a cracking line of light that scorches a tent pole two feet to my left. The flash sears my vision, but I don't stop. Florence is too far out now. If another bolt hits nearby, it'll ground through her.

"Florence!" I roar, but the wind eats my voice. She doesn't even glance back.

I sprint harder.

Another flash.

Too close.

The air shifts again, humming violently. A high-pitched whine fills my ears, and then the crack. Lightning tears straight toward me. I don't even have time to react; I see it before I feel it, but someone slams into me from the side, knocking me into the mud so hard the breath leaves my lungs.

A heartbeat later, the bolt strikes exactly where I'd been standing, and the impact explodes. My ears scream. Everything smells like burnt rubber and metal.

I groan and try to sit up, still dazed, when a hand grabs my collar and yanks me upright. "You're welcome," Wilder mutters, his tone anxious despite the sarcasm. His blond curls are soaked, and he's bleeding from his temple. "Next time you wanna play hero, maybe don't pick a lightning storm."

I stare at him, stunned, chest heaving. He *saved* me. "I didn't need your help. Hell, I was saving *your* girlfriend. Where the hell were you?" I snap, shaking out of his grip.

"I was on my way. And you're welcome," he says again, louder this time. He turns and launches back toward Florence, who, of course, is still trying to pull the tarp off the seed crates like an idiot.

To my left, another bolt hits a tent, obliterating it into nothingness. I stare blankly, realizing that's exactly where I placed Sage only minutes ago. There's nothing left but a patch of blackness on the ground.

I'm frozen in place, unable to move, unable to *breathe*.

They didn't even have time to scream.

I thought I was saving her.

I put her in that tent. I sealed her fate, and there's not even a body left to bury. My heart clenches, my chest so excruciatingly tight that I'm gasping for air, struggling to choke it down. Power surges through my blood, raw and hot and relentless, begging me to let go.

A hand closes around my arm, yanking me forward, but all I can do is stare at the patch. Wilder has Florence and me now, and he drags us into another nearby tent. Four other people are inside, huddled and trembling. When he finally lets go, I notice his hand is red and blistering.

He shouldn't have touched me.

There's nothing to do but wait and hope that our tent isn't the storm's next victim. Around an hour later, the air finally seems to still and the world goes quiet. I instruct everyone to stay inside while I check, then poke my head outside the tent. From what I can see, at least four tents are scorched to the ground, and several of our buildings have been knocked down by the wind, but the storm has passed.

"It's safe to come out," I call out to the rest before starting to walk the perimeter. So much destruction. Since my arrival at Solis, I've only ever seen one voltage storm, and it was far enough from camp that it didn't cause any damage. This ... this is catastrophic.

I see Keelan limping through camp, his leg singed in several places. "Slade!" he yells, and I run to him. We embrace, his body trembling. Or perhaps it's mine. "We lost so many."

"Sage," I confess. "We lost Sage. I don't know how many others."

"We'll take count in the morning when we can see. Get everyone settled for the night. There will be quite a few who lost their tents, so others may have to share. Once the injured are tended to, we'll rest. Unfortunately, I can't do much on this leg, so you'll have to start without me." As if they can smell the injury, Caius and his Stag come walking toward us, offering to tend to Keelan while I carry out his orders.

After two hours of checking tents and helping people get back where they belong, I realize we're missing at least twenty-four people, including Sage. That's more than we've ever lost in a single day.

I toss and turn, trying to find sleep, but it won't come. *"You cannot possibly blame yourself for her death. No one could have known it would hit that very tent. You're not responsible for this guilt,"* Vesper tries to soothe me, but the pain refuses to ebb. Sage spent fifty-two years up here after surviving exile, just to die because I placed her in the wrong tent at the wrong time.

"All this power and yet I was utterly useless tonight."

"Power is not the answer to every problem. Sometimes things just are."

Dawn is here before I know it, and I'm up and ushering people toward the center of camp so we can get a tally. Keelan comes striding out of his metal home not long after, his leg already vastly improved thanks to Caius. "How many?" he asks.

"Twenty-four so far. I'm having everyone head to the central hall for breakfast so I can get a better count." He looks broken, disheveled. I'm sure we all do right now.

The central hall is essentially several tents combined to form a large space, covering several long tables and benches. It's one of the few places we can fit the majority of the camp at the same time, and where we typically serve food, though I'm not sure anyone's going to feel like eating today.

When everyone gets settled in, Keelan moves to stand in

front of the tables, addressing the crowd. "Solis. We suffered a great loss yesterday. There are several structures that need to be fixed, and though we're still trying to get a total death toll, it appears that we've lost at least twenty-four members of our camp. This terrible news can only be cushioned by the knowledge that our training helped prevent those numbers from being higher." He stops and gives the crowd a moment to breathe. The silence is thick except for a few quietly crying in the crowd.

"We will hold a ceremony later this evening for those we've lost, once we get an official record. If you are missing someone, please let us know. I won't pretend this isn't hard. It is, but remember who we are. Every person in this camp has already survived the unthinkable. We were cast out, left behind, told we didn't belong, and we lived anyway. We built something here. Something worth protecting. Something worth mourning. That strength, the one that got us this far, hasn't gone anywhere." He lifts his chin. "We will grieve today. We will remember them tonight. And tomorrow, we will rebuild because *that is what we do*. We survive. We rise. *Together.*"

I have to admit, he's always had a way with words. It's hard not to feel pride when he frames it that way, to feel the importance of making the lives we've lost count. Right as Keelan steps away, I see Opie flag his attention and pull him aside, and I instantly join, refusing to let him sink his teeth into an already vulnerable camp. "You need to give them the option to go to Exion. After what they experienced last night, they deserve to know there's an alternative," he presses.

Keelan looks up as I approach, his eyes tired. "Trying to take advantage of their fear to funnel more people into your little trap?" I snap.

"It's because they're afraid that they should be informed of their choice. You not telling them makes you no different than the Regime."

I sneer at him, my jaw ticking.

"Is that so? Because I'd say emotionally manipulating frightened people is something the Regime would do."

"Enough," Keelan barks, looking between us. "We lost lives last night. Does that matter to either one of you?" Like two scorned children, we both stop talking and drop our heads.

"Opie's right, Slade. I understand how you think it could be manipulation, but the truth of the matter is, they'll never be safe from things like that out here. If they want to go, they should."

"Shouldn't we run this by the council?" I ask.

"The only members left alive are you, me, and Caius," he replies dryly. I hadn't had time to stop and consider that we lost half of our council. "Caius has already voted to tell our people and let them make their choice. I will go with Opie and whoever else follows. You're welcome to stay here or come with us. The choice is yours."

"Keelan, you can't be serious—"

He cuts me off. "I can't *live* like this anymore. I won't. If there's a chance this place can keep our people safe, I'm taking it."

"Let them go," Vesper coos. *"Forcing people to stay will only fuel unrest and make them despise you. It's their decision."* Wonderful, now everyone is against me. *"I am not against you,"* she adds, and I sigh. *"I only want you to understand both sides."*

Keelan walks back toward the crowd despite my pleas and whistles, quieting them down once more. "I know some of you may have been wondering why Opie has returned, and where he's been for the last three years. The truth is, he found a city called Exion, a place built for unbonded. As you know, the war that destroyed the Earth was survived by the bonded through moving underground, but what we didn't realize is that some of the unbonded survived. Exion is their form of the Burrows, only with far greater amenities. It's safe, with real homes. They're willing to take us in and allow us to integrate into their society."

A few dramatic gasps ripple through the crowd, and some clutch at their hearts as if it's the most insane thing they've ever heard. Some people still struggle to grasp how much the Regime lied to us. Questions pour out rapidly.

"Who are these people?" one yells.

"Where are they? How do we know it isn't a trick?" says another. I give Keelan a sidelong glance at that one, thankful I'm not the only one sharing the sentiment.

"Why have they waited so long to help?"

Keelan holds up a hand. "I will be joining Opie on his return there. You each have a choice: stay here with Slade, or take the trek to Exion, where we are allegedly going to be welcomed with open arms and given everything we need to survive. This is *your* choice. No one else will make it for you. We don't know these people in Exion, so there's always a risk that what we're walking into isn't all that it seems. After what transpired last night, it doesn't feel right to keep this choice from you any longer. I trust Opie when he says their intentions are true, and when he says that it's real. It's up to you whether you want to take that gamble with us. You have until tomorrow morning to decide." He walks off the platform, leaving the crowd in an absolute uproar as they begin trying to make sense of what they were just told.

CHAPTER 12

LENNON

I can't speak. I can't breathe. I can't even see straight.

What the hell is he doing? What did he take that has nearly every guard in the Burrows running after him? I'm out the door before Stick and Stump realize I'm running, slamming it hastily behind me.

My feet pound on the tile floor, catching stares from countless elites and Nexus workers alike. I don't care; I have to get to him; I have to somehow talk our way out of this.

I burst through the gate, fully expecting guards to yell at me for my abruptness, but there are none. Oh. Whatever he's done is *bad*, so bad that they've left the Nexus unattended. Something bumps my leg, and I look down to see Kaleu glaring at me. I'd be lying if I said I hadn't momentarily forgotten about him when I took off.

"You should at least tell me when you're going to take off, especially if you intend on going up against an entire army," he grumbles.

I'm still sprinting, trying to make it to the back corner of the Burrows where I saw him on the cameras. *"I'm sorry. All I can think about is getting to Shiloh. Can you hear anything? Do you have any idea what's going on?"*

"*I know no more than you. Breathe. We will not let them take him, no matter what kind of trouble he's gotten himself into.*" I try to let his words comfort me, but they don't. I'm already on thin ice with Blane, so I highly doubt whatever my brother has done will be easily forgiven by begging. "*I don't mean through begging. I mean by force. They will not take him,*" he adds.

By force. We will fight if necessary. Okay, I can handle that. Even if I don't have any useful powers at the moment, and I saw firsthand how well that went for me when they tried to take Wilder. I shake my head as if that can clear it. All that matters is getting to Shiloh; we can figure the rest out after that.

We fly around a corner, my heart threatening to beat out of my chest, and nearly run straight into the back of a guard. No, not one guard. All of the guards. Hundreds are blocking off the street, standing in a uniform position, shoulder to shoulder, weapons loaded.

Weapons loaded. What the hell did Shiloh take?

I try to push through, but they don't budge. They don't even bother looking at me. "Excuse me!" I shout, attempting to wedge myself between them. "That's my brother up there! Let me through!" One pushes me backward, nearly knocking me to the ground, and I close my eyes and center myself, tapping into the rage both from now and the day they took Wilder. It consumes me, boiling my blood to the point that it's almost painful. My hands tremble with the effort, but this time, when I reach to push through, I know they'll move.

My right hand grabs a guard's shoulder, and he breaks from formation with a choked scream, clutching his arm like it's on fire. Webs of blue and purple branch out from where my fingers touched him, spreading fast beneath his skin. His uniform has stiffened and fused with his flesh, the fabric cracking and flaking.

I move forward, seizing the next guard, then the next. Each one falls, shrieking as their limbs turn various shades of color. By the time I make it through the first three rows, the rest are opening a path for me. I suppose the screams of pain from the others are enough to make them comply.

They have Shiloh on his knees, his wrists handcuffed behind his back. His head jerks upward as I approach, his expression surprisingly resolute. President Blane stalks out from the shadows, his bear nowhere in sight, thankfully.

"What is it with you Benfields always causing trouble? Is it truly that difficult to abide by the rules of the Regime?" I'm about to bite back when Shiloh spits on the man's boots. Right when I think this can't get any more insane, he takes it a step further. Who is he right now? Where is my sweet, sensible little brother?

He grabs Shiloh's chin firmly, to the point where I can see it pains him. I lunge toward Blane and instinctively grab his arm, forgetting about my violent touch. He screams, and it's only then that I realize that I've made it far, far worse.

I've injured the President of the Regime. Our leader. The most powerful person down here.

From the way he's looking at me, I know he will make me pay for that.

Kaleu puts himself between us and Blane, his teeth dripping with saliva. Suddenly I'm back in the arena, standing in front of Wilder while Kaleu protects us both. "I'm sorry. I'm so sorry, Lennon," Shiloh whispers from behind me, but I ignore him. There will be time for that later.

"Stand down, Miss Benfield. *Now*." Blane still clutches his arm, face expressionless as he stares at me.

"What did he do? Why are you taking him? And *where* are you taking him?" I demand, holding my hands out in front of me like a weapon. Several of the guards point their guns in response, and I do my best not to let it unnerve me.

"Your brother stole something vital to the Regime, and he will pay for his crime with exile. We have few rules here, but your brother has managed to break almost every single one within a mere hour. I will not have troublemakers set on tearing down our city within our walls. As for you, I'm going to assume that this wound was accidental. We do not exile bonded, especially not elites, but you will suffer the consequences of your actions."

Kaleu lunges for Blane, and a guard shoots at him. A guttural scream slips past my lips. He falls to the ground, and the bond I've grown so accustomed to fades rapidly. I crouch beside him, checking his white fur for any signs of blood or wounds. Instead I find a small dart, no larger than a pen. I pull it out and stare at the blood coating the needle.

He's just asleep.

I breathe a sigh of relief, right before the panic sets in. There's no way Shiloh and I can win this fight. I try to summon more magic, more anger, but it's like it's been completely drained out of me. They slip a collar around his throat, then lock it shut with a key.

I'm just a girl protecting her little brother now; there's nothing special about me that can save us anymore.

CHAPTER 13
SLADE

All but twenty within our camp are packed and headed toward Exion the next morning. I try not to let my anger flare at the smug smile Opie gives as they follow him out, but it's an effort. Keelan says his goodbyes, telling the rest of us that we can always come in the future should we need to. I remind him they can always come home too, if things aren't all they seem to be.

I hope they are, for their sake.

Twenty-one left, including me. To my absolute annoyance, Wilder and Florence both stayed behind, likely to torture me. I'm fully aware that it has to do with his incessant desire to bring the rest of the Burrows up, but he stays quiet about it for today at least. He saved my life, yes, but that doesn't make him any less of a nuisance.

There are only three others whom I know relatively well: Lief, who was in my class of exiles; Brina, a girl who was exiled two years prior but is well-known around camp; and Caius. I suppose moving to a city full of unbonded people who despise the bonded isn't enticing enough for him to leave, either.

We gather at the center of Camp Solis, all staring at each other silently. They look to me for instruction, but I'm not sure what to say. I've always been the enforcer of the rules, not the creator.

"Alright, *Chancellor* Slade, what do we do now?" Lief says, earning an eye-roll.

"I'm *not* the new Chancellor. I will keep my role as Warden, and do my best to keep things in order, including continuing to enforce the rule about leaving the Burrows alone." I glare directly at Wilder as I say that. "But I'm not in charge of any of you. I do, however, think it's best if we all work together to stay alive. We have plenty of supplies now to last us through winter, and we can even combine tents to make larger ones, or move into the bigger ones if you'd like. With so many of them damaged from the storm, I think it's best if we toss what remains of them outside the gate, and repair the larger ones." I don't miss the flirtatious glance between Wilder and Florence, and I can't help but carry a twinge of jealousy.

I wonder what it's like to be loved like that. To be wanted.

"You're turning awfully sentimental on me," Vesper teases, and I block her out of my mind. The last thing I need when I'm already on edge is her provoking me.

"The only other suggestion I have is setting up a patrol and reassigning roles. I don't know why any of you stayed, but personally, I don't trust Opie or Exion's intentions. With fewer responsibilities around camp, I think it would be beneficial for at least three of us to do a biweekly patrol of the outside perimeter to ensure we aren't being watched or targeted. I'll set out on the first one tomorrow. Any volunteers to join me?" Lief and Brina both raise their hands without hesitation, and I thank them before setting out to find a new tent.

Caius chooses to stay in his old tent, given it's already massive compared to the others, and I snag the next biggest, which is actually Keelan's old home. It's more fortified than the others, reinforced by various scraps of wood and metal. The inside is a luxury compared to my old tent. Not only is it *triple* the size, but the bed is twice as big, it has an entire *bathtub*, and even a real-looking sink. In two years, I've never stepped foot inside. He always met me outside or came to me. I figured it was because he liked his privacy, but maybe it's because he was hiding all of *this*.

I move my stuff over and watch as the others do the same, all shifting to the central part of camp. Most of the larger structures were made by the original founders of Solis, so they're all right beside one another. Wilder and Florence move into a tent together, and she has quite possibly the biggest smile I've ever seen on someone's face as they carry their stuff in. What she sees in him, I'll never understand ...

Once I'm settled, I help tend to our crops, picking anything that's ripe and canning anything that can be canned. With our numbers so small now, it's even more critical that I master my abilities, so following lunch, I head out to train.

I pick a new field to potentially destroy, filled with tall grass and purple flowers that stretch for miles. My tether to Vesper snaps back into place as I let her back in, and my bag slips down to the dirt below.

"Block me out one more time and I'll rip off your arm," she growls, snapping her teeth at me.

"Quit being such a loathsome beast and I won't have to. Now, what will it be today? Shadows or Flame?"

"Considering you scorched an entire field with your flames last time, perhaps shadows are a safer option for the greenery." I scowl at her before turning around to face the open landscape.

Though flames are the most powerful and, therefore, destructive, shadows are by far the most fun to play with. I let my emotions coil through my body, radiating from one end to the other until I can taste it. Then I face my palms upward and let it roll out of me in steady tendrils like thick, black streaks of darkness.

There's a small tree growing on the edge of the field, and I extend my shadows toward it, grasping into the earth to find its roots. Then, carefully, I remove it from the soil entirely and take it to the other end of the field. I send another thread into the soil on this side and easily dig a hole big enough for the tree and its roots before setting it inside and reburying it.

I turn back to face Vesper, my smile wide and hands moving in a sweeping motion before I bow. *"See, I'm the picture of control. Impressive, really."*

"I'd hope so, considering you've had two years to figure it out." I frown, then use a shadow hand to tussle the hair on her head. She bites at it and turns a snarling head toward me.

I tilt my head playfully, motioning my hand for her to come and get it. She pounces, knocking me to the ground and stripping me of all the air in my lungs.

Despite being unable to breathe from the impact, I'm laughing as she stretches out and enjoys the sun against her fur. I haven't had the luxury of enjoying most things in life: love, friendship, family.

But she has given me all of that, even if she is a thorn in my side most days.

CHAPTER 14

LENNON

The guards surround us on all sides and begin to press in now that Kaleu is down, knowing my magic is disabled.

One of the guards grabs me by the throat, and I panic, searching for someone to help, but all I see are guards. They've done an exceptional job of blocking the public's view. He lifts me off the ground, and I kick and claw and punch, desperate for release, but it's no use. My vision blurs, my mind slipping in and out of consciousness.

I try to reach out to Kaleu as the darkness consumes me, screaming into the bond, into the void, but the tendril of gold that usually hangs between us is now devoid of color.

I'm unsure how much time passes before I wake up in an all-white room. It reminds me of the one I met Kaleu in: no windows, no furniture, and only one door.

But there is no Kaleu this time.

I pull my legs close to my chest, fighting off the chill creeping through my body. Something is tight around my throat, and I reach a hesitant hand up to investigate—a collar, like the one they put around Kaleu's neck before I lost consciousness. My throat burns immensely, and each shift of the collar only amplifies the pain.

In the corner of the room, there's a camera whose mechanical eye squeaks as it zooms in and out. "Where is Kaleu? Where is my brother?!" I scream at it, the words raw and strangled. "Where are they!?"

I keep shouting until the sound stops coming out altogether and curl back against a wall, my head falling into my hands.

If they've done something to them, they'll pay.

I've been here for hours. Or at least I think it's been hours; I can't be sure. I cling to the fact that I'm alive, and therefore Kaleu must be too, wherever he is. If they're hurting him … they can't be hurting him. If he's hurting, I'd feel it. I'd know. Wouldn't I? And Shiloh … What have they done with him? Did they lock him up? Torture him? Exile him?

No, I can't think like that. He's fine, he has to be fine.

Suddenly a jolt pulses through my neck, and I collapse, hitting my head against the polished marble. My body convulses as the current burns through me, rippling through muscle and bone alike. I try to pry the device off my neck, but my hands are shaking too much to grip it. I'm completely at its mercy.

Moments later, Lyric Calwyn enters, her curls bouncing as she walks toward me, her lips painted a deep red color. She smiles, but it isn't remotely sincere. "I think you and I have some things to discuss, Lennon," she says, crouching to look me in the eye. "Sorry about the shock, but I can't risk you trying to hurt me. You went a little bit crazy there before the guards knocked you out."

Her hand extends toward me as if to help me up, but I ignore it and force myself up on my forearms. The muscles in my arms twitch uncontrollably, making the movement far more difficult than I anticipated. My eyes are so heavy, but I force them open, refusing to back down.

"Where are Kaleu and my brother?" I croak, boiling with rage.

"Your wolf is safe, still knocked out. We couldn't let you have your powers right now, and the last thing we need is him biting people. Do you know that we have eight guards in the infirmary because of your actions today? As for your brother, well, he's made some pretty bad choices. There's no saving him, so don't waste your breath."

A sob crawls its way up my throat, but I kick it back down. "What did he do?"

"With all the trouble *you* have caused us, it's no secret we've had extra eyes on you. What you likely don't realize is that we also placed extra eyes on your family. Your brother, however, did surprise us a bit. He began digging through the archives, researching a wide range of ...*unusual* topics. When he didn't find what he needed, he broke into the restricted access area and stole materials that were confidential. I don't know what he was looking for or why he wanted it, but he will die for his decisions today. We will not allow some rogue child to cause chaos and unrest within our city."

My fingers graze the collar as a memory of when I first met Kaleu flashes through my mind. *"What if you had to sacrifice one for the good of many?"* My brother's life for the secrets of the Regime.

"He's just a kid. He's barely sixteen. *Please*, don't do this."

She reaches to brush a strand of hair from my face, and I recoil. "You'll understand one day—our reasoning. Your brother has already been sentenced and is being prepared to go up shortly. We're not in the business of being cruel, so we're going to allow you the privilege of saying goodbye to him. If you attempt in any way to interfere, we will utilize the chip in your arm to collectively end both of your lives. Do you understand? We're doing you a favor by letting you see him. We're trying to show you that we aren't your enemies. Do not make us regret showing you this kindness."

Goodbye. She's going to *let* me say goodbye. "Please, he's only sixteen." The words are beginning to sound more like a whisper, and I can't tell if she can even hear my pleas.

Her piercing eyes narrow at me, sending a chill down my spine. "Do you understand? Or should I tell them you're not stable enough to say goodbye to him? The choice is yours, but it would be such a shame if you didn't pull yourself together. That poor boy is absolutely terrified and could really use his sister right now."

My heart physically aches, threatening to stop beating at any given moment from the pain. I nod, lowering my gaze to the floor.

"Good!" She claps, then reaches for a key. "I'll get this off of you and take you to your wolf. Then you can see your brother. We only have about thirty minutes before the plat-form will rise." I sit silently as she removes the collar, not bothering to touch the burns that are already bubbling on my skin. "Oh, and the President wants to see you again when we're done here. He isn't pleased that you've disrespected him a *second* time. Not to mention what you did to him; I'm sure you'll pay for that, too." I flinch, then force my expression neutral. I hate that man with every fiber of my being. I should have gone for his throat.

She leads me out of the room and into another where Kaleu is starting to come to. Each step towards him is excruciating, as if my entire body has been beaten to a pulp. Maybe it has. It's hard to tell. His nose twitches as he smells me, and immediately, my body is flooded with relief as the bond returns. I run to him, my feet smacking on the cold tile floor in hurried, sloppy movements. The second my face is buried into his fur, I allow myself a moment to cry. Just enough to get me through the next hour. I won't let Lyric or Shiloh see me like this.

"I'm so sorry, little wolf," he says softly, easing away some of my pain. *"What have they done to you?"*

"I'm fine. It's Shiloh … they're sending him up. They're allowing us to say goodbye, but I couldn't save him. I couldn't keep him safe." My body fights my mind for release, but I won't allow it. I help him up slowly, his body teetering with the lingering aftermath of whatever they gave him. He's so heavy and I'm so weak that my legs nearly give out, but I force myself to stay steady.

"Time to go," Lyric says, giving us a smug smile. I hate her. I hate how much she looks like she enjoys this. I hate her *Auryth* that hangs out of her pocket like a toy. I hate the way she's willing to sacrifice my little brother's life over one mistake when he's a *child*.

We follow her out of Kaleu's room and down a long corridor, winding through countless hallways. Finally, we reach a set of stairs I didn't know existed. "We'll head up three flights to get to the platform level. I want to remind you that everything you've been told tonight—your brother's exile, and what you will see—is all classified information. If you attempt to share it with anyone, we will have to activate your chip. Do you understand?" How could I not, when it's the same damn threat every time?

I nod once more and begin the trek upstairs. Each movement fills me with dread, my legs becoming more leaden with each step. Kaleu stays glued to my side, never faltering despite his exhaustion.

When we reach the top, the floor gives way to a giant, metal cage. It looks rusted and beat to hell, and my brother is in the middle of it. Shiloh looks worse off than I feel. His face is bloodied and bruised, his hands still secured behind his back. He sits on his knees, struggling to keep upright. The moment his eyes meet mine, a cry leaves his throat that will haunt me for all of my days. "Len," he breathes, falling onto his butt as sobs wrack his frail body.

I run to him, dropping to my knees and pulling his head to my chest as he shakes. "I am so sorry." Kaleu lies down next to us, putting his head in Shiloh's lap. A sharp pain shoots through the bond, and I nearly break at the realization that it isn't my pain this time, but Kaleu's.

"It's—my—fault," he gets out between desperate sobs, and I pull him tighter to me as I shush his apologies.

"You have three minutes, then we need to leave," Lyric says, staring down at her watch as if this is the most boring interaction she's had all day.

"I'm scared," Shiloh says, staring at me with red-rimmed hazel eyes that likely match my own right now. "I don't want to die."

"I know. It's going to be okay," I tell him, though I'm not

sure even I believe that. "Wilder will be waiting for you in the sun. You won't be alone. He'll meet you there." My lips quiver as I speak. Each word is painful, but I force them out. He needs to hear this.

"Two minutes," Lyric calls out, pacing the entryway to the platform. I look between her, Kaleu, and my brother, trying to think of a way out of this, of any other option.

There are no weapons. Nothing I can use to knock her out and keep her from calling for backup. Not even a damn chair. Shiloh is trembling so severely I think it might break me, and Kaleu won't stop looking at me like he's waiting for me to say something.

What is there to say? What can I do? *Kill* Lyric? Then what, follow Shiloh to our mutual destruction? End Kaleu's life so my brother doesn't die alone? It's not like I can fight her; even if I win, the Regime will never let him stay. They'll simply flip my kill switch and send Shiloh on his merry way.

She won't let us go to the surface with him out of the goodness of her heart. The Regime wants me here. I'm useful to them, a pawn in their game. No matter what direction I go, someone is going to die.

"Kaleu, I need you to do something for me."

"Anything."

"I need you to rip out her throat." There's no hesitation in my voice, no remorse. It's a selfish thing to ask, both because I'm too afraid to do it myself and because it would mean I'm choosing death for us, too. Kill her, or let Shiloh die alone. That's the choice.

Injuring her would just result in another fight, and I won't let them hurt Shiloh or me ever again. He's all I have. There is no other family, no purpose, no *home* without him. I've lost *everything*—my mom, my dad, Wilder … I won't lose him, too. I can't. I won't survive it.

So we'll go together.

Kaleu doesn't bother questioning my motives; he has full access to my thoughts, as he always does.

And just like that, I've answered the very question Kaleu asked me on Convergence Day: *"Would you sacrifice one life for the good of the many?"* I'd sacrifice Lyric's, Kaleu's, my own, and anyone else who stood in my way if it meant Shiloh didn't have to die alone.

In fact, I'd sacrifice many lives for the good of one.

He moves so quickly, I barely have time to register that it's over until his white fur is stained crimson and her head is rolling on the floor beside us. A stream of blood makes its way toward my bare feet, grounding me back to reality. I yank off Lyric's boots and slip them on, just in case the ground is alive. Shiloh screams, but I run toward him and clamp my hand over his mouth.

The platform squeals and shifts as it moves toward the surface. "I won't let you die alone," I tell Shiloh, holding him tightly. I'm so tempted to grab him and run back inside, where it's safe, but I know there are far more people besides Lyric who want my brother dead—who will want me dead now, too. Being bonded won't be enough to save us from the repercussions of this. There will be no more chances, and I refuse to let Blane hurt me or the people I love ever again.

Maybe the Regime lied about the Earth being survivable. Hell, they've lied about everything else so far, so why wouldn't this be part of it? They definitely lied. They lied, and when we get up there, it's going to be beautiful, and Wilder is going to be waiting for us. We are not going to die today.

Kaleu squeezes next to me, the three of us clinging to one

another for our final moments. *"I'm so sorry,"* I tell Kaleu, my voice shaking.

"From now until our dying day, Lennon Benfield," he replies. I squeeze my eyes shut the entire way up and prepare for the end.

"I'll meet you in the sun," I say aloud, hoping Wilder can somehow hear me, wherever he is.

CHAPTER 15
SLADE

Lief, Brina, Vesper, and I leave at daylight with backpacks full of food, a change of clothes, medical supplies, and anything else I can think to bring, just in case. You never know what sort of things you'll run into outside the walls of Solis.

"So," Lief starts, and I roll my eyes in preparation for his hundredth question this morning. "How come you got to bond an *Auryth*? I thought we were all deemed unworthy or whatever. Seems a little unfair, don't you think?" I give Vesper a sideways glance, finding myself somewhat thankful the group can't hear her responses.

"I don't know, Lief. She chose me. I guess I'm special." Vesper's annoyance surges through our bond, and I fight to keep from laughing.

He scrunches his face up in contemplation and opens his mouth to say something else, but Brina cuts him off. "If I were an *Auryth*, I definitely wouldn't bond to you, Lief. You'd get yourself, and therefore *me*, killed in a matter of days. It's a wonder you've made it this far, honestly." I snort at that, and they both look at me like I have two heads.

"Would you look at that!" Lief shouts. "The dark, mighty Slade *does* have a sense of humor!" I shake my head as we continue down the path, keeping a watchful eye on the wood-line for any lingering wild *Auryths* looking for a midday snack. He looks at me seriously, and I sigh, bracing myself for his next words. "Can you ask Vesper what I need to do to bond with one? Is there some sort of, I don't know, call or something? Maybe a ritual? Personally, I'd love to bond with a fox, a red one, to match my hair, but I'll take what I can get at this point."

"No, Lief, I'm not going to ask her that."

It's scorching today; the sun appears to have some sort of vendetta against us. Sweat soaks through my shorts and shirt, which are now sticking to me like a second skin. One positive about everyone leaving Solis is that in Exion, they'll *allegedly* have all the clothes they'll ever need, which means more hammy downs for us. The shorts are a bit too short for my liking, which Lief got a massive kick out of this morning, but it's better than walking all day in stuffy pants. I can tolerate some teasing if it means I can feel the breeze.

"So what, exactly, are we looking for?" Brina asks, holding a hand up as if to block the sun from her face.

"Hopefully nothing."

We're moving in the direction of the platform since the other sides of camp are cut off by either woods or deep, hilly drop-offs. This will be the only side on which we'll potentially find people spying, unless they're brave enough to camp out with the wild *Auryths*, and if they are, all the more power to them. I have no interest in checking for that.

Vesper stops suddenly, her nose twitching in the light breeze as if she's caught a scent. *"What is it?"*

"I smell a wolf. And blood—lots of blood."

"Where? The woods?"

"Near the platform." I stare blankly at her, confused as to why in the world there would be blood near the platform. Has the Regime sent someone up? They've never done that before, not outside the day of the Convergence.

We're still a few miles from the platform, so I quickly inform Lief and Brina of what Vesper told me and change directions. As we get closer, we slow down to avoid scaring whatever—or whoever—it is.

The platform is positioned on our right as we crest the hill, and I wave my hand at Lief and Brina, telling them to get down silently. If there is someone on the other side, they must have done something particularly heinous to warrant the wrath of the Regime. Not to mention the smell of blood.

Vesper links her ears to mine, allowing me to listen in. There's yelling—a woman's voice, raspy and exhausted. "You better tell me what the hell it was and have a damn good explanation as to why you took it."

I quickly peek my head up over the hill, now lying on my stomach to avoid being seen, and find a girl, seemingly around my age, screaming at a younger boy with similar features.

That's not what makes me stop breathing, though. There's a massive white wolf at her side, its head nuzzled up against her leg as she gives the boy a good tongue lashing. *"What the hell is going on? Are they bonded?"*

"You're hearing the same thing I'm hearing. I know no more than you. Stop wasting my time with stupid questions." I turn and glare at her, though I suppose she's right.

The girl throws her hands in the air, then covers her face before slumping to the ground. It's difficult to get a clear view, but there appears to be something else on the platform. *"Do we approach?"*

"She's rather agitated, and she's bonded to a wolf. We may put ourselves in a bad situation if we interrupt right now."

I'm so distracted by my conversation with Ves that I don't notice Lief get up until he's strolling directly towards them. What the hell is he thinking? Brina gives me a sympathetic look that says, "I tried to tell him," and I groan. *We either go now or risk her obliterating Lief, and we're already kinda low on people."*

We get to our feet and watch as Lief approaches her, his hands held in surrender. "Hello!" he says sweetly, and her wolf positions itself in front of her and the boy, snarling. "Nice wolfie, please don't bite me. I'm friendly. I'm not here to hurt you." I place a hand to my sweaty forehead, both slightly amused and anguished at this entire interaction. Leave it to Lief.

"Who are you?" she shouts. "What do you want?" She holds her hands out in front of her, a motion far too familiar to me, and out of instinct, I release a stream of shadows to create a shield around Lief.

He whips his head around, his brows furrowed. "I had it under control!"

"Clearly," I say sarcastically, approaching closer and slowly evaporating the blackness. Her eyes are wild now, looking between Vesper and me with the utmost confusion. "And to think I thought I was the only one bonded to a wolf."

Her body is shaking, and I can see clearly now that the other *thing* lying on the platform is a human head. Blood coats the platform and her wolf's white fur. She's surprisingly small up close, though I've never been one to underestimate opponents on the basis of size—especially when they have magic. I point to the decapitated head behind her. "Did you do that?"

Her head turns to see where I'm pointing, then whips back towards me. I notice what appears to be handprints around her neck, splotchy and red. Some are even bubbled up as if something has burned her skin. She protects the boy desperately, pressing him further behind her back. "Yes."

I tilt my head. "Tsk, tsk, tsk. One day above ground and you're *already* killing people? That's not very friendly."

"She's not from here. She's from the Burrows," she seethes through gritted teeth.

"Was," I correct. "She was from the Burrows. That is, before you took her head off." Oh, she's angry now. Her face is red, her hazel eyes narrowed on me with malice. Good. I want to see what she's capable of.

"What the hell is this arrogant prick's problem?" a voice says into my mind, and my eyebrows nearly fly off my face. It certainly wasn't Vesper's voice, and she must've heard it too from the way her head snapped toward me.

"Name-calling isn't very polite, you know," I speak into her mind, then watch as her mouth falls open. Two-way mental communication. Interesting. It must be a wolf thing. I can tell by the way she's scrunching her face that she's focusing on trying to do it again, but to no avail.

Curious, I reach out a tether in three directions, building an intricate line between the girl, me, and Vesper. I have no idea if it will work, but it's worth a shot. *"Testing, testing. Can everyone hear me?"* Both the girl and her wolf look at me, and I don't need them to confirm it worked.

This should be fun.

CHAPTER 16

LENNON

The platform groans as it rises upward, and Kaleu presses his body in front of Shiloh and me, squishing us up against the back wall as if he can protect us from this. It slams to an abrupt stop, toppling us all over. The gate shifts open slowly, releasing a horrible screeching noise.

How long will we have before the air suffocates us? Will it be slow? Painful?

The sunlight meets my skin like a golden caress, and despite my fear, I relish it. I've never felt anything so warm and inviting; even my dreams never concocted anything so sweet. My nostrils fill with an overwhelming number of new senses, many of which I don't even have a name for.

"We should at least look outside. If we're going to die, we might as well enjoy the view. There's nothing we can do to stop it anyway," I tell Kaleu. He gently moves off of us so we can stand, and I help Shiloh to his feet.

He's still a little unsteady thanks to the handcuffs. There wasn't time to think about getting a key for them, and up here there don't seem to be many options for removal. "I'm sorry, Shy. I know that can't be comfortable."

He doesn't respond, but instead stumbles off the platform and into the grassy field that surrounds it. I follow behind him, taking in the vast landscape filled with blooming flowers and weeds sprouting every few feet. On the horizon, I see a massive forest lined with countless, monstrous trees. There's a buzzing in my ear, and it takes me a moment to realize that it's coming from a swarm of insects flying overhead. *Insects.*

The ground is alive. It's survivable.

"It's not dead." I look toward Kaleu, who has his head pointed toward the sky, his eyes squeezed shut as his nose twitches uncontrollably. A delirious laugh slips past my lips.

We're alive. "IT'S NOT DEAD!" I scream, turning in circles underneath the warmth of the sunlight. After processing the lack of impending death, I turn to face Shiloh again. "You are so lucky we're alive right now! What did you take from them?"

He stares at me with crazed eyes, though I'm not sure if it's from the adrenaline of being alive or the last twenty-four hours he's put us through. "It was nothing."

"Nothing? NOTHING?! You better tell me what the hell it was and have a damn good explanation as to why you took it." Though I'm angry, I'm also curious as to what was so detrimental to the Regime that they decided to immediately exile him for taking it.

"A book."

"*A book?* What the hell kind of book would send the Regime on a full-blown manhunt after you? You didn't seriously think they wouldn't catch you and take it back, right?"

"This book," he says slyly, pulling out a small, leather pocketbook with the Desmos Token engraved on the front and three triangles behind it. "I made a copy and switched them, then made a cover slip for this one so when they found it on me, they'd think they stole the right book back."

I open my mouth to scold him, but Kaleu growls, low and deep. *"There are others—humans and Auryth."* I scan our surroundings, searching for any sign of life, but there's nothing there.

"Where? I can't see anything."

"Not far. They must be hiding somewhere. I can smell them." Right on cue, someone emerges from the hilltop, the sun bouncing off his red hair like a beacon.

He attempts to introduce himself, then proceeds to call Kaleu "wolfie", which only makes him want to bite his hands off. I'm immediately on defense, unsure if my powers have even returned but desperate to make myself appear threatening.

"Who are you? What do you want?" I shout at him, despite the soreness still aching in my throat. Out of nowhere, shadows encompass the red-haired man, blocking him from my view. Fear simmers through me, and I swear the air has suddenly grown colder.

Then, as quickly as it arrived, the darkness is gone, revealing the man again as three more figures head towards us, one of which is a *massive* black wolf, nearly as big as Kaleu. My breath is knocked from my lungs at the sight of it stalking toward us.

There's a man and a woman with it, though it isn't difficult to tell which one is bonded to it by the way it's glued to the man's side. He's tall and muscled, his face entirely emotionless as he takes in the sight of us. His hair is dark brown and shaggy, and his eyes are a shade of green almost as vibrant as the trees in the forest behind us. His features are sharp, his expression hard and calculating as his gaze flickers between the three of us. He's built like he could kill us without magic, and his wolf is no exception. Even the way he walks oozes confidence, like he's in charge and everyone around knows exactly why.

If I have to take him on, I have little hope of winning that fight. Then again, I have Kaleu, and he just ripped a woman's throat out without a second thought, and I'm the one who told him to. Maybe I need to give us a little more credit. I push Shiloh behind me, desperate to put as much ground between him and this man as possible.

"Did you do this?" he asks, and I realize he's pointing toward Lyric's decapitated head behind me. I'd almost—*almost*—forgotten it was there. I turn to face the consequences of my actions and cringe at the sight of it, bloodied and unsettling.

"Yes," I choke out, the word sticking in my throat. As far as first impressions go, I'd say this is arguably the worst-case scenario.

"One day on the ground and you're already killing people?" he says, and a spark of fire ignites under my skin. My power is back, humming like a silent weapon, right when I need it.

His forest-green eyes glint with mischief as I attempt to explain that she's from the Burrows, but it's clear he isn't really looking for an explanation. No, he's toying with me, trying to rile me up. I will not give him the satisfaction. I choke the anger back down.

"*What is this arrogant prick's problem?*" I ask Kaleu, then watch as the man's face goes blank.

"*Name-calling isn't very polite, you know,*" a voice responds, and now it's my jaw that drops. Did he just … *respond* to me? How did he hear my snide comment in the first place?

"Testing, testing. Can everyone hear me?" the voice says again, only this time I know in my bones that Kaleu heard it, too.

"Kaleu?" I ask, more for clarification than anything.

"I've heard that those bonded to wolves can communicate with one another telepathically, but there's never been anyone else to test the theory with … until now, I suppose." Fantastic.

"Don't listen to him," the redhead says, giving me a lopsided smile. "He's always grumpy. My name is Lief, this is Brina, and that is Slade and his wolf, Vesper. Now, what are your names? And what did you do to make the Regime mad enough to exile you?"

I side-eye Slade, then turn my attention back on Lief and Brina, choosing to focus on them rather than the million questions I have for him. "I'm Lennon; this is my brother Shiloh; and my wolf, Kaleu. Technically speaking, I wasn't exiled; Shiloh was. I just decided to force my way up with him." Lief's mouth hangs open in disbelief, and Brina looks rather impressed.

"Risky move," she says.

"Alright, enough of this small talk. Why did your brother get exiled?" Slade says, looking as if this entire interaction is boring him.

I turn and face Shiloh, a little more bite in my tone than intended. "Yes, do tell them, Shiloh."

He stares at his feet, avoiding all of our stares. "I stole a book."

"A book?" Slade raises a brow, narrowing his eyes skeptically. "I highly doubt they exiled you for that."

I glare in his direction.

"What's the matter, sunshine? Have to resort to giving me mean

looks since you can't figure out how to respond?" I refuse to acknowledge him. Pompous, egotistical—

"It is the truth. I stole a book on the Desmos token." Every head whips toward Shiloh.

"Why would they keep a book on the Desmos token locked up?" Lief asks.

"I don't know. I can't explain it. All I *do* know is that I started having these visions about it, like it was *calling* to me somehow. It showed me where the book was and how to break into the restricted area. Unfortunately, it didn't tell me how to sneak back out. And before you ask, *no*, I didn't get to read any of it before they took it back." He plops down in the grass, sighing deeply. My eyes narrow at my little brother. Smart, not telling the strangers that he did, in fact, steal the book and brought it with him.

"Visions? What do you mean by 'visions'?" I ask, kneeling next to him.

"The nightmares I was having, well, they weren't exactly nightmares. They were more like clues, leading me to the book. I don't know why or how, but I knew I had to find it."

I look at Slade. "Have you ever heard of such a thing?" In all of my research and time spent in the Burrows archives, I sure haven't.

Slade claps his hands together. "Nope, and I don't really care, either. We have a healer back at camp; you can ask him if that'll make you feel better. We have about four hours before it starts getting dark, and it's at least that long a walk to get back. Let's go."

I pause, staring down at the small bump under my skin. "Can you get this chip out of my arm first? And my brother's handcuffs off? I doubt they can reach me up here, but just in case ..."

He gives me an all-too-eager grin and pulls out a small pocket knife. "I'll be gentle." He digs it lightly into my arm over the small knot and squeezes it out, then holds the bloody thing between his fingers. "Interesting." Then he melts it down to nothing between his fingertips. Turning to Shiloh, he puts his hands on the metal shackles and heats them until they snap. "Now, let's go."

Okay, kind of fascinating, kind of terrifying. He starts walking, and the three of us follow along; it's not like we have anywhere else to go, anyway. "How many people are there at your camp?" I ask.

"Twenty-one," he says plainly.

"Twenty-one?! Where did everyone go? That's less than half of the class that came up months ago! Are they all *dead*?" Is the air still poisonous? Or are there other factors up here that make it difficult to survive?

He lets out a frustrated groan, then rubs his face with his hands. "No, they're not dead."

"Then where are they? And do you have someone by the name of Wilder Ray in your camp? He should have come up with the last group of exiles. Blond hair, blue eyes."

The look he gives me tells me if I ask one more question, he might put me on the platform and send me back down to the Burrows. "Yes." My shoulders sag with relief. He's here. He made it, and he's *alive*. We both are. We'll actually meet each other in the sun. It doesn't feel real. "I'll take you straight to his tent when we return." Every nerve in my body teems with exhilaration.

"Lennon, can you ask Kaleu what a man's gotta do to get an *Auryth* to bond with him? I asked Slade to ask Vesper, but he said no," Lief says.

I look at Kaleu, then decide my answer is probably a lot

nicer than whatever response he'll give. "Kaleu says he unfortunately can't offer advice because every bond is different. He also says not to give up hope; your match is out there somewhere."

"I certainly did not say that," Kaleu grumbles, and I stifle a laugh.

"How long have you been bonded to Vesper?" I ask Slade, quickening my pace to catch up with him at the front.

"Two years."

"How long ago were you exiled?"

"A little over two years ago."

He must have bonded not long after arriving here. I lean in slightly, my voice lowering. "What powers do you have?"

"I'd say it's a pretty good bet that I have the same powers you have."

"Right. Well, we're both very powerful then." I slow my pace and move back toward the others, not wanting to give away the fact that I know next to nothing about how powerful "we" really are.

Within a few hours, we arrive at the camp. I'm unable to let myself take in the sight of it all, too wrapped up in what it will be like to be back inside Wilder's arms again. I turn around to face Slade. "Take me to him."

"Follow me," he says, walking through the gate.

CHAPTER 17

LENNON

Slade stops abruptly in front of a large tent, extending a hand outward as if inviting me to go inside. *"After you,"* he says, and I'm so wrapped up in my excitement that I don't bother being annoyed at him for speaking into my mind. I rip the tent flap open, tears already sliding down my face at the reunion only steps away.

Nothing could have prepared me for what I see.

There's a large bed situated on one side of the room, and in it is Wilder and a light-haired, beautiful woman, curled up together as if they don't have a care in the world. His hand traces her cheek lazily, and her eyes are locked onto him. His blue eyes widen in shock as he sees me, and I find myself lost for words, stumbling backward out of the tent to avoid seeing any more.

"Lennon?!" He shouts after me, but I'm already back outside, slamming straight into Slade, who's grinning like a cat. Then I'm moving again, trying to get as far away from them all as quickly as possible.

It's as if I'm moving in slow motion, every step I take sluggish and lagging. It's difficult to breathe, like my rib cage and lungs are collapsing in on my fractured heart as they realize there's nothing left to protect.

Did he even mourn the idea of never seeing me again?

It's painful, so much more painful than I could have ever anticipated it to be. Kaleu is with me, trying to calm me down, but I can't hear him anymore. All I can hear are the words in my head telling me how stupid I am for ever thinking I'd be enough for him, or that he could ever love me in that way.

I'm running through camp now, trying to find my way back to the front gate, but I don't know where I am, and everything is so blurry from my tears. I finally find the opening and take off, not sure where I'm going; all I know is I need to be away from this place, away from Wilder, away from *her*.

Right as I make it outside the gate, my arm is yanked backward, nearly throwing me off balance. Wilder. He's saying something, but the ringing in my ears is so deafening that I can't make out the words. I tear from his grasp and keep running. I can't stay here. I don't want to be here.

"Breathe, little wolf. I know you are hurting, but you have to breathe through it." Kaleu pierces through the cacophony of noise inside my mind, and I drop to my knees, dry heaving into the grass.

"Lennon!" Wilder shouts. I'm crying uncontrollably, suffocated by my grief. My throat is practically being torn open and clawed to death, and each gag or sob only makes it that much more agonizing. I'm trembling, unable to stop the anxiety racking my bones.

"Do you want me to get rid of him? I can do so easily," Kaleu asks.

Yes. No. I don't know what I want. I don't understand why this has affected me so much. Maybe it's everything—Lyric's death, the Regime, Shiloh, not dying when we reached the surface. The one constant I've always had in my life is Wilder, and now he has someone else.

It's like I've been betrayed and replaced all at once, but I also know I have no right to see it that way. He was never mine, and I was never his.

No. That's not right. He was mine, and I was *always* his. He had to have known that. Right?

Wilder's hand finds my back, attempting to rub soothing circles to calm me down. I sit on my butt and bury my face in my knees. "Lennon, what is going on? Why are you and Shiloh here?" The tears start to fall, trickling down my face in steady streams while my body heaves from my desperate breaths. "I'm sorry I didn't say more when you came into my tent. I was … shocked. I mean, can you blame me? You were about the last person I expected to see today."

I can't form words. There *are* no words that can encompass what I did to get here. What the Regime put me through for trying to save him, or the things I've done to keep those I love safe.

He moves beside me and tugs me to his chest, and the sobbing intensifies. I'm a blubbering fool. "Hey, hey, hey. It's okay. You're safe now. I'm here. There's no need to cry." Something about him not even realizing why I'm crying makes it that much worse. I've been delusional in thinking he ever saw me as more than a friend, to believe that he wanted to be with me. Even if he was going to kiss me that day, it was goodbye. Nothing more.

Like a light switch, my sadness and desperation are replaced with rage. I tilt my head back and place a hand to my forehead, my entire body going numb as I force myself to dissociate. I hate letting him see how deeply his betrayal has affected me. "I spent my entire life loving you. Cherishing you, *admiring* you. That day, the day they took you away from me, I thought you felt it too. I got your letter, and in some twisted way, I convinced myself I wasn't alone in the way I felt. But now I understand."

"Len ..."

"No." I cut him off and take a steadying breath. "You loved having me around because it made you feel wanted. *I* made you feel on top of the world because you knew, no matter what, that I'd do anything for you. We may not have ever been together, but you knew how much I loved you, and you let me believe you felt that way too. Just like you said in your letter, you knew you wouldn't bond and I would, so why not give the poor, lovesick girl a taste of happiness? It's not like you'll ever see her again anyway, right?"

"That's not fair, and you know it," he seethes.

"Don't talk to me about fair. Did you even think about me when you got up here? Or was I simply a forgotten part of your past life?" My tone is icy, my bones filling with a strange yet familiar chill to match. "You didn't try to let me know you were okay. You didn't try to get me out. I had to *mourn* you. Mourn! I felt your death every single day. I carried it with me like a brand. I still do."

His eyes fill with tears as he stares at me, anguish carved into every angle of his face. I don't care. I twist the knife deeper. "Did you even wonder if I was okay? Surely you didn't think the Regime would just let me off after what I did for you. Did you ever question if I was still alive? If they had me locked away somewhere, begging someone to come save me?"

He reaches for my face. I jerk back like his touch is poisonous. "Did they hurt you?"

I laugh dryly, the sound hollow and frigid. "Don't pretend to start caring about me now, Wilder."

"I never stopped caring about you. I never thought I'd even see you again."

The words break something open, and from the hollowed space, my power floods in. It surges up my throat, down my arms, electric and cold and furious. I stagger upright, my hands shaking with the effort to contain it.

"Uh, Lennon?" Wilder's voice is tight. "Your hands ..."

I look down. A pale white mist curls from my fingertips slowly. It coils outward, frosting over the earth beneath me. Lightning splits the sky, and a storm wind howls awake. The sensation is unbearable—burning and freezing, agony and ecstasy. I can't tell which is which anymore. I can't stop. I drop to my knees, shaking, my hair whipping across my face. Trees bend; leaves rip from limbs and fly freely. The clearing groans around me.

"Lennon!" Wilder shouts, but the wind devours his voice.

I am the storm. I am in control.

Only I'm not.

The power wants him. Wants to carve my heartbreak into his skin the way I've worn his memory on mine. "You never cared about me!" I scream.

No one has.

He tries to speak. I don't let him. I hurl a blast of power in his direction. He barely rolls out of the way, the ground erupting in a frozen crater where he stood, ice veins splintering through dirt and rock.

Still. Not. Enough.

I reach deeper, my body trembling from the cold that's

burrowing inside me. The mist grows denser. My breath fogs in the air. I can't stop shaking. And then … darkness. Total. Smothering. Immediate. Everything drops. My power chokes out. The wind dies.

I spin in place, panic starting to crawl into my throat until a voice cuts through the void behind me. "Wow," the voice drawls. "You do this often, or does he just have this effect on everyone?"

My head jerks toward him. Slade. Shadows slide off his shoulders like smoke, his eyes gleaming faintly in the dark. "What the hell are you doing?" I seethe.

He quirks a brow, completely unfazed. "Keeping you from accidentally turning Loverboy over there into a human popsicle or who knows what else. You're welcome, by the way."

I lurch to my feet, fists clenched. "Get out of my way."

"Yeah, not really in the mood to have any more dead campers today, even if it *is* Wilder, but thanks anyway." His gaze flicks over me, unimpressed. "Unless you'd like to see what else I can do, I'd suggest chilling the hell out." The shadows loosen, light seeps back in, and suddenly the cold inside me feels unbearable.

I stagger back, chest heaving, as the last of the mist burns off my skin. Wilder stares at me in terror, still scooting backward to distance himself from me. Not exactly what I intended, but it will do.

What *did* I intend to do?

I should feel guilty, but I don't. I feel numb. "How about we go get you and your brother a tent?" Slade asks, looking between Wilder and me. Kaleu nudges up against my legs, a subtle reminder that he's still here, even if I've lost everything else.

I nod, then follow him back to camp without bothering to look back.

We find Shiloh and get ourselves adjacent tents, though I ensure mine is as far from Wilder and his new girlfriend's as possible. It's larger than I thought it would be, with a twin-sized bed and even a small desk inside. It's certainly a far cry from my home in the Third Ring, but at least I don't have to worry about the Regime watching my every move.

No one comes to check on me, and I'm grateful for the silence. I'm convinced I won't be able to sleep, not with my mind running rampant with the aftermath of the day, but exhaustion tightens its grip on me.

I'm out as soon as my head hits the pillow.

CHAPTER 18
LENNON

The sound of bells jolts me awake, and Kaleu's on his feet before I can sit up.

"What is it?" I ask.

"It appears to be some sort of alarm. I can hear—" The sound of screaming cuts him off.

I'm up, throwing on yesterday's clothes and slipping on my boots, instantly concerned about Shiloh. I rip his tent flap open to see him sleeping peacefully, not remotely fazed by all the chaos. "Shiloh," I whisper, shaking him lightly. "Wake up."

He blinks his hazel eyes slowly, his face twisting into confusion as his ears catch up. "Wha-what's going on?"

"I don't know, but stay here. I'll come back when I know more, but stay alert just in case." I look around his room for some sort of weapon, locate a cast-iron pan, and set it in his lap before sprinting back outside. It's not much, but it'll do in a pinch.

People are running frantically in every direction, and it doesn't take long for me to find the cause. There's a group of lions right outside the perimeter, seeming to contemplate just how sturdy our gate is. Slade and Vesper stand at the opening, using his shadows to build a second barrier around the camp with impressive speed. An older man with a white stag is heading toward them, his cane dragging into the dirt with each hurried step.

Another bonded up here? How many are there?

Kaleu and I follow after them. "How can we help?" I call, breathless as we reach the gate.

Slade doesn't even turn. "You can't. Back to the tents —*now*."

The first lion crashes into the black wall of shadows. It shudders under its weight but holds. If it breaks, there's nothing stopping them from coming in and ripping us to shreds. The rickety pieces of wood they call a fence will be more of an annoyance than an obstacle for them.

"I will kill them all," Kaleu says, and as much as I want to believe that's true, there's only him, Vesper, and a stag versus at least eight lions.

Wilder, Lief, Brina, and the girl from Wilder's bed have arrived now, each looking just as confused and terrified as we are. Slade whips around, locates Lief, and yells, "Drag Lennon back to camp, and the rest of you go find somewhere sturdy to hide. NOW!"

Wilder grabs the blonde girl by her shoulders, his panic palpable. "Florence, go back to the tent." So that's her name. *Florence.* The moment reminds me all too much of the one we shared on the day of our Convergence, when we almost …

Another body slams against the shield of shadows, and panic floods in as I watch the entire thing crumble into broken fragments. I reach inside, trying to locate the hum of my power. Even if it isn't controllable, it's still *something*, and something is better than nothing ... right?

What is wrong with these animals? It's like they're going out of their way to attack us. Not out of necessity or from provocation, but simply for the hell of it. The man with the white stag stumbles forward right as the shadows fall, revealing several snarling, angry lions. One sprints toward us, never missing a beat. My stomach drops, and my eyes meet Wilder's for only a second before the man's stag bleats, then he slams his cane into the dirt with enough force that I swear I feel the ground tremble.

Roots shoot up like spiked chains, ensnaring the lion in midair and yanking it back down. It snarls and thrashes, but the earth swallows it whole like it was never there. The others pause, looking between the man and the spot their companion disappeared into. A tree explodes upward from right underneath the pack a moment later, splitting bark, blood, and bone in one breathless, brutal strike.

It takes out four of them.

As it turns out, the gift of chloromancy can be quite terrifying.

The rest run like hell ... directly towards us. They want blood. One leaps over the gate and heads straight for Kaleu and me; my first instinct is to run, but instead I extend my hands in front of me, hoping to draw my power out, but nothing comes. I find myself staring directly into the eyes of a lioness as she prowls toward me, begging my power to show the hell up so we don't die. I did not survive exile for this. Slowly, I step backwards, widening the distance between us, but Kaleu stops, standing his ground and daring the lion to take one more step.

The lion launches, but Slade's there before it can reach us, shadows flaring. He drives a jagged spike of darkness through the creature's side, knocking it off course mid-leap. It hits the ground hard, twitching and snarling. Lief finishes it off by bringing a machete down on its neck.

"Thank you," I breathe, my body trembling.

"I told you to go back to your tent," Slade seethes.

"And I told you I wanted to help!"

He turns and runs back toward the gate, ignoring me. I count the lions again. Three left. Another springs over the broken fence, its massive paws landing with a thud near Vesper's back. But she's already locked in a vicious fight with one while Slade and the man with the stag deal with the massive third beast. It tears a gash across her side before she can twist away, and she yelps, cornered.

"VESPER!" Slade's voice cracks as he tries to pivot, shadows lashing from both hands in an instant. They race toward the lion closest to her, but it's too far, too late. They won't make it in time.

But Kaleu will.

He lunges forward, slamming his body full-force into one of the lions. The two go down hard, claws and teeth flashing. I scream, unsure who's winning, until I see Kaleu sink his teeth deep into the lion's throat. Then the second lion charges.

Slade lifts both hands, palms outward, and fire erupts from his skin. It doesn't just burn—it *consumes*. Flames roar to life like they were waiting for permission, curling through the air in long, controlled whips. They wrap around the charging lion like ropes and slam it backwards, rolling it across the dirt before detonating in a controlled *blast* that sends ash and scorched grass into the sky. There's nothing left but charred, smoking ground where it once stood. Kaleu limps away from his kill, blood on his mouth, panting hard. It doesn't get back up.

"Vesper!" Slade rushes to her side, dropping to his knees. She growls softly, wounded but conscious.

I hesitate a moment before jogging over. "Is she—"

"She's okay," he says sharply, his hand pressed over the worst of the gash. "Thanks to you." His eyes flick to Kaleu. He doesn't say anything more, and neither do I. His hand stays on Vesper's wound, fire gently flickering along his fingertips. It isn't wild or angry this time. It's controlled, healing. Like he's trying to cauterize the wound.

The man with the stag finally steps forward. His cane sinks into the earth like it's all that's keeping him upright. "They're dead," he says hoarsely. "All of them."

The walk back to our tents is silent, all of us trying to regain our nerve and wondering how the hell we can prevent that from happening again. "Why were they attacking?" I ask, unable to stand the quiet any longer.

"I don't know," Slade says bluntly.

My eyes fall on Wilder and his girl sitting on a wooden bench as he checks her over for injury. I wish I could remove the twinge of jealousy in my stomach. "Does this happen often?"

"No. It's the first time they've ever crossed the woodline." Well, that's just fantastic. The man with the stag—Caius, I've learned—has already slunk back to his tent, likely exhausted from the aftermath of using his powers. I hadn't the slightest idea that chloromancers could be so ... violent. I've only ever known them to be healers or growers in the Burrows.

"Listen up, everybody," Slade shouts, gaining everyone's attention. "Let's start cleaning up and reinforcing any parts of the gate we can. I don't know how to keep this from happening again, but we need to try to come up with some alternatives for protection. With so many gone and after today's events, we need to reestablish some ground rules and assign jobs. If we all do our parts, we'll keep this place running smoothly and be far ahead of the game when winter comes. Lief, Brina, and Cass, you're on guard and cleanup duty with me. Patrols every other week and night watch rotations. In our spare time, we'll help with camp maintenance."

Lief groans dramatically, shooting a hand into the air. "Do I at least get a fancy title for this? Maybe 'Lord of the Night Watch'?" If looks could kill, he'd be dead from Slade's right now. He lowers his hand and scratches his chin, averting his gaze.

"Crop duty goes to Delilah, Florence, and the rest of you already handling food preservation," Slade continues. "Make sure everything's harvested and nothing goes to waste. Work *together*." I tense unintentionally at the sound of her name. Will it always be like this?

"Patching will fall to Jonah's team," he continues. "Wilder, you're with them. Stick to fixing necessary things, especially the gate and any tents that need reinforcements. All of you who know where you're going are dismissed."

"Who the hell put you in charge?" Wilder cocks his head at Slade, and my brows scrunch in confusion. I assumed from the moment I arrived that he's in charge from the way people listen to him, the way he instructs and directs.

"No one put me in charge, but clearly I'm the only one interested in providing directions for keeping us alive. Feel free to take over, Blondie." The air is tense, like there's some sort of rivalry going on here that I haven't been informed of. He doesn't bother saying anything else before walking off with the rest, leaving only Slade, Brina, Lief, and me.

Slade turns his attention toward me. "You'll be helping Florence and Delilah with the crops."

My stomach drops. "Are you kidding me?" All of these possible roles, and he's going to put me with Florence? What the hell did I do to him to deserve this?

"I need everyone to pull their weight, and we could use the extra hands for harvesting. If that's going to be a problem, you're welcome to volunteer for night watch with Lief instead."

Lief chimes in instantly, a mischievous grin splitting his face. "Oh, please say yes. We'll have a great time bonding over horror stories and surviving whatever wildlife tries to eat us."

"I'm not working with her," I bite out, ignoring Lief's suggestion.

"Yes, you are." His voice is devoid of sympathy. "I don't care what kind of stupid, childish grudge you're holding against her. She hasn't done anything wrong. Out here we survive as a team, or we don't survive at all. Do your part. Grow up. Play well with others."

"Fine," I seethe.

"Good," he replies, turning to the rest of the group. "If there are no other questions, get to work."

I make my way to the crop fields and find Florence, who's already bent over the soil, pulling some stubborn plant free. She looks up as I approach, her smile bright. "Hi, Lennon."

"Hi," I reply, kneeling down beside her. My fingers instinctively find the earth, pulling at weeds and searching for roots. The smell of dirt takes me back to the greenhouse, to Quor and Miko. Somehow it feels like an eternity since I was there.

Florence shifts beside me, brushing her hands on her pants before speaking. "Listen," she starts, and my stomach twists into knots. Here it comes. The conversation I've been avoiding.

"I hope I didn't get off on the wrong foot with you," she says. Her tone is soft, hesitant. "Wilder has always spoken so highly of you, and I know you mean the world to him. The last thing I want is to overstep, but I thought you should know that the distance between you two has been killing him. If there's anything I can do to help you two reconcile, I'm happy to help." Oh. She doesn't know. She has no idea about my confession, my humiliation, or the rage I've been harboring since.

Of course she wouldn't. Why would Wilder tell her about any of it when he didn't even realize why I was angry in the first place? "I don't think it's something anyone can fix," I say, keeping my voice steady as I yank a handful of weeds free. "Sometimes people ... grow apart."

Florence tilts her head, the sunlight catching in her blonde hair as her brows knit together. "I think any friendship as strong as yours is worth fighting for."

Her words hit like a knife to the chest. "I appreciate you saying that," I say, the words bitter on my tongue. My hands dig into the soil, finding potatoes hidden beneath the surface.

I really didn't want to like her.

When I make it back to my tent, I do my best to scrub my body down with a bucket of water and a rag. I let myself miss the running water of the Burrows for only a minute, then crawl into bed as night begins to fall.

I was so useless today. The other two bonded saved all of us, and I just stood there, *hoping* my powers would emerge. If this happens again, I need to make sure I can be an asset to our camp. Jumping out of bed, I slip on my shoes and head to

Slade's tent, dreading the idea of begging him to train me but knowing it's a necessary evil.

I come face to face with Wilder, who apparently was coming to pay me a visit. "Hey," he says softly, scratching the back of his head. "Can we talk?" I guess Florence told him about our conversation earlier today, but I'm not interested in hashing this out. Not tonight.

"Later," I say curtly. "I'm busy." I keep walking until I reach Slade's tent, then let myself inside.

CHAPTER 19
SLADE

My tent flap rips open, and Lennon enters, her eyes narrowed like she's on a mission. "No," I say bluntly, twisting my finger in a circle. "Turn around. Out. I'm not getting dragged into whatever this is."

"I want you to train me." Each word seems like an effort, like asking for help isn't something typically ingrained in her vocabulary.

"*You should do it,*" Vesper coos, and I groan. Kaleu makes himself at home, already lying down next to her in my bed like this is some sort of slumber party.

"No," I reemphasize, sitting up in bed.

"Lennon!" Wilder shouts from outside my tent, making my teeth clench. I lean my head backward, pinching the bridge of my nose. Why me? What did I do to deserve this?

I stand, not caring that I'm only in my boxers, and yank the flap open. "Can I help you with something?" I ask, and his eyes nearly bulge out of his head.

"You can't be serious. You two? She's been here for two

days. Lennon, I know you're just trying to get back at me. Come out so we can talk."

"Hell, that's longer than it took you to bed Florence," I add, with a grin that I have no doubt makes his blood boil. "She doesn't want to see you, and she's staying with me tonight. If you have an issue with that, take it up with someone who cares." I let the flap drop in his face and turn back around, crossing my arms while leaning against the tent pole. "I feel used," I tell her, letting the sarcasm drip off every word.

The flap rips back open, and I slowly pivot back around to find a very enraged Wilder. I think he's going to say something else and begin preparing my snarky response, but instead, he punches me straight in the mouth. My finger touches my lip, wiping away the small trickle of blood running down my face.

Oh, I'm going to kill him.

I drive my fist into his cheekbone, hard enough to knock him back a step. He recovers faster than I expect and barrels into me, tackling me into the tent pole. The whole structure groans. Lennon is screaming at us to stop, both of the wolves staring as if entertained by the entire ordeal. I get in a clean shot to his ribs before he lands one to my jaw that makes my ears ring.

"Enough!" Lennon screams, positioning herself between the two of us, her hands extended as if to keep us separated. "Wilder, leave. *Now*."

His face drips with betrayal as he looks between us, and I just can't help myself. "Yes, Wilder. Do leave." His face is already swelling, and I don't miss the way he clenches his fist. She pushes him forward, outside the tent. I smile, knowing that hurt him a lot more than any punch could.

"I'm sorry," she murmurs, staring at the ground. "Why didn't you just use your magic and avoid the entire fight?"

"I prefer to fight fair."

She sighs, taking a seat on the edge of my bed. Kaleu scoots forward, extending his back legs behind him. "I don't know how things turned so sour between us."

"Yeah, I'm not really interested in hearing about that," I say, shrugging. "He's gone now. You're safe to crawl back to your tent. Highly doubt he'll come lurking around again after that."

She sniffles, a tear sliding down her face as she looks up at me. "Can I stay here? I'll sleep on the floor for all I care. I really don't want to run the risk of seeing him again tonight."

I sigh, dragging a hand down my face. "You take the bed, I'll take the floor."

She blinks up at me, clearly surprised. "Really?"

"And miss an opportunity to infuriate Wilder more when you walk out of here in the morning? Not a chance. It seems you and I have a mutual dislike for him now. You could even say we're in 'cahoots.'" I grab a blanket and pillow and make a pallet on the floor. Vesper and Kaleu stay in the bed next to Lennon, and I roll my eyes. My back is going to hate me for this tomorrow.

The sound of rain against the tent starts slowly, then turns into a steady stream. Lennon sits up in bed, and I throw a light orb out so I can see. "What is that?" she asks, her voice cracking.

"Rain." I stand up and extend a hand toward her. "Wanna see it?" She hesitates before accepting, then stumbles outside with me.

She tilts her head upward and lets it drip down her face and neck, her hair soaked within seconds of standing in the downpour. There were no clouds in the sky earlier today, no indication that a storm was brewing. No, this has to be from her, and she doesn't even realize it. What is she capable of?

A small gasp leaves her lips as she stares at the sky, a hand hovering over her heart. "I used to dream of seeing the stars, back in the Burrows. We'd—I'd pretend the twinkling lights that hung from the cave ceiling in the Burrows were them, just so I could feel less trapped. It's so surreal, actually seeing them."

I feel myself begin to soften at the sentiment and decide I'm vastly deprived of sleep. "Alright, let's get back inside." I pull her in, both of us dripping wet, and allow my power to surge through me, instantly drying up the lingering dampness.

"Did you just—how did you do that?" she stutters, staring at me in amazement.

I give her a crooked smile. "That's upper-level stuff. I don't need you accidentally burning yourself to death. Here." I throw her a rag to dry herself with, one of my T-shirts, and a pair of boxers, which I figure may fit her better than my shorts. She raises an eyebrow as she looks down at the clothes. "Don't worry, they're not mine. Extra hammy-downs from people who are gone now. They're probably clean."

"Did you just say 'hammy-downs?'" she asks, cocking her head at me. "It's 'hand-me-downs.'" I give her a sweet smile as I extend a middle finger in her direction. "Go outside so I can change," she demands, and I find myself slightly baffled. "You're your own personal towel, stop acting like the rain is going to kill you." I scratch the back of my head and do as she asks, wondering when, exactly, I found myself complying with the demands of not one, but two females, if you include Vesper.

This is all dangerous territory—stirring up discord within camp, letting her stay in my tent, and the nonchalant flirting, though it is rather entertaining.

"You can come in now," she says, and I do. She's curled up under my blankets, her head on my pillows. I snuff out the light orb as I take my place on the floor, then listen to the sound of her breathing as she slips into sleep.

"You don't always have to be the egotistical brute, you know," Vesper says.

"I'm well aware. I'm not entirely monstrous."

"Oh, I'm aware. I just wanted to remind you."

"Fine," I say into the darkness. "I'll train you. We start tomorrow morning."

"Thank you," she whispers, and I roll over and close my eyes.

At dawn, I hurl my pillow straight at Lennon's head, and she yelps, shooting me a dramatic scowl. I have to ensure a delicate balance of flirting and berating. "Get up. Time for the training you so desperately wanted." To my surprise, she doesn't argue. Instead she disappears into her tent and returns moments later, dressed and ready to go.

We reach the training field as the sun rises, painting the sky in streaks of gold and fiery orange. She stops, her breath hitching, then drops into the grass to soak in the view. I've seen my fair share of sunrises by now, but something about the way her gaze softens makes me pause. I sit beside her, silent, letting her take it in.

"Alright." I break the silence. "Let's get going, you have a lot to learn. We'll start with light orbs. They're the easiest. Hold your palm out in front of you." She does as directed. "Now try to summon an emotion. It can be pretty much any of them, but try to imagine yourself forcing all of it into the

191

orb. I'm sure you have plenty of pent-up anger you can use."

Her jaw tightens, and I swear I see a flicker of fire in her eyes as they snap open. "Shut up."

"Relax, sunshine." I sit down and lean lazily against my pack, crossing my arms as she scowls at me. "It's just a suggestion. Unless, of course, you aren't mad anymore? Did watching me kick his ass last night quell some of your rage? I can always do it again, if you ask nicely."

Her glare could melt steel, but she doesn't take the bait. Instead she closes her eyes and raises her hand as instructed. Her fingers tremble slightly, and for a brief moment, a faint, golden glow shimmers in her palm.

"Good," I say, softening my tone. "Now let it grow. Focus on that feeling. Let it fill you, and then guide it into your magic." The light sputters, then flickers weakly before dying out.

Lennon lets out a frustrated groan, dropping her hand. "This isn't working."

"Try again," I push. "Practice makes perfect." She scowls at me. "Fine. Try it, don't try it. It doesn't matter to me." I lean my head up to the sky, letting the sunlight warm my face.

The air around us grows tense, the energy crackling like static. I look to find her holding a hand outward with deadly concentration. The shimmer returns, bright and golden, even against the midday sun. Lennon's breathing quickens as the orb takes shape, hovering just above her palm.

"Good," I say softly. "Now hold onto it. Don't fight it— just let it exist." The orb stabilizes, and she stares at it in awe, the tension in her shoulders easing ever so slightly.

"That's more like it," I say, my smile returning. "See? All it took was a little attitude adjustment."

She rolls her eyes, but there's no denying the pride flickering in her expression. "If this blows up, I'm aiming it straight at you."

"I wouldn't have it any other way."

"I hope it blows up," Vesper says, and I pretend not to hear her taunting.

Kaleu curls up a few feet from her. They're still rather skeptical of one another despite him saving her life. Personally, I think it's the fact that they both have egos big enough to fill a thousand light orbs, and neither can stand the idea of the other being more powerful. It's easier for them to ignore one another than to find out the answer to that question.

"Alright, now that that's out of the way, teach me how to keep you," her finger points at me, "and him," then at Kaleu, "out of my head."

"And what about Vesper?" I ask, and the large, black wolf tilts her head at us.

"Vesper is the only one of you three who hasn't annoyed me. She's welcome in my mind anytime. But you two? Not so much." I try, and I mean really try, not to find amusement in our little training arrangement, but it's the first conversation I've had that doesn't involve camp matters in as long as I can remember.

I fold my arms and give her a slow grin. "Mental blocking, huh? Are you sure you're ready for that? It's not exactly *beginner-level* stuff. You can barely handle orb-making."

Her lips twist into a frown. "Considering the alternative is letting you two invade my brain every five minutes, I think I'll manage."

"Fair enough." I stretch out my legs and pat the ground beside me. "Have a seat. This one's going to require some focus."

She hesitates, eyeing me warily before finally plopping down a few feet away, crossing her legs beneath her. "Alright. How do I start?"

"First, you need to understand how this works. Mental blocking isn't about shutting down your mind completely. It's about building a barrier between your mind and anything trying to get in. Think of it like a door. You decide when it's open or closed, and you're the one who holds the key."

She narrows her eyes, clearly not understanding my explanation. "And how am I supposed to 'build' this magical door?"

"Visualization. You have to imagine something solid. A wall, a shield, a vault, a door. Whatever works for you. It needs to be something you believe is inaccessible."

"That's it? I think about a door, and you two can't get in without permission?"

"Not quite. You also have to push back. When someone tries to breach your thoughts, you'll feel it, like a pressure or a tug. You have to focus on keeping them out."

Her gaze shifts to Kaleu, who's now sluggishly watching us with one eye open. "And what happens if they're stronger than me?"

"That's where practice comes in," I say, leaning forward. "The stronger your mind, the harder it'll be for anyone to get through. And lucky for you, I'm an excellent sparring partner."

She groans, rubbing her temples. "Great. More time spent dealing with you."

"Careful, Lennon," I tease. "You're starting to sound like you enjoy my company."

"It's not like I have any other options for companionship right now."

"Alright, fine. Let's get started." I close my eyes and take a deep breath. "First, clear your mind. Focus on your breathing. Steady and even. In through your nose, out through your mouth." I hear her huff, but she follows my directions, her breaths slowing after a few moments. "Now, imagine that barrier. Something strong. Something I can't break through." A long silence follows, and I risk cracking one eye open to see her sitting perfectly still, her nose scrunched in concentration.

"What kind of barrier are you picturing?" I ask.

"One where once you're in, the door disappears until it's ready to reappear. No one will be able to make it reappear but me," she mutters.

"Interesting," I tell her. "Now, hold onto that image. Make it real in your mind. Picture every detail: the texture, the weight, the way it feels to slam it shut, and the energy it takes to make it disappear."

I close my eyes and reach for the thin, golden tether that pulls me into her mind, overpowering it with my own dark and twisted version with ease. *"Nice attempt, but still not good enough to keep me out."*

She lets out a half-groan, half-growl and throws her hands up in defeat. "This is useless."

"Your patience and resilience are astonishing, Benfield," I say, getting to my feet. "That's enough for today anyway. Let's head back to camp." I reach out a hand to help her up, but she ignores it and hoists herself onto her feet. She walks ahead of me and the lazy wolves by my side, pretending we don't exist. When she does get a handle on her powers, she's going to be a handful.

Hell, she already is.

CHAPTER 20
LENNON

Wilder and I have been avoiding one another for the last week, though I don't miss the angry glances he gives every time he sees me with Slade. Our training has been going well, and though I'm nowhere near as controlled as he is, I'm getting better. Learning to let myself feel enough to unleash my powers without feeling too much is a tricky line, but I'm getting there.

I head out of my tent to check on Shiloh; some mornings he sleeps so deeply that if I don't wake him, I'm convinced he'll sleep all day. As I approach, I hear muffled crying and then words. Slurred, low, like he's speaking underwater.

He's trembling when I enter, soaked in sweat and tangled in the sheets. Kaleu quickly moves to be at his side, laying his heavy head on his chest. His mouth moves with frantic energy, even though his eyes are still shut.

"When moon meets marrow ... and blood seals stone ... the beast shall wake with fire in its throat." I freeze. His voice is flat, mechanical, like he's reciting something.

"Shiloh?" I whisper. He doesn't wake. His hands twitch against the bedding, fingers curling like they're grasping something that isn't there.

"Slade!" I scream. "Caius! Someone!"

Slade runs in seconds later, his shirt still missing, his hair tussled wildly from sleep. "What? What's going on?"

"When moon meets marrow ... and blood seals stone ... the beast shall wake with fire in its throat," Shiloh repeats.

Slade raises an eyebrow, looking to me for answers. "What the hell does that mean?"

"I have no idea. He keeps saying it. Where is Caius?" Right on cue, Caius enters, his eyes wild as he takes in the sight of Shiloh.

"He keeps saying the same thing over and over again, like he's in a trance. Have you ever seen this before?" I ask, and he shakes his head, moving to Shiloh's side.

"No. What does he say?"

"When moon meets marrow and blood seals stone, the beast shall wake with fire in its throat," Slade says effortlessly. I was struggling to remember despite hearing it twice, so I'm grateful at least one of us has a good memory. Caius unlocks his medkit and pulls out a small vial, then asks Slade to fetch him a small bowl with water. "This is somnar root. It will help lead him back to slumber and hopefully draw him out of this trance."

"Do whatever you need to," I tell him, touching a rag to Shiloh's sweaty forehead.

"It sees me, it sees me, IT SEES ME," Shiloh screams, his body moving furiously as if trying to get away from someone. My throat becomes tight, and Slade helps pin Shiloh's body down as Caius raises the bowl to his lips.

The tent flap opens, and Wilder and Florence peek their

heads through. "Lennon?" he says, staring at all of us. "Is he okay? What's going on?" He runs to the bedside, scanning us frantically. Florence stays near the entrance, trying to keep out of the way.

"He's in some kind of trance. Caius is giving him a sleeping solution to try and knock him out of it." He drops to his knees on the other side of the bed, worry etched into every line of his face. He might be a jerk, but Shiloh's his family, too.

A few minutes later, Shiloh's body stills, his breathing balances back out, and he begins to snore. "Everyone out," Caius directs, and we listen.

Once we're all outside, I ask Slade for a pen and paper and begin writing down everything Shiloh said, marked with today's date. I don't know what it means—if anything—but documenting it feels right.

"Lennon, stay with him today and call for me if there are any more issues," Caius says, exhaustion evident in his features. Poor man can't catch a break.

"I will."

"There's still a lot to do around camp," Slade says, looking at Florence and Wilder. "You two get back to your roles. I'm going to run a patrol. Lennon, let me know if you two need anything." For once, his words are sincere and *not* packed full of sarcasm.

Everyone disperses, and I pull up a chair next to Shiloh's bedside. His snores are almost peaceful; it's better than listening to his screams. I stare at his rumpled blankets and stand back up to straighten them out. When I get to the other side of the bed, I notice the mattress is slightly elevated, like something is stuck underneath it. I wrench my hand in and feel around, then pull out the leatherbound book he'd brought up with him.

I'd completely forgotten it existed.

The Desmos Token on the front is etched in a deep, radiant gold, untouched despite the cracking leather. What is it about this book? Is this what's been triggering these ... visions? I sit back down and crack it open, squinting at the small words filling every page.

It'll take me months to go through this entire thing, and even then, I have no idea what I'm looking for. Maybe there's some correlation between the things he's said during his hallucination and what's inside, or a way to stop it—whatever *it* is.

I make it all of ten pages before I pass out. Reading has never really been my thing; it always puts me to sleep. Wilder wakes me up, shaking me slightly. I startle, jerking backward until I realize I'm still in the chair. "I'm sorry, I didn't mean to scare you. I just wanted to check on him."

"How long have I been asleep?" I ask, noticing the setting sun outside from the cracked entrance.

"I'd say at least a couple of hours. You needed it. You both did."

I place the book and my papers onto Shiloh's desk, then attempt to rub the grogginess from my brain. He drags the other chair directly across from me, placing an arm gently on the bed.

"What is that?" he asks, his eyes trained on the book.

"That would be the book Shiloh stole that got us both exiled," I say bluntly. No use in hiding it. Having more people to help can't hurt right now.

"Oh," he says, shifting on his feet. "Shiloh isn't the only reason I stopped by. I'm sorry about how things went down between Slade and me. There's some … history. We aren't particularly fond of one another."

"I gathered that much." I stifle a yawn, then pull my legs underneath myself.

"I'm also sorry for hurting you. I didn't expect to come up here and fall in love." Love. He loves her.

"Well, there's nothing we can really do to change things. No use in mulling over it. Besides, I've got bigger problems right now." My eyes stay trained on Shiloh, and I place a tender hand on his forehead, ensuring he isn't feverish.

I turn back to face him, finding his sad eyes locked on me. "I'm sorry, Lennon. If it's any consolation, I always loved you, too. I was always afraid of saying it, afraid you wouldn't feel the same. I was a wreck when I came up here, and I swear I tried to get word to you, but they wouldn't allow it. Slade threatened my life if I did. When I met Florence, she was a friend who tried to console me. I was a mess for a long time."

I nod slowly, the words sitting heavily in the space between us. I want to point out Slade's comment about bedding Florence on the first day. Or the fact that he just told me he *loves* her, and he's only known her for a month. I want to emphasize that he could've tried harder to get to me and make him understand how wrong he is, but I don't. There's no use in arguing about it. "Yeah," I say at last. "Well, we all did things we regret."

Wilder swallows. "But I never stopped—"

"I'm not doing this," I interrupt, more softly than he probably deserves. "Shiloh's losing his mind. Something's happening with him, with this book, and now he's quoting cryptic death poetry in his sleep. I don't have space in my head for old love stories right now."

He leans back slightly, hurt flickering in his eyes. But to

his credit, he doesn't push. "Right. I just … I thought you should know."

"I do know," I say. "I've always known. That was never the issue."

There's silence after that. Not an angry one, but full. Full of things neither of us has the strength or time to unpack. There's no use arguing over something dead.

He gives Shiloh one more glance, brushes his fingers lightly against his wrist like he needs to confirm his heart is still beating, and stands. "I'll let you sleep," he says. "Yell if anything changes."

I stare after him for a moment, the weight in my chest feeling heavy.

Is there something wrong with me? We've spent eight years side by side, the best of friends, and he never once told me that he loved me. He's known this girl for a month, and yet he's already willing to tell the entire world?

Why wasn't I enough for him?

CHAPTER 21
LENNON

S lade retrieves me the next morning for lessons, claiming I need to release my "pent-up tension" in the form of magic.

"Alright," he says, clapping his hands together. "Let's make today interesting. I've seen a little bit of what you can do, and you certainly seem fascinated by my powers. Care for a demonstration?"

I roll my eyes dramatically. "Fine. Show me what you've got."

He pivots on his heel, then braces his feet shoulder-width apart. His magic flares hot and wild as he stretches his hands out, unleashing twin streams of black flames into the air.

Twisting his wrists, he weaves the fire into intricate knots and spirals, keeping it afloat and away from the ground. I'm in disbelief as I watch, consumed by fascination and a little bit of terror. Then he closes his fist, the flames dissipate entirely, and he turns to face me with a mischievous grin. A small, black ring forms above me, then moves and encircles me in darkness. I turn in a slow circle, remembering this cocoon from when I tried to attack Wilder.

"So, sunshine. What's your best guess? What does being bonded to a wolf *mean*?" He pulls the shadows back, and they seem to absorb into him. I find myself more confused than ever.

Every person bonded to the same species has a similar gift. Sure, there are variations of it, and some are stronger than others, but how can ours be so vastly different? "So you have flames and shadows, and I have weird ice-thing and ... storms? Why are our powers different if we're both bonded to a wolf?"

He steps closer. "When have you felt closest to using your power? When is it the strongest in your veins?"

My brows knit together, and I rub at my temples in frustration. "I don't know. Can you just *tell* me? It's been a long few days, and I'm too tired for riddles."

He takes another step, his face now mere inches from mine. "The truth is, I don't know why our powers are different. All I know is that my powers are fueled by my emotions, and so are yours. That's why you're stronger when you're *feeling*." He circles me like I'm some sort of prey, now standing behind me. I can feel his breath on my neck. "That, Benfield, makes you both powerful and dangerous if you don't learn how to keep your emotions in check."

I look down at my hands. "So, now what?"

"Now," he says, stepping away from me, "you practice. Pick a power to focus on." His voice is calm, steady, the kind of steady that makes me want to punch him. Why is he always so calm? So put together?

"Ice," I say plainly. Less destructive. Or at least I think it is.

"Good choice," he says with a small nod. "Let it fill you. Let it take over until it feels like it's going to split you in two. Then push it out through your hands. Toward the field, not me. I'd like to keep my blood warm." He steps behind me, resting a light hand on my shoulder to guide me forward. "Now, go. Let your emotions in, then let them out."

I extend my hands in front of me, hesitating as they tremble under the weight of the rage I didn't realize I've been suppressing. It's not just anger. It's sadness, grief, frustration, all of it tangled and suffocating. The air thickens around me, heavy with something I can't name.

Above us, the sky darkens. Clouds churn and gather, snuffing out the sun. The first drops of rain splatter against the earth, quickly growing to a relentless downpour as the wind howls, tearing through the trees and whipping the rain sideways.

Fantastic. I can't even control which power I want to use. I'm summoning a damn storm.

Light flashes across the sky and I flinch. I've never seen anything quite so … terrifying. My legs tremble, and before I can stop it, I collapse into the mud, my knees sinking into the earth. The storm above rages on, mirroring the one inside of me: the fury, the sadness, the loss. It's overwhelming and freeing all at once, and for the first time in weeks, I let it all in.

A raw sob rips from my chest, followed by a scream, tearing free with every ounce of pain I've bottled up. Torture. Loss. Wilder. Shiloh. Lyric. Coming here and losing Wilder again in a way I didn't think was possible. Becoming a murderer and sacrificing my own morals for the sake of the people I love.

It all pours out, unstoppable.

Kaleu slams into me, his warmth grounding me as he presses his head into my chest. *"Breathe, little wolf,"* he murmurs, his voice soft. *"You are not alone in your pain."*

I wrap my arms around him, burying my face in his fur as the storm ebbs. The wind dies first, then the rain slows to a gentle drizzle before stopping entirely. The clouds peel back, leaving a calm, clear sky behind them, as if the storm had never existed.

When I finally lift my head, Slade is staring at me, his eyes wide with alarm.

"I'm sorry," I stammer, my voice hoarse. "I don't know what came over me. That was ..."

"A bit dramatic for my taste." He cuts me off, a slight smile playing on his lips.

"Why can't I control it?" I shake my head, glancing at the soaked ground around us. "I was trying to tap into ice, not storm. How are you always so controlled?"

He raises his eyebrows. "Our powers are tied to our emotions, which means they sometimes overtake our magic. For me, it's almost always flame that overtakes me, especially when I'm angry. For you, that seems to be storms."

"I hate that," I tell him, crossing my arms tightly to my chest.

"Alright, I think that's enough for today."

Now I'm the one raising my eyebrows. "Already? Why?"

"Because I said so." He picks up both of our bags and trails back toward camp, completely silent. "We need to get back and check on everyone."

"Where did the rest of our people go?" I ask, quickening my pace to catch up with him. There's never a good time to ask, and when I do, he never seems to want to give me an answer.

"There's another city of people that survived the war. It's full of unbonded." His tone is dry, emotionless, but the way his body tenses at the question makes me think there's more to the story.

"I'm sorry, *what*? Unbonded survived the war? How? Why didn't you go with them?" So the Regime was wrong about the unbonded, just like they were about the ground being survivable. But how did they survive the chemical fallout? And what does it mean if we aren't the last ones left?

"Because I like it here. And I don't trust people I don't know."

"You weren't even the tiniest bit curious how they survived? How many people do they have? Didn't you want to make sure they got there safely? If they're real, there's no telling how advanced they are. What if their technology could help us survive? Isn't that what we *should* want? Survival?" Blane said the unbonded's greatest purpose was creating weapons to use against the bonded, but the Regime also used that very technology to their advantage. What if they have a way to help Shiloh? Or at least a way to diagnose what, exactly, is going on with him?

He stops walking and lets out an exasperated sigh. "I'm aware, but no. Up here, everyone has the privilege of choice. That's the beauty of no longer being under the Regime's rule: we're free to do what we want up here."

"Right, and that's why you're giving us *assignments*?"

He places a hand to his forehead as if I'm the most stressful thing he's ever encountered.

"You talk a lot."

"You avoid questions a lot." He ignores me and continues on his merry way, my bag swinging over his shoulder as he walks.

Something about his attitude irks me, and I make the arguably stupid decision to try to portray control. I let my emotions creep back in, but only a little bit this time. Calm, controlled, collected. I can do this.

It is not the time to play, Kaleu warns, and I block him out. His golden eyes narrow on me as the door slams shut, and I realize, for the first time since we bonded, I've managed to block him out entirely. My body tingles with that cold, odd sensation, and my heart flutters against my rib cage as I extend my hand just to the left of Slade—for research purposes, of course.

A beam of cold, white frost flies from my hand and slams into the ground beside him, fracturing the earth and leaving it in shambles. Slade stays deadly still as if he didn't even notice the blast, and my shoulders tense a little when he finally starts turning around.

I guess ice can also be destructive. Interesting.

"What the hell are you doing?! You could have killed me!" he shouts.

"Sorry!" I throw my hands up in surrender, giving him a sheepish grin. "I didn't think anything would *actually* work. I was testing a theory."

"You could have seriously hurt someone, Lennon. Were you even thinking?"

"I said I'm sorry. You're *fine*. Everything is fine." His eyes look almost dead as they bore into me, and my skin nearly crawls off my body.

His lips curve into a firm scowl, his tone ice-cold. "Everything is *not* fine. You don't think. You're reckless, impulsive, like some overgrown child throwing tantrums. What if you did that to someone in our camp? What if you hurt somebody?"

I take a step back, his words hitting harder than I'd expected, but he doesn't stop. "You let your emotions control you, wearing every one of them on your sleeve like some badge of honor. You let everything—*everything*—get under your skin, and that makes you dangerous. You did it with Wilder, and here you are doing it to me. The fact that you thought it was a good idea to try that after literally summoning a storm minutes ago? It's ignorant. Tell me, did you kill Lyric because you had to, or because you were acting on impulse?"

The words are a punch to the gut, and I can't stop the rage flowing through me as he moves closer. "Me? I'm the problem? Look at you! Maybe the reason everyone left is because they couldn't stand to be around you. I may be overly sensitive, but you're incapable of feeling anything at all. You pretend to be some arrogant prick to try and protect yourself, but the truth is you're afraid of anyone getting close to you because they'll see underneath the facade, and you know they'll hate what you're hiding."

To his credit, he doesn't bite back. Doesn't summon any of his power, doesn't even bother looking at me. He just walks away, which only enrages me further. "What, you can't even have a conversation? And I'm the overgrown child." Kaleu and Vesper walk a few feet away from both of us, clearly doing their best to stay out of it.

He whips around, his eyes dark as he clenches his fists. "Do not push me. For your sake, and for mine."

Something twists in my stomach at the tone of his words,

and I clamp my mouth shut despite everything inside screaming at me to push. He's a prick, yes, but this? He *snapped* at me, his words cruel and pointed.

Maybe there is some truth in what he said. I am erratic, impulsive.

But at least I'm not like him.

CHAPTER 22

LENNON

I'm so angry as I approach camp that I nearly walk right past Shiloh who's standing facing the woods, his shoulders squared and back rigid. He isn't moving, his head quirked to one side like he's listening to something.

His condition has been declining rapidly since his vision last week, and I often find him mumbling to himself or staring as if his mind wanders. Him being outside the gate, however, is a first.

"Shiloh?" I start, but he doesn't respond. I take a few steps closer. His breaths are loud, harsh, and uneven, but that's not what grabs my attention.

He's whispering. "When moon meets marrow."

I sigh. If I have to hear this mantra one more time without getting any further context as to what it means, I'm going to lose *my* mind. He speaks like he's trying to remember something. Each line is rougher than the last, like it's been scraped from his throat.

"And blood seals stone." His body begins trembling, his hands twitching uncontrollably out in front of him. "The

215

beast shall wake." His voice rises, nearly a shout. "With fire in its throat."

I reach for him, but he flinches before I can touch him, blinking hard like he's trying to wake from a dream. "Where did she hide it?" he breathes—not to me, but to the woods. "She *had* it, I know she did, it was *hers*."

"Shiloh."

His eyes snap to mine. Wide. Wrong. But just like that, it's gone. He exhales, swallows hard, and wipes at his nose where a small trickle of blood has run out. "I'm fine."

"You're not."

"I said I'm fine." His jaw tightens. "I just haven't been sleeping."

"Clearly." I wrap my arm around his waist and usher him back to camp, his body still quivering. It was one thing to watch my father deteriorate before my eyes after my mom died—at least I had Shiloh and Wilder by my side. It's a whole other ordeal to watch my brother become a shell of the person he once was, knowing there's nothing I can do to stop it and no one left to care but me.

I get him settled back in bed, write down his newest revelations, then flip through the Desmos book until my eyes hurt and Wilder shows up to relieve me. We don't say much outside of swapping watches, which I'm grateful for on both accounts.

"You need to eat something," he tells me, and I bite back the urge to tell him it's none of his business what I do. He's trying to be nice.

"I'll bring Shiloh back a plate," I reply, giving him a soft smile. There. I can be nice too.

The sun is setting, leaving pink and orange streaks over the treetops. Despite the constant fear of attacks and death, it's beautiful out here, even a little bit peaceful. I dreamt of this exact scene my entire life, and I can't help but sit and soak it up some nights. Who knows when my last sunset might be with all the different things trying to kill us.

I overhear shouting, which ruins my relaxing moment, and I pivot toward the noise. Slade is standing with Lief by the weapons shack, screaming at him with a bite that makes me shiver.

"Are you seriously that stupid?" Slade snaps. "I knew you were lacking in the intelligence department, but this? This is next-level."

Lief's holding a training blade awkwardly. "It was already cracked. I was just trying to—"

"You don't *try* with something you don't understand!" Slade steps forward, fast. "You ask. Or better yet, you leave it the hell alone." Vesper snaps at Lief's leg, nearly clamping on to it.

Lief jumps back instinctively, startled. I am, too. "It's just a blade," Lief mumbles.

Slade laughs, the sound cold and humorless. "Right. Just a blade. Next time, it's our crops. Or our tents. Or someone's *life*." He shoves the weapon into Lief's chest hard enough that he stumbles. "Don't touch what you're too dumb to fix."

"What the hell is your problem?" Lief barks. Without hesitation, Slade extends his hands, wrapping a loop of shadow around Lief's throat and dangling him a few feet off the ground. Lief's legs kick aimlessly as he claws at the phantom hand, desperate for release.

"Slade! What the hell are you doing?!" I scream, trying to draw his attention as I race toward the pair. He turns toward me, and for half a second, his eyes look … off, like he isn't himself, but it's gone just as quickly.

He straightens and smooths his expression before turning and walking off. "He needs to learn," he mutters.

Lief looks at me, confused. Embarrassed. I can't tell if he's shaking because of the encounter or because of the night air. Hell, *I'm* shaking. What was that? I should go after Slade, but I don't. I'm not so sure I want to be another victim of his temper today.

"Are you okay?" I ask, kneeling next to him as he takes in large gulps of air. I know that feeling all too well. He nods, seeming more frightened than injured. "Let's go grab some dinner." I help him up and drag him towards the food tent, scooping what I'm pretty confident is lion stew onto my plate and his. I don't ask; I'd rather not know.

Slade catches me on my way back to my tent, hiding up against a tree with Vesper. "Care for a walk, sunshine?"

I scoff. "With the mood you've been in today, I can't help but think you're trying to lure me away from camp to kill me. You hurt him, Slade."

"I'm sorry. Really, I am. For what I said earlier to you and for what I said and did to Lief. I don't know ..." He sighs. "Is he okay?"

"You should probably be asking him that question."

His hands clench and, for a moment, I ready myself for another fight, but then his shoulders soften and he smirks. "If I promise not to kill you, will you come with me? There's something I want to show you. It is a bit off the beaten path, though. I figured it's best to tell you that now since you already think I'm leading you to your death. I could really use the fresh air."

"It might be nice to stretch my legs," Kaleu says, and I roll my eyes.

"Fine. But if you try anything, I'll turn you into a human

popsicle. I'm getting pretty good at this control thing, you know."

"As your trainer, I'd have to strongly disagree with that."

I scowl and cross my arms. "You are so bad with people. How the hell you ended up in charge, I'll never know."

"I'm not--" He stops himself, following my line of sight to Lief who is staying as far away from us as possible while trying to return to his tent. "Give me a minute, okay?" I nod, taking his place against the tree.

I watch as they converse, but they're too far away to eavesdrop. The interaction ends in a hug, which I'd assume means it went well enough. He gives me a soft smile as he approaches, holding his hands up as if in surrender. "I promise, no funny business. Ready?"

I roll my eyes, then gesture for him to take the lead. He starts walking toward the gate, and I follow after him like an idiot, curiosity outweighing my reasoning. Once he's outside the gate, he goes straight into the woods like a crazy person. Even Shiloh, in his delusional state, didn't cross the threshold. Yet here Slade is, walking in like he owns the place.

I stop, and he turns around to see what I'm doing. "Aren't you coming?"

"I'm pretty sure one of the main rules you ingrained in all of us was to *never* go into the woods because it's wild *Auryth* territory and will likely get us killed, no?" Kaleu, the traitor, walks in after Slade and Vesper.

"Considering they attacked us in our own camp, I'd say that rule doesn't really matter anymore. Plus, it only really ever applied to unbonded. For whatever reason, they tend to leave Caius and me alone. At least until the lion attack, that is. Now come on, scaredy-cat. It'll be worth it." I let out a dramatic huff, then follow him into the woods.

219

We hike for what must be at least a mile before I finally understand what he wanted to show me. A pale green glows faintly from the undersides of leaves like bioluminescent veins, while mushrooms bloom along rotted trunks in clusters that shimmer like stars. Even the moss growing on rocks and trees emits a subtle, hazy light.

"Whoa," I breathe. "What is it?"

Slade glances back, a smirk tugging at one side of his mouth. "It's a radiation zone, or at least that's what we think caused it. The chemicals tainted everything, but some of it … adapted." He nudges a glowing fern with the tip of his boot. "Most things here survive by becoming something else."

"It's beautiful," I say, and it is, but in a haunting kind of way. Like the forest remembers what it's endured and decided to glow in spite of it.

Kaleu takes off running through the woods like a pup, sniffing everything as if he's on some kind of mission. His fur is giving off a faint, bioluminescent glow from all the pollen that's rubbed off on him, making him look like a giant ball of light. Behind us, Vesper gives an exaggerated yawn and snaps at a floating beetle, then looks back at Slade like she's bored with the whole endeavor already.

"Yeah," he murmurs. "Even poison has its moments." For some reason that makes me laugh, and he stares at me like I have two heads. We walk around for a while in comfortable silence. For once, he's not being agitating, and I'm not gearing up for a fight. There's a quiet reverence here that neither of us wants to break.

Finally, I ask, "Why'd you bring me out here?"

He doesn't answer right away. Instead, he sits down at the base of a tree, his black pants glowing in spots. I sit down across from him. "I don't know," he admits. "I think I just needed to get out of my own head. And maybe I thought you did too."

I study him in the strange light. His jaw is tight, but his eyes look … tired. Fractured. "Is something bothering you? You've been a major prick lately."

He snorts, but there's no humor in it. "I'm always a prick."

"I'm serious."

"So am I," he says, more quietly.

He leans back, looking up through the glowing canopy. "Sometimes I hate what this place brings out in me. The pressure. The expectations. The fear of not keeping everyone safe." He pauses. "You know, it wasn't always like this. I used to be able to *know* when something was wrong. Make decisions based on instinct and logic. Now everything feels warped. Off. Like now that Keelan's gone, I have to focus on doing his job and my old one, and I can't keep up."

Delilah filled me in on Keelan and how he led Solis before he left. She also told me that she thought it broke something in Slade, being left alone.

"Sometimes I look at people and I can't tell if I'm angry because of something they did, or if it's just … something in me. Like there's something dark and evil inside that I can't shake. Vesper feels it too, sometimes." His voice cracks slightly, and I blink. I've never heard him this vulnerable.

I want to ask what he means. I want to press. But I don't.

So instead I say, "Then don't lose the part that still knows the difference, even if it's small. Even if it's buried."

He looks at me for a long time. The glow paints his features in golds and greens, softening the hard lines he usually wears. "You're slightly enjoyable to be around when you're not being annoying," he says eventually, almost smiling.

"And you're tolerable when you're not being a raging jack-ass," I reply, leaning back on my elbows. A pause. Then, more softly: "Thanks for showing me this." I look up at the stars, still breathless at the sight of them, especially out here. I could have never imagined something so magnificent; the flickering lights didn't even come close.

He nods. "It helps. Seeing something that's survived worse. Makes you think that no matter what we face, there will still be something good that comes out of it." The wind stirs through the glowing trees, rustling the leaves. I don't say anything else, and neither does he.

For the first time, we just sit there, not as enemies or even allies, but as two people who are trying—not entirely succeeding, but trying—to hold on to the parts of themselves they still recognize.

CHAPTER 23
SLADE

For the first time in a long time, I find myself excited as I walk to Lennon's tent to retrieve her for training. It's a peculiar thing, having someone around whose company is almost always enjoyable. She makes me feel lighter, like the weight of all the things I carry around with me are a little less heavy.

The last three months have been blissfully good. No arguing, no voltage storms, no wild *Auryths*. I find my temper is the most difficult thing to deal with these days, and even that has seemed to diffuse quite a bit. That, or I'm getting better at keeping it in check.

I stop at Shiloh's tent to check on him first, something I've been doing each morning since his first vision. I've even tried helping Lennon decipher that stupid book, but I'm absolutely useless when it comes to things like that. I've mulled over everything he's said and claimed to have seen a million times, but I can't come to any real conclusion. Half the time I wonder if he might truly be going insane, though I'd never tell her that.

"Ready?" I call from outside her tent.

She's pulling her hair up as she walks out, Kaleu practically underneath her feet. "Ready."

I grin, tossing a small wisp of black flame from my palm, letting it dance around her head mischievously. "You sure about that? Last time, you barely kept up."

Lennon smirks, raising a frost-coated hand. "Last time, you got lucky with those shadows. Let's see if you can handle a storm."

We head out to our training field, the sunshine bright against her soft features. She throws her bag to the ground, getting right into the thick of it. This is how it's been lately: Lennon growing stronger—eager to master her control and pummel me daily—and me, willing to be her practice dummy if it means I get to spend a few extra minutes with her alone.

The ground between us hums as she summons a gust of icy wind, swirling flakes around her like a living halo. I flick my wrist and the shadows bend, snaking up like fingers, trying to snatch the freezing air from her grip. The black flame in my palm flares, pushing back the chill, steam rising where fire and ice meet in a furious clash.

She laughs, a breathy sound, eyes sparkling with challenge. We circle each other, powers weaving in a chaotic dance; her storm whipping up crackling electricity, ice sliding and stabbing; my flames licking shadows that twist and shift like plumes of smoke. The air thickens with humming energy, every breath sharp with cold and heat.

Combining our powers into one has been our newest obsession. Ice storms and flaming shadows are quite the sight to see, and quite the weapon. Or they would be, if we were actually good at using them together. Most of the time we just end up canceling each other out.

I catch her wrist with a shadowy tendril, pulling her close a heartbeat longer than necessary. "You seem distracted today."

She leans close, her voice low and teasing in my ear. "Maybe it's a ploy." She zaps the side of my head with a miniature lightning bolt, and I yank away, furrowing my brows at her in annoyance, though I can't help the smirk that curls my lips.

I could do this for hours.

I let my shadow flames loose into the dirt, melting her icy patches into pools of mud. It backfires, spraying both of us from head to toe with the concoction. She screams, then laughs, staring at me through mud-caked eyes. "I'm going to kill you for that."

"I'd like to see you try."

Kaleu and Vesper are less than entertained by our foolery, especially now that Kaleu's white coat is painted brown. *"We will be stopping at the pond on the way back to rinse off,"* he sends down our four-way channel. Lennon snorts, and I throw a shadow hand out and knock her off her feet, straight back into the mud.

She screams, her hair and face now coated. "You absolute jerk," she says, half laughing, half threatening.

I raise my hands in surrender, shadows flickering harmlessly between my fingers. "Truce?"

She narrows her eyes, and for a second I think she might actually launch a spear of ice at my chest. But then she grins and grabs a fistful of mud, flinging it straight at my face.

I dodge it, but barely. "Oh, that's very mature of you."

The sparring turns playful again, more mud than magic now. We're both soaked, breathless, grinning like idiots, until Kaleu sends a pointed huff through the link again. *"Enough of this. You both smell disgusting, and you're getting even more mud on me. Pond, now."*

Vesper chimes in. *"Before I drag you both in by my teeth."*

Lennon rolls her eyes but slings her bag over her shoulder. "Fine, fine."

We walk the short path in silence, the tension from training still crackling faintly between us, like the leftover static of her storms. The sun filters through the trees in patches, catching on the wet strands of her hair, the sheen of mud drying on her jaw. She looks like chaos, and yet, somehow, she's never looked more like herself.

The pond comes into view, crystal clear and undisturbed. Lennon kicks off her boots and steps to the edge without hesitation. She wades in to her knees, then drops lower, submerging fully for a few seconds before resurfacing with a gasp. Her dark lashes are clumped with water, and her skin is flushed. She wipes a hand down her face, then looks over her shoulder at me. "Well? You coming in or just gonna watch like a creep?"

I smirk. "Didn't want to get in your way."

"Liar." She flicks water in my direction.

I step in, boots and all, wading toward her. The water is cold, but still a relief from the glaring midday sun. She's watching me now. Not teasing, not glaring, just … watching. I go under, shaking some of the dried mud from my hair.

When I come back up, she's still staring at me. "Why do you pull back when we fight?" she finally asks.

I blink. "What?"

"We both know you're stronger than me, yet lately it's almost always an even playing field. Why do you do that?" Her voice isn't accusatory. It's soft. Curious. Maybe a little bit offended.

I take a step closer, my body moving in slow motion from the weight of my wet clothes. "Maybe I don't want to hurt you."

"Or maybe you aren't going easy on me and I'm just that good," she says, tilting her head, a spark of that usual Lennon mischief flickering beneath the words.

My shadows curl around the water beside us, drifting lazily like smoke on the surface. "Maybe."

Her eyes flick to my lips, and I can't help but do the same to hers. No. We can't go there. It's a horrible, terrible idea. Isn't it?

She ducks under the water again, breaking the tension with a laugh as she resurfaces. "You've still got mud on your face, by the way."

I shake my head, swallowing the strange knot that's taken root in my throat.

CHAPTER 24

LENNON

Shiloh hardly leaves his bed anymore, his brain fractured by these visions. Though the more they progress, the more I wonder if they might mean *something*. They have to mean something. He repeats the same phrases, the same words, over and over, but the only thing I have to work with is the book Shiloh stole from the Burrows.

I know he took it for a reason, but most of it's in a language no one recognizes, and though the text is occasionally accompanied by hand-drawn illustrations, they don't offer any help.

I run my fingers along the ink, tracing the sharp lines of what I think is a jaw, lined with ragged teeth and hidden in shadows. Two piercing eyes look back at me through the pages, soul-sucking and filled with rage. Each drawing is more chaotic than the last, as though the illustrator was slowly losing his mind with each stroke of the pen. Eventually, I have to close the book.

"I'd love to hear your thoughts on the matter," I tell Kaleu, who's pretending to be asleep next to Shiloh to avoid

helping me. Another fake snore. *"I know you're not sleeping. When you actually snore, you sound more like a grizzly bear than a wolf."*

He lets out a low huff. *"I don't know, but that book smells like trouble. I wouldn't go digging around in old fables, you never know what you'll find."*

"I need to know why Shiloh is having these … visions. Maybe if we can figure out why he took the book, they'll stop."

"Maybe. Or maybe you'll end up like him."

I scowl at Kaleu. *"There is nothing wrong with my brother. He's just … sick."* A shiver of apprehension pulses down the tether between us, and I know Kaleu believes my words about as much as I do.

Caius has tried countless herbal remedies and can usually knock Shiloh out of his daze by putting him to sleep, but nothing seems to completely eliminate them. They've been happening less frequently the last few months, which is a plus, but I'm not naive enough to think they're gone for good. His mind … it hasn't been the same since the day I found him near the woods.

Slade, Wilder, and I take turns watching over him, dispersing the burden so it doesn't all fall on me. I'm thankful; sitting in that tent all day long would be a surefire way to make me go insane, too. Slade shows up to relieve me, his dark brown hair wild from the humidity. "You need a haircut," I tell him.

He smiles, rolling his green eyes. "Have at it."

"Later. I need to get out of here and stick my hands in some dirt, feel the sun. *Something.*" I stand up and offer him my chair, which he takes joyfully. It's been nice seeing him this way. Happy.

Florence is in the fields, giving me a dirt-smeared smile as

I approach. Her hands dip into the soft soil as she rips out lingering weeds. "Good training session this morning?"

"You could say that. Glad to be back here, though," I reply, kneeling on the dirt beside her. I cup my hand into a makeshift shovel and get to work digging, thankful for the distraction.

"Is there something going on between you and Slade? I only ask because he appears to be rather smitten with you." My mouth drops open. "I mean, Slade is *hot*, so I wouldn't blame you. A little scary, but in a hot kind of way. I think you guys would be cute together."

I laugh. "I would not let Wilder hear you say that; he'll never let that one go. The last thing we need is them fighting again after finally finding a state of peaceful resentment. And, anyway, there's *nothing* going on with me and Slade." I'm still shaking my head at the idea.

Slade's a good *friend*, nothing more. Hell, we're just now getting to a point where we aren't at each other's throats every second of the day. And, yes, he's *conventionally* attractive, if you're into the whole "dark and brooding, always has an attitude" thing. Though he has been less broody lately, I have to give him that.

"How are you and Wilder?" I change the subject, the words foreign to my tongue.

"Good. Really good, actually. Thank you for asking." Her face flushes red, her smile so big it must hurt her cheeks.

"I'm really happy for you guys," I say, and mean it.

We should all be so lucky as to find happiness in this broken world of ours.

When I get back to Shiloh's tent, he's awake. Slade, on the other hand, is asleep in the chair. I reach my hand out and let frost blossom at my fingertips, then tiptoe toward him. Shiloh stays dead silent, staring at me like *I'm* the one who's lost *my* mind.

I press my fingertips to his neck, and he jolts upright as if I've shot him, knocking the chair to the ground. His shadows instantly fill the tent, and I double over laughing at his frantic movements. "Seriously, Lennon?"

"Shouldn't be falling asleep on the job." Vesper narrows her eyes at me, clearly annoyed that my shenanigans have disrupted her sleep.

"I'm not a job," Shiloh interjects, and I instantly feel guilty.

"I know you're not. I'm only joking. I'm sorry." I stumble over my words as he glares at me. If there's an award for the worst sister of the year, I'm certainly in the running.

"I'm not insane," he says quietly, staring out of the tent opening.

"I don't think you're—"

"I'm not insane," he repeats, cutting me off. "I'm not insane, and I know how to stop it from getting out." My eyes slide to Slade, who looks as unnerved and confused as I am. "Opposite sides of the same coin. One above, one below. It can't—I can't. I can't. I can't." He crawls out of bed, scratches his head profusely, and begins pacing the ground, speaking to himself.

Suddenly, he stops and grabs my arm harshly, staring straight into my soul. His eyes are no longer hazel, no longer *human*. They're pools of endless white. "They can't exist. They can't exist. Above, below. She hid it because she knew. She knew. She *knew*."

I freeze, my body trembling. Normally I would never be afraid of him, but I'm not so sure who he is anymore. "Who knew? What are you talking about? I need context, Shy." It's like he doesn't see me; he's here, but not really—not in mind.

"Let her go, Shiloh," Slade says sternly, looking between us.

It happens so fast. One minute, I'm trying to wrench free from his grip, trying to get through to him as he continues shouting louder and louder. The next, he slides a blade out of his pocket and plunges it into my stomach.

My own brother. Everything moves in slow motion. Slade's face as he watches me fall. Kaleu's panicked whine. "I'm sorry, I'm sorry. I can't let it out. I can't let it get out," Shiloh says as he stands over me, the blade still firmly gripped in his hand, coated in my blood. My ears are ringing, and my vision is struggling to keep up with my movements.

It doesn't hurt. I always thought being stabbed would be painful, but it isn't. I look down at my stomach, at the blood pooling out over my hand and dripping onto the ground. I hadn't realized I was holding pressure on the wound.

When I look back up, I realize that Slade has Shiloh in a chokehold of shadows, suspended midair. His eyes are so dark, so void of life or empathy. Shiloh lets out horrible gasps for air that make me violently ill, and I open my mouth to beg for his life.

The words won't come out. I feel dizzy, queasy, and tired. So tired.

I search for the tether between Slade and me, desperate to reach him with every ounce of energy I have left. *Please. He didn't know what he was doing. He isn't in his right mind. Slade, look at me!* His head flinches slightly, but his eyes are still glazed over with that blackness and his shadows only grow. *You let him go, NOW, or I swear I will kill you myself,* I demand.

"No." There's no emotion in his tone, no inkling of

empathy or concern, just pure rage and my heart shatters. He's going to kill him.

Kaleu tries to lunge for Slade, but Vesper pins him to the ground, gaining the upper hand due to my injury. *"I've reached out to Caius,"* he tells me. *"Do not go to sleep, little wolf."*

I take deep, staggered breaths, calming myself. Slade isn't budging, and I'm so weak I highly doubt my powers will be much help right now. I only need to stay alive long enough for Caius to get to me.

I look toward Vesper, desperate. *"Please make him st-stop."* It's an effort to hold the mental bond. "Or let Kaleu go so he can ... Kaleu?" I whisper, my eyes growing heavy. I can't see him anymore. There's a choking sound coming from Shiloh now, like he's struggling to breathe. "Slade ... I won't forgive you for this," I say, the words difficult to force out. *"Slade."*

My head hits the floor, and everything fades to black.

CHAPTER 25
SLADE

I would like to say that I didn't want to kill him, but that would be a lie.

I don't do well with liabilities, not in this camp, and I sure as hell don't do well with people that try to kill their own sister. Lennon and Wilder can plead by reason of insanity on his behalf all they want, but I can tell something sinister has been brewing inside of him.

I know this because it's inside of me, too.

That darkness becomes suffocating, removing everything else of importance piece by piece until it's the only thing consuming you. Fighting it is not an easy feat, yet I do it daily. Shiloh must have given in.

Sometimes I wonder if it's some sort of disease or illness that's infiltrated our camp. Did we obtain it from our food or water supply without realizing it? Are others affected like we are, or were we the only two it deemed breakable?

I would have killed him had Caius not entered and stopped me. He threw a tree root at me like some sort of net, then threw a powder in my face that knocked me right out. I woke up back in my bed an hour ago. Lennon still hasn't.

Caius said he was able to repair most of the damage and that, thankfully, it hadn't hit any major organs. That being said, she lost a lot of blood, and her body needs rest. She *will* wake up, though, and that's the important part.

Shiloh is being detained inside his tent, tied to a chair and forced to stare at the pool of blood where his sister lay as she nearly bled to death. It was the only form of punishment Wilder and I agreed on. I'm not allowed in the tent, given I almost killed him once already, and I'd more than likely try again if I got close.

Fair enough.

So instead I sit by Lennon's bedside. I'm not so sure she'll actually want to see me when she wakes, but at least I'll know she's okay. More than likely, she'll try to kill me for what I did to Shiloh, which is slightly ludicrous given that *he* tried to kill *her*.

At this point, I'll drop to my knees and give her an easy target.

"I told you not to hurt him," she croaks out, her voice raw and raspy. I lean my arms on her bedside as her eyes slowly blink open. "I thought you were my friend."

I don't know what to say. How can I explain that there's a darkness brewing inside me that likes to come out and take over at the worst possible times? Or that when he hurt her, I only saw *red*. Not her little brother, but an enemy of one of the few people in life who's been kind to me. Instead, I simply say: "I know."

Her words come out strangled, like she's fighting back tears. "Is he alive?"

"Yes," I say bluntly. "Caius stopped me." No point in lying.

I have no doubt Wilder will fill her in later, if only to make her hate me more and him less.

"I'm taking Shiloh to Exion." I stare at her in disbelief. She sits up, wincing in pain. "He needs help, and I don't want to spend another second near you. You're a *threat*."

A threat. It isn't the first time I've been called that, but it cuts deep coming from her. "He tried to kill you. I was *protecting* you."

"One, I don't need anyone to *protect* me. I am not yours to protect. Two, you knew he was struggling. You watched over him all these months. You saw how his visions overtook him. He's the only person I have left, and yet you were still going to kill him. I begged you to stop, and you said *no*. Your decision was perfectly clear."

I reach a hand toward her arm, but Kaleu snaps his teeth at me. Vesper growls in return, but I put a hand up to stop her. "I thought I was doing what was right. He's not only a danger to you, but to this entire camp. Clearly, whatever visions he's been having are getting worse, and are now trying to convince him to *kill* people. We don't have the kind of manpower to watch over him constantly, and it's no life for him to stay locked up."

"Considering what you've now done to two people in this camp, I'd say you're the real danger. But it doesn't matter. I'm taking him to Exion, and we won't be your problem anymore."

"How will you get there? Do you plan on spending days and nights with him alone in the woods after he just tried to murder you? Tell me, what is your plan, Lennon? You've clearly thought this through. You're acting like a child." I hate how betrayed I feel.

Her expression goes cold, and her eyes narrow. "I don't need to explain anything to the likes of you." Ouch.

I should apologize. Beg for her forgiveness, come up with some sort of plan for Shiloh. Instead, I say, "if you set foot outside that gate, don't bother coming back. You will no longer be welcome in Solis." The words taste bitter on my tongue, but they come out all the same.

"If I could walk right now, I'd already be gone."

My hands twitch as my power begs to be released. There are a million things I should say, that I want to say, but I don't. Instead, I leave and walk up to our—*my*—training field and let my flames swarm the field with an insatiable hunger.

CHAPTER 26

LENNON

It's two days before Caius clears me to walk again. I'm not exactly cleared to walk who knows how many miles to Exion, but I refuse to spend another minute in Solis. Not when Shiloh is getting sicker. Not to mention every time I see Slade, I have a horrible desire to make him hurt the way he hurt Shiloh. The way he hurt me.

Others have been joining Slade's thirst for vengeance, demanding we sentence him to death to eliminate the "threat" to our camp. Sometimes I feel like I'm back in the Burrows, surrounded by the Regime as they sentence unbonded to their deaths for that very same sentiment. As it turns out, you can change the home, but you can't always change the people.

Shiloh has refused to speak since stabbing me. No apology, no fragmented warnings or prophecies. Only silence, though his eyes have returned to their normal color. I can't get the sight of those hollow, white irises out of my mind.

"Lennon?" Wilder calls from outside my tent as I cram

things into a backpack. Kaleu's ears fold back; he still isn't particularly fond of him. Neither am I.

"What?" I snap.

He slides in, hesitating just past the flap like he's afraid I'll bite. His hair looks like he's run a hand through it a thousand times, and dark rings have settled below his eyes. "Florence and I want to come with you."

I pause my packing, my grip tightening on a shirt. "No." Maybe it's foolish to turn down his help; who knows what kind of fight Shiloh's going to put up in the woods, and I'm still injured, but ... The idea of watching the two of them in love for several days, up close and personal, makes my skin crawl. I think I'd rather let Shiloh stab me again.

"He's my brother, too. Maybe not in blood, but still. I want to make sure you guys get there safely. Besides, there's nothing left for me here anyway."

"I ..." The words stick in my throat. "I can't spend days in the woods with the two of you. I'm healed, but not *that* healed."

He looks down at his hands as if the words he's searching for are hidden in the cracks of his palms. "You shouldn't go alone. Take somebody. Lief, Slade—"

I scoff. "If I never see Slade again, it'll be too soon."

"That's not fair, and you know it. I'm nowhere near his biggest fan, but he was defending you. Your *life* was at stake." He sighs deeply. "Sometimes I think you look for reasons to push people away."

My head snaps toward him. "You weren't there! You didn't see the look in his eyes when he was strangling the life out of my *brother* or hear me beg him to *stop*. Say what you want, but you would've never hurt Shiloh. He could've knocked him out, hurt him bad enough to disable him, *anything* but try to kill him."

"Is that what you were thinking when you asked Kaleu to kill Lyric? Shiloh told me what happened that day, what you had to do. I'm not saying you were wrong for your decision, but it's a bit hypocritical, don't you think? Why did her life matter less than Shiloh's? Because he's your brother?" Kaleu snarls as he prowls toward him, every hair on his back standing up.

"Get out," I seethe. "GET OUT!" He takes a step backward, and Kaleu takes one forward. He disappears out of the tent, leaving me to my silence once more.

I sit on the bed, folding the shirt over my lap.

He's right. In the game of life and death, I was the judge, jury, and executioner, choosing the person I loved over her. Despite her being entirely awful, I have no doubts she had people who loved her, and I took her from them. But that was different. Slade doesn't love anyone but himself.

"Would you sacrifice one life for the good of the many?"

I was so sure when I answered him that day—so naive.

"You did what you had to do to keep those you love safe. That doesn't make you a bad person." Kaleu attempts to calm me.

"It does when I'm willing to kill for it."

I shake my head in an attempt to clear it, throw the rest of the supplies into the bag, and head to Shiloh's tent. He's lying in his bed, his hands still bound. My eyes drift to the bloodstain, and I quickly divert my attention. No use in dwelling on it.

"You and I are going to Exion," I tell him. "For both of our safety, I've got to keep your wrists bound. I think they can help you there. I'm willing to bet their medical team is better than what we have here, hopefully closer to what we had in the Burrows." He doesn't say anything, only stares at me blankly. "I don't blame you for what happened. I know it wasn't your fault. I've packed us enough clothes and supplies for the few-day hike." Still, nothing.

Well, this will certainly be a quiet trip.

"Get up," I command, and he ignores me. I grab both of his legs, and he squirms against me. "Shiloh, *stop*. We have to go. Please don't fight me on this."

He goes stiff, and I grab both of his legs and move them to the ground before pulling him upward by the ropes encircling his wrists. I keep my grip on the ropes, then yank him upward so that he's standing. He scowls at me, but at least we're making progress.

"Will you walk behind me, or are you going to make me drag you the entire way?"

Another death stare. Fine. Dragging it is.

I loop my hand through the rope and yank him forward a little harsher than necessary, hoping he'll become agitated enough by my pulling to walk like a normal person. Whatever has overtaken him is not a fan of mine. Maybe it knows that I'm a murderer. Maybe it sees the dark parts of my soul that Kaleu missed when he chose me.

As we make our way out of the tent, Slade steps in our path, Vesper right behind him. "You don't even know where you're going," he says.

"Actually, I do. Your friend Opie left Wilder a map in case anyone else wanted to join our people later." He looks surprised by the revelation, his head tilting in curiosity. "Now get the hell out of my way."

"You're making a mistake." His voice is like a caress against my mind, tender and sincere.

"My mistake was thinking I saw anything good in you." I push past him, Shiloh stumbling behind me.

When we reach the wood line, I can't help but hesitate. *"Slade said the wild Auryths typically stay away from bonded, right?"* I ask Kaleu.

"He did, but I'm not so sure they're following protocol anymore. Don't fret, little wolf. I'll keep us safe." I think about the lions— the way one tore into Vesper, and the sheer number of them.

I am not the same person I was that day, though. My power is strong; I'm in control.

We step into the woods, not bothering to look back at what we're leaving behind.

CHAPTER 27

LENNON

According to the map, it should be a three-day hike to get to Exion—if it exists, that is. Considering no one has returned, I'd say that's a good bet. That, or they're all dead.

Though I prefer to put my beliefs in the former.

Apparently, Shiloh's visions have also made him mute now, but at least he's following me without complaint, and we made it through the first night without him trying to kill me. Sometimes I swear he looks at me as if he's plotting it, though.

We stop every so often to eat some of the canned food I brought and drink water from our canteens. It's unbearably hot, and I'm beginning to think the sweat-smell will cling to my skin for a lifetime.

By midday, the trees begin to change. The thin pines that surround Solis are replaced by massive, spindly trunks that tower at least fifty feet over us. Moss and weeds carpet nearly every surface, and tufts of briars and entangled vines snatch at my feet, determined to knock me off balance. I hear

Shiloh stumble a few times behind me, but I don't turn around. As long as I know he's back there, that's enough for me.

The air is different here. Sweet yet metallic, unlike anything I've encountered before. I'm scanning for any plants or flowers that may be the culprit when I notice the mist.

At first, I think it's just humidity bouncing off the vegetation mixed with the sunlight seeping through the canopy of trees, but then I realize it's *moving*. It snakes through the base of the tree trunks, hovering right over the dirt and lapping at my ankles. I turn around to see that Shiloh has stopped walking and is staring at it.

Either we're both crazy, or he sees it too.

Kaleu lets out a shrill whine that makes the hair on my neck stand up, then takes off through the woods without hesitation. *"What do you see? What is it?"* I ask, but there's no response.

"Lennon?" A voice calls out to me, but it's not Shiloh. I pivot in a circle, desperate to lay eyes on its owner. To my right, over the clearing, is a figure standing in the sun. Her brown waves nearly reach her hips, her smile soft and kind and everything I remember it to be.

"Mom?" I call out, the words choking on the sobs crawling their way up my throat. I look at Shiloh, desperate for him to confirm that he sees her too, but he doesn't move. His eyes are fixated on something else that I can't see.

"Lennon, come to me," she calls, and I snatch Shiloh by his rope, trying my best to drag him along with me. He puts up a fight, digging his heels into the dirt and trying to move to our left.

"Shiloh, it's Mom. We have to go to her," I plead, but he still refuses to cooperate. I use all of my strength and snatch him forward, nearly knocking him down in the process. "We're coming. Please, wait!"

A yelp pierces through the trance, grounding me back to reality. Kaleu. I search all around, but I can't see him. *"Where are you? What has happened?"*

"Lennon," my mom calls again.

I'm at a crossroads. I look between my mom and the direction I saw Kaleu take off in, then back at Shiloh. This can't be real. My mom is dead. She died when I was ten in the Burrows. It wouldn't make any sense for her to be up here, not like this.

"Kaleu!" I scream into the open, desperate for him to make another sound so I can go to him. A whimper, small and faint, fills the silence. I run toward the sound as fast as my feet will carry me, Shiloh still in tow. A figure appears in front of me so fast I skid to a halt, and Shiloh slams into the back of me.

Lyric. Her ringlet curls are matted with blood, her neck gashed open and exposed. "You're a murderer," she says, a hand sliding to her throat. No, no, no. This isn't real. This isn't real. This isn't real.

I take off, sprinting straight through her; her body dissolves back into the mist, and I keep going until I can breathe again. The woods open up into a wide clearing, and in it I see Kaleu spinning in a slow circle, snarling and snapping at the air. *"It's not real,"* I tell him desperately. *"It's not real."*

His head turns toward us, his teeth still barred. Slowly, he closes his mouth, lies down, and buries his head between his paws. I approach slowly, extending my hand out in front of me. *"It's just me. I'm real. It's Lennon."*

When I reach him, I place my hand on his head, attempting to ground both of us back in reality. I hear something loud and large moving through the woods, cracking limbs and leaves as it grows closer. When does it end? What is this?

I release Shiloh and push him behind Kaleu and me, then hold my hands out in front of me, letting my emotions pour into my magic. Is this some sort of weapon? A way to disorient your opponent, then come in for the kill? Or is it a wild *Auryth* coming to tear us limb from limb?

Either way, they're going to get one hell of a fight.

A crawler comes barreling through the woods, straight for us. Or at least I think it's a crawler. I've only ever seen them in history books: massive vehicles built for transporting people and *Auryths* of all sizes. It's black, round, and comes to a squealing stop a few feet from where we stand.

A girl with a halo of kinky black curls jumps out, panic etched on her face. "Are you guys okay? I heard yelling while on my patrol." I blink, still trying to decide if she's real or another product of the mist. "I'm Harlow. You're okay, the mist is gone now. Its effects don't typically linger." I open my mouth to respond, but no words come out. I can't stop thinking about my mother, about what Kaleu saw, about Lyric coming back to haunt me. "Sorry, do you speak English?" the girl presses, leaning back against the crawler.

"We do," Shiloh says, startling me. I turn to face him, surprised to see his face softening.

"Sorry," I say breathlessly. "The mist ... I think it messed with our minds."

"Yikes," she says, wincing. "Yeah, that stuff is no joke. I'm pretty sure that's what makes the wild *Auryths* so unhinged. Anyway, where are you trying to go?"

"Exion. I believe the rest of our people are already there."

Her eyebrows raise, her mouth gaping slightly open. "Holy

smokes, you guys are from the Burrows?" I nod. "Yes, your people made it. Is it just the ..." She pauses, looking over Kaleu. "Three of you?"

"Yes."

"I can take you guys the rest of the way, if you want. It's only about a thirty-minute ride from here. Beats walking, unless you're enjoying the many wonders of these woods." She climbs back into the vehicle, rolling the rest of its windows down.

"I think a ride would be a nice change of pace," Kaleu quips, and I swing one of the doors open, dragging Shiloh toward it.

"Can I ask why you have a prisoner with you?" she asks.

"He's not a prisoner," I say quickly. "He's my brother."

"I tried to kill her two days ago," Shiloh interjects, and I swear my eyes nearly pop out of my head.

"Noted. Yeah, let's keep him tied up then," Harlow says, giving me a nervous smile. Kaleu and I climb in after Shiloh, and I let myself breathe once I shut the door behind us.

"What are your names?"

"I'm Lennon Benfield, this is my brother, Shiloh, and this is my *Auryth*, Kaleu." I catch her stare from the little mirror hanging from the roof. "You don't seem very afraid of him for someone who comes from a city of unbonded."

"We're taught not to fear them. Plus, he's not the first I've encountered or that's been inside Exion's gates."

The woods are so different from this view: flashes of greenery and fresh air against my face. When we finally break through the dense line of trees, my breath catches.

Exion looms before us, a stark contrast to the scrappy remains of Camp Solis. It isn't just bigger; it's older. Ancient, even. This place has to have been around long before the war, its massive structures standing as a testament to whatever civilization built them. Towers of tarnished metal rise taller than the trees that encircle them, their surfaces rough with age. Some are rounded and smooth, while others are jagged as if they've been pieced together.

The buildings stretch as far as I can see, their edges fading into the horizon. It isn't a camp. It's a fortress, nearly fifty times the size of our little makeshift base. Between the structures, narrow pathways wind like veins, illuminated by soft, pulsing lights embedded in the ground.

The gate at the front is massive, constructed of interlocking panels that gleam under the filtered sunlight. It looks impenetrable, as if it's been built to keep the world out—or to keep something in. A group of officers stand rigid at its base, their dark uniforms blending with the shadows.

And they're armed.

My stomach twists as I catch sight of the weapons slung across their chests. Guns. Not the crude makeshift weapons we use at Camp Solis, but huge, sleek, deadly firearms that make my throat tight. I've seen guns before, back in the Burrows, close enough to know how much damage they can do.

Seeing them here, in a place that's supposedly safe, according to the mysterious Opie, throws my anxiety into overdrive. Beyond the gate, I can make out movement. Figures darting between the buildings; the faint hum of voices carries on the wind. The air is different here, too, sharp with the tang of metal and something bitter I can't place. It's a world apart from the soft, earthy smells of our forest camp.

"They have guns," I tell Kaleu, my heart pounding against my rib cage.

"I have eyes," he retorts, and I glare at him. Now is not the time for sarcastic remarks.

"*Do you think we're safe here? Can you hear anything? Smell anything?*"

"*What choice do we have? Shiloh needs help, and you made enemies in Solis before we left.*" I lean back against the seat's headrest and squeeze my eyes shut.

"One second," Harlow says, opening her creaky door. "Let me tell the guards I picked you guys up." It's not like we have any other options.

I look over at Shiloh, who looks suspiciously chipper, even wearing a faint smile across his face. Something about it unsettles me.

"Alright, we're good to go! I need to take you guys to medical first so the doctor can examine you for any illnesses or ailments, then I'll get you set up with your rooms." Kaleu and I open the door and jump out, leaving Shiloh stuck for a minute.

"Can I talk to you for a second?" I ask her, and she nods and walks a few feet away. "My brother is sick. Not physically, but mentally. He's been having these … visions. I don't know why they started or how to stop them, but when he tried to kill me, I knew we had to get him help. That's why we're here."

"Gotcha. Yeah, that doesn't sound good. I'll pull Doc aside when we get to the medical building and fill him in. We have special rooms designed for patients struggling mentally, so we'll get him set up there where he can't hurt himself or anyone else."

I breathe a deep sigh of relief, feeling the tension leech from my body. "Thank you."

She helps me get Shiloh out, and he follows behind her, Kaleu and I taking up the rear. I do my best not to tremble at the sight of all the guards and guns, but it's an effort. Upon seeing us, two of the guards move away from the gate, and it begins to open, moving forward to let us enter. It has to be electrically operated, which only fuels my curiosity. How have they managed to build such a facility with no magic? Or did they take it over after surviving the chemical war? How did the city *survive* the war?

True to her word, Harlow leads us straight through the gates and into the heart of the complex. The buildings grow larger the closer we get, their exteriors a patchwork of metal and concrete. Some walls are etched with intricate patterns, runes, or marks I can't decipher. Vines crawl over a few structures, their green tendrils weaving through gaps and cracks.

Our footsteps crunch against the ground, accompanied by low huffs from Kaleu. Around us, the camp buzzes with activity. People move in groups, their clothing a mixture of practical uniforms and ordinary clothes. They carry crates of all sorts of things: food, plants, metal parts, and things I don't have names for. More vehicles zoom past us in the street, ones I don't recognize from any of the books I read in the Burrows. They're smaller than crawlers, slimmer, like they were built to navigate through the busy city.

We pass a structure with a partially open door, revealing a room filled with monitors and blinking lights. Inside, a handful of people work at desks, their eyes flickering between screens. If so much is in that one room, what in the world is inside all of these other buildings?

"Almost there," Harlow says softly, her voice cutting through my thoughts. She gives me a reassuring smile.

The medical building is unlike the others. It's smaller, though still impressive, with outer walls that gleam metallic silver. A symbol I don't recognize is etched above the entrance in black: a hexagon with four triangles inside it, each one tucked neatly within the other, getting smaller as they go inward. On the outside of the triangles in the open space are little lines connected by dots in various patterns. The words PER MENTEM are written above it, and the words NON VINCULUM are written below.

The doors slide open as we approach, a quiet hiss of air escaping, and a cold breeze hits my face. The antiseptic smell accompanying the breeze is overpowering, mixed with the metallic tang that seems to linger throughout the city. The walls are smooth and painted a light shade of gray from where I can see, and the pearly white floors are pristine. I can hear the faint beeping of machines and the murmur of voices coming from somewhere inside.

Harlow points to a bench near the entrance. "Wait here. I need to let them know you've arrived." More like she needs to let them know about Shiloh's condition.

I take deep breaths in and out, trying to quiet the unease clawing its way up my throat. Opie says it's safe here, and the rest of our camp trusted him enough to follow, but I have yet to see a single person I recognize. Not to mention I've yet to meet the infamous Opie himself. Will they accept me if I'm bonded to Kaleu? Allow me to walk their streets, bonded and full of magic?

Bonded and unbonded have been at war for centuries. Why should I expect it to be any different now? Especially when I haven't seen a single *Auryth* inside these walls. The Regime still holds a grudge. Who's to say these people don't?

Approaching footsteps sound through the building, seeming to bounce off the floors. I straighten, my heart pounding. My instinct is to fight or grab Shiloh and run, but I'm in no position to do either. He needs help, the kind that I can't give. We're completely at the mercy of these people and can only hope they're nothing like our own.

A man emerges from the open door, holding a clipboard and wearing a long, white coat. His hair is light brown but has streaks of silver that show his age. "Lennon Benfield," he says, his voice calm and soft. "And you must be Shiloh. It's good to meet you both. Welcome to Exion. I'll take you both back for a full check-up, then we'll get you reunited with your people."

He begins walking inside, and we follow closely behind. As my eyes adjust to the stark brightness of the medical building, the cool air biting against my skin, I hear something beyond the hallway ahead: a scream. It's faint but unmistakable, seeping through the cracks of a partially closed door at the end of the corridor.

"Kaleu, did you hear that?" I ask as goosebumps prick my body.

"I did," he replies, *"and there is a smell accompanying that room. It reeks of death."*

Before I can ask him to elaborate, the man pauses, turning his head toward me with an unreadable expression. "Don't worry." He leans in, his voice merely a whisper. "We have everything we need to help your brother. Some of our patients in other rooms are in far worse conditions than he is." His smile doesn't reach his eyes.

CHAPTER 28
SLADE

I just watched her leave. No argument. No begging her to stay. No confession that the thought of not seeing her every day makes me feel like I'm suffocating.

It's better this way—for both of us. I'm not sure I can contain myself when it comes to *anyone* threatening her safety, and if that's not something she can understand, then the distance is for the best.

Sitting on a log bench, I stare at the sparks flying from the fire and think about all the things wrong with me. Wrong with her. Wrong with me for ever thinking there could be an ... us.

"You should go after her," Wilder says, sitting down next to me.

"I'm not in the mood. Now go away and bother someone else." I raise a hand, letting shadows flicker at my fingertips. Not quite threatening, but enough to get my point across.

He doesn't move. Just sits there with an insufferable calm, like he thinks if he waits long enough, I'll come around. His hands go up in surrender. "I'm not trying to agitate you, but I know her. She cares about you, even if she won't admit it. You should go find her and fix this. She can't be far, and she shouldn't be going to Exion alone. You and I both know that."

"He's right," Vesper adds.

I tense. "She doesn't want to see me. She made that pretty clear."

"Since when did you start caring what other people want?" He's got me there. Why *do* I care what she wants? But maybe he has a point. At the very least, I can make sure she gets there safely.

"Fine, but I'm not going to drag her back here if she doesn't want to return." He smiles, looking far too satisfied with himself. I shoot out a black flame near his foot, and he jumps straight off the bench. "I still don't like you."

"The feeling is mutual," he shouts as he walks off.

Vesper and I take off toward the woods, my chest full of anxiousness more than anger. Every step feels heavier than the last, and yet for some reason we're moving faster with every stride. She was so clear about never wanting to see me again, and she has every reason, but I still don't regret what I did. If I could rewind time, I think I'd do it again. Shiloh hurt her. He tried to *kill her.* I don't care that he's her brother. If it were anyone else, would she still have the same reaction?

If it *were* anyone else, I would've snapped their neck in an instant.

I did what I had to do to keep her safe. Protected. He's the one who drove a knife into her stomach, and yet I'm the one she hates. I push the guilt down because I don't know what to do with it. Guilt's not an emotion I'm used to. But this ache? The silence where she used to be? It's loud. Painful.

"I'm not going to beg for her forgiveness," I tell Vesper. *"I just want to make sure she's not stupid enough to get herself killed."*

"Whatever you say."

I turn around to glare at her just in time to see the dart lodge itself in her side. She yelps, then drops to the ground like she's dead weight. Out of instinct I reach for my power, desperate to prepare for a defense, but it's like my tank has been depleted. The trees are silent, and I can't see where it came from. No sound, no movement. No source.

I try again and again to call my magic, but it never comes. I can feel our bond slipping, like something is tearing it to shreds. The shimmering black that normally hangs between us is fading into silver.

Then I feel something hit my shoulder, and my vision fades as I hit the ground beside her.

CHAPTER 29
LENNON

They separate Shiloh and me, despite my begging. The doctor said it's necessary since he needs additional care, but I don't want to let him go. A nurse introduces herself as Margo and promises to get him the best care possible as she leads him away, though her words do little to quell my panic.

The doctor takes me into a room with the same white floors and metal walls as the main area, only this space is accompanied by a hospital bed and a few beeping machines. The bed isn't all that different from what we have in the medical building in the Burrows, but the technology they've acquired here is far more intricate. I thought we were advanced, but everything inside this place makes us look hundreds of years behind.

First they place a small device on my finger that apparently tells them my heart is beating appropriately. Then they put me inside some sort of machine that feels like a tunnel to "check me for diseases." After what seems like hours of being poked, prodded, and examined, I'm finally cleared. The doctor bandages my arm where they drew blood and gives me a soft smile.

"How did Exion survive the war?" I ask, unable to keep my questions to myself any longer.

"Our original founders developed an energy barrier to absorb the radiation and heat from the chemicals. It protected our people from harm, though I can't say the same for the rest of the Earth. You'd be amazed at how much has changed in the last forty years alone."

"And the symbol on the outside of the building? The one with the grey triangles?" I continue, blood rushing to my head as he helps me off the table.

"We call it the Cognis. It represents the *separation* of humans and *Auryths*." I steal a glance at Kaleu. I can hardly remember what life was like before our minds became linked. It's strange to be in a place where being unbonded is celebrated after spending eighteen years in a place where it was supposed to mean death. "You'll find it in nearly every building in our facility and many other places, too. It's also on all of our guards' uniforms."

"What do the words in the center mean?"

He pauses, smiling to himself. "Ah, yes. *Per Mentem Non Per Vinculum*. In English, it means: Through mind, not bond."

"Is *anyone* here bonded?" I press as he opens the door, leading me back into the hallway.

"I am," a voice says from behind me.

I turn and freeze.

A man, probably in his early twenties, leans against the wall like he's got nowhere better to be. His wavy blond hair falls neatly across his forehead, not a strand out of place. Everything about him is polished, from the clean shine of his boots to the crisp collar of his shirt. He looks like he belongs on the Third Ring in the Burrows. Handsome, but almost certainly thinks he's better than everyone else.

At his feet, his panther is the opposite of charming. It's massive and still, muscles coiled as if ready to pounce. Its coat is sleek and black, and its yellow eyes narrow on me, unblinking. Kaleu lets out a low growl. My gaze drifts back to the man. Green eyes. Bright, curious, *unreadable*.

"You seem to have a bit of a staring problem," he says, tilting his head slightly.

My face heats. "Sorry, I just didn't expect to meet anyone else bonded."

"Don't apologize. Selene here is used to people admiring her beauty." His smile widens. "I'm Opie. And you are?" My jaw nearly hits the floor.

He's the one I've been looking for. The one who led our people here.

"Where are they?" I blurt. "The ones you brought over from Camp Solis?"

His brows lift, mischief flickering behind his eyes. "You're from Solis?" He gives me and Kaleu a once-over that makes the hair on my neck stand up. "Where are the rest of you? I figured Slade would've driven the rest of you out by now."

I wince at the sound of his name. "Still there."

"So why did *you* come?"

"Her brother needs our help. Now, quit torturing the poor girl and take her to the Solis Complex," the doctor interjects, shooting Opie a warning look.

Opie's mouth twitches, like he enjoys being scolded. "As you wish, *sir*." He motions toward the hall, giving me a subtle wink. "After you." We follow him back down the corridor and head for the main entrance, passing the room with the phantom scream from earlier, its door now firmly shut.

"Lennon," the doctor calls out right as my foot passes the threshold to outside. I turn, my entire body buzzing with nerves. "I want you to know that I'm going to take good care of your brother. You're welcome to visit him anytime you'd like as long as it doesn't interfere with his progress." I nod, swallowing the knot in my throat.

Opie walks ahead with an ease I can't wrap my head around, boots crunching against the gravel path, hands tucked in his pockets casually. He gives me a tour as we walk, show-casing their greenhouses, farmland with growing crops, mechanical shops, surveillance buildings, and so much more. The place goes on forever.

He points to a long row of houses nestled on the far right side. "That's where most of our permanent residents stay. We have somewhere around ten thousand people living here."

"Ten thousand?" I ask, eyebrows raised.

He shrugs. "Give or take. Hard to keep an exact count with so many. But yeah, it's not small." Not small is an understate-ment. Exion makes Solis look like a backyard shelter. Hell, it even makes the Burrows look minuscule.

As we approach where I'll be staying, he explains that the buildings towering several hundred feet into the sky are what they call "apartment complexes" and contain anywhere from fifty to one hundred rooms apiece. Apparently, he's taking me to Complex D, where the rest of our camp has been placed.

The doors open automatically as we approach, sliding out of view. Inside is a short man wearing a round, blue hat and a matching uniform. "Welcome to Complex D! We're so excited to have you stay with us here in Exion." His smile is too prac-ticed, too perfect. "My name is Corwin. If you need anything during your stay, don't hesitate to ask."

In some ways, he reminds me of Archie—that is, if Archie

were creepy and a little *too* polished. "Thank you, Corwin," I say politely, forcing some warmth into my voice.

"This is Lennon. She's from Solis and will be staying with us for a while. Can you check her in?" Opie asks, leaning his forearms on top of the desk.

"It would be my pleasure!" Corwin says, his smile never faltering. "Give me just a minute to get everything together." Opie begins drumming his fingers on the desk incessantly as Corwin works, which only heightens the buzzing in my veins.

I can't stop thinking about Shiloh. What if they can't help him? What if leaving Solis, coming here and having them do who knows what kind of testing is all for nothing? How can I be a sister to a brother who wants me dead? How can I protect him when the thing he needs protection from the most is himself?

I wrap my arms around myself as if it can warm the internal chill.

When Corwin finally hands Opie a keycard, he straightens and offers it to me between two fingers. "Room 305. Elevator's down the hall."

I stare at the very platform-looking elevator, my stomach twisting. As much as I'd like to pretend it doesn't haunt me, Lyric's decapitated head rolling across that platform lives on repeat inside my mind.

Opie gives me a sideways glance. "You look like someone about to be sacrificed. We don't do that here."

"Stairs would be great, thanks."

He laughs, giving me a lopsided grin. "Can't say I blame you. After you get exiled, moving platforms aren't really all that anymore, are they?"

"You could say that."

We climb three flights of stairs, the silence between us

broken only by our footsteps, and when we reach the room, he points at a small device above the handle. "Put your card up against it, and it'll unlock."

I do as he directs, and a little light in the device turns green right as I hear the mechanisms; I turn the handle and push it open. Inside, the room is simple: a bed, two nightstands, a small desk pushed up against a window, and a bathroom tucked off to the side. Kaleu steps in first, sniffing the corners, pacing once, then settling near the window.

"Not bad, right?" Opie says behind me, resting a shoulder against the doorframe. "We usually reserve these for people we actually like."

"Lucky me."

He chuckles softly. "Lucky you."

I cross my arms. "Do you always flirt with people you just met?"

He tilts his head. "Only when they stare first."

I hate that I smile.

CHAPTER 30
SLADE

I can't move.

Thick straps pin my entire body to a cold metal table, holding me down like I'm something dangerous. I reach inward for Vesper, but there's only a thin, silver strand between us. Not silence. Not resistance. Just ... emptiness. It isn't like when we block each other out. This feels final, like the connection has been severed entirely.

But she can't be dead. If she were, I would be too. Unless I am. Maybe this is what comes after—some twisted afterlife built for people who've done terrible things like I have.

I drag my gaze across the room, only able to see so much from the angle I'm stuck in. White walls. Marbled floors. It smells like antiseptic and steel. A few machines sit in the corner, humming quietly, but otherwise, the room is empty.

I'm alone.

I struggle against the restraints, twisting and pulling until my muscles ache, but it's pointless. They don't budge. I feel weak, as if every ounce of energy has been drained from my body.

With a frustrated sigh, I let my head fall back against the table, eyes fixed on the blank ceiling above. Nothing but white. Still. Bare. Like the inside of my own mind.

I start tracing back through everything that led me here, choice by choice, mistake by mistake. What's the last thing I remember?

Lennon.

I was going to find Lennon and make things right.

A dart. Vesper going down. Something hitting me, then darkness.

So this is purgatory, then. I wonder if whoever runs this place will make me suffer for everything I've done. I hope they will. I deserve to.

The door creaks open, and I'm able to twist my neck enough to see a man in a white coat walk through, a clipboard in his hand. My heart thunders in my chest, and for the first time in a long time, I feel true panic. I reach for my power, but still come up dry.

"Glad to see you're awake, Slade. Do you know where you are?" He asks, his lips twisted into a sickening smile.

"Dead?" I guess, straining my wrists enough to rub them raw as I try to slip a hand free.

"Not exactly," he says, stepping closer into my line of sight. "But you'll wish you were."

He sets the clipboard down and takes his time adjusting his sleeves, like we have all the time in the world.

CHAPTER 31

LENNON

As much as I hate to admit it, I haven't slept this well since my first night on the Third Ring. The bed is comfortable, the air conditioning is heavenly, and the sheets are buttery soft.

I wake up to a knock at the door and dig through the fully stocked dresser to grab some shorts. They're a little big, but the drawstring keeps them from falling off completely. Good enough.

I half expect it to be Opie returning to annoy me, but I'm surprised to find Harlow instead. "Sleep well?" she asks, giving me a wide grin.

"I did, thanks."

She lets herself in and heads straight for my bed. When she sees Kaleu still curled up, she hesitates, standing awkwardly by the wall. "Sorry, I'm not sure what proper etiquette is around *Auryths*," she says in a near whisper, as if Kaleu might smite her for saying it wrong. "The only one I've ever met is Opie's panther, Selene. He always says they're a projection of the person."

I laugh. "Then I must be a grumpy old man."

Harlow grins. "Honestly? He kind of fits you." Kaleu snorts. I contemplate whether she meant it as a compliment or an insult.

She glances at him again, then down at her hands. "You up for a walk?"

I raise a brow. "Where?"

"Nowhere crazy. I was going to grab something from the mess hall and figured you might want to come. Your people will probably be there for breakfast."

"Your mess hall?" I repeat. "Like an entire building dedicated to food?"

Harlow stands, brushing imaginary dust off her pants. "You'll see. We need to get you changed first, though. Let's dig through your closet."

I follow her, mostly because she's already opening drawers and poking around like this is her room too. The closet lights up when she slides the door aside, revealing rows of clothing hung in neat arrangements by color and purpose.

She pulls out clothes and throws them at me, turning away so I can change. It's a soft, fitted top and a pair of tight, matte-black pants that cling like a second skin but are surprisingly comfortable.

I follow her through the quiet hall, down the stairs, and past a still-smiling Corwin until we get outside. She navigates through the busy streets with ease, sticking to the sides and chattering away about the variety of foods they have.

The mess hall is *massive*. Nearly as big as the Bowl in the Burrows, only rectangular instead of round. At the entrance are two huge, wooden doors with black iron handles. "Ready?" she asks. All I can do is nod as she opens the one on the right.

I'm hit with the overwhelming smell of food and the sound of chatter and laughter echoing from every corner. Long tables stretch the entire length of the building, packed with what must be thousands of people. Along the far right wall, rows of tables are stacked with a plethora of meats, breads, fruits, and even sweets. People stand in line, patiently shuffling along and stacking their plates with more food than I've ever *dreamed* of consuming, even on the Third Ring.

"We do this for breakfast, lunch, and dinner," she shouts over the noise. "Follow me." She hands me a white plate. It feels like paper, but much sturdier. I'm at a loss for words. So many people and yet no rationing, no segregation, no too-thin bodies. It's like I've walked into a dream. My nose draws me forward, a smile tugging at my lips as I wander past a tower of sweet-smelling, chocolate-colored ovals. They're piled one on top of the other, reminding me of the pines surrounding Solis, and when I get closer, I notice the gentle steam rolling off them. In all my life, I've never seen something so magnificent.

The rest of the table is no less astounding. Large bowls overflow with fluffy, freshly cooked eggs, according to Harlow, and beside them sits a variety of soft-baked breads: crescent-shaped rolls, buns, and biscuits. Fresh, colorful piles of sliced fruits are stacked on platters far bigger than my head, and a tower of apples so tall it dwarfs me. The sights and smells are dizzying. I stare at the feast, my hand frozen over the plate, unsure where to start.

"Just take one of everything," she directs, catching my stare. "There's plenty to go around." I do as she instructs, feeling guilty but absolutely *starving*.

When my plate is piled high, she leads me through the maze of tables until she finds the one she's looking for. Every head at the table turns toward me. No, not me—to Kaleu. A man stands up and climbs off the bench, heading straight for me.

"Are you from the Burrows?" he asks, glancing behind me.

"Yes," I tell him, my voice a little shaken. "Are you from Solis?"

A nod. "Did the others come with you?"

I shake my head. He looks ... disappointed. "My name is Keelan. Welcome home." Home. The word feels foreign.

The rest of breakfast consists of Keelan and the others asking a million questions about how I ended up exiled despite being bonded, why I left Solis, and why the others didn't join. I leave out the part about Lyric, claiming to have snuck onto the platform during Shiloh's exile instead. When Keelan brings up Slade, it isn't difficult to tell what he means to him. He seems physically pained by the fact Slade stayed behind, like a father separated from his only child, so I decide to leave out the parts about Slade's attempt on my brother's life. No use in creating fresh wounds.

I become an expert liar, weaving tales of Shiloh's illness, Slade's determination to keep Solis running for future exiles, and the rest of the camp not wanting to leave his side. They buy it, and the prodding eventually stops when plates are being emptied and discarded.

"Can you take me to see Shiloh?" I ask Harlow, desperate to see how my brother survived the night.

She looks down at her hands, avoiding my gaze. "The doctor thinks it's best if you give it a little time before seeing him again."

"But he said I could visit whenev—"

"I know," she interjects. "He told me that, too. As it turns out, Shiloh still has a desire to kill you. Even the sound of your name sends him into a spiral, and the medical team is worried it will offset any potential progress as they work with him. He asks that you try to understand. They only want the best for him."

Right on time, Opie walks up holding a heaping plate of the oval, brown stuff—*sausage*, Harlow called it. "I brought this for Kaleu," he says, putting it down in front of him like a peace offering. Kaleu devours it in seconds. Selene licks her lips, and Opie gives her a knowing look. "I might need to grab him a second plate. Her, too."

"So," he continues, "what are you sulking about? You've had real food, you slept in a comfy bed last night, and your clothes are clean and look rather nice, by the way. What could you possibly be so sad about?"

"Now's not the time, Opie," Harlow warns, giving him a dirty look.

He plucks a piece of leftover fruit off my plate and pops it in his mouth. "The way I see it, you can stay here and continue being the queen of brooding, or you can join me on a little tour of the grounds. A *real* tour, not the sorry excuse for one I gave you yesterday. If you're nice, I might even break you into the medical facility. Though in your current state, I think we can probably count that one out."

"*I like him,*" Kaleu says, gobbling down another plate Opie made someone bring over.

"*You only like him because he's feeding you.*"

"So, what'll it be?" Opie asks, extending a hand to me. I look at Harlow for help, but she only shrugs.

"*Take the tour,*" Kaleu demands, popping his head up to lock eyes with me. Crumbles of sausage stick to his white fur, but his plate is licked clean.

I accept his outstretched hand, and he gently pulls me to his feet, then extends his elbow to me instead. "Proper tour etiquette," he says with mock formality. "We're nothing if not civilized here in Exion." I roll my eyes but link my arm with his. Kaleu follows close behind, tail swishing, full and happy.

The grounds are larger than I thought. The further we walk, the more I realize how much I haven't seen. Towering buildings line the walkways, some made of stone, others of sleek metal, many interconnected by arched pathways and hanging greenery. Opie gives half-explanations as we go, pointing at things with exaggerated flair.

"That's where the tech team likes to pretend they're superior," he says, motioning to a domed building with shimmering glass panels. "And over there? That's the water treatment facility. Smells like dirty socks but keeps everyone hydrated at least." I laugh, and he looks like he's won something.

"Oh no, don't start laughing now," he says sarcastically. "You'll lose your title of queen of brooding if you keep that up."

We pass what looks like a greenhouse and some kind of open training yard. A few people sparring catch my eye. Guard training, maybe? They're using swords instead of guns, which feels outdated given the rest of this place. Or at least until one of the blades *flares* to life.

A bright blue glow hovers along the edge, crackling with energy that I can feel through the air. Not just swords, then. Something more. Something dangerous. I want to ask more, but Opie's already dragging me further along.

"Do you still want me to break us into the medical building?" he asks, giving me that mischievous grin. "It'll be difficult, might get us both into some trouble, but what is life without a little *roguery*?"

I consider it for a minute, thinking about what Harlow

said and the doctor's explanation. Being the subject of Shiloh's rage is one thing; being the reason he doesn't get better is something else entirely. If I want it to work, I have to let them do their jobs, even if not seeing him is killing me inside. "I think it's best I let them help him."

"That's very big sisterly of you," Opie replies. A few steps pass before he opens his mouth again, this time with a little too much casual interest. "So, why'd you really leave everyone behind? I highly doubt *no one* wanted to come."

My gaze hits the ground as I question my options. It would be nice to have someone who understood. A place where I could talk without trying to sort through all the lies, but telling him the truth would mean exposing Slade ...

"When you spent time in camp, did you meet Slade?" I ask, the name acid on my tongue. No. I owe him nothing. Especially not my protection when he's not even here.

"Unfortunately."

Well, at least he has a similar impression of him. "My brother was haunted by visions for months before he finally snapped. We kept a close eye on him, Slade included. When Shiloh stabbed me, he was having a full breakdown. He wasn't himself, and we all knew it. Still, Slade tried to kill him. I begged him to stop, but he didn't. Not until someone was able to physically *force* him to. I left because I knew Shiloh needed help, and no one followed because they're either scared of Shiloh or too afraid to leave Slade."

"I'm sorry," he says. "Truly."

"It's behind us now, I suppose. Not much we can do about it, and Shiloh's finally getting the help he needs. That's what's most important." We stop in front of a large, white building with wide steps that lead to an arched entryway and a path beyond framed by trees.

"I'm afraid this is where I must leave you. Governor Gideon would like to meet you and discuss some ground rules in case you decide to officially move to Exion." My body tenses, my mind flashing back to President Blane and how well my "visits" with him and his henchmen went.

Noticing my panic, Opie touches my arm gently. "You have nothing to worry about here. This isn't the Burrows, and Gideon is not Blane. No one will hurt you" In my defense, people don't typically tell you when their government is evil and preparing to torture you. No, those are the kind of things they tend to keep to themselves.

I swallow hard, and he offers to walk me to the door, which I agree to gratefully. When we reach it, he knocks twice, and a guard in a freshly pressed uniform opens it. He stares at us with a monotone expression. "Name?"

"Lennon Benfield."

He whips out some sort of paddle-like contraption, then hovers it all around Kaleu and me. "All clear. You may enter. Not you." He points at Opie.

"I'll catch you later," Opie calls as the door shuts behind us.

I suck in a deep breath and watch my feet shuffle against the stark-white tile floor.

CHAPTER 32
SLADE

I've been in and out of consciousness for what feels like days. There's no real way to tell how long I've been strapped to this bed, but it's long enough that I've started to consider the possibility that I'm losing my mind. They perform test after test on me, but they never bother to explain what, exactly, they're testing for.

I still haven't decided if I'm in purgatory or if I'm somehow still alive. The man in the white coat comes in often, sometimes bringing others with him. Assistants, he calls them. They hardly ever speak, but I always find myself screaming before they leave. My entire body hurts, covered in sores from fighting the restraints and whatever the hell they've been doing to me: injections, machines, some sort of device that messes with my mind.

None of it is pleasant.

They never let me have peace. They never let me rest. I haven't seen Vesper since I arrived, and the bond is still completely silver. I long for that shimmering black tendril to return to me. If she is alive, I hope they're treating her better than they're treating me. I hope she isn't suffering the way that I am.

I'd endure this for a millennium if it meant she didn't have to live in agony.

The door creaks open, and I recoil. The white-coat-wearing man enters, holding some sort of electronic square in his hands that I haven't seen before. It's big enough that it takes both of his hands to hold it, but small enough to be passed around easily. The assistants follow behind him, their eyes curious.

I'm a project, an experiment. For what, I have no idea, but whatever it is, I know it can't be good. "Good morning, Slade," he says, and the horrible scent of antiseptic and lemon fills my nostrils. He always smells like that, and my body nearly retches every time he gets close to me. How is it already morning? How long have I been here? Has anyone noticed that I'm gone?

I doubt they'd notice. It's better for them this way—with me gone.

I don't speak. This is our routine, he and I. He pokes and prods, causes me excruciating agony, and I never say a word. If this is my penance, I'll learn to accept it. If it's not, then I refuse to give this man the satisfaction of thinking he's won something through my words. If only I could keep the screams from forcing their way past my lips …

I've had a lot of time to think in here about my choices and the harm they've caused. Sage. Shiloh. Lennon. Lief. I've hurt everyone I've touched.

"We're going to try something new today. I'd like to see how advanced our technology truly is, and how much progress we've made. Our team has been working very hard on our new improvements," he says, smiling over me. A needle enters my arm, and everything around me goes fuzzy.

It isn't the same feeling I get when they give me the sleeping injection; I'm still here, still able to see and hear despite the blur. Instead, my body feels heavy, like someone has filled me full of rocks and left me to sink.

I watch hazily as his finger slides to something on the small device, and my body instantly goes numb. I try to wiggle my fingers and toes, but they refuse to move. One of the assistants comes to my side, and I can hear the sound of unbuckling as they undo my restraints.

Is this some sort of game? A sick joke to offer me freedom, only to inject me with a paralytic that makes it impossible to run? There's no power thrumming in my veins. No Vesper. No fight left in me.

The man in the white coat leans over, inspecting my face. His pale blue eyes are bright with fascination. "Remarkable. You're still in there, aren't you?" he says, tapping the side of my temple repeatedly. "Eyes tracking. Breathing steady. Brain activity. Very much awake. *Excellent*." He's talking to the others now, not to me, like I'm some fascinating animal they've cornered and caged. "This is the latest prototype of our neurological override. We needed a bonded subject they would consider easily disposable to test its full potential. I don't know why any of the bonded are worth keeping, but Gideon said it had to be this way, and what he says goes."

One of the others, a young female with black hair, shaky hands, and nervous eyes, looks at me with something close to pity. "He's ... conscious?"

"Oh yes," White-coat says casually, as if he's discussing nothing more than the weather. "Fully aware, but completely paralyzed. Every nerve still functions, but he has no say in how. Instead, that luxury is now ours to decide."

He turns the square device toward them, revealing a tangle of lights and pulse-like waves that shift across the screen. "You can see that it's all tracked here. Silas, would you do the honors?"

The male assistant, Silas, steps forward, eyeing me with the same excitement. This must be White-coat's prodigy. Silas extends a hand and swipes at one of the digital bars, smiling as he makes patterns. Pain explodes behind my eyes: raw, searing, electric.

I can't scream. Can't even blink. The agony is a storm in my brain, lighting every pathway on fire. I'm trapped in my own skull with no way out.

"It's like tuning an instrument," the White-coat says calmly. "We're still trying to figure out where pain and memory intersect. And, of course, how far we can go with it." He takes the tablet back from Silas and offers an eerie smile.

Then, he slides his finger upward on the device, and I watch in horror as my own arm shoots straight into the air. He's controlling my movements. Whatever technology this is, it's dangerous. First it's an arm, then what? What will they force me to do? My lungs feel heavy as I suffocate in the silence. I can't breathe fast enough to chase the panic away.

Vesper.

The name floats like a ghost in my mind. Still no bond. No warmth. Only silence. Wherever she is, I hope she's free.

I'm not.

I'm a body on a slab.

A machine in human skin.

A lesson in punishment they haven't finished writing yet.

CHAPTER 33

LENNON

The air inside is cool and smells faintly of citrus and polished wood. Light pours through tall windows that stretch nearly from the floor to the ceiling, softened by sheer white drapes that billow slightly from hidden vents.

It almost makes the entire encounter feel less threatening. Almost.

Everything gleams. The floors are dark wood, and the walls are adorned with minimalist art that feels intentional rather than decorative. There are some portraits of humans, but none that I recognize.

I step forward cautiously, Kaleu brushing against my hip, right as a door at the end of the hall opens. A man steps out, and I freeze. He's tall and dressed in a sleek lavender suit, not a wrinkle in sight. There's something in the way he walks, the way he looks directly at me with no hesitation, demanding my attention. Close-cropped, black hair, perfectly trimmed. Sharp features, but not unkind, and when his eyes land on me, they soften even more.

"You must be Miss Benfield." His voice is low and soothing. "I'm Governor Gideon. Welcome to Exion."

"Thank you for allowing us in and for taking care of my brother." My voice wavers slightly, but I force myself to hold his gaze.

"Of course." He inclines his head, a gesture of practiced warmth. "We pride ourselves on giving sanctuary to those the Burrows have abandoned." I nod, unsure how else to respond. "You, however, are … unusual, aren't you?" He lets the word settle before continuing. "My sources tell me you were bonded before you ever reached the surface."

My spine straightens. "I was."

"Well, I doubt they'd exile one of their precious bonded. So why did you give it all up?" Kaleu's ears twitch, but he doesn't growl.

I rest a hand on his fur. "For my brother. I didn't want him to die alone."

"So you risked death for the sake of your brother? Surely you didn't know the ground was survivable when you made that choice," he says, heading in my direction.

I exhale slowly. "No, I didn't."

He gestures for me to walk with him. "I admire your courage and loyalty. You, your brother, and your Companion are welcome here. We've already welcomed the rest of your people inside our walls. We don't believe in exiling people because they're different than us, but there are rules to ensure peace and the safety of everyone."

Well, being welcome is a good start. "No magic inside Exion," he continues. "It's a non-negotiable. Use it here, and you forfeit the hospitality we've offered and your brother's treatments. You're welcome to go outside the gate anytime to do that, if you wish. Just not within these walls. I trust that won't be a problem?"

I swallow, then shake my head. "No. It won't."

"I'm glad to hear that. The second is that if you wish to become a permanent resident of Exion, you must submit to a chip placement." Panic etches her sharp claws into my chest.

No more chips. Not after everything in the Burrows. I've seen what they can do, and considering this place *thrives* off its technology, I can only imagine what their version is capable of. "I can't commit to that. I've been chipped before, and I won't put myself in a position like that again."

He looks confused, his head tilting curiously. "They chipped you in the Burrows? Why?"

"I suppose it depends on who you ask. According to them, safety. I believe it had more to do with control than anything, though."

"Interesting," he blurts, then immediately collects himself. "Apologies. I understand your experience with that was likely not a pleasant one. I just mean that it's interesting they used technology in that capacity, given their history of disdain for it. Or their disdain for us, rather."

"I suppose their fear of uprisings made it an easy decision. They figured out control is more convenient than integrity, which is why I can't accept your terms," I counter. "Is there something else I can do? Some other way to prove myself?"

"It isn't about control here, I assure you," he presses. "I know trust is likely a difficult thing for you to give, but I have to put my people above all others. Our chips are for medical purposes only. They can detect illness and disease the moment they develop, preventing us from having potentially widespread, devastating loss of life. They're how we've been able to not only maintain, but also grow our population, despite Earth's many challenges. Our own people are chipped when they're young, and all of your people have agreed and received theirs as well."

"Can I have some time to think about it?" My voice trembles.

He considers this for a moment, sliding his hands into his pockets casually. "One week. If you haven't agreed by that point, we'll have to remove you and your brother from our city. If it's any consolation, the rest of your people from Solis did some thinking as well, and all agreed. Maybe talk to them about their experience. It might give you some clarity."

The front door opens, and he gestures for me to exit. "We are not the enemy, Lennon. We don't believe in violence and death like your people do. In the original war, we only created those weapons to stop our people from being massacred. Our ancestors never wanted to hurt anyone, but they needed the killing to stop. I hope you can understand our perspective, and I encourage you to visit our library and review some of the history inside. I believe you'll find a very different lesson than what you learned down below."

That's the problem with history: every city, every civilization has a different story and a different person documenting it. If I've learned anything, it's that documenters of history have a real issue being neutral.

I have one week to decide if I want to go down that path again. One week to determine if their helping Shiloh is worth risking losing my control again when there's no guarantee they can even fix him. I've been surrounded by so many liars in my life that it's difficult to believe anyone has good intentions—especially those in power.

I turn back to address the governor one final time. "I will."

The door closes behind me with a soft click, and I find

Opie standing at the bottom of the steps, giving me a lopsided smile, Selene at his side. "He's a little different than Blane, don't you think?"

Sometimes I forget Opie once lived in the Burrows. If it wasn't for his *Auryth*, I'd think he was born and raised inside of Exion. "Question," I say, walking toward him. "Did you live on the First Ring in the Burrows, or was your family from a higher station? I'm going to guess Third Ring. And when, exactly, did you bond with Selene?"

"That's *two* questions," he quips, and I roll my eyes. "Yes, I'm from Ring Three. How did you know?" He raises an eyebrow at me. "Both of my parents were elites. I think that's why it was so surprising when I didn't come out bonded. As for Selene, I met her a year after I arrived in Solis, right before I left to search for Exion."

"Why did you leave Solis?"

"You are *full* of questions today," he says, grinning. "Though I suppose it's better than your quiet sulking."

"Answer the question."

He shrugs. "Selene came across Exion when she lived in the Wildwoods. I didn't believe her when she first told me about it. I needed to see it for myself. The way Solis was going … I knew I needed to find somewhere our people could be safe."

I hesitate. "You let them chip you?"

"Yeah. But it's not what you're thinking. It's nothing like the Burrows. No trackers, no surveillance. It just keeps us healthy. It's how they keep their people safe from outsiders like us. I barely notice it."

"So you're saying I'm overreacting?"

"I'm saying you've been through hell, and you don't trust

anyone yet. Which—" he flashes a crooked smile, "—is fair. But maybe don't lump me in with the bad guys just yet."

I stare at him for a second, then glance toward the walkway leading deeper into the city. "I want to see the library."

Opie blinks. "Now?"

"Yes, now. If they're going to keep trying to convince me they're different, I need to see it for myself."

He nods, then gestures for me to follow. "Come on. It's this way. Just don't get mad when you finally figure out that I'm right."

"We'll see about that," I mutter, but follow him anyway.

CHAPTER 34
LENNON

T he library is a twisted, blossoming rose in this city
of precision. Unlike the other buildings, it's been
untouched and kept in its original form, likely from
before the war.

It's round and separated into three tiered rings, all sporadically painted in hues of yellow and white, each growing
narrower as the structure grows taller. The first tier is
composed of bricks that curve into six identical archways,
spaced evenly apart. The second is circled by pairs of white
columns, the space between each set adorned with tall
windows. The third and highest tier includes a dome-shaped
top with an entire gate around it, and six small windows
decorating the sides.

It's one of the most breathtaking things I've ever seen.

"You really do have a staring problem, don't you?" Opie
jokes, holding the door open. "Buildings, people, *Auryths*."

I ignore his teasing and follow him inside, only to find
myself even more enthralled by the interior. It smells like dust
and old pages. Not musty, but warm. Like something that's

been well-loved and left undisturbed for a long time. The floor is a dark, weathered wood that creaks under our steps, and the walls are covered in a combination of paintings, random symbols, and languages that I don't understand or recognize.

Light streams in from the upper windows, hitting the shelves in uneven patches. There's no obvious order to the rows. Books seem to be stacked randomly, some leaning, others piled flat. A few have colored threads wrapped around their spines, and some are so old that the titles have faded off the spines completely.

I run my fingers along the edge of one of the shelves and stop when a book in a pale green color catches my eye. The pages are frayed, but the spine holds firm when I pull it free. The feel of it settles into my hands as I flip through the pages, admiring the flourished type scouring its pages.

I grab another, with a cracked leather cover and gold etching along the edge that reads, T*he History of Bonded and Unbonded*, and add it to the first—It's a little on the nose, but it'll do—before adding third. It's smaller than the others, and reads, *How to Ensure an Auryth Chooses You.* It makes me think of Lief. Maybe if I ever see him again, I can give it to him.

"You planning to start a collection?" Opie asks, eyebrows raised.

"Maybe," I say, hugging them to my chest. "I like how they smell. And I have a lot of questions that need answering."

He laughs, then stacks two more on top. The pile nearly reaches my chin. "I had the same questions you did when I came here. These two are on the history between bonded and unbonded, and where it all went wrong. If you're picking up books to *learn*, that is."

"I am." I offer him a small smile. "Thanks. So what,

exactly, do you do here besides give tours to new people?"
I ask.

"I volunteer on guard and patrol, and sometimes I help
out in the greenhouses. Once you get clearance, you can
pretty much do anything you want." Interesting. Maybe I can
pick up gardening again, especially with the advancements
they no doubt have in their greenhouses. I miss the feel of
dirt between my fingers.

He closes the heavy library door behind us, and we begin
our walk back to my apartment. "Do you think about your
parents a lot?" I ask him, trying to keep my books from
toppling over.

He pulls a few off the top of the stack, lightening the load.
"Sometimes. You?"

"My mom? Every day. But she's … gone. My dad, not so
much. I doubt he even realizes Shiloh and I are missing."

He cocks his head curiously. "I think even if I saw my
parents again, they'd still be disappointed in me. Even if I do
have Selene now."

I wince. "I'm sorry. That sucks."

He shrugs. "No use in feeling bitter about it. Besides, it's
better to surround yourself with people who actually *want* to
be around you than force people who don't just because
they're family."

I look around us playfully. "Sorry, do you *have* any of those
people? I was under the impression everyone was just as
repelled by you as I am." He snorts and rolls his eyes.

We reach the apartment complex, and he stops before the
automatic door. "Want me to help you get these up?"

"No, I've got it. Just put them back on top of the others.
Thank you for today."

"Anytime. I'll catch you later," he says as he walks the other direction.

Back inside the apartment, I settle beneath the window with my knees tucked up and the books piled beside me. The room is quiet, and for a while, I just read. I'm not normally one for reading, but there's got to be *something* useful in all these words. Unfortunately for Lief, the tiny book on *Auryths* and bonding was less than helpful. In fact, I think I now have questions about how the hell I bonded.

A knock at the door breaks the silence just as the sun begins to dip behind the buildings.

Harlow stands on the other side, arms hugged tight across her chest. "I hope it's okay I came," she says, eyes flicking past me like she's unsure whether to actually step inside. "I, um … I went to check on Shiloh for you."

I blink. "Why? Is he okay?"

She nods quickly. "He's … hanging in there. Not great, but not worse. He remembered me, which is something. I just thought … I don't know, maybe it would help to know someone's checking on him since you can't go."

Something in my chest eases. "Thank you," I whisper.

"I'll keep going, if you want me to," she adds. "And keep you updated."

"That would be amazing," I say, feeling the tension leech out of me.

She steps inside like she belongs there, kicking the door shut behind her and plopping down beside Kaleu on the bed. "Now," she says, eyeing the stack, "why in the world do you have so many books?"

I sit down across from her, pulling my legs beneath me. "I met Governor Gideon today."

Her eyebrows shoot up. "Oh. And how was that?"

"He was very formal. Polite. He told me about the chip. Said we have to get one if we want to stay here and get Shiloh treatment." I run my thumb along the spine of the green book. "I asked for more time to decide. I don't know if I can do it. So I'm doing some research. Weighing my options."

Harlow leans back, resting her head against the wall. "I've had one since I was five. Never really noticed it. But even so, it's your body, Lennon."

"You don't think I'm being paranoid?"

"No," she says firmly. "I think you've earned the right to be cautious. Just make sure it's a decision, not a reaction. Do your research. Talk to people. Don't just say no because you're scared. Say no because you're sure it's not what you want."

I study her for a moment, then nod. "That's actually helpful. Thanks."

She shrugs like it's no big deal, then nudges a book with her toe. "Still doesn't explain why you've built a fortress out of reading material."

I smirk. "Well, considering my brother's stuck spouting cryptic prophecies no one can understand, I figured I'd at least try to crack the code. I'm hoping one of these has the answers I'm looking for." Harlow's expression softens. "Actually," I add, "next time you visit Shiloh, could you write down anything he says that seems off? You know: visions, strange phrases, anything that might be part of a pattern. I've been keeping my own running list."

She sits up straighter. "Yeah. Of course. I can do that."

"Even if it sounds like nonsense. *Especially* then, actually."

"I'll keep a notebook with me," she says. "If he says something weird, I'll write it down word for word. I promise."

"In the meantime," I say, reaching into my drawer, "you

wanna see what I've got so far? I could use a second set of eyes." There's a strange level of comfort with Harlow, like I've known her my entire life, despite it only being a few days. I hand her the Desmos book and my journal. Her fingers skim over the worn leather, tracing the lines of the engraving on the front.

"What's it like?" she asks quietly. "Being bonded to an Auryth?"

My eyes drift to Kaleu, sleeping peacefully nearby. Just looking at him makes everything feel a little less heavy. "It's the best feeling in the world," I say. "It's knowing you'll never be alone for the rest of your life, no matter what."

She smiles faintly. "Sometimes I wish we had the chance to bond with one. I always hoped one would find me on patrol, though I doubt Governor Gideon would ever let me back inside if it did." She laughs, but there's something uneasy about it.

She flips open the book, then pauses. Her brows knit together. "This is in Eronaeic."

I blink. "Huh?"

"Eronaeic. It's an old language, used way before the war. A lot of historical documents were transcribed using it."

"Can you read it?"

She grins. "Actually, yeah. I can." Flipping to a page with an image of a wolf, she traces her finger on the lines below it, reading, "Ena sovrae, ena inrae. Ta vestra shaleth draveth na an ignar en suae gorath."

My brows furrow. "And that means?"

"Well, I remember Ena means one, so that covers two out of fourteen words." She laughs, running a hand down her face. "Ta means the, an means a, and ignar means fire. I need to think a minute on the others, it's been a while."

I copy the lines into my notebook, then begin the translation below based on what we have so far:

Ena sovrae, ena inrae. Ta vestra shaleth draveth na an ignar en suae gorath

One sovrae, one inrae. The bestra shaleth draveth na a fire en suae gorath

I show her what I have, and the visual causes a gasp to escape her lips. "Oh! Sovrae and inrae! Above and below!" I don't need her to translate the rest; I've heard these particular phrases more times than I can count.

One above, one below. The beast shall wake with a fire in its throat.

Shiloh's visions aren't just visions. They're from the book. A book far older than the Burrows, likely older than the war itself. That's why he took it, but what exactly is he trying to tell us? A beast? Fire? Is it an old story? A fable like Kaleu thought?

"Lennon, look," Harlow says, pointing to another page. "Ta innecta shaleth necteth qua inpoteth esse necta. The unbonded shall bind what cannot be bound." Her brows knit together and then she looks over at me. "I think … I think it's a prophecy."

CHAPTER 35
SLADE

I'm a puppet from one of the shows about Earth they used to put on in the Burrows. Only these people don't use strings. They use technology.

Every day, they push it further: forcing my legs to walk, my hands to wave, my eyes to blink. There isn't a drop of power left in me. Only numbness. A body on autopilot.

"Today we're moving to Phase Four," the man in the white coat says, jabbing another needle into my arm with barely restrained excitement. "I've been looking forward to this step for months."

I have not.

Wait. Did he say *months*? That can't be right.

They unstrap me from the bed again, then prop me upright. The man holds the device he calls a tablet and tilts it toward me enough that I can see. A diagram of a body fills the screen, marked with symbols and numbers. He presses a button and drags his finger across the right leg of the outline.

My leg lifts in response. Immediate. Precise.

"Fascinating," he whispers, then runs a few more motions like a kid playing with a new toy. I can't speak; my tongue is useless.

He swipes the diagram away and pulls up a blank box. Into it, he types: "My name is Slade Whitlow." Then, he holds a circle on the screen down until it turns green. The words come out of my mouth, but I didn't say them. I emit them like a damn speaker.

He lights up, spinning in place and clapping like he's won something. I try to speak on my own. Nothing. I can't even twitch. This is worse than death. Worse than purgatory. I'm a shell. A vessel. A tool for their display. My mind is screaming, yelling into the void, but my body is theirs.

"You, my boy, are the result of an experiment gone right," he says, watching me like I should be proud. "You've been given a purpose. You should be *grateful*."

Grateful.

If I could move my hand, I'd wrap it around his throat and show him just how grateful I am. If I could feel even the smallest flicker of a bond between Vesper and me, I'd claw my way out of this hell. But there's nothing. No powers. No connection. No sign that she's even alive except for my beating heart.

Sometimes I like to focus on the sound to keep myself grounded, a small slice of reality. I'm alive. That has to count for something.

"We've been working on this for a long, long time." He stands over me, smiling in a way that makes my skin crawl. "If we can control the bonded, we'll never face a threat again. And with the addition of your little friend and her wolf to our camp, I have yet another subject once we perfect it. If something goes wrong with you, there's no one to miss you. Hell, we've had you here for days, and no one's bothered to even ask about you. She, on the other hand, has an unfortunate number of people looking out for her. We need to get it right before we take her."

I'm not dead. I'm alive. And she's here.

Lennon.

He's going to use me. Control me. Make me a complacent soldier. I want to open my mouth, to say something, anything, but all I can do is stare.

"And that's the best part." He grins. "You can't even talk. I love how far we've come." He claps, then barks orders at his team to strap me back down in case I somehow regain control, even though I haven't had an ounce of it since I arrived.

At the door, he turns back one last time. "I'm sure you're wondering about your wolf," he says like an afterthought. "We've been using similar tech on her for much longer than what you've endured. Have you ever wondered why a sudden darkness crept into your chest? Why she suddenly snapped? Why you would suddenly snap?" My stomach twists. "She's a fighter, your wolf. Took more precautions than we've ever needed with a host and multiple chip variations to create something that could finally break her. But she won't be an issue anymore."

What does he mean by "anymore"? What has she silently endured? And how did I not know?

And then he's gone.

I just stare at the door, unmoving, a tear sliding down my cheek. She was never evil. They tried to make her that way, and she fought it.

What have they done to her? Where is she now? I feel like

I need to be sick, but I can't even twitch a finger, let alone vomit. I can only lie there, drowning in my own silence, paralyzed in a body that no longer feels like my own.

The thoughts are worse than the pain. They don't shut off. The ache in my chest bleeds like an old wound cracking open, and my mind drifts to the day she chose me.

Keelan and I had gotten into it over something stupid; I don't even remember what. Words were thrown like knives, and his disappointed looks had sent me over the edge. I hadn't waited for it to settle. I stormed out, past the edges of the camp, past the gate.

I think I wanted him to chase me. Wanted someone to come looking for me, but he didn't. No one did.

I'd made it to the woodline before my anger folded into sadness. I dropped to the ground in a heap, pressing my forehead into my knees, and sobbed.

I wasn't the type to cry, not even as a kid. I was taught not to. My parents didn't know what to do with their own emotions, let alone mine. I was simply a product of their duty to the Regime, not something they ever truly wanted. The day I was exiled, no one looked surprised that I didn't bond. Even I wasn't.

No one cried for me when they took me away.

But that day, under the trees, I cried hard enough that I'm sure everything in a five-mile radius heard me choking on air. And then, the sound of crunching leaves pulled me from my sobs. I looked up, and she was there, standing at the edge of the clearing like a shadow painted in sunlight. Her slick black coat gleamed as she stepped forward, and those amber eyes seemed to soften when they found me.

She didn't move to attack. She didn't flee. She laid down, slow and deliberate, her front legs stretched out like she was inviting me in. I didn't understand it, but something inside me shifted.

I stood, barely breathing, and approached with caution, my arm extended out in front of me. My hand trembled, but she waited patiently. Then, right before I touched her, she leaned in and pressed her snout to my palm.

The bond exploded through me like lightning across a stormy sky.

It wasn't just power. It was understanding. It was being known. Being *seen*. Every empty corner I'd carried for years lit up at once, filled with something far more meaningful. My knees gave out, but she caught me before I hit the ground.

Her voice was quiet in my mind, soft and soothing. It vibrated through my entire body. *"My name is Vesper,"* she said. *"And you will never be alone again."*

She was the first thing that had ever chosen me. Not out of duty or pity or utility, but because she saw me, even when I didn't. We haven't left one another's sides since that day.

Sometimes I'd wake in the middle of the night, drenched in sweat, haunted by memories I'd never spoken aloud, and there she'd be: watching, silent, steady. One nudge of her head and the panic would quiet. One rumble in her chest, and my hands would stop shaking.

She kept me tethered when I wanted to disappear. She called me back to reality when I wandered too far into the dark.

The weight in my chest has turned into a hollow, growing thing. My mind screams her name, but my lips can't move. My fingers stay still. My body no longer belongs to me.

They used her to control me. *All those months*, she was fighting. Fighting for me, and I didn't even notice.

What did they do to her now? Where is she? What is left of her?

The silence stretches until it feels like it might crush me. Not the silence of the room, but of *absence*. Of severance.

She promised I'd never be alone. Until now.

And the loneliness is almost worse than death.

CHAPTER 36
SLADE

Their new goal is to utilize my powers without me controlling them. How that's even possible considering my powers are fueled by emotions, I have no idea, though I'm sure they'll figure it out. They've spent the last week attempting to get my powers to respond at all. Or at least I think it's been a week; it's difficult to keep track when there are no clocks or windows.

"What if we utilized technology to incite memories that induce emotions?" Silas asks, staring sideways at me.

They discontinued the paralytic, needing the bond between me and Vesper active, but replaced it with two round-the-clock, heavily armed guards. I was hopeful I might be able to reach out to Vesper or even Lennon and Kaleu—but it's no use. Either I'm too weak, or they're blocking my ability somehow.

"That could work," the doctor says, pacing the small, square room. Terror grabs my heart and yanks it right out of my chest. I know they can control my thoughts, my movements, but to incite memories?

My mind is a tangled spiderweb of things I've long since kept hidden. I've locked those doors for a reason, not wanting to ever think about them again. Even when I pull on those emotions, I only use surface-level feelings when I can, unless absolutely necessary.

This is a new type of torture. I can handle pain; I can handle threats and blood. I'll gladly accept any of those things over being forced to relive my worst days.

They pull out the tablet again and swipe to a new screen. The doctor turns it toward me, which has become one of his favorite routines. It's a way to explain how exactly I'll be tormented that day so that my mind can simmer on it first. "Go to hell," I spit.

"Oh! We seem to have finally struck a nerve with this one. What's the matter, boy? Have some things in that mind of yours you don't want to relive?" His tone is overly mocking, and his smile is sinister.

I glue my mouth shut, refusing to let him see just how shaken I am. "Fine!" he continues. "Speak, don't speak; I couldn't care less. You'll still serve your purpose. Lucky for you, Silas here is going to take the lead since it was his idea. I have some other business to attend to today."

I furrow my brows, and he laughs. He's never let anyone experiment on me beyond himself. "As it turns out, Lennon made a deal with Governor Gideon for permanent residence here and the healing of her brother. Isn't it funny? We're testing on you so we can learn how to control them, and once we figure it out, we'll already have the chips in place. Half of our work has been done for us!"

Lennon. They're using me to learn how to control *her*, and there's nothing I can do to stop it. I've heard them mention Gideon before—the man in charge.

So this corruption goes all the way to the top. Why does that not surprise me.

I lunge for him, discovering a newfound energy in my rage. My shaking hands pin him to the white wall by his neck as he laughs through struggling breaths, his eyes never leaving mine. One of the guards tries to attack from behind, but I throw out a wall of shadows to pin him in place.

My power is back.

There's no point in sitting here idly if they're going to hurt her regardless of whether I cooperate or not. The time for wallowing in self-pity is over. Now it's time to fight.

And then, just as quickly as the idea blossoms, a needle pricks my arm from the other side, and I turn to find the female assistant staring at me with wide eyes. She's small and fragile. My first instinct is to throw her against the other wall before I slip into whatever coma they've induced today, but she looks apologetic, like she's only doing what she has to. I suppose there's no use adding more bodies to my death toll if I'm going down either way.

Exhaustion leaks through my body, causing my hand to slip off the doctor's neck and my shadows to dissipate. They sling me back onto the table and tighten my restraints, my body too tired to fight it.

"That attempt will cost you," the doctor says, his words thick with hatred as he paws at his throat. "On the bright side, Nora utilized a mild version of our sleep injection. It will make you drowsy but still alert enough for that bond of yours to stay intact so Silas can experiment on you." He leans down so close to my ear that I can feel the heat of his breath. "And I hope it hurts."

He shuts the door behind him, and the two assistants stare at me with wild eyes. Silas pulls a chair up beside the bed and reopens the tablet. "We're going to start by tracing through your memories and finding the ones that trigger the best emotional responses," he tells me, averting his gaze.

I close my eyes and try to build my walls. Maybe if I can build a shield, I can keep them out of my mind. I can show them this isn't possible, and my people—she—will be safe from them.

But I'm too weak to even do that.

He places a small, metal band around my head, then activates it. I can feel it slicing through my mind with ease, and memories flash through my mind in rapid succession. They zoom through to the beginning, then backtrack to a point where I can actually remember enough to feel.

My parents and I are sitting at our dining table; I can't be older than ten. My father slams his fist down as my mother ridicules him for his tardiness. "I spent hours preparing this supper, just for you to show up late *again*? Were you with *her*?"

He stands, his face and neck red with anger. "I didn't ask for this marriage. I didn't ask for him." He gestures to where I sit, quietly picking at the food on my plate. "I never loved you, and you never loved me. What the hell does it matter?"

My little eyes well with tears, and I sniffle to keep my nose from running. He's on me in an instant, pulling me upward by my shirt collar. "Men do not cry. You are a sorry excuse for a son, and I wish I had never had you. If it hadn't been for the duty of the Regime, I wouldn't have. I can't wait for you to turn eighteen so I can finally be rid of you."

He releases me and walks out the door, slamming it so hard it rattles the walls. My mother pulls a bottle of pills out of her bag and takes three of them, then returns to her room while I sit there silently for two more hours, refusing to let a single tear slide down my face.

I try not to let it bother me. I've bounced that particular scene around in my head so often that I should be numb to it by now. If I can keep their screens from tracking a spike in my emotions, they lose.

They pivot from that memory to more recent ones, zooming in on one particular morning on the plateau with Lennon. Her brown waves are tangled from the wind, her freckles more prominent from being in the sun.

My stomach grows uneasy at the reminder of this day, of the storm that came after. I don't want to watch this. I don't want to remember the way she used to look at me when I know she'll never see me that way again.

But they stay here, forcing me to watch the entire thing.

They move further in the day to when I pin Shiloh by his throat as he gasps for air, and Lennon screams and screams at me. Begs me not to go through with it, to stop, but I can't.

I watch her bleed out on the ground, the life draining from her hazel eyes. I watch myself walk toward her on unstable legs, every piece of me broken and confused as to what I did. How did it all go so wrong so fast?

Then she looks at me again with such hatred, such fear, and leaves Solis for good.

I want to explain, to tell her I never wanted this. I want *her*. I want to apologize, but it's like I'm unable to.

It doesn't matter anyway; she's already gone.

It isn't until the assistants are shaking me, trying to wake me up, that I realize I've been screaming her name out loud.

CHAPTER 37

LENNON

I t's been four weeks and two days since I accepted the chip.

My brain is packed full of horror stories of cruelty on both sides of the war. Bondeds, taking out entire villages and families with their magic and *Auryths*; unbondeds, retaliating by creating weapons to disable their magic and murder their *Auryths* right in front of them.

If there's one thing I can say about Exion, it's that they didn't leave anything out. I have to give credit to their historians: they seem to have stayed neutral. Even the unbonded's wrongdoings were inscribed word for word, not a detail left unturned. By the end of it, I wasn't on anyone's side, but I did find myself grateful that they allowed me to form my own opinion with all of the details. Or what I think are all of the details. Call me cynical, but I still struggle with the idea of *trusting* a government, even if Gideon is kind and Exion has given me no reason to think otherwise.

Harlow visits Shiloh daily for me, and even in the first week, they saw progress. She says his visions have slowed, and he's even cracking jokes again. It didn't feel right to deprive him of a chance to get better, so I accepted Gideon's terms. It wasn't painful; in fact, I hardly felt it. Just a small injection into my arm, and that was it—though it was eerily similar to the one I received in the Burrows. Or maybe that's just my paranoia talking.

I don't spend as much time with the others from Solis as I had hoped. I feel more like an outcast with everyone except Opie and Harlow. It's funny: all I ever wanted was to be bonded in the Burrows, to be "chosen," and now that very thing has everyone here treating me like I have a disease even my new chip can't detect.

"There's a party tonight," Harlow says excitedly.

"I've never been to a party," I tell her as I comb out my tangled hair. Kaleu is snoring in the bed, twitching softly in his sleep.

"Never?! Then you have to go. They're so much fun. We get to dress up, dance, and drink. There is nothing better, in my opinion."

I laugh, turning to face her fully. "No one here wants me to show up at a party. Besides, I don't want to leave Kaleu."

She narrows her brown eyes at me. "And why can't Kaleu come?" At the sound of his name, Kaleu's ears twitch upward, but he doesn't lift his head. Sneaky beast, listening while pretending to still be asleep.

"Oh, I don't know, probably because everyone's terrified of him? Most still aren't used to being around an *Auryth*."

"Opie and Selene don't care if people are afraid of them. Why do you? Besides, that's actually great for us. It'll give us more room on the dance floor." She shrugs.

"I just don't think it's my type of thing."

"How do you know if you've never been to one?" Harlow

asks, a playful smirk on her lips as she leans back against the doorframe. Damn, she's got me there.

Besides, it might be nice to get out of this stuffy apartment for a change. We've spent nearly every day and night trying to crack Shiloh's code. As it turns out, when Harlow said she could read Eronaeic, she meant "kind of," so it's taking a lot longer than we'd anticipated.

I throw my head back and groan, acknowledging my defeat. "Fine."

She claps her hands excitedly and jumps up and down a few times, making me laugh. "Perfect. There's so much to do! I'll find you a dress, and then I'll be back here in two hours for us to do our hair and makeup! Promise me you won't be a killjoy tonight!"

I roll my eyes. "I promise."

She's out the door before I can consider changing my mind.

I glance back over at Kaleu, whose snoring hasn't returned, but his eyes are still squeezed shut. I pick up a T-shirt off my dresser and chuck it at his head, smiling as it lands perfectly on top of his ears. He shakes his head and snorts, then narrows his golden eyes at me. The white fur on his head is sticking up sporadically from the static, and I let out a wheezy giggle at the sight.

"Some help you were! I know you were only pretending to sleep, you sly beast." He yawns, showcasing all of his canines, and stretches his back legs behind him until they're nearly straight.

"I don't know what you're talking about," he says, and I scrunch my nose at him.

I decide to use my extra two hours to shower and blow-dry my hair, another luxury I'm still learning to get the hang of. It wasn't something we had access to, even in the Third Ring—too much electricity. It's certainly one of my favorite small improvements. Being in the cooler weather with wet hair is not for the faint of heart.

There hasn't been snow yet, but I look out my window every day, hoping it will finally fall. It's getting colder, but apparently, we still have a few months before we can expect it. Then again, crazier things have happened, and you never know what the weather might do in a world once destroyed by chemicals.

Opie and Harlow both tell me I'll regret wishing for it, but I can't help myself. The idea of it sounds so unrealistic, so unimaginable, that I know I'll have to see it, feel it, before I believe it. Harlow tells me that no two snowflakes are the same and each has its own design, but I won't be able to tell unless I look at it under a microscope. Then she likes to tell me how people are like snowflakes: all of us different and unique in our own ways. Sometimes you have to look a little closer to see it.

She's always saying things like that.

In exactly two hours, she returns, holding not one but three dresses in her hands. I put my hands on my face as she bubbles over with excitement. Her radiance is contagious. It's impossible to feel low around Harlow. She has that way about her that makes you want to live, even when almost every internal piece of you yearns to die.

"I brought three options because neither of us has a clue what you like," she says as she hangs them on the back of the bathroom door. "There's one in green, blue, and a very sexy red." I stare at each gown, mesmerized by the detailing. I'm not sure where to start or how to choose; they're all stunning.

"What are you going to wear?" I ask her as I walk over to feel the different fabrics.

"I'll choose from whatever you don't like!"

"Why don't you choose first, and then I'll pick from the rest?" I ask, furrowing my brows at her.

"Because this is your *first* party, and I refuse to have you feeling any less than spectacular." She nudges me with her shoulder, her smile growing bigger by the minute. "Now go try them on; I'm dying to see them!"

I hesitate before grabbing the red dress and heading into the bathroom. The fabric feels soft and smooth against my skin as I slip it on, and I turn to face the full-body mirror attached to the door before going out to face her.

It hugs me in all the right places, its silky fabric flowing down to my ankles like a river of fire. A slit runs up one side, exposing enough leg to make me want to immediately peel it off, and the neckline plunges deeper than anything I've ever worn, leaving very little to the imagination.

I step out of the bathroom, and her face lights up instantly. "If you don't wear that one, I will," she says, clapping her hands together. "You look amazing!"

"It's … a little much for me," I admit, glancing down at my exposed skin.

"Fair enough," she says with a grin. "At least you made my decision easy. Next!"

I duck back into the bathroom and reach for the blue dress. This one is simpler, with a high neckline and delicate lace sleeves. It's probably the fanciest thing I've ever worn. I think back to the day I moved to the Third Ring and the lady on the platform in her blue dress—I used to dream of wearing something this elegant.

When I walk out, Harlow tilts her head. "It's lovely," she

says slowly, "but it's almost too proper. You need something that says, 'I'm a lady, but I like to have fun, too.'"

I laugh, shaking my head. "What does that even mean?"

"You'll know it when you see it," she replies with a wink, waving me back toward the bathroom.

I sigh and reach for the last dress: the green one. When I slip it on, something feels right. The fabric is soft, with intricate embroidery that shimmers faintly under the light, and the skirt flows freely, grazing the floor without being too heavy. The fit is perfectly flattering without being overwhelming, and it's not so bright green that people will stare, but more of a dark green like the grass Slade and I used to train on.

Almost like the green of his eyes.

No.

I step out hesitantly, and Harlow's jaw drops. "Lennon," she breathes, her voice softer now. "That's it. That's *the one.* It makes your eyes pop!"

"Okay," I say quietly, a small smile tugging at my lips. "This is the one, then."

Harlow whisks the red dress into the bathroom and then returns, looking unbelievably stunning. Her hair has been pulled into a perfect, messy bun, and the red dress complements her features perfectly. "You look beautiful!" I breathe as she does a quick twirl, one arm stretched behind her head for added flare.

"Don't I know it?" She laughs, and I realize that this may be the first time I've ever had a friend besides Wilder.

"Let's get going," I say, looking over at Kaleu, still sprawled out on the bed. "You too, old man. Get up." He grumbles but follows nonetheless while I try to keep my hands from shaking.

CHAPTER 38

LENNON

Harlow is dragging me through the busy streets of Exion by my hand, squealing with delight. Kaleu is at my heels, and people move to the other side of the street just to avoid us.

I can hear the music blaring as we approach, a luxury we rarely had in the Burrows, but one I always adored. Radios don't work underground, and apparently, no one considered taking any records, CDs, or instruments down when they went either. It broke my heart to learn about all the pieces of history they left behind and didn't deem important enough to save. The only music we had access to was human made. Acoustic vocals accompanied by hand drums or other makeshift instruments, but even those were rare occurrences. Everyone had a job to do down there; there wasn't time for such "trivial" things, I suppose.

The beat seems to vibrate through my body, starting in my ears and shooting all the way down to my toes. My body sways to the rhythm involuntarily, immediately filling with joy as we enter the hall.

It's breathtaking. The main room is painted in bright gold with intricate moldings lining the walls and ceiling. A stunning wooden staircase leads to a second floor above, and a balcony stretches over half of the space. A few people look down from it at the crowd below.

People are everywhere: at least three hundred, from what I can see on this floor alone. Servers in full suits carry trays of drinks and food around, offering them to anyone they come into contact with. When one approaches us with drinks, Harlow grabs two and thanks the man before he rushes on to the next group.

"Here, take this," she says, pressing the crystal glass into my hand.

I accept and take a whiff before drinking. It smells sweet, like some sort of fruit and flower mixture. "What is it?"

"Does it matter? It'll make this entire experience a million times better. Now, drink up!"

I do as she asks, and to my surprise, it goes down smoother than I thought it would. My stomach immediately feels warm and bubbly, and I give Harlow a mischievous smile as she finishes hers in one sip.

Alcohol.

I'd be lying if I said I hadn't snuck sips of my dad's moonshine from time to time, mostly to see what all the fuss was about. I never cared for the taste, and I certainly didn't care for the way it made him behave. But I am also not my father, and I promised not to be a killjoy.

"Try not to get too out of control, Lennon. We still don't know these people," Kaleu warns.

"Yes, Grandpa," I tell him, earning a low grumble through the bond.

As we move further into the room, I realize it keeps going.

Harlow was right; I'm immediately grateful that people are terrified of Kaleu. They quickly move out of our way, creating an open path for us as we meander between the rooms, until we eventually reach the dance floor. Bodies are pressed against bodies, and drinks are spilling out of cups.

Harlow begins dragging me onto the floor, but I dig my heels in. "Come on!" she says, tugging hard. I shake my head, and she stops, placing a hand on her hip. "Lennon Benfield! You promised you wouldn't be a fun-killer tonight!" Like clockwork, another person with a drink tray approaches us, and she grabs two more. "Chug this, and let's go. It will loosen your nerves." I sigh, look at Kaleu apologetically, and drink.

It's so hot in the middle of the dance floor with all of the moving bodies, despite the cool air they're funneling in through vents. People keep bumping into me, their sweat touching my skin, and my anxiety begins to spiral out of control. My mind keeps flashing back to the platform, the rolling head, the woods, the mist, Slade, Wilder.

Opie.

My eyes find him as he moves through the crowd, Selene at his side. I nearly leap into his arms, his presence instantly providing not only relief but an out.

"Opie!" I yell, pointing in his direction so Harlow can see. She begins jumping, waving, and doing some very question-able dancing in between that tells me the drinks might be hitting her a bit harder than they're hitting me. Then again, my head is spinning, and my stomach is practically upside down, threatening to make me spill its contents on the floor.

He gives me a big smile as he approaches, his muscular arm instantly drawing me against his chest for a hug. "You look fantastic," he says near my ear, eliciting a shiver down my spine. Pine and citrus fill my senses, and I instantly feel a bit more at ease.

"I need air," I yell back, and he raises an eyebrow before placing a hand on my back to lead me away. He whispers something to Harlow that makes her laugh, and she waves her hands to dismiss us in response. Now I'm the one with a raised brow, curious as to what he could have possibly said to get her to allow us to leave without a fight.

I take deep, hungry breaths of air as we step outside, desperate to fill my lungs with something other than the scent of alcohol and sweat. "Not enjoying your first party, huh?" he asks, his green eyes staring at me with pity.

"I think I drank too much, too fast. Plus, I'm not the biggest fan of crowds, and neither is Kaleu, which only … amplifies things. And my feet hurt from these damn shoes Harlow made me wear." I point toward the nude heels that are currently ruining my feet. He extends an elbow to me, and I loop my arm through, allowing him to lead me to a bench.

The moment I sit down, he kneels to remove my shoes. Opie is good—pure, like Harlow. At first, I thought he was trouble with all the flirting and mischief. Now I know that's just who he is.

"There we go," he says softly. "That better?"

I nod. "Yes. Thank you for saving me."

He smiles up at me in that roguish way he does, and I can't help but return it. "Anytime."

It isn't that I don't like Opie. In fact, I do like Opie. A lot … just not in the way that Harlow speculates he likes me. Harlow isn't wrong either; he's certainly hinted a time or two that he wants more, but he's respectful and never pushes when I brush him off.

Sometimes when I'm around him, I can't get Slade out of

my mind. Not because I want or miss him, but because I once thought he was trouble too, then I thought I saw the good in him before he proved me painfully wrong. I can't go down that road again. I don't *want* to go down that road again.

The small radio on Opie's belt begins to crackle with static before words begin pouring out. "All guards, please report to front the gate immediately. We have around twenty people claiming to be from Solis."

I'm running barefoot toward the gate before he has time to react.

The gravel bites at my heels, my dress tangles around my ankles, but I don't stop. I can't. The name Solis triggers something in me: *my people are here*. They're here, and I can tell them it's safe to stay. I hear Opie behind me, shouting for me to wait up, but I don't. He'll catch up.

The wind claws at my face as I sprint toward the gates, my breath ragged in my throat. I have Opie here. I have Harlow. I have Kaleu. But I've never felt more alone.

I miss Lief, Delilah, and Florence. Hell, I even miss Wilder.

Slade is a different story. I can handle him now. Or at least I think I can, now that Shiloh is getting the care he needs. At least he can't use magic inside these walls without risking getting kicked out.

The gates come into view, a cluster of people standing right beyond the bars.

I spot Wilder instantly. His fingers are interlaced with Florence's, and he's smiles when he spots me. Those familiar dimples cut into his cheeks, flashing like nothing's changed. My chest stings, but only a little this time. Not like it used to.

"I had to see if it was true. Tell them to let me out, *please*," I beg Opie as he sprints up behind me.

He walks toward the guard station and says something I

can't hear. Whatever it is, it works, and the gate shifts open. I run toward Wilder out of instinct, eager to wrap my arms around him and apologize for everything, but I hesitate when my eyes land on Florence.

"You guys made it." My voice cracks with emotion.

Florence lets go of Wilder and wraps her arms around me, squeezing tightly. "I was so worried you hadn't." My shoulders relax as I slowly wrap my arms around her, feeling awkward but grateful all the same.

As she pulls away, she sets eyes on Opie. "I see you met Opie," she whispers, raising a brow. "Where are Shiloh and Slade?"

Now I'm the one with raised brows, looking between her and Wilder. "Shiloh is in medical getting treatment, but I haven't seen Slade. I thought he was with you guys in Solis."

Wilder steps forward. "He left to apologize an hour after you did and never came back. We just assumed he went with you."

Lief overhears our conversation and quickly joins our little group, panic etched in his expression. "Then where the hell is he?"

CHAPTER 39
SLADE

I keep having this recurring dream.

Lennon asks me to take her back to the radiation-lit forest after training, and I can't help but say yes. I head to my tent, the air still thick with the scent of her—wild earth and something faintly sweet. I wash off quickly, but it doesn't erase the way her touch lingers on my hands, the way her presence burns in my mind like a brand.

She's driving me mad in the most exquisite way. Fearsome, relentless, brilliant. She's everything I shouldn't want, everything I can't stop needing.

She meets me at my tent, a backpack full of apples and a grin that's all mischief. "Do you think if I push you in the pond down there, you'll start glowing too?"

I raise an eyebrow and pretend to contemplate the question with expert precision. "I'd say it's a good possibility. That, or it'll kill me."

"Well, we wouldn't want that, would we?" she quips, bumping me with a hip.

By the time we make it down to our spot, night has

already fallen. The glowing plants and water make her shine even brighter, and I choose tonight to confess the way that seeing her but not being able to *have* her tortures me.

My hands are shaky, my heart erratic. What if she doesn't feel the same, and I ruin everything? What if she's seen what's underneath my facade and hates me for it?

But if I don't tell her, I'm afraid I'll combust. I can't live like this anymore.

So I wait until we're quiet, staring down at the fractured moonlight caught in the pond. She's still talking, but her voice is drowned out by the roar of my own nerves.

"Lennon," I say in almost a whisper, turning to face her.

"What?" She looks at me as if she's concerned, as if seeing me this way is strange.

"There's something I need to tell you ..."

"What?"

I grab her face and kiss her tenderly, softly, just enough to provide an explanation for the words I can never get right. Then I step backward, fully prepared to be wrapped up in a blizzard or storm, or for her to actually push me into the glowing pond. To my surprise, she blinks, startled, and throws herself at me, returning the kiss desperately.

And then I wake up in this room, stare at the white walls, and wish I were dead.

CHAPTER 40

LENNON

"Whater's going on?" Opie asks, walking up to our clearly panicked group. I turn to him and shake my head, still trying to piece it all together.

Slade is *missing*.

He might be a loner, but there's no way he'd leave everyone in Solis behind without an explanation, even if he'd found me in the woods and decided to come along for the journey. Not that I would have let him.

All my anger and resentment towards him briefly washes away, replaced by a concern that something's actually happened to him. Could he be lost? Trapped in some hole in the woods somewhere? Did the mist get to him?

Is he dead?

I close my eyes and search for Vesper and his dark tendril, but it's like it doesn't exist. *"Do you feel anything?"* I ask Kaleu.

"No."

Lief is in a full-blown panic now, putting his arms on top of his head and pacing around while mumbling to himself. Wilder and Florence are discussing how their group would have seen or heard him if he were lost in the woods some-where, considering they walked the same path he intended to.

"We'll send out a patrol in the morning to search for him," Opie interjects, silencing everyone. "For now let's get everyone inside, cleared at medical, and into some warm beds. Sitting here and panicking about it isn't going to help the situation."

"Why do you care? You hate Slade," Wilder accuses. I remember asking Opie if he knew Slade, but all he ever said was "unfortunately." I didn't think that was code for despising the man, though.

"Wait, what? You *hate* him?" I ask.

He whirls to face me. "*You* hate him. Wilder hates him. Is there anyone in the camp who actually likes the guy? There's a line of people that had more than enough reasons to want him gone."

"I like him," Lief says quietly.

"Do you know something?" I press Opie, crossing my arms over my chest.

"No. I'm only saying—"

"You know what they say about guilty people?" Wilder cuts in. "They always over-explain."

Opie takes a step forward, almost nose-to-nose with Wilder. "Do you have a problem?"

I step in between them, putting my arms out to create some distance. "That's *enough*, both of you!" Everyone freezes, and Lief even stops pacing. I exhale slowly, then say, "Opie's right. Blaming each other isn't going to help. We'll rest, and in the morning, we'll search. Maybe he's stuck somewhere. Maybe he's just being Slade. Either way, we'll find him. He has to be out there somewhere."

They finally quiet down and agree, then Opie leads

everyone through the gate and straight to medical. My dress is coated in dirt and beyond annoying at this point, but I keep trudging forward.

Harlow.

I am the worst friend in the entire world. I left her there all alone, thinking I was going to get some fresh air outside with Opie, and then all of this happened. After the others meet the doctor and begin their screenings, I tell them I'll catch up with them later and head back to the party to check for her there first.

People are still streaming in and out of the hall, some throwing up in the bushes, and others are plain annoyed by their puking friends. *"Do you smell her anywhere?"* I ask Kaleu.

"Between the vomit, sweat, and all the bodies, that's an impossible ask."

Fair enough. I circle back around to the dance floor area, but only see a few stragglers hanging around. "Should we check her house?"

"I think that would be wise."

We head to the far right of Exion, where the actual houses are. It's around a ten-minute walk from the hall, but with my scraped feet and my maddening dress, it takes me twenty. Her porch light is off, but she could be sleeping. I walk up the gravel drive to her bright-red front door and grab the key she keeps hidden under a black rock.

The door creaks as I open it, and inside is an intact, sleeping Harlow, passed out on her living room couch. She didn't even make it to her bedroom. I grab a blanket off her bed and place it over her before tucking it in. "I'm sorry I didn't come back to make sure you got home safely," I whisper, though the sound of her snores drowns it out. Kaleu checks the rest of the house and gives us the all-clear before we lock it behind us and head back to medical.

Around half of them have made it out so far and are standing outside the building, waiting patiently for the rest. I see Caius and his stag talking to Delilah to the far right. So that's how they made it past the wild *Auryths* without Slade. I'm thankful he came with them. Wilder's made it out, but I don't see Florence anywhere. I walk straight toward him, my mind still swimming with questions about Slade.

"Hey, Len," he says, pulling me into a hug. I'm stiff as a board as he squeezes me. He pulls away and gives me a side-long glance. "What's your deal? You've been acting so strange since we arrived. I thought we were past all that."

I rub my face. "We are. I just … I want to make sure I'm being respectful to Florence and of your relationship."

"Yeah, I don't think giving you a hug is going to throw Florence over the edge. She's pretty cool and actually wants us to be friends, remember?"

I shrug it off and redirect toward Opie, desperate to be as far away from this conversation as possible. "Tell me, Benfield, does every man just swoon at your feet?" Opie says, looking toward Wilder.

"Only the ones with unresolved emotional issues," I counter.

He laughs at that, and I take a seat on one of the benches surrounding the medical center to rest my feet for a moment. "Have you been barefoot this entire time?" he asks.

"Yeah. You took off my heels, remember?"

"Barely. That can't be good. Let me carry you back to your room once the others are cleared." He gives me a boyish smirk.

"Thanks, but I'll pass."

"Why, because you're afraid he'll see?" Another pointed look at Wilder. "I figured that'd be a good thing."

"Because I've had a long enough day without having to play the desperate damsel for your ego." I stand, slow and stiff. "Besides, you don't look all that strong anyway."

The rest file out with the doctor, who gives me a smile. "All-clear. They have one week to decide to go back to Solis or stay here and receive their chips, same as you did."

We lead them to Complex D and introduce them to the ever-happy Corwin, then get them each a room assignment. Once they're settled, we promise to discuss everything in the morning at breakfast and reunite them with the rest of the camp.

I have no doubt Keelan will be desperate to search for Slade, and the more numbers we have, the better. There's no telling what could go wrong inside those Wildwoods.

CHAPTER 41
SLADE

The doctor has not returned today. Instead I'm left with the two assistants and two overly eager guards, still strapped to this bed. On the bright side, the assistants are so determined to provide the doctor with a monumental discovery that they've forgotten to give me the serum that suppresses my power. I'm not stupid enough to try to utilize it to get out again, at least not with the guns pinned on me, but maybe I can send a message.

They're still monitoring my thoughts and memories, and I have no idea if they can track mental conversations, so it needs to be casual. Something only she can decipher to make her understand. A way to tell her that I'm here too, but also a warning so that she gets herself and the others out. At least I don't have to worry about her wanting to rescue me.

I reach out for her tether, nearly releasing a sigh of relief when I find the golden shimmer. *"Hello sunshine,"* I say nonchalantly. The assistants are facing the other direction, chatting away about my emotional response levels or something.

"Slade? Where are you? Are you—"

"Do you remember the day you came up on the platform?" I cut her off, hoping to steer her in the right direction and away from asking questions I can't answer. Not if I want to keep her safe.

"Of course I do."

"You asked me to do something before agreeing to come with me to Camp Solis to make you better. I'm glad you weren't changed without it. I was thinking about Lyric today and how unfortunate it is that she's gone. GG reminds me so much of her. They would have been great friends. I just wanted you to know that. Don't worry about me. I'm safe."

I snap the tether closed behind me, building up my shields quicker than I've ever done before. I hope she'll understand the message I'm trying to convey, though I'm certainly not the best at speaking in code.

The two assistants haven't even noticed their tablet is going off with notifications of my increased brain activity, so I decide to close my eyes and pretend to sleep. She'll figure it out. Hell, she's probably already halfway to the answer. Maybe that's the push of information she needs to connect the dots. Either way, I know she won't sit idly by and watch our people's lives get destroyed by Exion, especially not after already escaping one prison.

If she can figure it out, she'll do what's right. I can count on that. I can count on her. That, or she'll ignore the message entirely since she hates my guts.

The door swings open harshly, and I open my eyes, expecting to see the doctor walk in.

"Hello, Slade. It's good to see you again." I stare in disbelief as Opie walks toward my bed, a twisted smile on his face and his panther by his side. "It's such a shame things had to turn out like this, but there can't be two alphas in the same pack, and I'm much better at this game than you are. You two, leave. *Now.*" The two assistants vacate the room without question.

Great, he has power here.

I have no words. No, scratch that I have words, but none I'd be dumb enough to throw at him while helplessly strapped down to a medical table. I *knew* my gut instinct was right about him, and here he is, working for the enemy. Of course he is.

"Lennon's doing great," he continues, squatting down to get level with my head. "In fact, I just got done visiting her. She loves it when I stop by. Actually, she really loves it when I … well, I'll save you the dirty details. It looks like you're being tortured well enough for now."

"Is that so?" I ask, unable to help myself. "Because I don't really think you're her type. She prefers men who don't reek of desperation." And then, because I really *am* that dumb, I smirk at him.

He punches me square in the jaw, and my mouth immediately fills with the familiar taste of blood. I laugh. I've hurt his feelings with that one. How interesting. "What the hell do you know? I highly doubt you're the person to get advice from on the inner workings of Lennon Benfield's mind. She *knows* you're missing, and she isn't looking for you. What kind of message does that send?"

Damn, my jaw hurts. "It's kind of a coward's move to hit someone when they're literally pinned to a table, don't you think? Untie me, and we can settle this on an even playing field."

"Oh, no, I'm not an idiot. I'm well aware that you're

capable of holding your own against me. And I wouldn't call this cowardly; I'd call it smart," he scoffs.

"So what's your master plan then? Keep me locked in here? Use me as your own personal errand boy? Or are you only keeping me up because you know if I'm out there, you'll lose your shot with her?"

His jaw tenses. "No. You're serving your purpose right now, but once they get all the kinks straightened out practicing on you, we'll kill you off and get started on the rest. There's no reason to keep dead weight around now, is there? As for Lennon, well, you do a great job taking yourself out of the equation without me needing to do it for you." If I could get my hands free, I'd show him what the hell dead weight feels like.

On the bright side, the two assistants didn't give me my meds, and with Opie entering the room and ordering them out, they didn't bother to track my cognitive data either. I can feel the power simmering inside, the heat radiating through my blood, begging to be released. Just a little bit and I could singe these straps, get myself out, and kill him.

I force myself to slow down. Lennon is chipped, and who knows what their intentions are with the rest of our people. If I break out of here, will they really kill all of their potential puppets? Probably not, but they very well may torture her if I escape and can't get to her first. Not to mention he's powerful and hasn't been tortured for weeks like I have.

There are too many what-ifs. Maybe if I keep my cool and don't try anything, they'll leave me in here tonight without my meds. Then I can come up with a better plan, but fighting Opie and two guards only to get so far doesn't seem like the best choice right now.

I slide my eyes toward him. "And what purpose is it that

you serve, Opie? You're nothing but a washed-up exile from the Burrows, just like the rest of us. Why do you think they're giving you power here? You're nothing but a martyr. Someone to blame if things go terribly wrong—a bonded, doing their bidding."

He narrows his eyes at me, his cheeks turning a light pink. "I am the reason they have all of you. I made you make mistakes. I forced the wild *Auryths* closer to your camp. I *took* you from the woods after days of watching, hoping you'd be dumb enough to go after her."

"You're an idiot," I tell him, forcing my body to still as he inches closer.

"You don't know the first thing about me," he seethes.

"I know that Keelan loved you like a son. What will he think of your betrayal?" He's on me quickly, shoving some type of fabric he pulled from his pocket into my mouth. Point taken. Not utilizing the ever-growing power at my fingertips is borderline killing me, but I have to keep my composure for a little longer. The best attacks are the ones they don't see coming.

"I'll enjoy killing you," he continues. "Don't worry, though. I'll take great care of Lennon." I bite down on the fabric in an attempt to distract from the anger.

I'll be damned if he's going to get near her ever again.

His lips tilt into a sadistic grin before he leaves the room, and I do my best to breathe slowly through my nose. Once he's gone, the assistants return, and the girl, Nora, removes the fabric from my mouth.

I won't forget her kind gesture when I burn this entire place to ash.

CHAPTER 42
LENNON

I jolt awake, heart pounding against my ribs. Slade. His voice echoes in my mind, soft as breath and just as impossible. Kaleu startles beside me, claws extending and gripping the blanket in alarm. My eyes dart wildly around the room, searching every shadow, my breath already catching in my throat.

"*Hello, sunshine,*" he says gently. And for just one breathless second, I forget I ever hated that nickname. He's *alive.*

"*Slade? Where are you? Are you—*"

"*Do you remember the day you came up on the platform?*" I pause. His tone. It's all wrong. Careful, deliberate, like he's threading a needle with his words.

"*Of course I do,*" I say slowly. And then he keeps going, throwing out random words and phrases, reminding me of the chip I asked him to remove without actually saying it. Bringing up Lyric, of all people, then this "GG" person. Then … connecting them to Lyric? What does one have to do with the other? And why in the hell would he say it's unfortunate she's gone? He hated her more than I did.

Then that one phrase in particular that I can't get out of my head: *"I'm glad you weren't changed without it."* Did he mean the chip? Why would I be changed *without* it?

Normally I like to pride myself on being reasonably intelligent, but none of this makes any sense to me, and for him to just *happen* to send me a message the day we realize he's missing? Seems slightly odd. Not to mention, he didn't bother explaining where he actually is. Couldn't he have at least given some useful information? If this is some sort of code, he picked the wrong girl. We've been trying to crack Shiloh's for months and have still gotten absolutely nowhere.

"What do you suppose that was?" I ask Kaleu.

"Maybe we should break it down, piece by piece?" he suggests. I reach for my journal and flip to the back, not wanting to mix this with what I have written for Shiloh.

"Right. Okay, he said he did something for me when we arrived on the platform and that he's glad it didn't change me. I'd assume he's talking about the chip."

"I'm inclined to agree."

"Okay, then he goes down the rabbit hole of Lyric and this 'GG' person and how it's unfortunate she died—which I know good and well he doesn't believe—and that the two would be great friends. Who is GG?"

"I believe in some families that is a nickname they utilize for 'grandmother,'" Kaleu says very matter-of-factly.

I rub at my temples. *"Kaleu, why in the world would it make sense for Slade to say his grandma and Lyric are alike? I don't even know if he has a grandma."*

"None of what he said makes any sense. Don't act like I'm unintelligent because he's overtly terrible at sending coded messages."

"Think back to Solis. I can't remember anyone whose name starts with a G, and there were only twenty of us. Could he be hinting at

someone from Solis who moved here with Keelan and the others? Maybe someone left and took him for some reason?"

"We could try asking Keelan. He seems to be one of the few who actually like Slade."

Okay, now we're getting somewhere. I still don't know Keelan all that well, but I believe he genuinely cares about Slade. Not to mention, he'll undoubtedly be the best source for answers to my millions of questions—especially when it comes to identifying someone that may have been in his camp.

Two hours later, I've managed to gather Keelan, Harlow, Opie, Wilder, Florence, and Lief into my tiny apartment.

"You wanna tell us what this is about, or are you going to leave us hanging?" Opie asks, leaning up against my doorframe.

Keelan stands with his arms crossed next to him, Harlow is in the bed with Kaleu and me, Wilder and Florence are sitting on the floor, and Lief is cautiously attempting to talk to Kaleu, who's baring his teeth at him.

"Lief, leave him be," I direct, rolling my eyes. "Slade sent me a message last night. A rather cryptic one, if I'm being honest. I need your help in trying to dissect it."

"He's alive?" Keelan breathes, his eyes watering.

"Yes, but I still don't know where he is. All he said is that he's fine, but something felt off about the entire ordeal." I cross my legs and grab my journal, flipping to the page where I wrote it all down. "He mentioned our first interaction, when he removed my chip from the Burrows, and how he was glad it didn't change me."

I scan the room, bracing myself for the confession the next piece carries. There's no use in hiding it anymore. "There's something I have to explain to the rest of you about how I actually ended up exiled with Shiloh. Lyric Calwyn was the director of post-bonding affairs in the Burrows. When Shiloh got caught and was scheduled for exile, they locked Kaleu and me up too for trying to save him. They agreed to let me say goodbye, but when I saw Shiloh sitting on that platform ... I just couldn't let him go alone."

I swallow hard, trying to eliminate some of the trembling in my voice. "She started counting down, and I panicked, deciding to go up with him. She'd already threatened to use my chip, and there was nothing around that I could use to knock her out. I couldn't risk her calling for help or having time to activate my chip, so I killed her."

Part of me thought confessing my darkest secret would give me a kernel of relief, but it doesn't. Wilder looks at me like he has no idea who I am, his disappointment more than evident. Keelan looks more surprised than anything, and Harlow grips my arm in solidarity.

It's Florence, though, who surprises me. She steps toward me, her eyes brimming with tears. "I can't imagine how impossible that decision must have been for you," she starts, her voice cracking. "I am so sorry you've been carrying this all alone."

It's the sheer kindness in her tone that finally breaks me down. A strangled gasp escapes my lips, and I have to fight to keep from crying. I breathe deeply, reeling myself back in and trying to maintain my composure. Now is not my time to grieve. There are more important things to discuss. "I did what I had to do to keep him safe. I'm not saying I was right, and I carry a lot of guilt because of it. But the point of telling you that is to say that Slade brought her up, and he knew what I did. He said she and someone he nicknamed 'GG' would have gotten along great. Whoever it is, I think he intends to tell me that they're not who we think they are. I don't know if they took him, if they have him now, or what, but that's all I've got."

"Governor Gideon," Opie breathes, and we all turn to look at him.

"What?" I say, confused as ever. "But how would Slade even know who he is? And what does that mean for all of us?"

Keelan steps forward, anger flashing across his face. "It means they have him here, and we're all a bunch of fools."

CHAPTER 43

LENNON

My bedroom is a war zone.

"Why would they take Slade?" I press.

"I don't know. There has to be something we're missing," Keelan adds, pacing. If they're right—if Exion has Slade and has been using us this entire time—then what have they done to Shiloh?

And I handed him over willingly.

I turn toward Harlow, my tone coming out far more accusatory than I intended. "When was the last time you visited Shiloh?"

Her eyes widen, and I can see the hurt on her face. "This morning. He's doing well. Better, even. He has good days and bad, but the visions only occur once in a blue moon now. What does that have to do with anything?"

"Why would they offer to help him? Why do they have Slade? Why did they *force* our damn hands to put these chips in our bodies?" Oh, I'm panicking now. Everything I thought I was doing to help Shiloh, to help our people, to help *myself*, is crashing and burning right before my eyes. My eyes drift between Harlow and Opie, not knowing who I can trust anymore.

"Lennon, breathe," Opie instructs, holding his hands out in front of him. My power is a tangible, burning thing inside my veins, begging to be let out. It's been so long since I've felt the sweet taste of release. "What motive would Harlow have to hurt your brother and betray you? You aren't thinking clearly. Calm down."

Wilder's eyes narrow at him. "You've been the director of this entire thing, Opie. You suggested we come here. *You* brought our people here because you said it was safe. Was this the plan all along? Shower us with food and safety to get us to let our guard down, all while destroying us from the inside out?" His voice rises. "What's your endgame? What are you getting out of it?"

"Shiloh's visions," I say breathlessly. "They're not just visions. They're prophecies. But how would they know that?" I grab the book, my hands fumbling over the numerous tabs and papers sticking out from the worn pages. "This book was from the Burrows. Shiloh took it from the Regime, so how would Exion know anything about it?" Then my eyes land on the intricate symbol etched into the front of the book. The Desmos token, centered in front of three, shrinking triangles. "It was theirs." I breathe, my head swimming as realization hits. "This book belongs to Exion. Or did at some point. This is their symbol, behind the token."

"Slade never wanted to come here," Keelan interjects, grabbing the book. "He doesn't trust anyone but himself. They wanted to eliminate him, because if you eliminate him, the rest will come. And you all did."

I look toward Opie. "Would they have kept him alive?"

"Probably," he says plainly. "They'd need leverage. If he is here, and that's still a big 'if', he'd be in the medical wing. There isn't a prison here, or at least not that I know of. In medical, they can keep him sedated. Keep his magic from becoming a problem."

Suppress his magic, like they did to Kaleu and me in the Burrows. "They can suppress magic? And you never thought to mention that to me?"

He shrugs. "You never would've chosen to stay if I had. They keep it in case a bonded ever turns and tries to wipe them out. Can you blame them?"

No, I can't. I cup my face, my head spinning. "Is there a way to remove the chips?" The thought of them having an off-switch to Kaleu and me is making my skin crawl.

"I don't know," Harlow says.

"Could Opie be wrong?" I ask, directing my attention toward Keelan now. "Is there anyone from Solis who would fit 'GG?' Is there any other possibility? Because once we go down this path, there won't be any turning back."

Keelan shakes his head. "No. None that rings a bell, anyway. Besides, I can't imagine what motive one of our own would have to take him. Not to mention all of the other messages Slade sent you. Gideon is the only thing that makes any sense."

This is so, so bad. We're locked inside a fortress with chips in our arms with no idea what they can do. I should have trusted my gut. I should've never let them put one inside of me. When will I start trusting my instincts?

"Tell them what you have on Shiloh's visions," Kaleu suggests, nuzzling closer to me. *"Work as a team."*

My skin is itching, the frost biting at my fingertips. I breathe slowly, trying to force it away. Not right now. "We need to try understand why they'd want Shiloh."

I grab the book from Keelan and lay it open on the floor, sprawling my notes at their feet:

"When moon meets marrow and blood seals stone, the beast shall wake with fire in its throat."

"Where did she hide it?"

"She had it; I know she did."

"It was hers."

"Opposite sides of the same coin. One above, one below."

"It sees me."

"The gate. Don't open the gate."

"It's the key. It's the key to the gate."

"He's been stuck on those last two for a week," Harlow says. "Lennon and I tried to decode some of the book, but all we found were the same phrases Shiloh's been saying. Plus: 'the unbonded shall bind what cannot be bound.'"

"How long has your brother been having these visions?" Keelan asks, bending down for a closer look.

"Since before we arrived at Solis. He stole this book because he saw it in his visions. That's why they exiled him."

Keelan looks at me, something like recognition flashing in his eyes. "Your mother was Iris Benfield, wasn't she?" I nod, both confused and perplexed by the question. "Your mother saw the same things. She was a seer. A long-lost gift in the Burrows, wiped out by the Regime for 'security purposes'. Though your mother's visions didn't manifest until she was bonded. Your brother seems to be an exception. Perhaps, without the bond, his mind couldn't handle it."

I'm trembling, my breathing ragged and desperate. Something loud shatters the sky outside, startling us all. Then the rain sounds, hard and relentless as it bashes against the window.

He knew my mother. My mother was a seer, just like Shiloh. She was troubled by the same things he was. Did she really ever get sick? Or did they kill her for becoming a problem?

I'm overwhelmed, drowned by the sadness and confusion taking root in my soul. Here I am once more: the girl who can't control her emotions. But I can't stop it. Not this time.

There's shouting all around me, but I'm frozen in place. Keelan is shaking me, but it's no use; the pure power running through my veins is eating me alive, forcing more and more bitterness into my thoughts to fuel itself. I think Kaleu is trying to calm me, but I can't hear him. Someone is screaming, but I can't tell if it's me or somebody else. All I know is pain, hurt, power, and desperation.

"Get her in the bathtub and turn on cold water, NOW," a voice shouts, but I can't tell who it is. I can't see. I'm stuck inside my own mind, staring into nothingness as my body drains itself of everything I've been holding in. "Breathe, Lennon. You don't want to alert Exion to what's going on, do you? Think of Shiloh." I pause, considering the words. I *am* thinking of Shiloh. Of my mother. Of every decision I've made to get us to this very point. Every stupid, rushed, desperate decision.

My vision returns slightly as I drift my focus away from the power and onto Kaleu. I'm no longer sitting on the floor. Someone is carrying me. I'm set gently into a bathtub, and two cold hands grip the sides of my head firmly. "You need to breathe," Wilder tells me. I'm so, so tired. So close to nothingness, I can almost taste it. If I can get there, I won't have to remember it all: Wilder, my mother, my father, Shiloh, the torture, the pain, the killing.

It's all washing over me in waves of misery.

Freezing cold water drenches me, and something in my reality shifts as I'm snapped back to the present. Wilder stands over me, drenched in sweat, his face bright red and ... terrified. I can't remember anything since being on the floor, everyone surrounding the book. I scan the bathroom frantically. Kaleu nuzzles my hand with his snout, whining softly.

"You're okay, Lennon. You're safe," Keelan says calmly, kneeling beside the tub. "This happened to Slade more than once, and cold water usually does the trick." My clothes are soaking wet and clinging to me like a second skin. It's suffocating.

"What happened?" I ask, each word a struggle to get out.

"If I understand it correctly, your emotions are tied to the amount of magic running through your veins. When your feelings get out of control, so does your power. It's a blessing and a curse, I'd imagine." He gently brushes a clump of wet hair out of my face with genuine concern.

I find myself oddly envious that Shiloh inherited my mother's gift of sight—it would have been a way to truly be *connected* to her. Then again, that very thing drove him mad, so it feels a little insensitive to wish for such a thing.

Knowing what I do about the Regime, I have little doubt that they killed her. They don't exile bonded; that's what they told me when I tried to save both Wilder and Shiloh. Her "sickness" down below was so fast and undescribed; Shiloh and I didn't even get to say goodbye. One day she was there, and the next she was gone. If she'd made it up, she would've found the others ... right?

Is that why my father tried so hard to drink himself to

death? Did he know the truth behind her visions, her death, but couldn't go against the Regime without risking his children's lives too? He has to know about it; surely he would've noticed them if they were anything like Shiloh's.

My entire body still lingers with the sting of power, and as much as I'd like to fight sleep, it's far stronger than I am right now. "I'm so tired," I tell Keelan.

He loops an arm around me and helps me up. "Let's get you in bed. We can discuss this later."

Harlow offers to help me change, and the rest of them file out. She helps peel off my clothing piece by piece, silent as she works. My body is so exhausted that I can hardly stand without placing a supportive hand on Kaleu.

"I'm sorry," I whisper, swelling with guilt from my accusations.

"You didn't hurt anyone, Lennon," she says softly.

"Not for that. I'm sorry for thinking you'd hurt Shiloh or betray me."

She crouches down with a pair of shorts, signaling for me to place a leg in. "You've been hurt by a lot of people. I don't blame you. I'd never betray you, though. You're my friend."

"I know. And you are mine."

Once I'm dressed and she leaves, I curl into bed with Kaleu and sleep like the dead.

CHAPTER 44
SLADE

The door to my room slams open so hard I swear it cracks, and in walks a highly agitated Opie and his panther.

The doctor looks up from the tablet, stunned, and gives him a confused look. "To what do we owe this pleasure? And can you try opening the door a little softer next time? It's nearly impossible to get them to replace it."

Opie teleports from the door and reappears with a hand around the doctor's throat, suspending him in the air. "Do I have to do everything myself?"

Nora, the female assistant, approaches slowly. "What's going on? What happened?"

Opie's eyes are full of ire as his attention snaps to her, but he releases the doctor, who slams back down on his chair. "What's wrong is that in all of your surveillance and studying, you failed to realize that he can telepathically communicate with Lennon. Now he's sent her into a spiral, and they're trying to figure out what we're doing. I had no intentions of killing them, but you're making that an extremely difficult task to avoid now."

She got my message.

I didn't have enough energy to reach out and tell her about Opie after his visit, though, and now that tiny detail may very well be the death of everyone.

He picks up a syringe and slams it into my arm, eliciting a small groan from my throat. "You think you're so smart, don't you?" he seethes, standing over me. My body is already going limp from the paralytic, but I still force myself to smile, which only fuels his rage. "I'll admit that was a good play. But you missed the fact that she *trusts* me. I know all about your mental rendezvous, and I know about the book. If they come up with a plan, I'll know it before they can carry it out."

I force myself to stay composed. I refuse to let him think he's won something. A laugh escapes, slightly delirious and mostly calculated.

"What the hell are you laughing at?" he yells.

"You underestimate her," I say, my words slightly slurred. "And that will be your downfall. She *always* sees what's under the facade."

He whirls back around to the doctor. "You keep him sedated at *all* times. If he gets any more messages out, I'll let Selene rip you limb from limb. She likes it when her prey struggles." The panther licks her lips, slow and eagerly, to emphasize his point.

Then he storms back out without another word.

The doctor turns slowly and rises, bruises already blooming on his neck. "What have you done? You dare to make me look incompetent? You will pay for this, boy." Then he smiles to himself, that same smile he's worn nearly every time I'm about to endure something particularly abhorrent. "I think it's time to test our theories tomorrow night. Let's see how many different ways we can use you."

"Doctor, I don't think he's—" Nora starts, but he cuts her off.

"He's ready. We have the control, *not* him."

I have no idea what they intend to do to me, but I have an inkling that if I leave this room with them tomorrow night, I won't be returning.

"Prepare the other subject for testing. Take it to the Wildwoods, and prepare for us to meet you out there tomorrow night. Make sure you take the big lights out there; I want to see everything. Do not be late," he directs Silas. "You, Nora, will be with me and our friend here, getting him ready as well. It's going to be an excellent evening."

I nearly choke on my trepidation.

CHAPTER 45

LENNON

Aknock at the door wakes me from the sleep my body craves. I blink, looking out the window to find that it's dark outside. How long have I been asleep? It was only this morning that …

That I found out my mother likely went mad from the same visions Shiloh has, and that Exion's been lying to us this entire time. I can feel our impending downfall breathing down my neck. I'm starting to wonder if we'll ever feel safe again.

I rise, open the door, and find everyone standing outside, eager to enter; I gesture for them to come in and catch the faint scent of food. Harlow smiles, extending a plate stacked with dinner for me, and my mouth waters as I shut the door behind them.

"Back to business, guys," Lief says, and I raise an eyebrow at him. When did he start keeping people on task? He's normally the very reason we're *off* task.

"How are you feeling?" Florence asks, placing a gentle hand on my arm.

"Better. Thanks. Sorry about all of that earlier, guys. I

think my power has been bottled up for so long, it was bound to happen eventually."

"Are you ready to talk?" Keelan questions, taking a seat against the wall. I nod, shoveling forkfuls of food into my mouth. "Okay. Good."

I swallow, grab the cup of water from my nightstand, and wash it down before speaking. "How did you know my mother?"

"Iris was my mentor when I worked in the Burrows. I was sixteen, and I believe you were around nine at the time. She'd have these blackouts. Start saying things I didn't understand. I did my best to coax her down before anyone else noticed, and I never told a soul, but I'll never forget that one line: *'When moon meets marrow and blood seals stone, the beast shall wake with a fire in its throat.'* It's haunted me for years."

It's surreal to talk about Mom this way. "It haunts me, too," I tell him, suddenly losing my appetite. "Did you ever figure out what it meant?"

"Only bits and pieces from what I found in the archives. They kept most of the books created before the war under lock and key, but it seemed to be from an old fable. Something about a gate, which would make sense based on Shiloh's last vision. At the time, I had no idea it was a prophecy. I was just a kid, and seers weren't spoken of in the Burrows. It wasn't until I met Sage, one of the earliest members of Solis, that I realized what was happening to your mother. She'd been friends with someone very similar when she was a child.

"I tried to figure out what your mother's words for some time, but with no resources to help, I was at a loss, and eventually the memory faded from my mind as I turned my attention towards the exiles that were arriving each year. Then you arrived."

A silence falls over the room, suffocating me.

"Do you know what happened to her?" I finally ask, though I'm not sure I want to know. In some ways, it's easier to believe she got sick than to think that the Regime killed her. Then again, I need to know who my enemies really are.

"No. I always just assumed she lost her mind from the visions. All they ever told me was that she got sick." He winces like the words hurt.

"So all we know so far is that there's a gate and something behind it?" Wilder concludes, sitting up against the wall, Florence leaning on his chest.

"They killed her. They must have," I breathe. Everyone stares at me quietly.

"But why would they kill her and not Shiloh?" Wilder presses. "Isn't it possible she made it to the ground?"

"Let's think this through," Florence interjects. "Why would the Regime keep the book your brother stole locked up? And why did they *exile* him for stealing it? Seems a bit excessive to me."

"Did the Regime know Shiloh was having visions?" Keelan ask.

I shake my head. "No. Or at least I don't think they did."

He crosses his arms. "Maybe they thought your mother left him clues and that's why he stole the book. If they didn't know he was a Seer, exile might have seemed like a more humane option."

My brain is in overdrive. I grab my journal again and stare at the Desmos token on the front of the book, then flip back to the pages of Shiloh's fractured phrases. *It's the key. It's the key to the gate.*

"It's about the Desmos token," I say, not caring if it sounds insane. Everything about this is insane, anyway. "Think about it. The Regime threw the symbol in our face all the time, but never actually showed it to us. Shiloh's visions told him to steal the book on it, and it's consistently been the only thing that doesn't make sense and that we can't connect to the rest of the visions. All this time, we thought we had to translate the words to crack the code, but what if we had the answer right in front of our faces all along? What if the token is the key?"

"That tracks," Opie adds, moving to sit beside me on the ground. "Do you think it's still in the Burrows? Or would they have moved it somewhere else, somewhere safe?"

I hadn't really thought *that* far ahead. "I feel like they'd want to keep it close if they've put this much effort into hiding it. Not to mention we still aren't sure if they know the ground is survivable, so I don't know where else they would've hidden it."

"Shiloh said: '*Where did she hide it? She had it; I know she did. It was hers,*'" Harlow interjects. "I think he's telling us someone took the token and hid it somewhere, if we're on the right path of it being the key."

"So why does Exion want the key? What is hidden behind this gate?" I press. "That's the real question. If they're willing to kidnap Slade and use Shiloh to get what they want, it's got to be important. They must want to open it."

"We don't know that," Opie interjects, leaning back on his forearms. "What if the Regime wants to open it, and Exion wants to keep it closed? What if there's something behind the gate that could bring peace, and the Regime doesn't want that? How can we be certain they're inherently bad here?

How can you know which side to be on when we don't even know what each side wants?"

My eyes find Harlow. "I'm not saying they're all bad, but Slade said Gideon is. I don't take that warning lightly. And regardless of the gate situation, they've had Slade here for a month and haven't said a word to us about it. There's a reason for that."

"Slade's also not the best source of information," Opie replies, and Keelan tenses. "Not to mention Chancellor Blane isn't an exceptional human being, either. How do you know Slade isn't making all of this up to get back at you guys for leaving him? Or what if he did something to get himself locked up that we don't know about?"

"Opie, you can dislike Slade all you want, but if he's being kept locked away from all of us, it can't be good. He sent Lennon that message for a reason. I trust him." Something about the way Keelan defends Slade strengthens my resolve.

"I trust him, too," I say, surprised by the certainty in my voice. "He might be an arrogant prick, and he certainly makes poor decisions, but he's never lied to me. If he says Gideon is bad news, then he is. And we all know Blane is."

"Agreed," Wilder chimes in.

"I trust Slade with my life," Lief adds, earning a few sideways stares from around the room.

"Glad that's settled. Now what?" I say. "The Regime isn't going to let us back in without a fight, and even if we do get in, I highly doubt they'll willingly offer up any information they have regarding the prophecy. Lest we forget they kept this book locked away for over a hundred years and *killed* people to protect their secret. Plus, we won't be able to leave Exion peacefully once we take Slade and Shiloh."

"Right now, it seems like the Regime might be our best

bet," Wilder throws out, adding to the never-ending list of decisions. "We don't know what's behind this 'gate', but if it's a weapon and Exion wants it open, it could start another war. We know the Burrows wants to keep it closed, so until we know more, I'd say they're the safer option. I've been wrong before, though."

I consider everything before deciding. "I say we break into the medical wing, grab Shiloh and Slade, and force our way back into the Burrows. Once we get them out, we're going to need somewhere besides Solis to hide. I have no doubt that Exion will come for us if they're who we think they are. And even if they're not, we're undoubtedly going to cause some chaos getting our people out."

"I can steal weapons," Harlow practically whispers, and my head pivots toward her. She shrugs. "It's probably best we go armed with guns *and* magic."

"You're going to come with us?" I breathe.

"I don't know if there's a right side here, but I do know if we find the token first, we can decide what to do with it and make sure it doesn't end up in the wrong hands. Plus I've always wanted to see the Burrows."

I give her a small smile, grateful to have her by my side. "And you, Opie?"

"Considering I'm to blame for dragging everyone into this in the first place? Absolutely. Let's give 'em hell."

CHAPTER 46

LENNON

We formulate a plan quickly: break into medical, grab Slade and Shiloh, and get the hell out of Exion and down to the Burrows as quickly as possible. The details, however, haven't been quite hashed out yet. As it turns out, putting a bunch of people into one room and having them come to the same conclusion is a nearly impossible feat.

"Should we split up? Half of us go after Shiloh, the other half after Slade?" I ask, doing my best to ignore the headache throbbing at my temples.

"How can we be sure that Slade is in medical?" Keelan argues.

"We can't be sure, but what other choice do we have? Every day we don't do something is another day those two are locked up having who knows what done to them. We need to get them out. *Tomorrow.*"

They all stare at me like they're waiting for further instruction, but thankfully Opie interjects. "Harlow and I can retrieve Shiloh, weapons, and a crawler to transport us to the platform. No one will blink an eye if we walk in there. She's already been visiting him, and I can pretty much go where I want without question. The rest of you should go for Slade. He'll probably be guarded, so you'll need the numbers."

I consider this, thinking about all the ways it could go wrong. Most of all, I don't like the idea of entrusting anyone but myself with Shiloh's life—not even my friends. "I need to be the one to get Shiloh. I need to know he's safe. Not that I think you two won't protect him, but he's *my* brother."

"Lennon," Harlow starts. "We don't know if seeing you will trigger him. It might be best to get him out seamlessly. If seeing you restarts his visions, it'll draw attention to us. I know that hurts to hear, but it's the easiest way to ensure we all get out safely."

I take a steadying breath. "Okay. I know you're right. Just please …" My eyes slide to both of them. "Keep him safe."

"I'll protect him with my life," Opie declares.

"What do we do about the rest of our people?" I ask, looking to Keelan for an answer.

"I think it's best they remain oblivious for now. Most of them agree with Exion's ways, and there's no way we can get nearly a thousand of them out without notice."

"You don't think Exion will take it out on them? What about Caius?"

His face falls. "I don't know, but it's a risk we have to take. If we're right and we don't get to the Burrows, we risk either side using the token for their own agendas. Plus, Caius can protect them if it comes to that. I'll fill him in before we go." So we risk a thousand of our people dying if we're wrong. Fantastic.

"What about the guards at the gate?" I ask. "How will we get through once we have them?"

"There's a hole in the gate behind the medical building. We used it when we were kids to take unauthorized excursions," Harlow says, smiling as if reminiscing on those very trips. "They never fixed it. I don't know if the higher-ups even know about it, but I'll check again tomorrow morning to make sure it's still there."

So it's settled. We're doing this.

We agree to meet back here tomorrow night at seven, and everyone files back out to their respective rooms. I can hardly sleep with all my tossing and turning, considering the very real possibility that we won't all make it out of this alive. Exion is strong. They have guns and technology we can only *begin* to imagine. They've fought against magic wielders before, and I have little doubt they've created tools strong enough to destroy us should they choose to.

But all we have to do is get them and *run*. We aren't trying to wage a full-on war right now, and I can only hope that Exion doesn't use this as an excuse to attack our remaining people. They're innocent, and yet I've seen innocent lives taken for far less than what we're about to do.

The next morning, we go through the motions: breakfast, lunch, and a quick trip to the gardens. I stash some extra rolls in my bag, just in case we need them. Everything seems to be going according to plan: Harlow checked the fence, and the hole is still there; so far, we haven't been suspected of anything; everything seems calm.

At least for now.

When night falls, we pack our bags and reconvene back in my room, each of us carrying a bag with our essentials and what supplies we can afford to carry. Wilder, Florence, and I are still waiting on Keelan, but Opie and Harlow take off ahead of us to get cleared for their "visit" with Shiloh. It's better we separate, anyway. Big groups are easier to spot. I hug them both tightly, wish them luck, and hope this works out the way we planned. If it doesn't, this could be the last time we see one another.

Thirty minutes later, Keelan bursts through my door, sweat beading on his forehead, and a look of pure panic creasing his brows. "We have a problem."

"What? What happened?" I ask, instantly feeling nauseous. We haven't even started, and things are going wrong. This was a terrible, stupid idea.

"I overheard some guards talking, and one said they'd be busy tonight because she and another guard are needed in the woods."

My brows knit together. "For what? Why would they take guards into the woods?"

"They said there was some sort of 'experiment' going on, and they had to be there to protect the doctor if things went awry. I think they're taking Slade, but I don't know why."

Okay, that changes things, but at least he'll already be outside the gate, so that's one less obstacle we have to worry about. And now we know how many guards are with him. "Keelan, breathe," I tell him, shocked that I'm somehow the one coaching others to calm down. "This is a good thing. He's in the woods, alone and isolated from the rest of the camp. We can get him from there and not have to worry about causing a scene here. Now let's get going. Opie and Harlow already have a thirty-minute head start."

We walk casually through the city, doing our best to seem like anything but a group of delinquents looking to break out. Lief has no qualms with this, chatting away with any one of us that will listen and whistling. Once we reach the medical building, I shush him and motion for them to stick to the walls. They have cameras everywhere, but the fewer that see us, the better. Once we're out, we'll run like hell to find Slade.

When we reach the gate, I realize we have our first issue. It's been sealed. At first I think we must be at the wrong spot, but after checking every possible avenue, I come to the conclusion that Exion is on to us, which means we have even less time than we thought. I let my emotions flood my mind, then turn them into power. I work on freezing a space large enough for us to fit through, then begin kicking it with everything I've got, which isn't much.

Keelan slams his foot into it, and the piece crumbles. We slide through one by one, desperate to get as far away from Exion as possible and locate Slade. Kaleu picks up his scent immediately and takes off, all of us hot on his trail.

I can see lights shining through the trees in the same clearing where Harlow found Shiloh and me. *They have an Auryth positioned for slaughter. A wolf,"* Kaleu breathes, and my heart sinks.

"Vesper?"

"No. It's an adolescent. She's terrified. I'm trying to tell her we're coming. We've got to move, now." The despair in his voice nearly brings me to my knees.

"Don't worry, little wolf," he says, but I don't know if he's talking to me or the one preparing to die.

CHAPTER 47
SLADE

The doctor forces me to walk through the woods. Not by gunpoint. Not by dragging me. No. He forces me through the tablet in his hands.

My body obeys every command he enters, down to the exact angle of my step. My arms swing naturally; my breathing is steady. On the outside, I'm the picture of calm. But inside, my heartbeat is thrashing against my ribs like a dying thing, begging to be released from the cage of my chest.

Because I know what's waiting for me out here.

They called it a *subject*. Like it's nothing. Like it's disposable. Like it's not alive.

I wish they'd just kill me already. There's mercy in an ending. But this? Forcing me to be the weapon? To move against my will while my mind screams at every step? It's a different kind of torture. One that comes in slow, methodical pieces. One where I'm still breathing despite already being dead.

The doctor walks beside me, whistling some upbeat tune. It's light, cheery, and grotesquely out of place. He's grinning.

He *likes* this. He *wants* me to break, and I just might. Silas walks beside him, looking just as gleeful. Nora, on the other hand, doesn't make a sound. Her eyes stay locked ahead, lips drawn tight, hands clenched at her sides. At least I'm not the only one despising every second of this.

We reach a clearing with massive lights positioned in a perfect circle, pouring so much artificial daylight into the space that I keep forgetting it's night. My feet stop walking, and my head tilts up on its own. I don't want to look, but the command overrides me.

And then I see it.

A wolf.

Half of me desperately wants it to be Vesper, if only to lay eyes on her and know she's okay. The other half knows what they brought me here for and can only hope that it's not. As we grow closer, the picture becomes much clearer.

It isn't Vesper or even Kaleu. It's smaller. Light brown. Frantic. Tied to a stake in the ground. It turns in desperate circles, paws skidding in the dirt, a snarl stuck in its throat. It's not so much vicious as it is terrified. Its ears are pinned flat against its skull, and its eyes dart from face to face like it's trying to find someone, anyone, who might save it.

But there's no one. Only me. Or at least the puppet version.

Beside me, Nora gasps, then covers her mouth as if realizing her perfect-assistant act is shattering. The doctor glares at her, displeased, then back at me. "You are going to kill the wolf."

"He can't—" Nora starts, but the doctor whirls on her, cutting her off.

"He will do whatever *I* tell him to do. That's the point."

No.

The word screams through my head, over and over, deafening. No, no, *no*. Not this. Anything but this. Kill me. Rip my spine from my body and burn what's left. But don't make me do this.

One foot lifts and shifts forward, then the other. Each inch brings me closer and closer to its small body, and all I can do is hope it's strong enough to take me out first. *"Please,"* I beg, trying to tether mentally, but I don't know if it works. Vesper always handled that part.

"Please," I say out loud, not caring if they listen. "You have to kill me first; I can't stop this." It crouches lower, teeth bared. Their usage of the magic suppressor instead of the paralytic means I can speak, which is at least a small win.

"Now, now. There's no need for all of that, Slade. She's been starved for a week and locked in a cage her entire life. There's no way she'll be a threat to you."

My throat tightens. Is this what they've been doing to Vesper? Is she locked in a cage somewhere, alone and hungry? Anger surges, and I hear the doctor "woo" behind me. "Don't stop on my account. The more emotion, the better!"

I'm giving him ammunition, and he knows it. That's why they chose this scenario to test their big theory on. How could I stand here and feel nothing? How could I not want to murder the doctor and every single person who's had a hand in setting this up?

My hand extends before me, right toward the now-shaking wolf. I try to fight it. I choke down the emotion, try to bottle it up inside with a lock and key, but it does me no good. My power surges through my body, tingling with the desperation for release. Over a month of pent-up magic; if she's in my line of fire, there will be no saving her.

I'm screaming: screaming at the little wolf, screaming at the doctor, screaming at myself. Please, please, *please*.

My flames shoot out of my hand, straight for her little body, which is now curled into a ball as she tries to appear smaller. "MOVE!" I scream, but she doesn't even lift her head. I can't close my eyes to prevent myself from seeing it. That's a luxury I'm not privy to.

Suddenly, my flames snuff out, sending curling plumes of smoke into the air. I can see a figure moving toward the wolf through the smoke, and then the little wolf runs toward my right, straight for the woods. Someone must have cut it loose. I can't move my head to see, but I don't need to. There's only one person who has magic strong enough to counter mine.

Lennon.

The moment my eyes meet hers, my hands begin to rise, and though I can't stop them, I can feel the power pulsing through my veins, determined to take her out. The doctor laughs from behind me, and I realize what he's about to make me do.

"I can't stop this," I tell her.

"I know," she says softly, kindly.

"He's control—" I'm cut off by my own black flame erupting toward her like a storm, relentless and unrestrained.

She raises both hands and creates a massive sheet of rain, slamming it up like a shield just as the flames reach her. It hisses as my black flames crash into it, steam exploding outward in a choking white cloud. I can't even cough. My body keeps moving forward, hands pushing harder, feeding the fire with everything in me.

Her jaw clenches as she focuses. Lightning flickers across her skin, bright veins sparking down her arms. She forces the rain forward in a violent spray, and the impact shoves me back a step, only for my shadows to lash out behind me, anchoring me in place. I don't command them. I don't want this. And still they move, twisting around my legs like chains and digging into the ground.

"Slade, you have to fight it!" she shouts through the smoke, her voice raw. I can't. I can't fight this. I'm too tired. Too weak. It would be so much easier if she'd just *kill me*.

She slams her foot into the earth. Ice erupts in jagged spears, ripping up through the dirt and spearing toward me in a deadly crown. She's trying to box me in, but my flames melt through most of them while others sink into the ground.

"You're going to have to kill me, sunshine. It's the only way."

"You're not getting off that easy," she says sarcastically, then slams an electric bolt in my direction. She's fast—too fast, and I hit the ground, my body convulsing as the electricity thrums through me.

"Get up!" the doctor screams, and I feel my body instantly rise despite the twitching. A shadow extends out of me, a phantom hand that reaches for her throat.

No, no, *no*.

She isn't strong enough to fight it off. Whatever energy she had, it's depleting quickly. The shadow slips around her throat and yanks her into the air. Her hands claw at it, desperate for release. Her feet kick, and a horrific gargling noise escapes her mouth as she stares at me with watery eyes. I'm watching the life drain out of her ounce by ounce, and there's nothing I can do to stop it.

Then, like the wave of beautiful chaos she is, her hand opens and closes, and an icicle slams through my shoulder. I smile as I watch the shadow release her and breathe a sigh of relief when she hits the ground, gasping for air. My vision blurs, and as my body begins to fall, I memorize every inch of her face. A hand falls to my wound, and when I pull it back to look, I realize how much blood there truly is.

My knees hit the ground, and even the doctor can't make me get up this time. *"Thank you,"* I whisper into her mind.

She's up before my eyes can close, throwing another icicle at someone behind me. I hear a body hit the ground with a heavy thud, but I can't turn to see who it is. I hope it's the doctor.

She kneels beside me and puts pressure on my wound. This would be a good way to go—her face being the last thing I see. I'd be happy with that, I think. *"I told you that you weren't going easy on me in training. I really am that good,"* she says, and a breathless laugh escapes my lips.

"You, assistant lady, get over here and help me now," Lennon yells sternly, and Nora is instantly at my side with a little med kit. Where she got it from, I have no idea, but she begins working on my wound.

"I'm so sorry," she says, her eyes glassy. "This isn't how things were supposed to go." I nod at her, a gentle acceptance of her apology, and she props me up to get a better angle on the wound. "I've destroyed the tablet," she continues, now looking at Lennon. "So he should regain control soon. It looks like this is a clean wound, in one end and out the other. Essentially, he'll live and this medpatch should make him feel a hell of a lot better. It won't heal him completely, but enough where he can walk and not be in excruciating pain."

Lennon smiles over me. "Hear that? You're stuck with us." She brushes my hair off my forehead. "And you really do need a haircut."

I'm not going to die. I'm not going to die, and she saved me. My eyes drift to her throat, where bruises are beginning to form in the shape of red, swollen fingerprints. *"I'm so sorry."*

"It wasn't you, so you have nothing to apologize for." She leans down and kisses me softly on the forehead, and it seems to ease the pain for a moment.

Nora slams the medpatch into my wound with a little more force than I feel is necessary, eliciting a scream from my lips. Once she's finished, though, the pain immediately lessens, and I'm able to sit up.

Keelan, Lief, Wilder, and Florence are all behind me, staring wide-eyed at the three of us. My eyes move back to Lennon's face, soaking in the sight of her alive and well. "You got my message?"

"I got your message," she replies, a grin plastered to her face.

"Where's the little wolf?" I ask, looking around.

"She took off into the woods. Can't say I blame her. She's okay, though. You didn't hurt her. I promise," she assures me.

The doctor remains motionless on the ground, now nothing but a corpse with a melting icicle lodged in his throat. Lennon catches my line of sight. "I was wrong. Not every life is worth saving."

The woods rustle to my right, and I turn, hoping to see the little wolf returning. Instead I find Silas, beelining it towards Exion, desperate to get away from us. "Not so fast," Keelan says coldly, sprinting through the woods after him. A few moments later, he returns, dragging Silas by his legs as he screams and thrashes.

"What do you want to do with him?" Keelan asks me as I force myself onto my feet. I'm still stiff, both from the wound and being controlled, but the more I move, the more comfortable I get in my own skin.

"Where is my wolf?" I ask Silas as Keelan pins him with a foot.

His mouth is a bloody mess, that sickening smile still stuck on his face. "Even if you were to get to her, it'd be too late. We defanged her a long time ago."

Before I can lift a finger, Kaleu is on him, ripping his throat out with a viciousness I hadn't realized he had.

Silas's screams become silent, and his body goes still. Kaleu is covered in blood but looks more triumphant than ever. *"I will not accept the mistreatment of her or any Auryths,"* he says plainly, a growl still on his lips.

"He was lying," Nora interjects. "I know where she is. I'll take you to her."

"I have to go," I tell Lennon, not wanting to leave her again but also desperate to get Vesper back. "Where's Shiloh?"

"Opie and Harlow are retrieving him now and grabbing weapons. Oh, and a crawler. They're supposed to meet us right before the mist section of the forest. You two should have plenty of time to get to Vesper, though. Even if we don't, they'll wait on us. We're not leaving without you."

My fist clenches. "Lennon, we need to get back there *now*. Opie's not on our side. He's the one who brought me to Exion. He's with them."

CHAPTER 48

LENNON

I'm beginning to wonder if I'll ever grow out of this naive, overly trusting version of myself. Mistake after mistake. Lie after lie. Terrible choice after terrible choice. Deceiving friendship after deceiving friendship.

Opie betrayed me, and I hadn't the slightest idea that it was coming. Now he has not only Shiloh, but Harlow, too. That is, if she's actually on our side. Clearly, I can't be trusted as a good judge of character, so there's no way to tell right now.

I'm running as fast as my legs can carry me, desperate to get there before it's too late. Not to mention Vesper. How did I not consider they'd separate her and Slade?

Keelan and Florence stayed behind. The fewer bodies we have moving through the city, the better. And if we don't come back, we still have a few that can go down to the Burrows and keep the plan rolling.

So that leaves Kaleu and me, Lief, Nora, Wilder, and Slade. In other words, the last group I would've ever expected. Wilder and I steer the others toward the gate opening I created and barrel through. We try to take a little extra caution once inside, sneaking back around the side of the building before letting ourselves inside the medical wing.

It's so quiet. Two bodies are lying in the hall, both wearing white coats. Not Harlow or Shiloh. Not Vesper. Not Opie, either. Nora begins giving orders. "Slade, you and Lief come this way. This is where they keep the *Auryths*. Lennon, the psychological ward is to the left." My body tenses at the plural use of the word *Auryth*. How many do they have here, locked up for their little "experiments"? What kind of things have they put them through?

Slade seems to understand my unspoken words and says, "I'll get them *all* out." Then they're off, veering right while Wilder, Kaleu, and I head to the left.

We turn down three corridors before Kaleu catches Shiloh's scent, and then we're running again as he tracks it. We skid to a stop in front of a massive black door with a silver handle, and I cautiously turn it, extending my hand in front of me in preparation for a fight.

Inside Opie, Harlow, and Shiloh are surrounded, a total of eight guards closing in on them with weapons drawn. To my surprise, Opie stands in front of the pair, shielding them while Selene shows her fangs to any guard that gets too close. I reach for my ice, funneling it out toward the first two to my left while Wilder knocks one on the right to the ground and takes his gun.

It's a bloodbath. My frost isn't just freezing skin—it's creating razor-sharp icicles that slide through muscle and bone with grace, dropping the guards to their knees in puddles of their own blood. Wilder attempts to shoot one of the others, but his shot goes high, and the guard returns fire, catching him right in the leg. He screams out, and my head swings toward him in a panic as he falls.

"*Focus,*" Kaleu demands, and I try to level back out. Wilder is down and there are three guards left standing.

The barrel of a gun swings towards Shiloh, and time itself halts. All I can see is a seven-year-old boy running through the Burrows with a stick in his hand and a smile that lights up my world. He's my everything. I would do *anything* for him. Kill, steal, lie. Not everyone is worth saving, but some people are worth killing for.

People like Shiloh.

A scream rips past my throat as my magic expands past the confines of my body in a blast so big it almost brings me to my knees. Two of the three guards drop with a sickening thud as my icicles tear through their chests and just as I reach for the third, she takes aim.

And fires.

Bullets are shockingly fast, much faster than my magic can comprehend. I breathe, accepting that this is where it ends. I've had a good run—at least the others will get out of here, and Slade is safe. He and Nora will find Vesper, they'll get out, and they'll get to the Burrows. They'll protect my brother. I've done my part.

But bullets are no match for *his* magic.

Opie teleports across the room, throwing himself in front of me without hesitation. The guard stares, dumbfounded, and Harlow takes the opportunity to pick up another weapon and shoot her down.

I catch him as blood spews out of his mouth with each breath, trickling down his chin in a steady stream. He's heavy, but I cradle his head as his body goes down. He gives me that mischievous smile, and I brush a strand of hair from his face.

"Why would you do that?" I say as my tears mix with the blood coating his cheek.

"Y-you were th-the on-only friend I've ever had," he gets out, a peaceful smile on his lips, but I know what the words really mean. They mean goodbye. His breathing is shaky, each breath slower than the last, and his eyes blink in slow motion as he struggles to keep them open. The bullet went right through his chest. A true kill shot.

"I tried to fight it," he adds breathlessly.

I press my lips to his forehead tenderly, the tears falling heavier now. "Thank you."

Selene lets out a horrific moan, and I hear her hit the ground next. Shiloh walks to her, lifts her off the ground, and places her gently between Opie's legs. We crowd around the two of them, hugging them tightly as they take their final breaths, sobbing desperately.

When all is quiet and their hearts are no longer beating, I vomit on the floor.

CHAPTER 49
SLADE

Nora is running her heart out, and it still isn't fast enough. What if Opie's done something to Vesper? What if the doctor did before I left? And who knows what they've put her through over the last month. The thought makes my head spin.

I nearly slam into the back of Nora as she skids to a halt, peeking around a corner. She points, and I slide my head around to see what it is. A guard stands posted outside the door, half asleep. I launch a shadow toward him and quickly, quietly, snap his neck. There is no room for hesitation today. We have suffered enough, she and I. They deserve to suffer a little, too.

His massive keychain hangs out of his pocket, holding more than thirty keys. I look at the door, down at the keys, and then at Nora.

"Screw this." I melt the lock off and slam the door open, anger rushing through my veins as I take in the scene on the other side.

The smell hits me first: urine, feces, unwashed bodies,

and *death* suffocate my nostrils. There are more than a hundred cages, stacked on top of one another from floor to ceiling. Every *Auryth* looks emaciated and trembles at the sight of me.

A familiar whimper sounds from my right, and I run towards it. She lies curled up in the back of her cage, her coat so dark it'd be difficult to place her if it weren't for those amber eyes staring back at me. "Ves," I say, dropping to my knees. "I've got you." Sorrow and rage fill my veins, and I let it build in the form of power.

I grab the lock with a flamed hand, letting it melt into nothing in my palm and yank open the door before reaching for her.

She instantly snaps at my hand. "It's me, Ves. It's Slade." Her head lowers to the floor of the cage, and I try again, pressing my hand to her head just like I did the first day we met. This time, she lets me pull her out.

The feeling of her in my arms, so frail and light, devastates me. She looks like she hasn't eaten in weeks, and her fur is matted with things I don't even want to imagine. Her eyes barely stay open, and she's certainly too weak to stand. Nora and Lief are running around, doing their best to open cages using the dead guard's keys and trying to coax terrified *Auryths* to safety.

I look at all the cages, at the body in the hall, at the fear and desperation weighing heavily on every *Auryth* in this room. Closing my eyes, I allow the pool of rage inside my chest to flood my magic. Shadows pour out of me without even needing to extend a hand, then separate into hundreds of strands, each becoming no larger than a key. Focusing my mind, I push one strand into every lock, then twist and unlock every damn cage in the room simultaneously.

"Woah," Lief says, staring dumbfounded at me as I open my eyes. "I didn't know you could do that."

A sigh of relief leaves my lips. "Neither did I."

We get to work coaxing the animals out of their cages, most still too afraid to leave the safe corner of the only home they've ever known. That, or too afraid that our hands will be no different than the cruel ones they've become accustomed to. "We're not going to hurt you, I promise," Lief tells one of them, talking in a soft, high-pitched voice. "No one is going to hurt you ever again." I give them a minute, hoping they'll get as many out as they can before we have to go.

Another guard comes barreling around the corner, spots us, and raises his weapon. Without hesitation, Nora reaches into her pocket, pulls out a knife, and slings it straight into the guard's neck. It sticks with perfect accuracy, spraying blood all over the doorframe and floor.

Lief stares at her in disbelief, his arm still inside a cage. "You are a fascinating woman," he breathes. She rolls her eyes and returns her attention to the *Auryths*.

"We need to go, guys. We can try to get them to follow us and into the woods, but if we stay any longer, we risk getting caught," I tell them.

Lief pulls an injured, red fox from the back of an upper kennel, its front leg clearly mangled. "Not all of them are … alive. A lot of them are injured. I'll carry as many as I can."

I reach for that tether, needing to know my other girl is okay, too. *"Lennon, check-in time. Are you okay? Did you find Shiloh?"*

"Yes."

"Is everyone okay?"

"We'll meet you at the clearing." She does not sound well, but at least she's alive. Clearly avoiding the question about

everyone being okay, but I don't have time to ponder that. We need to go, and we need to go now.

An alarm screeches overhead, and all of the animals shrink back into their cells. "You guys have to come with us! Please! We'll take you to safety, to the woods!" Lief begs, grabbing a small turtle and rabbit, while still clinging to the fox. I think back to the little wolf in the forest. This must be where she was from.

"Can you hear me inside that head of yours, Ves?"

"I'm here." The sound of her voice feels like home, and oh, how I've missed it.

"I know you're beyond exhausted, but any chance you can give your furry—and not-furry—friends some direction to follow us? If they stay here, they'll be massacred."

She doesn't say anything else, but a minute later, *Auryths* of all species funnel out by the masses, waiting for our instruction. The more seriously injured ones that can't walk are carried by one of us, and the rest limp alongside as we race for the gate with what must be one hundred *Auryths* in tow.

CHAPTER 50

LENNON

My hands are still coated in his blood.

I can't speak. Can't move. Can't leave him here. I don't understand why he did what he did, but he saved me. I can't just leave his body here.

A strangled cry from behind me finally snaps me back to reality. Wilder.

I snap around to see him gripping his thigh, blood spilling between his fingers. I stumble to one of the fallen guards, unhook the belt from his waist with trembling hands, and cinch it tight around his leg. "This'll slow the bleeding. It's not great, but it's something. Can you walk?"

He gives me a tight grimace, trying to get up. "Kind of?" It's a lie. He's shaking. He won't last long on foot.

Shiloh loops an arm underneath his shoulder and takes some of the tension off. He and I haven't spoken since we arrived in Exion. They kept saying seeing me would trigger him, but he seems perfectly fine to me. Another one of their lies? Or is he healed? What have they put him through?

I turn back to Opie one last time and lean down, brushing

my fingers across his eyelids to close them. "You didn't have to save me," I whisper. "But you did. I will never forget that."

No one says anything as I stand. There's nothing left *to* say.

We move fast through the corridors, guns now strapped to every one of our sides. I glance over my shoulder more times than I can count, expecting Exion's soldiers to come storming through the hallways any second.

We're not going to make it. Not like this. "Any chance we can still get a crawler?" I ask Harlow, my voice hushed. If we have to run, they'll hunt us like animals.

"Yes," she says. "But we need to move *now*." She leads us back into the open city, and every step we take feels like a gun pressing into the back of my skull. The lights are too bright, the air too loud. I flinch at every sound, desperate to cling to the shadows of night.

She stops in front of a steel-paneled building. "Stay here. If I don't come back in five minutes—"

"Don't finish that sentence," I cut in. "You're coming back." Her eyes flick to me with something like sorrow. Then she slips inside.

We wait, and every second drags my mind deeper into darkness. I hear Wilder stifle a groan. I keep replaying Opie's voice in my head, the way it cracked around the word friend. Why would someone like him die for someone like me? Was our friendship really all a lie, or did he mean it? What am I missing?

What did he mean by "I tried to fight it?"

A side panel slides open to our right, and a crawler backs out slowly. We squeeze our bodies up against the siding, doing our best to stay out of sight.

"Get in," Harlow whispers through the open window. We

scramble in, pressing ourselves down to the floor. Harlow tosses a tarp over us, then climbs back into the front.

My heartbeat pounds in my ears as the crawler jerks to a stop. "Patrol?" a voice asks. It must be one of the guards at the gate station, though I'm not risking a peek to confirm.

Harlow doesn't miss a beat. "Alarm's going off near the medical wing. They sent me to loop the fence perimeter, see if anyone got out. All other guards were called to the scene."

A beat of silence. Then I hear the gate start to open, the engine groans, and we're moving again. I don't breathe. Not until the crawler's tires crunch onto fallen leaves and sticks. Not until Harlow says it's safe to come up for air.

Within a few minutes, we're back at the clearing. Keelan and Florence are both sitting, waiting for us. To my surprise, the little brown wolf is beside Florence, and her hand rests on its back gently.

When she sees Wilder, she jumps to her feet and runs to him, crying like she was worried she'd never see him again. Then she assesses his leg and begins searching for remedies to help.

I feel Slade's familiar tug on my mind, asking if we're all okay and if we found Shiloh. No. We aren't *all* okay. Opie is dead. Selene is dead. I will never be the same. But instead, I tell him yes, then tell him to get to the clearing. Everything else hurts too much to explain, and I'm not so sure he'll care that Opie is dead anyway.

Keelan's sad eyes meet mine, and I quickly look at the ground. "Opie?" he asks, the name sending a shudder through my body.

"He died saving Lennon," Wilder says for me.

"So Slade was wrong? He wasn't on their side?" Keelan presses.

"He was," Harlow says, and my attention snaps toward her. I hadn't asked. I wanted to, but I couldn't. "He was the one who fixed the hole in the gate. He's been working against us the entire time. When I went with him, he took me prisoner. I think originally he was going to do the same with Shiloh, but something in him snapped. I can't explain it, but after that, he started protecting us instead."

I hear the sound of footsteps, and not just one or two. It sounds like there are hundreds of people racing toward us. "Everyone in the crawler!" I scream, moving to the front with Kaleu, prepared to fight.

Instead I see *Auryths* running toward us, all grouped around Slade, Lief, and Nora. In Slade's hands is Vesper, who has undoubtedly been abused for some length of time. She looks so frail, even from several feet away. Kaleu turns his head up to the moon and lets loose a shiver-inducing howl that I feel all the way to my toes.

It's the first time I've ever heard him do it, and I know without asking that it's for her. For what she endured. Her black ears twitch slightly as the howl echoes, and she slowly, painfully turns her head toward us. *"I missed you, too,"* she says to us both, and my heart sinks.

My attention circles back to the nearly hundred *Auryths* now surrounding all of us, all far too skinny, many limping, and a few being carried. I notice Lief has a red fox curled up in his arms, holding it tightly to his chest. Despite everything, I let myself smile at them. They did it. They freed them all.

"You guys ready to go?" I ask as the rest of them file back out of the crawler.

Lief looks at me, teary-eyed and desperate. "I don't want to leave her." I look at Slade for help, unsure what to do.

"She should come," Kaleu rumbles. *"She has chosen her bonded;*

he belongs to her now. Once she is healed, the bond will solidify." Now I'm the one with glassy eyes, my heart swelling for the boy who always dreamed of this day. The red-haired boy and his fiery little fox.

"Bring her with us," I tell him, my voice softening. "Kaleu says you are hers now."

Lief looks down at her so tenderly, brushing her small head with his hand. "I won't let anyone hurt you ever again."

"What about the others?" I ask, staring at all the new faces. "Won't Exion just capture them again?"

"With everything that happened today, I doubt it'll be at the top of their list, especially without Doc. At least now they have a chance to get as far away as possible," Nora adds.

"Alright," Slade interjects. "We need to go while we still have a head start."

"Hang on," Nora says, stepping toward him and Vesper. "I need to remove her chip. No more controlling the two of you ever again. And anyone else that's chipped, I'll remove them when we're safe."

"Why did Vesper get chipped, but they chipped me instead of Kaleu?" I ask, wincing as she makes a small incision on Vesper's neck and digs for the microchip. This is about as far as you can get from a sterile environment.

"Because Vesper was part of their project. They'd take certain *Auryths* from the Wildwoods, chip them, then release them back into the wilderness in hopes that they'd bond with someone from Solis. Vesper was chipped long before she met you, Slade." She pulls out the microchip, her fingers dripping with Vesper's blood. Harlow hands her some alcohol out of a medkit, a needle, and thread.

"Could … could they have been controlling Opie?" I ask, my voice wavering.

"Yes," Nora replies, and I try to ignore Vesper's pained whine. "I would say he almost certainly was being controlled, though I was never privy to that information."

That's why he betrayed us time after time. Why he protected Shiloh and Harlow after fighting against it. Why he saved my life.

He was never bad. He was forced.

I see the lights flashing through the trees before the sound of rumbling engines reaches my ears. They're coming.

"We need to go, *NOW*," I scream, ushering everyone to the crawler.

"Finally, time to go home," Slade says, grinning at me. "Back to Solis."

"We're not going to Solis." I sigh, stepping into the crawler. "We're going back down."

EPILOGUE: IRIS

I fall quietly to my knees, staring at Lennon and Shiloh. If this is the last time I'll ever see them, I want to remember every detail of their perfect faces. How has it come to this? How can I leave them behind?

Tucking a strand of hair behind Lennon's ear, I lean down and kiss her gently on the forehead. She breathes deeply, and for a moment I worry she'll wake, but she doesn't. Shiloh is curled up in a ball, his mouth hanging open as he sleeps. I kiss him, too, then stand in the doorway until my eyes are too watery to see straight.

"It's time," Malcom says, his hand wrapping around my waist from behind. I turn around and bury my face into his chest, hoping he might force me to stay.

No. I can't stay. My children's future depends on my not staying. "One day they'll know what I did, and they'll hate me for it," I tell him, my voice a mere whisper.

"No," he says, placing a hand on my head as he tugs me closer to his chest. "They'll know that you did it for them. For all of us. I'll make sure of it." Twelve years isn't enough with him. It'll never be enough. Why does it have to be me? Why can't it be someone else? Anyone else? Why do I have to walk away from everyone I love?

"Because most wouldn't do what needs to be done," Cora says, and I sigh, turning to find her perched on a dining chair, her beady eyes locked on me. *"And he's right, it's time to go."*

So many things tonight could end up with us dead, and that's before we even make it to the ground. "You remember the plan?" I ask Malcom, placing a hand on his cheek.

He lets his head fall into it, smiling softly. "Yes, my love. I won't let you down."

"No one should ever love anyone the way I love you," I tell him, a tear slipping down my cheek as I drop my hand.

He wipes it away. "And I you." I kiss him deeply, as if it's the last time I'll ever get to. Because it is.

I slip a cloak over Cora and me, then pull the hood over my head. Get in, get the token, and get to the platform. I can do this. We stick to the darker parts of the Burrows, avoiding the walkway and overhead lights.

When we reach the archives, I slide the door open and slip inside. It's the middle of the night—there are no people and no guards. Why would they bother guarding the place when no one knows there's anything worth stealing?

A misstep on their part, but good for me. I walk past the shelves that stretch from floor to ceiling, packed with the pieces of literature and history they allow us to have. I wonder if there will be similar places up there, places with written words that haven't been edited or altered.

"Focus," Cora demands, and I continue to the back where the classified materials are locked up and slip a key out of my pocket. So many betrayals this week, but all necessary. Maybe Maggie will forgive me if she ever learns I took it

from her father. Hopefully their family won't be punished for this.

Shifting the painfully creaky gate open, I head straight to my left, finding the small display case and the coin inside. I suck in a breath and open the case, grab the coin, and give myself only a second to ensure it's the real thing. Gold. Ancient. Round. The eight elite *Auryths* carved inside. The familiar words rounded along the edges. The sun in the center.

It's real.

Alarms begin squealing through the building, red lights flashing with every screech. I can feel Cora bristle underneath the cloak as I take a calming breath; we planned for this. We knew this would happen, though I didn't expect it to be so loud. I carefully place the replica I had made weeks ago into the display case and close it shut, stopping the alarm.

I nearly laugh at the fact that it worked, but I keep moving instead. We aren't done yet.

Locking the gate behind me, we slip back through the archives into the dead streets and toward the Nexus. This is the trickier part—getting out of the Burrows before they can stop the platform and without Pip, Malcolm's ferret, getting caught. I'd searched for three months before I found a tunnel entrance that got me inside, then another two studying the guard rotations.

The tunnel entrance is located in an alley behind the Bowl, and I slip through quickly before closing it behind me. I run, holding Cora tightly to my chest, sticking close to the walls until it's safe to run to my next spot. When I finally reach the staircase, I'm breathing heavily, my legs shaking. So, so close.

My hand slips into my pocket, confirming once more that the Desmos Token is still there. Without it, this is all for nothing. When I feel it, it gives me the last bit of energy I need to get to the top of the staircase and push open the door.

It's dark, so I throw out a few light orbs until I find the cage. "Pip?" I whisper, my chest tight with the thought that he hasn't made it.

A little white body steps into the orb light, and I squat down, holding out a hand. "Tell him I love him. Don't let him go to his dark place; he has our babies to look after." Though Pip can't say it, I know he'll give Malcom the message.

I close the gate behind Cora and me, press up against the back wall, and hold on for dear life. "Now, Pip," I say, and the little ferret flips the switch to activate the platform. Tears run down my face as I watch everything I've ever known fade into blackness.

Every vision, every confirmed prophecy, has led me here. I know what I have to do. I know where I have to take the key, and I'll kill anyone who tries to get in my way.

For my family. For the *Auryths*. For the *good* people in the Burrows.

The beast shall wake with a fire in its throat.

ACKNOWLEDGMENTS

Firstly and above all else, thank you to my Lord and Savior for blessing me with the opportunity to follow my dreams. All Glory to You.

Thank you to my husband, Sawyer, for being the kind of support system every girl dreams of having. You always push me to be better, to follow my dreams, and to believe in the impossible. You are the light of my life, and there aren't enough words to describe my gratitude for you.

To my family: thank you all for your endless support and encouragement. Having people in my corner throughout this journey has made all the difference.

To Gillian Collins: I feel incredibly lucky to have met you and have you as my editor. The work that you've put in on this novel nearly matches my own, and we both know it would be nowhere near where it is now without your constant support and correction. Thank you so much for agreeing to take me on and helping me start over more times than we like to count! For my Token and Cover Design Team:

Thank you, Cole Sanders, for creating the original token and helping formulate my idea into actual artwork. Thank you to Pinkerchu on Instagram for taking that design and bringing it to life so fully that I couldn't resist utilizing it for the cover. And finally, thank you, designbyseventhstar on Instagram, for creating the cover of my dreams! It truly takes a village, and you all contributed beyond belief to make my vision come to life!

Thank you to my beta reading team. When I started writing this book, I had no idea where I'd end up. These girls went above and beyond to help me navigate improving the story, read countless versions, helped me bounce ideas around, built maps, social media content, and, most of all, offered words of encouragement when things got hard. I feel incredibly lucky to have them all in my life and to call them my friends, and I'm listing them below:

Shanelle Krumbhols

Megan Phillips

Mary Beth Gould: @marybeths.book.nook

Kat Feilner

Mira: @bookish.mira

Samantha Johnson

Jamie Fischer: @jamiesreadingspace

Lyndsey Morris

Catalina Hidalgo

Abi Walker

Jessie

Moria Montoya

Beck Davis

Sydney Antonius: @sydneyantonius

Maddy Rice

Jessica: @probably.athome.reading

Emma Hickman-Garcia

Amber Wilhelm

Brittany Piland

Kayla

Henna: @takemeoutsidee

Jasmine: @shush.im.reading

Heather Walker
Griffin Maddox
Emma Schuessler
Macey Hawkins

"Everything is possible for one who believes." — Mark 9:23

About the Author

Kearstin Dunn has spent most of her adult career as a sales representative because she enjoys yapping so much, and now she gets to do it with written words, too! When she isn't writing, you can find her spending time with her husband and two dogs (a very spoiled boykin spaniel and an adopted bully). She's a huge advocate for the animal fostering community and has personally fostered over 30 animals (and managed to only keep one)!